The Poetics of Internatio

A cutting-edge contribution to the aesthetic turn in international relations scholarship, this book exposes the role of poetic techniques in constituting the reality of international politics. It has two symmetrical goals: to illuminate the nonempirical fictions of factual international relations literature, and to highlight the real factual inspirations and implications of contemporary international relations fiction.

Employing narrative theory developed by Hayden White, the author examines factual and fictional accounts of world affairs ranging from the anarchy narrative, central to mainstream international relations research, to novels by Don DeLillo and Milan Kundera. Chapters analyzing factual literature flesh out its unacknowledged inventions, while those dedicated to fiction explain its political roots and agenda. Throughout, the distinction between factual and fictional representations of international relations breaks down. Social-scientific narratives emerge as exercises in rhetoric: the art and politics of persuasion through language. Artistic narratives surface as real pedagogical lessons and exercises in political activism.

The volume challenges the autonomy of academic international relations as an exclusive purveyor of serious knowledge about world affairs and calls for active engagement with literary art. It will be of interest to scholars of international relations, political theory, historiography, cultural theory, and literary studies and criticism.

Milan Babík teaches international politics at Colby College. His research interests include narrative theory and critical historiography. His first book, *Statecraft and Salvation* (2013), examined the religious foundations of Wilsonian liberal internationalism.

The Poetics of International Politics

Fact and Fiction in Narrative Representations of World Affairs

Milan Babík

Routledge
Taylor & Francis Group

LONDON AND NEW YORK

First published 2019
by Routledge
2 Park Square, Milton Park, Abingdon, Oxon OX14 4RN

and by Routledge
52 Vanderbilt Avenue, New York, NY 10017

Routledge is an imprint of the Taylor & Francis Group, an informa business

First issued in paperback 2021

British Library Cataloguing-in-Publication Data
A catalogue record for this book is available from the British Library

Library of Congress Cataloging-in-Publication Data
Names: Babík, Milan, 1979– author.
Title: The poetics of international politics: fact and fiction in narrative representations of world affairs / Milan Babík.
Description: Abingdon, Oxon; New York, NY: Routledge, 2019. | Includes bibliographical references and index.
Identifiers: LCCN 2018032414 (print) | LCCN 2018047291 (ebook) | ISBN 9780429437472 (eBook) | ISBN 9781138346123 (hardback)
Subjects: LCSH: Politics in literature. | International relations in literature. | Politics and literature.
Classification: LCC PN3448.P6 (ebook) | LCC PN3448.P6 B33 2019 (print) | DDC 809.3/9358—dc23
LC record available at https://lccn.loc.gov/2018032414

ISBN: 978-1-138-34612-3 (hbk)
ISBN: 978-1-03-209439-7 (pbk)
ISBN: 978-0-429-43747-2 (ebk)

Typeset in Times New Roman
by codeMantra

Mým dětem, Kyliánovi a Matyášovi

Contents

Preface

The four years it took me to write and publish this book, from 2014 to 2018, were full of personal trials and change. Luckily, just when the various developments threatened to overwhelm me, I realized that the key to coping with them lay right on my writing desk. In Vico's *teoria dei corsi e ricorsi storici* and its postmodern progeny, Hayden White's tropology of human consciousness, I recognized a framework enabling me to interpret not only the world of international politics, but also my private experience.

According to White, historical reality is intelligible only to the extent that we tell stories about it, and the plot structure of these stories changes over time. In the Romantic mindset, we celebrate the triumph of the human will after extensive ordeals, expressing our belief that there are no limits to what we can achieve. In the Comic phase, we become aware of the obstacles in our path and acknowledge the threat of disruption to our lives, but we regard any upheavals as temporary misunderstandings sure to be clarified in due course, setting us back on the path to eventual success. In the Tragic mode of consciousness, the obstacles surface as insurmountable: we realize the irreconcilable element of human affairs and mourn the loss entailed when values collide, adopting a posture of survivors warning about past disasters in an attempt to mitigate their repetition. In the Satirical frame of mind, we finally reach the conclusion that life displays no meaningful patterns and is governed by blind chance, which foils all our designs and leaves us with only one option: ironic laughter at the folly of existence.

When I commenced drafting the manuscript in the early months of 2014, I was convinced that I was en route to a bright personal and professional future. There were abundant indications: I had just published my first book, moved my family to a beautiful country home in coastal Maine, and received an attractive entry-level appointment as Visiting Professor of Political Science at Williams College. Not that life was easy. My regular weekly commutes to Williamstown, located three hundred miles away, were exhausting. But my wife and two little children were enjoying a stable and comfortable foothold, and I was teaching bright undergraduates at the finest liberal arts institution in the United States. Besides, the time spent in the car, six uninterrupted hours once every three days, afforded me ample opportunity to think. The Introduction and Chapters 1, 3, and 4 were thus born on the road: I composed entire sections in my mind while following Deerfield River into the mountains of western Massachusetts and then typed them up from memory after arriving at my one-bedroom apartment in town.

My subsequent move to Dartmouth College, where I spent the academic year 2015–2016, gave my professional career further room for growth, but my excitement was tempered by the increasing awareness of the hard realities of the academic job market in the United States. I was hoping for more than just another one-year job offer. Where did all the tenure-track positions disappear? Why were so few of them advertised each fall? I was no longer a Romantic. Nonetheless, it would have been difficult to regard an Ivy League appointment, even if only temporary, other than as an encouraging sign. As for my long-term prospects, I remained confident that ultimately hiring committees would see past my gender, sex, and skin color, which were clouding their minds in a manner of Comic misapprehensions, to what truly mattered: my resume, teaching evaluations, and letters of reference. Instead of western Massachusetts, I spent the year commuting to western New Hampshire. Chapter 2 was conceived during weekly treks across the White Mountains and committed to paper in a small studio apartment in Fairlee, Vermont.

By the spring of 2016 the manuscript was nearly finished, but my spirits were darkening. In March my eight year-old son suffered a serious medical emergency, and I spent a week sitting by his hospital bed. In April it was my turn to visit the emergency room: sleep-deprived and overworked, I collapsed during one of my lectures. Worst of all, as the academic job market continued stagnating, no new job offers came my way, and I was left to my devices as a de facto single father to two small boys. These setbacks no longer struck me as temporary difficulties. They manifested implacable forces and constraints too large to overcome, against whose background my situation emerged as Tragic. I pretended not to notice, instead focusing on drafting the last remaining portion of the manuscript: Chapter 5 on Milan Kundera. But his novel *The Joke*, a story about a university student whose life is suddenly destroyed through no fault of his own, pushed me to consider the possibility of a Tragic future anyway. On Friday, February 23, 2018, that future became reality when my children and I fell victim to a heinous legal ambush and were forcibly separated from each other.

My memory of the first few days following this traumatic event remains fragmented. It took me a while to gather myself. But gradually a most unexpected thing happened: I started laughing! I was overcome with the kind of mordant laughter described in Kundera's *Book of Laughter and Forgetting*, which I was reading together with *The Joke*. It grabbed me infrequently at first, then more often, eventually permanently and uncontrollably. Tragedy morphed into Satire. There was plenty to laugh about, above all myself: my prior Romantic worldview, which had been propelling all my personal and professional efforts up to that point, for at least fifteen years. Their outcome, exactly the opposite of what I had intended, was so absurd that my sense of injustice evaporated. I became mesmerized by the Satire the way one gets mesmerized by roadkill. Its twists and turns began filling me with pleasure. My ironic detachment grew to such proportions that it affected even the manuscript. The draft was now complete, but instead of pitching it to academic presses I simply shelved it. What was the point of trying to publish it? What was the point of *anything*?

No sooner did these debilitating questions enter my mind than help began arriving. Heather and Dan Wyman of Appleton, Maine, took me in without a moment's hesitation when I appeared at their doorstep that February night. Dozens of others got in touch to offer food, shelter, vehicles, and money, but only Melanie Goodman—perhaps thanks to her long history rescuing dogs—understood that my most immediate need was at once much simpler and infinitely more difficult to find: sleep. After years of nightmares, I found it in her arms. Meanwhile, Jennifer Yoder and Joe Reisert, my former teachers and now colleagues in the Government Department at Colby College, worked relentlessly to bring me aboard as a full-time faculty member and were entirely unfazed by the personal catastrophe that befell me halfway through my first academic year back on campus. Particularly in Jennifer's case, a professional relationship has morphed into something much more akin to personal friendship as a result of her undisguised affection for my children and of her willingness, from her senior position at the head of the department, to let me tailor my work schedule according to the boys' needs. Thanks to all these individuals and their support, my parents, Milan and Marie, and closest friend, Michal Stryk, had less to worry about while regularly checking in on me by phone from the distance of my native Czech Republic. I picked myself up and, among other things, sent the manuscript to Routledge, where Rob Sorsby and Ella Halstead, respectively my editor and his assistant, quickly put it under contract and expertly shepherded it through the publishing process. I owe everyone mentioned here a massive debt of gratitude.

Vico and White held that the ironic mindset was not terminal and that history did not end with it. In due time, the devastating laughter of rational critique, what Vico called *barbarie della reflessione*, would engender a *ricorso* from the age of Satire back to a new epoch of Romance—at a higher level of consciousness. This is where I stand today: aware of the dark shadow of my recent past, but no longer its prisoner and much richer and wiser for having lived through it. My children hugged me with urgency bordering on savagery when we reunited; clearly our shared Tragic downfall was not the conclusion of our epic, but just the prologue. As for my professional outlook, Colby has recently appointed me to spearhead a new partnership with Salzburg Global Seminar, which will involve spending part of the academic year at Schloss Leopoldskron. It does not get more Romantic than this.

Kyliáne a Matyáši, tuto knihu věnuji vám. I hope that you always see your lives and world as a story, stand up to every bully threatening to do the telling for you, and have courage to revise your tales when they cease to ring true to you, even if it should mean getting rid of half the chapters already written.

Acknowledgments

Some of the material in this book has previously appeared elsewhere. Chapter 3 makes partial use of Milan Babík, "Realism as Critical Theory: The International Thought of E. H. Carr," *International Studies Review* 15, no. 4 (2014): 491–514. Permission to reprint portions of this essay is hereby acknowledged with gratitude.

Introduction

Academic International Relations as a Discourse about Power

It is often said among culinary connoisseurs that there are three secrets to French cuisine: butter, butter, and butter. Connoisseurs of international politics—professional academics dedicated to its scientific analysis—may not be aware of the adage. They spend their days immersed in scholarly research, not in Julia Child cookbooks or Paul Bocuse's truffle soup recipes. Nonetheless, with one small tweak the dictum offers an excellent summary of the serious study of world affairs. There are three secrets to the discipline of international relations as it has evolved in the United States since its birth in the first half of the twentieth century: power, power, and power.

This is evident already from the titles of its canonical works, such as *The Tragedy of Great Power Politics, Soft Power, The Future of Power, Power and Interdependence*, and *Politics among Nations: The Struggle for Power and Peace.*[1] Initially, up until the 1950s, classical realism, which was the leading school of international relations theory at the time, justified the focus on power mainly with reference to human nature. Hans Morgenthau, the German-born thinker who emigrated to the United States during World War II and subsequently became the most influential international relations scholar of his generation, famously declared that "politics ... is governed by objective laws ... [rooted] in human nature."[2] Since for Morgenthau the essence of human nature was *animus dominandi*, as he postulated under the influence of Nietzsche's will-to-power metaphysics, it followed that among these objective laws "the main signpost that helps [us] to find [our] way through the landscape of international politics is the concept of interest defined in terms of power."[3]

Today's academic international relations course syllabi often list Morgenthau in the company of Hobbes, Thucydides, and other giants of Western political thought: a formidable entourage. Together, these thinkers are repeatedly invoked to remind students of world politics that human beings in the state of nature engage in a beastly dog-eat-dog competition making life nasty, brutish, and short, as Hobbes put it in his *Leviathan*, and that relations among sovereign collectivities are no better. Power is paramount in them.

"The powerful extract what they can," as Thucydides reports the blunt words of Athenian generals to their Melian victims during the Peloponnesian War, "and the weak grant what they must."[4]

In more recent decades, classical realism has been eclipsed by neorealism in mainstream international relations thought, but the focus on power has remained unchanged. If anything, it has intensified and assumed the mantle of a scientific law. Explanations of why power is essential in world affairs have shifted away from human nature, deemed indeterminate and anecdotal, to the ostensibly more objective structure of the international system: anarchy as the absence of world government.[5] According to the "lore of neorealism," as one of its critics has called the updated discourse, the international arena is profoundly different from the domestic arena.[6] At the domestic level, central government with monopoly over legitimate violence enforces order by punishing its transgressions, but in world politics "there is no higher authority that states can turn to for protection," according to John Mearsheimer, today's preeminent neorealist; "if you dial 911 in the international system, there is nobody at the other end."[7] This predicament generates widespread fear and paranoia among sovereign countries, driving them all regardless of internal differences to practice the same foreign policy: power politics. "[States] know that they live in a self-help world, and that (...) if they hope to survive, they have no choice but to compete for power."[8]

The world of international relations is therefore dark, menacing, and inhospitable. One hesitates to step into it. The grim inscription on the arch above the gate to Hell in Dante's *Divine Comedy* might as well hang above international departures gates at today's airport terminals: "All hope abandon, ye who enter here." Inside sovereign states, life of peace, justice, and progress unfolds; outside, no such progress is possible, for here existence eternally revolves around war, power, and bare survival. Domestic and international politics represent qualitatively separate force fields, which is also why they require separate scholarly toolkits. The centrality of power to international relations is in this sense intimately bound up with the status of academic international relations as a discipline apart from other areas of intellectual inquiry.

Power thus reigns supreme in mainstream international relations scholarship. Unsuspecting undergraduates walking into their first theory lecture humming the popular 1960s music hit "Love Is All Around" may be excused to walk out again an hour later with the song's lyrics—and their pliable minds—transformed beyond repair: "I feel it in my fingers, I feel it in my toes, power's all around me, and so the feeling grows." Never mind that in the vast majority of international relations literature the definition of power is merely implied and left up to one's imagination, hardly ever explicitly articulated. Never mind again that this seemingly self-evident concept is therefore vague to the point of empty: "one of those terms in political discourse that are so widely used as to have become almost devoid of meaning."[9] Even just a cursory glance reveals a bewildering variety of definitions, whose mutual relations are all but clear.[10] Despite this ambiguity, or perhaps precisely because of it, power looms large in academic international relations discourse. It is not the discourse's sole element, of course; issues of trade, morality, law, culture, gender, or environment all come into view in contemporary research. But it is the dominant ingredient without which this discourse would be unthinkable, just like Paul Bocuse's truffle soup without heaps of butter.

Academic International Relations as Discursive Power

Placed in the context of this discourse, this book may be characterized as at once traditional and subversive. It is the former in the sense that it, too, deeply concerns itself with power, seeking to illuminate its nature and map its operation. To this extent, it proceeds firmly within preestablished boundaries delineating the proper subject matter of academic international relations. At the same time, however, it unfolds decidedly against the grain of traditional thought, for in analyzing power it does not train its sights on the international system, state behavior, dynamics of conflict and cooperation, or other substantive issues and problems occupying mainstream scholars of world politics. Rather, it turns the lens of inquiry on disciplinary scholarship itself, approaching it as a locus of power in its own right: power to induce audiences, through the use of poetic techniques and narrative strategies commonly associated with fiction writing, to adopt a certain consciousness of political reality reflecting interests satisfied within the existing global status quo.

In undertaking this endeavor, the book claims no exemption from the workings of power, as more "proper"—traditional, social-scientific—international relations treatises do. In E. H. Carr's memorable verdict, "political thought is itself a form of political action."[11] This study, fully aware of its own nature as a literary artifact and poetic performance designed to sway minds in accordance with its own goals, could not agree more. In and through talking about power, it simultaneously and inevitably participates in it as one of its channels.

That this project may be defined with reference to academic international relations and its traditional concerns emphatically does not mean that the book accepts the discipline as a valid reference point: a discrete field with clearly defined boundaries. On the contrary, although the book certainly speaks to international relations scholars, it regards them as only one small segment of its intended readership and denies them their most cherished and closely guarded professional possession: their autonomy as a self-standing academic guild. After all, to cast academic international relations as a site of discursive power utilizing poetics to shape reality in accordance with certain interests is to cast it as the art of rhetoric and therefore as a subset of ethics. The conventional assumption that academic international relations represents an independent field of inquiry must be read in the context of this art: as a performance of self-legitimating power. Whatever else this field strives to persuade its audiences about, it must first of all convince them—*discipline* them—to accept it as the principal or even exclusive purveyor of true knowledge about world politics.

In doing this, the field simultaneously guides them to regard knowledge generated outside its borders as highly suspect: lacking in facts and science. "After all, what is a discipline but a learning of what *not* to do?"[12] Academic international relations is exemplary in this regard. "Every discipline ... is ... constituted by what it *forbids* its practitioners to do. Every discipline is made up of a set of restrictions on thought and imagination...."[13] Among other things, international relations students are quietly forbidden from looking for, let alone importing, valuable insights from art, fiction, and literary criticism. Reading *belles lettres* might be good etiquette or even a requirement, particularly at liberal arts colleges committed to interdisciplinary education, but for the purposes of serious international relations scholarship it is merely a distraction: a type of recreation and guilty pleasure. Rare is the international relations course syllabus with a work of fiction listed among its reading assignments. At most American universities offering the subject, it is perfectly normal for international relations majors to receive their degree without ever encountering a single novel, short story, poem, or dramatic play in their prescribed disciplinary coursework at all.

A Project in Critical International Theory

Efforts to analyze traditional international relations discourse as a form of ideological power are not new. Their beginnings may be traced to the late 1960s and early 1970s, a period marked in the United States—and academic international relations has been dubbed an "American social science"[14]—by dramatic social and political upheavals. The Civil Rights movement set out to end racial segregation and inequality, feminist activists raised the flag of sexual liberation, the New Left staged huge demonstrations against the Vietnam War, and everybody regardless of gender, skin color, or ideological orientation had their faith in America's political elites bludgeoned by Richard Nixon. The Watergate hearings were broadcast on national television gavel-to-gavel, all two hundred and fifty hours of them. The tragic shootings at Kent State University, where the Ohio National Guard killed four unarmed students protesting the US invasion of Cambodia, induced open trauma: "the country was convulsed and its system of authority was brought to the brink of a nervous breakdown."[15] A massive legitimacy crisis broke out on all fronts, engulfing the entire American society.

With its close ties to the country's political leadership and foreign policy establishment, ties personified by scholar-statesmen such as Henry Kissinger and McGeorge Bundy, academic international relations could not have remained unaffected. Within a decade, from the early 1980s on, a small number of younger scholars including Robert W. Cox, Richard Ashley, and

Andrew Linklater initiated a rebellion against the discipline's orthodoxies. Turning their attention from substantive problems of world politics to the theoretical framework governing their conceptualization, they placed traditional academic international relations research under the microscope and started identifying the various biases buried deep within its interior, in the form of silent presuppositions, value judgments, and other nonempirical content. Their works gradually coalesced into a counterculture to dominant modes of international relations thought. This counterculture, with which this book shares deep affinities, has become known as critical international theory.

The opening salvo and much of the subsequent initiative came from Robert Cox: "Theory is always *for* someone and *for* some purpose."[16] In this simple declarative sentence, Cox gave critical international theory its manifesto neatly summarizing its signature feature: emphasis on the historically situated, goal-driven, and ultimately political character of all theoretical knowledge. "There is ... no such thing as theory in itself," Cox argued, "divorced from a standpoint in time and space."[17] Although it is usual for theory to aspire to universal laws in an effort to transcend its original historical perspective, this perspective is irreducible and always present—no matter how much theorists may try to disguise, repress, hide, or otherwise conceal it. "Social and political theory is history-bound at its origin ... (and) always traceable to a historically conditioned awareness of certain problems and issues, a problematic...."[18] Exposing this problematic is one of the principal aims of critical theory and accounts for its hallmark trait: post-positivist reflexivity, or awareness of theory's "rootedness" in a particular nexus of sociohistorical forces which surrounded it at birth.

To elaborate this trait and its implications, Cox contrasted critical theory with problem-solving theory as the traditional methodological approach animating mainstream (social-scientific) international relations thought. Whereas problem-solving theory "takes the world as it finds it, with the prevailing social and power relationships ... as the given framework for action," critical theory "stands apart from the prevailing order and asks how that order came about."[19] The assumption of fixed social parameters lets problem-solving theory achieve considerable analytical precision as it goes about targeting discrete issues in an effort to harmonize the standing reality of international relations, but from the viewpoint of critical theory it also makes problem-solving theory static, ahistorical, and conservative: "serving particular national, sectional, or class interests, which are comfortable within the given order."[20] Critical theory is able to appreciate this because it is, by comparison, fundamentally dynamic and historical: "directed towards an appraisal of the very framework for action ... which problem-solving theory accepts as its parameters."[21] Rather than addressing particular problems within the given order, it approaches the order as a whole, denaturalizes it by revealing its historical construction, and in this manner introduces the possibility of its progressive reconstruction. Therefore, unlike problem-solving theory, "Critical theory allows for a normative choice in favor of a social and political order different from the prevailing order," and to this extent it contains a radical (idealist, utopian) impulse.[22]

Cox did not concoct critical international theory out of thin air. In introducing it to academic international relations, he drew heavily on western Marxist social theory: not the determinist current of orthodox or scientific Marxism alleging to know the iron laws of history, but rather the historicist current concerned with the role of ideas and consciousness in retarding or facilitating revolutionary action.[23] His work has been influenced by Antonio Gramsci and the Frankfurt School, especially Max Horkheimer's distinction between traditional and critical theory.[24]

Active during the 1920s and 1930s, these western Marxists shared an intellectual agenda focused on a key objective: "to come to terms with the new emerging forms of organized capitalism and to radically reconstitute the project of human emancipation that in traditional Marxist theory had been projected as the proletarian revolution."[25] The fact that this revolution, deemed imminent by scientific Marxists, failed to materialize during World War I, that capitalism survived the cataclysmic conflict intact, and that the international communist movement became "Bolshevized" posed a major challenge for them. It was necessary to diagnose the obstacles impeding the emancipatory project and formulate new strategies for its advancement.

Gramsci's diagnosis centered on the role of bourgeois hegemony: the consensual form of power embedded within standing social norms, values, relations, and general consciousness, of which the coercive bureaucracy of the modern capitalist state was only the farthermost expression. Thanks to this hegemony, a rapid proletarian revolution against the state's bureaucratic apparatus was likely to be short-lived in Italy and other European countries with well-developed civil societies, for the state represented merely "an outer ditch, behind which there stands a powerful system of fortresses and earthworks."[26] In due time, the inertia of bourgeois consciousness would reemerge from the interior trenches of civil society and stage a counterrevolution (as illustrated by Italian Fascism and German Nazism). Based on this diagnosis, Gramsci therefore suggested that a different, more gradual revolutionary strategy be pursued in the hegemonic state-societies of interwar Europe: a counterhegemonic strategy, one commencing from within the "fortresses and earthworks" of social relations and knowledge. In his view, "the struggle had to be won in civil society before an assault on the state could achieve success."[27] Gramsci's Marxist thought, self-consciously practical and political, constituted an active contribution to this process.

Horkheimer expressed the juxtaposition of hegemonic and counterhegemonic forces in the distinction between, respectively, traditional and critical theory. Traditional theory "presuppose[s] the present economy and [is] part of the total economic process as it exists under specific historical conditions," whereas "the critical attitude ... is wholly distrustful of the rules of conduct with which society as presently constituted provides each of its members."[28] The former type of theory, Horkheimer noted, acts to normalize and sustain the status quo; critical theory, on the other hand, "runs counter to the prevailing habits of thought" and serves to undermine them, functioning "not simply [as] the theory of emancipation ... [but] the practice of it as well."[29] In drawing the distinction, Horkheimer pursued the same overarching goal as Gramsci and other western Marxists at the time: to unlock, through immanent critique of the existing capitalist order and of traditional theory as its attendant mode of intellectual activity, mental space for progress toward a more egalitarian society conducive to the full realization of human freedom.

Half a century after Gramsci and Horkheimer, Cox applied their insights to world politics and, even more importantly for the purposes of this book, to the academic field consecrated to the serious study of world politics: the discipline of international relations. Whereas they concerned themselves mainly with domestic society in Italy and Germany after World War I, Cox focused on hegemony at the international level during the Cold War. Defining world hegemony as a tripartite—social, economic, and political—structure, he noted that it "is expressed in universal norms, institutions and mechanisms which lay down general rules of [international] behavior ... —rules which support the dominant mode of production."[30] As a self-proclaimed discoverer and repository of these ostensibly objective rules, traditional international relations scholarship, with neorealism as its most advanced form, constituted a prominent hegemonic discourse: one reflecting and legitimating the American-led Western liberal-capitalist world order established after World War II. In this vein, Cox wholeheartedly concurred with Stanley Hoffmann's characterization of academic international relations as an "American social science" and added that

> Neorealism ... appears ideologically to be ... at the service of big-power management of the international system. There is an unmistakably Panglossian quality to a theory published in the late 1970s [Kenneth Waltz's seminal neorealist *Theory of International Politics*] which concludes that a bipolar system is the best of all possible worlds.[31]

The application of western Marxist sociology of knowledge to traditional international relations discourse created a theoretical opening through which an entire host of alternative approaches quickly poured in, fueling the counterculture. From the outset the insurgency has been plural and diverse, making it more accurate to talk about a variety of critical international theories rather than a single monolithic one. Different scholars zeroed in on different (though frequently overlapping) hegemonic groups and biases. As a longtime International Labor Organization officer directly acquainted with the impact of free markets on global economic inequality and Third World poverty, Cox singled out the United States, casting traditional international relations theory as a rationalization of American dominance in world affairs. Feminists such as J. Ann Tickner focused on gender, arguing that mainstream international relations discourse derives from and propagates a masculine worldview and contributes to the ongoing exclusion of women from international politics.[32] And postcolonial critics such as Edward Said asserted that scholarly and literary representations of non-Western cultures are by the West and for the West: forged during imperial expansion, saturated with Western prejudices, and serving to justify Western colonial aspirations.[33]

All of them, however, have utilized a broadly identical method of analysis exuding western Marxist ideology critique, interdisciplinarity, a counterhegemonic thrust challenging the social-scientific mainstream, and reflexive post-positivist epistemology comprehending academic international relations as a site of discursive power and a form of political action. Said's remark is emblematic:

> No one has ever devised a method for detaching the scholar from the circumstances of life, from the fact of his involvement (conscious or unconscious) with a class, a set of beliefs, a social position, or from the mere activity of being a member of a society. These continue to bear on what he does professionally....[34]

All of them also evince a clear commitment to progress, equality, and emancipation of marginalized and excluded groups, whether these be underdeveloped Third World economies, women, or former colonial subjects such as the Palestinian people. The goal of transforming the status quo into a more equitable and just world order may very well be critical international theory's defining feature.

The Argument

This book contributes to existing critical international theory and post-positivist scholarship by fleshing out the role of poetic techniques and narrative composition in constituting the reality of world affairs. It has two interrelated goals: to excavate the nonempirical content inherent in mainstream social-scientific international relations literature by virtue of its narrative form, on the one hand, and to highlight the real political inspirations and aspirations of fine literature written by leading contemporary novelists, on the other. Put differently, this study lays bare the fictions of factual stories about international relations, such as the story of anarchy, and simultaneously points out the factual foundations and implications of fictional accounts of world events.

To accomplish this twin purpose, the book draws on cutting-edge narrative theory of factual representation developed since the late 1970s by historians, philosophers, literary theorists, and cultural critics such as Hayden White, Frank Ankersmit, William Dray, Louis Mink, and Arthur Danto.

This theory holds that empirical reality is unintelligible unless narrativized; that narratives are not found but crafted via poetics; that even factual narratives, ones fashioned entirely out of publicly verifiable singular existential statements, possess an irreducible nonfactual (aesthetic, ethical, ideological) dimension on account of their story form; and that in this form, if not in substantive content, factual and fictional narratives are indistinct.

In academic international relations today, most scholars are not familiar with narrative theory at all. This is because from the perspective of dominant approaches including neorealism, neoliberalism, and constructivism international relations is a social science whose job is to formulate hypotheses, test them against hard evidence, and in this manner gradually uncover the fundamental causal laws of state behavior. Nonscientific areas of intellectual activity such as "poetry, literature and other humanistic disciplines ... are not designed to explain global war or Third World poverty,"[35] so they do not receive any attention; "if we want to solve those problems our best hope ... is social science,"[36] in which all claims "need to be evaluated empirically before they can make a contribution to knowledge."[37] This prevalent conception of research is couched in a rationalist epistemology and regards language as a perfectly transparent window on political reality, which is assumed to exist independently of its human spectators. Mainstream scholarship, in other words, espouses a form of representation "seek[ing] to discover a truth ... that somehow escapes the necessity of interpretation (...) [and] aiming to capture world politics as-it-really-is."[38] Poetics and aesthetics have no place in this project.

In the discipline's periphery, however, among critical scholars shunning rationalist and positivist presuppositions in favor of reflexive epistemologies and ontologies, a different sentiment may be detected. From their vantage point, language does not simply codify the world but actively constitutes it. For many of these scholars, "political reality does not exist in an a priori way. It comes into being through ... representation,"[39] which consequently must be understood in poetic terms, as the process of narrating and figuring forth the international stage. This process unfolds in and through fine literature, visual art, music, cinema, and culture broadly speaking.

The relationship between these various forms of artistic activity and international politics is, of course, far from straightforward. In an attempt to impose some order on its complexities, Iver Neumann and Daniel Nexon have proposed four basic types of interaction: popular culture and its artifacts as direct causes and effects of international political events; as mirrors illuminating academic international relations concepts and processes; as sources of data about norms, ideas, and identities in a given state, society, or region; and as factors constituting these norms, ideas, and identities.[40] Within the latter category, the influence of popular culture may be further subdivided according to whether it directly determines political decisions; merely informs them by providing diffuse knowledge that people bring to bear on political issues; enables policies and behavior by furnishing legitimating frameworks of meaning; or normalizes particular viewpoints in the sense of making them seem natural and incontestable.[41]

There is no shortage of work illustrating the turn to culture in recent international relations and foreign policy scholarship, even if most of it comes from outside the United States. In addition to Neumann and Nexon, notable contributors include Richard Ned Lebow, David Campbell, James Der Derian, Roland Bleiker, Cynthia Weber, Christine Sylvester, Christopher Coker, Hidemi Suganami, and Alex Danchev.[42] To mention a few examples in detail, Aurélie Lacassagne has approached J. K. Rowling's famous *Harry Potter* novels not only as a literary phenomenon but as a sociological account: "an allegory of twentieth-century world history in all its violence and brutality," especially "of the historical atrocities and ideological discourses of the Second World War."[43] Emma Norman has used the same series of books to clarify key disciplinary conceptual and theoretical problems, specifically the nexus of identity, fear, security, and violence.[44] In the hands of Stephen Deets, *Harry Potter* became an international relations textbook providing an accessible introduction to power politics, ethnic conflict, and bureaucratic control.[45] Jutta Weldes has turned to *Star Trek* and emphasized its constitutive function, showing how the iconic TV and film series creates "a background of meanings that help to constitute public images of international relations and foreign policy" and how "Popular culture helps to construct [both] the reality of international politics ... and ... consent for foreign policy and state action."[46] Other scholars have taken various popular TV programs, science fiction novels, and other kinds of mass entertainment and analyzed them in relation to international political issues and phenomena such as *Realpolitik*, soft power, imperialism, diasporas, authority, hierarchy, class, race, and gender.[47] In keeping with the spirit of critical theory, most of this literature has a distinctly counterhegemonic thrust. It maps the relationship between popular culture and world politics as part of an effort to foster emancipatory change and transform the present into a more just, peaceful, equitable, and inclusive future.

As stimulating and apposite as it is, the scholarship on the constitutive role of aesthetics in international relations nonetheless contains important gaps, thanks to which it falls short of realizing its full potential. In the first place, most of its contributors have focused on works of art, which has prevented them from noticing that factual international relations literature, too, is saturated with aesthetic elements worth exposing. This neglect stems in part from the fact that Whitean narrative theory, the principal framework for analysis of the poetics of factual representation, remains largely unknown to them save for a few occasional parenthetical references.

This book addresses this problem. It takes White's tropology seriously, explains it in detail, adopts it as its central optic, and aims it at the very foundation of social-scientific international relations: the narrative of anarchy as the standard image of the international stage. This narrative emerges as a literary artifact involving specific poetic choices and commitments, namely a mechanistic mode of explanation, a tragic plot type, and a conservative ideological agenda.

A second missed opportunity emerges when one realizes that the aesthetic turn in academic international relations has directed most of its attention to a specific type of art: mass entertainment, exemplified by bestselling fantasy and science fiction novels such as the *Harry Potter* series, their Hollywood film adaptations, and other commercially successful TV and movie franchises, whether *Star Trek* or *Buffy the Vampire Slayer*. Not that these highly profitable cultural brands do not merit scrutiny. On the contrary, showing how they (re)produce hegemonic consciousness and existing global order is an important and valuable undertaking. However, it has precluded contributors to the aesthetic turn from engaging with a type of art that lends itself to their emancipatory agenda much more directly and immediately: historiographic metafiction. This species of literature concerns itself with actual historical occurrences rather than fantasy worlds, thematizes them simultaneously with the processes of their symbolic-narrative construction, and strives to resist the homogenizing pressures of the sovereign state and capitalist economy, not necessarily to achieve mass popularity and astronomical sales figures.

This volume thus steers clear of wizards and spaceships, keeping Harry Potter at Hogwarts and Captain Kirk aboard the USS Enterprise. Instead, it focuses on real political events as depicted in the novels by Don DeLillo and Milan Kundera, who have repeatedly used the tools of historiographic metafiction to deconstruct received narratives of the political past, suggest alternative readings, and in this manner foster counterhegemonic consciousness and change.

Overall, then, what this book brings to existing international relations literature is clear. Unlike mainstream scholars, who ignore fiction under the assumption that it deals in inventions and is therefore irrelevant to serious analysis of real-world international politics, the following pages show how and why fiction matters. From the perspective of Whitean tropology, insofar as the narrative form characterizes the vast majority of international relations scholarship, in their structural features serious accounts of world politics are no less fictional than their novelistic counterparts—and the latter are no less serious and worthy of academic attention than the former. Indeed, this book reveals that the two kinds of narrative frequently share not just the same structure, but also the same content. If international relations scholars produce their factual accounts of world affairs using the artistic form of narrative common to novelists, novelists in turn often weave their fictional narratives from the same factual content as preoccupies international relations scholars: in DeLillo's case, the September 11, 2001, terrorist attacks in New York City. What is more, both constituencies go about their respective tasks out of a shared desire to sway the minds of their audiences and thereby shape the life of the polis.

Several important implications follow from this book. Mainstream academic international relations discourse, its scientific pretensions notwithstanding, emerges as a province of rhetoric: the art and politics of persuasion through language. At the same time, literary artistic narratives of international affairs surface as real pedagogical lessons and exercises in political activism. The discipline's closely guarded professional status as an autonomous field and sole purveyor of true expertise about the international arena thus comes under challenge. The book issues a powerful call against specialization and for holism—not just across established divisions within the domain of factual knowledge about international relations, but across the much broader divide between fact and fiction, both of which it subsumes under the rubric of narrative. Insofar as novelists and international relations scholars alike rely on the narrative form, their projects are not nearly as dissimilar as common sense suggests. Both are engaged in storytelling, fashioning a certain consciousness of political reality through Aristotelian *poiēsis* and *mimēsis*. If there is a difference between the two groups of writers, it lies mainly in their sincerity and readiness to publicly admit the moral-aesthetic nature of their enterprise.

The Roadmap

The book's structure follows its argument, whose twin goal endows the study with a distinctive symmetry. The first half focuses on international relations theory and its factual representations of political reality. It reveals that they employ the same poetic and narrative techniques of literary composition as feature in novelistic writing, and it excavates their fictions. The second half focuses on contemporary fiction. It shows that novelists, even ones classified as postmodernist, craft their artistic representations of international political events out of the same stuff as international relations scholars—actual empirical occurrences—and, again like the professors, do so for didactic purposes: to instruct their readers, teach them certain lessons, and thereby mold social and political life.

Before any of this, however, the first chapter introduces narrative theory as the book's overarching theoretical-analytical framework. It commences by discussing its origins in Aristotle's *Poetics* and then presents its main contemporary proponents, above all the recently deceased American historian and cultural theorist Hayden White. The bulk of the chapter gives a detailed exposition of narrative theory's principal claims, such as that empirical reality is essentially chaotic and meaningless; that sense and action emerge in and through storytelling; that stories are literary artifacts fashioned through poetics and narrativization; that even factual narratives possess a nonfactual aspect—"content of the form" (White), "synoptic judgment" (Mink), "narrative substance" (Ankersmit)—on account of their artificial structure; and that, formally, factual and fictional narratives cannot be distinguished without a priori assumptions about what kind of truth each is supposed to deal in. As part of this exposition, White's tropological framework for analysis of factual narrative representations of historical reality is laid out at length. The chapter does not neglect to subject narrative theory to critical assessment probing its strengths and weaknesses. It fleshes out its western Marxist inspirations and emancipatory counterhegemonic politics, surveys and evaluates its main criticisms, and situates it in the context of modernist and postmodernist historical theory and literary studies.

Chapter 2 aims the machinery of narrative theory at the notion of anarchy in contemporary academic international relations literature. Initial sections demonstrate anarchy's status as a foundational concept underlying all mainstream social-scientific approaches to international relations; extract its meaning from canonical texts such as Waltz's neorealist *Theory of International Politics*; note the subtle variations in anarchy's neoliberal and constructivist definitions; and unpack its implications, such as that the domestic and the international are qualitatively different realms, that normatively driven progress is possible only in the former, and that academic international relations is an autonomous field of inquiry dedicated to the latter. In a key move, the chapter then approaches anarchy as a factual narrative of the international arena, analyzes it using White's tropological framework, and illuminates its hidden nonempirical content: a combination of mechanistic, tragic, and conservative tropes. Anarchy surfaces as a poetic creation and a form of discursive power. The chapter concludes by hinting at alternative ways to figure forth the international stage and at how they would alter conventional wisdom about the disciplinary autonomy of international relations scholarship or about the possibility of international progress.

Chapter 3 directs attention to disciplinary history—stories the field tells about its past—as a particular subset of factual international relations narratives. Within this subset, the chapter zeroes in on the well-known British scholar E. H. Carr and examines disciplinary representations of his legacy as one of the founding fathers of modern academic international relations. It begins by laying out Carr's standard image as an early realist, which is widely familiar to international relations students and forms part of the discipline's common sense, but promptly complicates it by noticing an alternative image: Carr as a progenitor of critical international theory, a perspective ordinarily deemed at odds with the realist approach. After unpacking this alternative image, the chapter performs a comparative analysis of the two representations and arrives at a curious discovery: although mutually incommensurable, both narratives of Carr's bequest are factually accurate. To solve this paradox, the chapter uses White's tropology of factual narrative discourse to suggest that the truth of each representation contains a nonempirical dimension and reflects the unique poetic style of its proponents: a blend of mechanistic, tragic, and conservative narrative strategies in the realist instance, and of organicist, comic, and liberal-radical ones in the case of critical theory. Just as anarchy in the preceding chapter, Carr thus emerges as a literary artifact. The chapter concludes by teasing out the justificatory function of Carr's images and disciplinary historiography in general in the ongoing struggle among competing paradigms of international relations theory today.

Leaving academic international relations and entering the world of fine literature, Chapter 4 turns from the fictions of factual narratives about international relations to the factual sources and implications of fictional treatments of world affairs. It opens by noting several famous novels about real international political events, especially wars, and then selects a case study: the September 11, 2001, terrorist attacks and Don DeLillo's *Falling Man*, respectively a watershed moment in contemporary international relations and its novelistic account by one of America's preeminent living writers. The chapter sets up the discussion of the plot, characters, and structure of *Falling Man* by first elaborating DeLillo's conception of the novel as an emancipatory art form engaged in immanent critique of the state and society. With this conception in the background, the chapter then explains the main political implications of DeLillo's book: a deconstruction undercutting the official (state-propagated) 9/11 narrative by revealing its plasticity and artificiality, coupled with a subversive counter-narrative collapsing the popular distinction between benevolent Americans and their evil Islamic enemies by pointing out the terror latent in American-led globalization. By virtue of these elements, and quite aside from its reception by most literary critics as nothing more than a psychological trauma novel, *Falling Man* surfaces as a prime example of political activism.

The leitmotif of Chapter 5 is in many ways identical to that of Chapter 4: an emancipatory critique, through the art of the novel as an instrument of counterhegemonic political action, of the totalizing tendencies inherent in the global spread of Western liberal democracy and market capitalism. This time, however, the critique comes from the pen of the acclaimed Franco-Czech author Milan Kundera. His reputation, forged during the Cold War, as a political novelist writing against the state is well known and has made him into a darling of the liberal West, as the chapter notes in a biographical sketch mentioning among other things Kundera's leading role in the Prague Spring of 1968 and his subsequent exile from Soviet-occupied Czechoslovakia. But this reputation does not do Kundera justice. What it conveniently ignores is that his artistic resistance is not tied exclusively to his anti-Stalinist dissent prior to 1989, did not cease with the fall of the Soviet empire, and in his recent fiction turns against the dictate of "imagology": Kundera's term for the homogenizing mass-media culture of Western capitalism as the ostensibly post-ideological climax of humankind's universal evolution toward freedom. The chapter recovers this forgotten part of Kundera's achievement by explaining the role of his poetic style, including irony, polyphony, and contrapunt, in cultivating a sense of tragedy and ambiguity against the triumphalist certitudes of the liberal-capitalist end of history.

Notes

1 John J. Mearsheimer, *The Tragedy of Great Power Politics* (New York and London: Norton, 2001); Joseph S. Nye, *Soft Power: The Means to Success in World Politics* (New York: Public Affairs, 2004); idem, *The Future of Power* (New York: Public Affairs, 2011); Robert O. Keohane and Joseph S. Nye, *Power and Interdependence: World Politics in Transition* (Boston: Little, Brown, 1977); Hans J. Morgenthau, *Politics among Nations: The Struggle for Power and Peace*, 5th ed. (New York: Knopf, 1973 [1948]).

2 Morgenthau, *Politics among Nations*, 4.

3 Ibid., 5. For Nietzsche's influence on Morgenthau, see Christoph Frei, *Hans J. Morgenthau: An Intellectual Biography* (Baton Rouge: Louisiana State University Press, 2001), and Ulrik Enemark Petersen, "Breathing Nietzsche's Air: New Reflections on Morgenthau's Concepts of Power and Human Nature," *Alternatives* 24, no. 1 (1999): 83–118.

4 Thucydides, *History of the Peloponnesian War*, trans. Benjamin Jowett (Amherst, NY: Prometheus Books, 1998 [1881]), 5.89.

5 Principal statements of this structural or neorealist position include Mearsheimer, *Tragedy of Great Power Politics*, and especially Kenneth N. Waltz, *Theory of International Politics* (Reading, MA: Addison-Wesley, 1979).

6 For the "lore of neorealism" (and a frontal assault on its "orrery of errors"), see Richard K. Ashley, "The Poverty of Neorealism," in Robert O. Keohane, ed., *Neorealism and Its Critics* (New York: Columbia University Press, 1986).

7 The quotes are, respectively, from Mearsheimer, "Conversations in International Relations: Interview with John J. Mearsheimer (Part II)," interview by Ken Booth et al., *International Relations* 20, no. 2 (2006): 232, and idem, "Conversations in International Relations: Interview with John Mearsheimer (Part I)," interview by Ken Booth et al., *International Relations* 20, no. 1 (2006): 120. Mearsheimer's initial discussion of what he calls the "911" problem is in his *Tragedy of Great Power Politics*, 32–33.

8 Mearsheimer, "Interview (Part II)," 232.

9 Chris Brown, *Understanding International Relations*, 2nd ed. (Basingstoke: Palgrave Macmillan, 2001), 88.

10 The same holds for concepts that incorporate power, such as balance of power: "no one can agree on what it means." (Brown, *Understanding International Relations*, 107.) Martin Wight and Herbert Butterfield have identified at least eleven distinct usages. See their essays in Wight and Butterfield, eds., *Diplomatic Investigations: Essays in the Theory of International Politics* (Cambridge, MA: Harvard University Press, 1966).

11 Edward Hallett Carr, *The Twenty Years' Crisis, 1919–1939: An Introduction to the Study of International Relations*, 2nd ed. (New York: Harper & Row, 1946), 5.

12 Hayden White, "A Conversation with Hayden White," interview by Ewa Domanska, *Rethinking History* 12, no. 1 (2008): 15. [Emphasis original.]

13 Hayden White, *Tropics of Discourse: Essays in Cultural Criticism* (Baltimore, MD, and London: Johns Hopkins University Press, 1978), 126. [Emphasis original.]

14 Stanley Hoffmann, "An American Social Science: International Relations," *Dædalus* 106, no. 3 (1977): 41–60.

15 Walter Isaacson, *Kissinger: A Biography* (New York: Simon & Schuster, 1992), 269.

16 Robert W. Cox, "Social Forces, States and World Orders: Beyond International Relations Theory," in Robert O. Keohane, ed., *Neorealism and Its Critics* (New York: Columbia University Press, 1986), 207. [Emphasis original.]

17 Ibid.

18 Ibid.
19 Ibid., 208.
20 Ibid., 209.
21 Ibid., 208.
22 Ibid., 210.
23 Ibid., 248. The differences between scientific and western Marxism and the latter's status as the principal intellectual origin of critical theory are discussed in Robert J. Antonio, "The Origins, Development, and Contemporary Status of Critical Theory," *The Sociological Quarterly* 24, no. 3 (1983): 326–328.
24 Mark Hoffman, "Critical Theory and the Inter-Paradigm Debate," *Millennium: Journal of International Studies* 16, no. 2 (1987): 237. See also Cox, "Social Forces," 241. Cf. Scott Burchill et al., *Theories of International Relations*, 2nd ed. (Basingstoke: Palgrave, 2001), 156–159.
25 Paul Piccone, "The Future of Critical Theory," in Scott G. McNall and Gary N. Howe, eds., *Current Perspectives in Social Theory*, vol. 1 (Greenwich, CT: Jai Press, 1980), 21.
26 Antonio Gramsci, *Selections from the Prison Notebooks*, ed. and trans. Quinton Hoare and Geoffrey Nowell Smith (New York: International Publishers, 1971), 238.
27 Robert W. Cox, "Gramsci, Hegemony and International Relations: An Essay in Method," *Millennium: Journal of International Studies* 12, no. 2 (1983): 165.
28 Max Horkheimer, *Critical Theory*, trans. Matthew J. O'Connell et al. (New York: Herder & Herder, 1972), 206–207.
29 Ibid., 218, 233. For an excellent discussion of Horkheimer's critical theory, see Hoffman, "Critical Theory," 232–234, and Richard J. Bernstein, *The Restructuring of Social and Political Theory* (New York: Harcourt Brace Jovanovich, 1976), 191–200.
30 Cox, "Gramsci, Hegemony and International Relations," 172.
31 Cox, "Social Forces," 248.
32 J. Ann Tickner, "Hans Morgenthau's Principles of Political Realism: A Feminist Reformulation," *Millennium: Journal of International Studies* 17, no. 3 (1988): 429–440. Far from comprising objective laws of international politics, Morgenthau's realist theory, Tickner contended (ibid., 431), "is based on assumptions about human nature that are partial and that privilege masculinity." See also Cynthia Weber, "Good Girls, Little Girls, and Bad Girls: Male Paranoia in Robert Keohane's Critique of Feminist International Relations," *Millennium: Journal of International Studies* 23, no. 2 (1994): 337–349. For gender analysis as a form of critical international theory, see Sandra Whitworth, "Gender in the Inter-Paradigm Debate," *Millennium: Journal of International Studies* 18, no. 2 (1989): 265–272.
33 Edward W. Said, *Orientalism* (New York: Vintage, 1979 [1978]).
34 Ibid., 10.
35 Alexander Wendt, *Social Theory of International Politics* (Cambridge: Cambridge University Press, 1999), 90.
36 Ibid.
37 Gary King, Robert O. Keohane, and Sidney Verba, *Designing Social Inquiry: Scientific Inference in Qualitative Research* (Princeton, NJ: Princeton University Press, 1994), 6, 16.
38 Roland Bleiker, "The Aesthetic Turn in International Political Theory," *Millennium: Journal of International Studies* 30, no. 3 (2001): 510–511.
39 Ibid., 512.
40 Iver B. Neumann and Daniel H. Nexon, "Harry Potter and the Study of World Politics," in idem, eds., *Harry Potter and International Relations* (Lanham, MD: Rowman & Littlefield, 2006), 6–17.

41 Ibid., 17–20.

42 Lebow, *A Cultural Theory of International Relations* (Cambridge: Cambridge University Press, 2008); Campbell, *National Deconstruction: Violence, Identity and Justice in Bosnia* (Minneapolis, MN: University of Minnesota Press, 1998); Der Derian, *Virtuous War: Mapping the Military-Industrial Media-Entertainment Network*, 2nd ed. (New York and Abingdon: Routledge, 2009); Bleiker, *Aesthetics and World Politics* (London: Palgrave Macmillan, 2009); Weber, *Simulating Sovereignty: Intervention, the State, and Symbolic Exchange* (Cambridge: Cambridge University Press, 1995); Sylvester, *Feminist Theory and International Relations in a Postmodern Era* (Cambridge: Cambridge University Press, 1994); Coker, *Men at War: What Fiction Tells Us About Conflict, from The Illiad to Catch-22* (New York: Oxford University Press, 2014); Danchev, *On Art and War and Terror* (Edinburgh: Edinburgh University Press, 2009); and Suganami, *On the Causes of War* (Oxford: Oxford University Press, 1996).

43 Aurélie Lacassagne, "War and Peace in the *Harry Potter* series," *European Journal of Cultural Studies* 19, no. 4 (2016): 318–319.

44 Emma O. Norman, "International Boggarts: Carl Schmitt, *Harry Potter*, and the Transfiguration of Identity and Violence," *Politics & Policy* 40, no. 3 (2012): 407–408.

45 Stephen Deets, "Wizarding in the Classroom: Teaching Harry Potter and Politics," *PS: Political Science and Politics* 42, no. 4 (2009): 741–744.

46 Jutta Weldes, "Going Cultural: *Star Trek*, State Action, and Popular Culture," *Millennium: Journal of International Studies* 38, no. 1 (1999): 118–119.

47 See, for instance, Jutta Weldes, ed., *To Seek Out New Worlds: Science Fiction and World Politics* (New York: Palgrave Macmillan, 2003); Giselle Liza Anatol, ed., *Reading Harry Potter: Critical Essays* (Westport, CT: Praeger, 2003); and idem, ed., *Reading Harry Potter Again: New Critical Essays* (Westport, CT: Praeger, 2009).

1 Narrative Theory

The Role of Stories in the
Representation of Reality

To most contemporary American international relations scholars, narrative theory is utterly foreign: nothing but a question mark. On the one hand, this is hardly surprising, given that the recent linguistic turn in humanities and social sciences has tended to involve exotic ideas steeped in semiotics and literary criticism, served in thick postmodernist sauce, and garnished with hard-to-pronounce French names such as de Saussure, Foucault, and Barthes. On the other hand, insofar as narrative theory's core concerns include the nature and structure of stories, their typology, their relationship to reality, their role in the production of meaning, and their function in society, these already preoccupied Aristotle, whose name regularly appears on political science syllabi and should make students of international relations at least vaguely familiar with issues of narrative representation.

Unfortunately, the specialization and anti-theoreticism of academic international relations in the United States have progressed so far that not even the great author of *Politics*, one of the foundations of Western political philosophy, rings a bell any longer. His wisdom lacks any direct pertinence to the complex mathematical models of alliance formation, foreign aid impact, energy security investment determinants, World Trade Organization litigation costs, reverse-engineering of Chinese censorship, and other similar technical, policy-relevant problems that win tenure at Ivy League departments, comprise the daily bread and butter of the discipline's star researchers, and fill the pages of its flagship journals.

However, those with broader horizons and more open—less *disciplined*—minds who continue to read the Greek polymath even today may be aware that he penned not only the *Politics*, but also the *Poetics*: the oldest surviving treatise on storytelling. In it Aristotle developed a model of emplotment which, despite its focus on ancient Greek tragedy, is applicable to every composition that may be called a narrative.[1] As such, his *Poetics* offers an excellent starting point for discussing the role of stories in the representation of reality in preparation for fleshing out the poetics of international politics: the fictions of the factual discourse of academic international relations, on the one hand, and the factual inspirations and implications of fictional narratives of world affairs, on the other.

Aristotle on Narrative as the Making of Action

Aristotle wrote the *Poetics* with a clear didactic purpose: to instruct Greek poets in the art of making plots. If this art boiled down to simple reproductions of reality, no sophisticated instruction would be necessary: poets would merely transcribe events and deliver their copies to the audience as epic poems (such as Homer's *Odyssey*) or dramatic plays (such as Sophocles's *Oedipus Rex*). But according to Aristotle, the poetic art is far more involved, as the phraseology of the original Greek text already reveals. From the opening expression, *peri poiētikēs*, to the concluding passages, Aristotle uses cognate words on a single root: *poiein*, "a strongly active verb that ... dominate[s] the whole discussion in the sense 'to make.'"[2] Examples include *poiēsis* (the process or activity of making), *poiēma* (a thing made), and *poiētes* (a maker). All of them indicate that in Aristotle's view, the poetic art requires intensive participation by and genuine contribution from the poet: a point lost in translation to English, whose structure and vocabulary are unable to accommodate the subtleties of Aristotle's ancient Attic Greek dialect.

The same problem plagues *mimēsis*, a second term central to the *Poetics*: "English has no word to match the processive implications that abide in the very form of the words *mimēsis* and *poiēsis*."[3] Aristotle uses *mimēsis* in several different ways and never defines it other than contextually, above all when stating that tragedy, for him the most serious kind of dramatic poetry, "is a *mimēsis* ... of actions—that is, of life."[4] But his usage reveals beyond any doubt that he abandoned the Platonic definition of *mimēsis* as passive imitation in favor of a much more active conception: *mimēsis* as a process of imaginative fabrication. In Aristotle's *Poetics*, *mimēsis* "becomes the closest neighbor to creation: not out of nothing—no Greek ever believed in creation *ex nihilo*—but out of carefully observed 'universal' human tendencies to thought and action."[5] Poets sculpt action using language as their material, according to Aristotle. To say that their plots "represent" action is appropriate only if one strips the notion of representation of its usual passive undertones and comprehends it in terms of a highly inventive performance.[6]

This qualification is necessary because, in Aristotle's view, reality does not come preformed in ready-made plots available for passive reproduction; it is essentially chaotic and unintelligible. Those in the business of merely recording *ta genomena*, what actually took place in its actual sequence, face an unpleasant and disorienting task: "disclosure ... not of a single action (*praxis*) but of a single span of time—everything that happened ... in that [period of time], and each of these [events] bearing to the others an accidental ... relation."[7] The flow of everyday existence does not possess any inherent logic or unity. Rather, it is shot through with randomness: what Prince Hamlet would later decry as "the slings and arrows of outrageous fortune"[8] and, more recently, the Romanian anthropologist of religion Mircea Eliade captured with the memorable phrase "terror of history."[9] Aristotle views bare temporal succession of events—an unceasing stream of surprises and arbitrariness confounding all expectations—with similar dismay: as lacking any sense. Throughout the *Poetics*, "[He] clearly regards time sequence as a weak link, and no substitute for the logical *necessity* postulated for the unity of action."[10]

To represent action, therefore, poets must *craft* it: skillfully chisel it out of the amorphous sea of occurrences. In the process, "selection and arrangement are of paramount importance [to *mimēsis* and *poēsis*]."[11] The result—the epic or dramatic plot—encapsulates a human achievement: a contrived victory of logical concordance over temporal discordance. "To make up a plot is ... to make the intelligible spring from the accidental, the universal from the singular, the necessary or probable from the episodic."[12] So central is the plot (*muthos*) to the poetic art that Aristotle proclaims it "the first principle of tragedy—the soul, in fact,"[13] and dedicates the bulk of his attention to spelling out its ideal characteristics. These include "a length such as can readily be held in memory"[14] and protagonists who are like us (neither morally perfect nor thoroughly evil) and "[come] upon disaster ... because of some mistake"[15] rather than because of sheer bad luck.

Above all, however, well-constructed plots possess wholeness, purpose, and unity. The first of these aspects refers to having a beginning, a middle, and an end, where

> A 'beginning' is what does not necessarily have to follow anything else, but after which something naturally is or happens; an 'end' ... is what naturally is after something else, either of necessity or usually, but has nothing after it; [and] a middle is what comes after something else and has something else after it.[16]

Plots that are whole, in other words, display internal necessity: they "neither begin at an accidental starting-point nor come to an accidental conclusion."[17] Sudden reversals of fortune (*peripeteia*) are permissible and indeed distinguish more sophisticated "complex" plots from "simple" ones, but their inclusion is acceptable only on the condition that they

> come from the structure of the plot itself, so that, from what has happened before it turns out that these things would necessarily or probably happen; for it makes a big difference whether things happen *because of* [what has gone before] or [merely] *after*.[18]

The reversal must emanate from the overall logic of the action, so that the unexpected engenders in the audience a powerful recognition (*anagnōrisis*) of its paradoxical inevitability and necessity; "strokes of chance that seem to arrive by design"[19] are the very pinnacles of poetic achievement. Tragedies featuring genuine arbitrariness are much less compelling.[20]

Wholeness, however, cannot be achieved without something more fundamental: it presupposes the presence of a clear overarching purpose (*telos*) guiding the plot in the first place. Without any specific moral goal or message in mind, the poet would have no criterion of relevance for event selection and no basis for identifying the plot's proper beginning. "Beginnings never come first, not logically"; if the plot's beginning

> describes the logical-relational placement of a certain event inaugurating everything that follows, ... [the] process of deciding on that inaugurating point can't possibly start there: everything is a 'beginning' of some tellable series, or more than one. (...) Beginnings are conceptually possible only as a function of endings.[21]

In this vein, "all narrative constructions are teleological ... in a fundamental way."[22]

The teleological requirement signals the practical-political role of plots and stories in ancient Greek society: to educate citizens and shape the life of the polis. By advancing a specific *telos* and communicating it in a convincing manner, properly composed dramas and epics functioned as instruments of power, specifically the power to persuade through language and narrative. Their ultimate purpose was to mold the audience's consciousness of political reality. In this vein, "The *Poetics* does not speak of structure but of structuration ... as an oriented activity that is only completed in the spectator or the reader."[23] The completion occurs in and through *catharsis*: an experience of deep pleasure which "is neither simply intellectual nor simply emotional, but has its roots in both realms. It is a pleasure springing from emotion, but an emotion authorized and released by an intellectually conditioned structure of action."[24]

If wholeness "guarantees that no part is missing which should be there," unity, another key feature of a well-crafted plot, means that "nothing is there which belongs somewhere else."[25] Expertly composed plots not only portray *praxis* driven by internal necessity anchored in a specific *telos*, but also omit everything else: all happenings and information extraneous to the action's driving logic.

> Constituent events [must] be so put together that if one of them is shifted or taken away, the whole [structure] is disrupted and thrown out of kilter. For a part that clearly does nothing by being present or left out is no *part* of the whole.[26]

Notably, unity is not achieved by writing about a single individual. "A plot doesn't get to be unified ... [simply] by being about one person," since

> a lot of things—an infinite number of things—happen to one person, and a good number of these have [*sic*] nothing to do with a single [action (*praxis*)]; and in the same way, there are many of one person's actions from which no single unified action arises.[27]

A complete record of an individual life would lack any meaningful action or message, for these depend on and emerge through poetic selection and arrangement.

In the pages ahead, this argument will gain crisp contours in the chapter excavating the fictions of competing factual representations of the late British historian E. H. Carr as a proponent of different schools of international relations theory: regardless of how contemporary scholars portray him, whether as a realist or critical theorist, they all necessarily filter out parts of his life and achievement, or else he would display no intelligible legacy and cease to be politically useful to them for the purpose of justifying their paradigm of choice. Before any of this, however, it is necessary to establish a key point: the applicability of the *Poetics* beyond fictional narratives to factual ones. In a crucial move, Aristotle announces that the subject matter of epic and dramatic poetry is not restricted to imaginary persons and events. True, typically "the poet's business is to tell not what is happening but the sort of things ... that, according to likelihood and necessity, *can* [happen]."[28] In this vein, "poetry deals ... with universals" rather than empirically based particulars, where "'Universals' means the sort of things that according to likelihood and necessity a certain kind of person tends to say or do."[29] But Aristotle adds unequivocally that

> even if it turns out that he [the poet] is making his work out of *actual* events, he is none the less a poet—a maker: for nothing prevents some actual events from being the sort of things that might probably happen, and in such a case he is the *maker* of those events.[30]

The implications of this passage are difficult to exaggerate. In it, "The paradox inherent in Aristotle's concept of 'imitation' [*mimēsis*] rises to a climax," since he claims that

> events are already there, they have happened, and yet the poet 'makes' them just as much as if he had invented them himself. What the poet 'makes,' then, is not the actuality of events but their logical structure, their meaning. Their having happened is accidental to their being composed, and vice versa. (...) A poet, then, is an *imitator* in so far as he is a *maker*, viz. of plots. ... Aristotle has developed and changed the bearing of a concept [*mimēsis*] which originally meant a faithful *copying* of pre-existent things, to make it mean a *creation* of things which have never existed or whose existence, if they did exist, is accidental to the poetic process. Copying is after the fact. Aristotle's *mimēsis* creates the fact.[31]

Whether plots work with imaginary or actual information, Aristotle effectively declares all of them poetic fabrications. Differences in content—whether it is made up or rooted in empirical reality—are secondary to the narrative form; the aspect of fiction inheres precisely in plot design. To the extent that they feature the structure of a unified story with a coherent beginning, middle, and end, even factual accounts are mimetic *creations* with everything this entails, such as that they have a practical-political purpose and serve as linguistic-rhetorical instruments for its dissemination.

Aristotle, his fellow Greeks, and many subsequent generations of heirs to classical learning considered this common sense. From antiquity to the late eighteenth century, the idea that historical narratives as specimens of evidentiary discourse are nonetheless literary artifacts featuring open invention and ethical agenda was a thoroughly unremarkable and unproblematic proposition. That it provokes controversy today as part of the widely decried postmodernist threat to serious historiography and social science is a result of recent changes, above all the professionalization of historical inquiry during the nineteenth century. In its course, *Geschichtsschreibung* was transformed into *Geschichtswissenschaft*, and the constitutive role of narrative became thoroughly occluded by the emphasis on verifiable data, transparent expression, and scientific method. Leopold von Ranke, who personified these developments as the preeminent shaper of modern historiography as it emerged in European and North American universities in the late 1800s, could thus maintain in the same breath that proper historical writing should rely on empirical sources, refrain from judging bygone events, avoid instructing the present, report the past *wie es eigentlich gewesen ist* (as it really happened), and do it all *in narrative form*.[32]

In light of Aristotle's teachings in the *Poetics*, such a methodological approach, no matter its current monopoly in professional historiography and social sciences including academic international relations, surfaces as confused to the point of self-contradictory. By the same token, the postmodernist challenge to it emerges as much less radical than commonly perceived. Indeed, some have suggested that "postmodern narrative analysis of history is grounded in the classical philosophic tradition in the earliest dissection of mimetic activity," that "Aristotle's *Poetics* stands as a foundational prolegomenon to the entirety of the linguistic turn," and that "the book ... could, without distortion, and with considerable gain in accuracy, be called Aristotle's *Narrative Theory*."[33] These claims are problematic on a couple of counts: contemporary narrative theory is not necessarily a strand of postmodernism, as will be seen shortly, and if it were, one wonders why it should feel compelled to search for its foundations in the first place, given postmodernism's "incredulity toward metanarratives,"[34] presumably including those of its own origins. But they are also perceptive and useful in that they hint at the extensive and generally unrecognized affinities between Aristotle's thoughts on poetic emplotment and many of the key ideas of narrative theory today.

Hayden White and the Narrativist Thesis of Historical Representation

As it has evolved since the late 1950s, contemporary narrative theory of historiography is a large and complicated animal: it wears many faces, speaks numerous tongues, and refuses to submit to simple summary. Thinkers who have engaged with the nature, function, and implications of narrative in factual discourse (especially but not only historical writing) are legion, including Paul Ricoeur, Roland Barthes, Fernand Braudel, W. B. Gallie, William Dray, Arthur Danto, Louis Mink, and Frank Ankersmit. In English-speaking circles, however, one figure towers high above all others: Hayden White. His work at the crossroads of historical and literary studies, the same area of inquiry staked out by Aristotle's *Poetics*, has revolutionized modern historiography and acted as a major catalyst for the recent linguistic turn in humanities and social sciences.

Born in a working-class family in Martin, Tennessee, in 1928 and raised with one foot planted in the rural South and the other in the industrial city of Detroit, where his parents moved during the Great Depression, White was an American cultural theorist and historian originally trained as a medievalist. After working at the Ford factory in his teens and serving in the US Navy in the late 1940s, he enrolled at Wayne State University, where he and many of his fellow class members—including Danto—came under the influence of the history professor William J. Bossenbrook. Charismatic and well-read, Bossenbrook mesmerized his students "really like some sort of shaman"[35] and imbued White with a lifelong passion for the study of the past as a form of human self-understanding and emancipation. After completing his doctorate at the University of Michigan with a thesis on St. Bernard of Clairvaux, White joined the academic profession and eventually arrived at the University of California at Santa Cruz, where he forged a long and distinguished academic career as the driving force behind the History of Consciousness Program and as a mentor to many future cultural and historical theorists. But it was already at the very outset of his academic life, during his initial postings at institutions such as the University of Rochester and Wesleyan University in the intellectually vibrant 1960s, that his scholarly interests began pivoting from substantive topics of historical research to the broader social and cultural function of history and, as a subset of this area of concern, to the ethical-rhetorical dimension of historical representation.[36]

Since then until his death in March 2018, inspired especially by Vico and Barthes, the latter of whom he described as "the greatest and most inventive critic of the postwar period,"[37] White had dedicated practically all his energies to mapping the poetics of composition of historical texts and to fleshing out the silent nonempirical content brought to them by virtue of their narrative structure. The results of his efforts have become known as "the narrativist theory"[38] of historical representation and garnered him widespread acclaim. In 1997, Dan Stone stated that White had made "the most important contribution to philosophy of history of the last three decades."[39] Writing ten years later, Patrick Finney enthusiastically endorsed Stone's assessment, "except ... we might now stretch the figure to four [decades]."[40] Robert Doran went further still:

> One would have to return to the nineteenth century to find a thinker who has had a greater impact on the way we think about historical

representation, the discipline of history, and on how historiography intersects with other domains of inquiry, particularly literary studies.[41]

Central to White's narrativist thesis is the notion that "Stories are told or written, not found."[42] Echoing Aristotle, White regards bare temporal existence as chaotic, messy, full of contradictions, and devoid of any meaning: "enthymemic," in a word.[43] "Reality is highly complex," White elaborates, "the more information you get, the less comprehension you can have of a situation."[44] Voicing a similar view, Mink has written that "life is not a story and does not have the form of one except insofar as we give it that form..."[45] Events and occurrences prior to narrative representation do not possess any kind of inherent logic or motif awaiting simple discovery, as traditional historiography and social sciences presuppose.

> It is sometimes said that the aim of the historian is to explain the past by "finding," "identifying," or "uncovering" the "stories" that lie buried in chronicles; and that the difference between "history" and "fiction" resides in the fact that the historian "finds" his stories, whereas the fiction writer "invents" his.[46]

From the vantage of the narrativist thesis, however, this conventional definition of the historian's activity "obscures the extent to which 'invention' also plays a part in [his] operations."[47] The inevitability of invention in historical writing springs precisely from the recognition that "Life has no beginnings, middles or ends; there are meetings, but the start of an affair belongs to the story we tell ourselves later, and there are partings, but final partings only in the story."[48]

Patterns, meaning, and action thus emerge only through poetics and storytelling, which is to say that they are constructed and imposed. History is "a species of the genus Story."[49] To the extent that "All stories are fictions"[50] and historians are professionally required to render the past in story form, their craft involves the imaginative mental processes and literary techniques of the novelist: narrative selection, omission, emplotment, figuration, troping, and so on. In a sense, the entire thrust of the narrativist thesis is to lay bare the "uniquely *poetic* elements" and "deep structural content which is ... linguistic ... in nature and ... serves as the pre-critically accepted paradigm of what a distinctively 'historical' explanation should be."[51]

Systematic analysis of this buried poetic apparatus led White to assert that "Historians' findings are arrived at by cognitive operations that have more in common with poetry than ... science."[52] As the product of these cognitive operations, historical texts may be regarded as pieces of literary art:

> The ... strategies [historians and novelists] use can be shown to be substantially the same. (...) Viewed simply as verbal artifacts histories and novels are indistinguishable from one another. We cannot easily

distinguish between them on formal grounds unless we approach them with specific preconceptions about the kind of truths that each is supposed to deal in. (...) History is no less a form of fiction than the novel is a form of historical representation.[53]

Neither White nor most other narrativists deny that historians or social scientists compose their stories out of different material than novelists: empirically based facts as opposed to imaginary events. The narrativist thesis does "not ... say that a historical discourse is not properly assessed in terms of the truth value of its factual (singular existential) statements taken individually and the logical conjunction of the whole set of such statements taken distributively."[54] But the difference in material should not obscure the identity in process and form, whereby both historians and novelists engage in narrative composition and storytelling—Aristotelian *poiēsis*—in the first place. "[W]hatever its subject matter," narrativization is "*inherently* fictive."[55] Whether it manipulates with imaginary events or real happenings, "the process of fusing [them] ... into a comprehensible totality capable of serving as the object of representation is a poetic process."[56]

Always touting the factual content of its texts in an effort to avail itself of the status of science, traditional historiography has failed to reflect on this process and consider the characteristics and implications of the literary structures conventionally utilized to integrate the content. It has focused exclusively on historical research and "almost entirely neglected ... the problem of how the historian *narratively* interprets the results of historical research."[57] Scholars working in the methodological tradition of Rankean empiricism, which is to say the vast majority of professional historians today, "favor the narrative mode for the presentation of their findings ... but ... do not understand the significance of their preference, (...) are ... incapable of analyzing the discursive dimensions of their writing," and indeed "positively repress the idea that there might be such a dimension."[58]

The seriousness of this lapse emerges when one recognizes that historians see themselves as much more than just detectives. Locating sources in the archives, corroborating evidence, and in general establishing the facts about the past is not their main task, but only a prologue to their main task, which lies elsewhere: in providing compelling "images" of the past. "Saying *true* things about the past is easy—anybody can do that—but saying the *right* things about the past is difficult."[59] In other words,

> all that is essential and interesting in the writing of history ... is not to be found at the level of the individual statements, but at that of the politics adopted by historians when they select the statements that individuate their "picture of the past."[60]

Were factual content the principal determinant of the value of historical texts, nobody would read Gibbon's *Decline and Fall of the Roman Empire*

any longer; today's historians of ancient Rome preside over far more accurate and extensive source evidence, not to mention incomparably more
sophisticated auxiliary sciences and detective tools such as radioactive carbon dating. But the enduring status of Gibbon's work as a widely admired
classic illustrates that "The historiographical value of a piece of history is
determined less by the facts disclosed ... than by the narrative interpretation of such facts."[61]

Some narrativists have taken this argument all the way to the conclusion
that the manner of interpretation is not just more important than the matter
interpreted, but all-important—for the following reason: "If various historians are occupied with ... the same research subject, the resulting differences
in *content* can just as well be described as a different *style* in the treatment
of that research subject."[62] From this angle, content is entirely derivative: a
function of the literary-stylistic form adopted for its composition and presentation. This position just about inverts the common wisdom of the empiricist mainstream, according to which linguistic form, when not perfectly
transparent, is merely ornamental and either way adds nothing to factual
content, whose truth alone defines the quality of the historical account in
question.

Excavating the Buried Poetic Content of the Narrative Form

The narrativist thesis shines the spotlight precisely onto the formal and
compositional features of historical works. The difference from traditional
historiography could not be starker. The standard historical method

> has resulted in the repression of the *conceptual apparatus* (without which
> atomic facts cannot be aggregated into complex macrostructures) and
> the remission of the *poetic moment* in historical writing to the interior of
> the discourse (where it functions as an unacknowledged—and therefore
> uncriticizable—*content* of the historical narrative).[63]

By contrast, in analyses undertaken by narrativist theorists, the buried
"content of the form" takes center stage, and the various "poetic and rhetorical elements by which what would otherwise be a list of facts is transformed
into a story"[64] surface to visibility in their full glory.

It is in and through this content of the form that fiction infiltrates factual
representations, which in order to pass for proper accounts of reality must
consist of "much more than a list of singular existential statements."[65] They
must feature narrative structure, and this structure "claims truth not merely
for each of its individual statements taken distributively, but for the complex
form of the narrative itself."[66] Historical understanding, in other words,
much like wisdom related by novels, is fundamentally a configurational
mode of comprehension evocative of Aristotle's requirement that well-
crafted plots be readily graspable in one's mind and memory. Its distinctive

feature is synoptic judgment, which enables the historian or social scientist to gather together events that took place in temporal sequence, conceive of them as a single complex whole, and communicate the mental image to the audience in the *narrative* sequence of a comprehensible story, whose form embodies the judgment.[67]

As the poetic content of the narrative form, synoptic judgment is typically silent and unarticulated, but it manifests itself in several familiar ways and implications. One is the non-detachability of historian's conclusions: a major difference from the research protocol in natural sciences, where results of particular analyses and investigations are readily detachable and facilitate cumulative growth of knowledge. By contrast, in historical writing and social-scientific treatises, "The significant conclusions ... are ingredient to the argument itself, not merely in the sense that they are scattered through the text but in the sense that they are *represented by the narrative order itself*."[68] They inhere in the topography of the story, as it were, which is unique to every text, reflecting as it does the author's unique poetic and interpretive standpoint. Another familiar implication is that narrative historical representations resist additive combination, something the traditional Rankean conception of the past as a totality of "what actually happened" should in principle allow. The content of the form again stands in the way: "Narrative histories should be aggregative, insofar as they are histories, but cannot be, insofar as they are narratives."[69]

The poetic-rhetorical element of historical and social-scientific narratives thus serves a constant reminder that they are works of *mimēsis* in the Aristotelian rather than Platonic sense. "Individual statements about the past may be true or false, but a narrative is more than a conjunction of statements, and *insofar* as it is more it does not reduplicate a complex past but constructs one."[70] For this reason, to talk about the historian's essential task in terms of providing "pictures" or "images" of the past—words suggestive of passive reproduction—is not, strictly speaking, appropriate. Rather, what results from the cognitive process of gathering disparate facts about the past and colligating them into unified stories such as "The Terrorist Attacks of 9/11" is narrative substances, whose fundamental characteristic is that they are self-contained in the sense of not corresponding to anything in historical reality.[71] "The narrative substance is a linguistic object we can refer to ... but that never refers to anything other than or outside itself. Narrative substances are truly semantic 'black holes' in the universe of the language we use."[72] They are intrinsically aesthetic, can be identified only by mutual contrast, and function not as copies of the past but as substitutes attempting to replace it.

On occasion, White has intimated that the content of the form of histories proper—their narrative substances or synoptic judgments—can be isolated by contrast with annals and chronicles, which only record events as they occur in time. "The chronological sequence," he has stated in this regard, constitutes "a kind of zero degree against which ... [to] measure emplotment."[73] Since they are un-narrativized and hence presumably free of any interpretive elements, annals and chronicles might function as a sort of light table: superimpose a narrative history covering the same events, and the extra poetic-rhetorical content added to the events by the history's plot structure surfaces to visibility.

But as windows onto the past, not even annals and chronicles are fully transparent. They, too, introduce opacity, involve figuration, and therefore actively constitute the past rather than just passively report it, as Danto has been the most adamant to emphasize. The idea that chronicles merely describe facts whereas proper histories additionally interpret them, he noted,

> is a distinction I am unable to accept. For ... history is all of a piece. It is all of a piece in the sense that there is nothing one might call a pure description in contrast with something else to be called an interpretation. Just to do history at all is to employ some overarching conceptions which ... go beyond what is given.[74]

Indeed, "even if we could witness the whole past, any account we would give of it would involve selection, emphasis, elimination, and would presuppose some criteria of relevance."[75]

The deep linguistic structural content, whose excavation and charting comprise White's main contribution to historical theory and the cornerstone of his intellectual legacy, thus may not be exclusive to proper histories. Poetic prefiguration might very well lie much deeper and begin much earlier: at a far more basic stage of historical consciousness and representation. In Danto's view, it occurs already at the point where the human mind encounters the world for the very first time and, attempting to make sense of its chaos and mystery, utters its initial descriptive sentence about it.

Narrative Theory and Historical Truth: From Logic to Tropologic

Narrative historical theory is far from monolithic, of course; it manifests numerous fissures and tensions. One notable controversy surrounds the question of whether plots originate within the mind or have any external existence: whereas narrative idealists such as White and Ankersmit espouse the former view, narrative realists such as David Carr propound the latter, arguing that "Narrative is not merely a ... way of describing events; its structure inheres in the events themselves."[76] Another gray area concerns the proximity of historical narratives to their counterparts in fiction writing: White and Ankersmit may agree that narratives are ideational, but only in White's case can there be any talk of an "'evaporation' of the borderline between ... history and fiction."[77] For Ankersmit, "the narratio," a technical term he reserves solely for narratives in historiography, denotes "a linguistic entity essentially different from other coherent systems of sentences such as poems, novels, sermons, mathematical proofs, and so on," even if novels— and historical novels in particular—come very close to it.[78]

Nonetheless, such disagreements do not detract anything from the numerous convergences, among which the most prominent is epistemological relativism. It arises in direct consequence of the central thesis that historical narratives are more than the sum of their parts and feature, in addition to the facts they present, structural content which is nonempirical and poetic in nature. This means that unlike individual facts, which can be evaluated as true or false on the basis of material evidence, structural content cannot: "at the level of the historical text and historical interpretation we cannot appropriately use the words truth and falsity."[79]

When it comes to assessing historical narratives, in other words, the standards of science and syllogistic logic, while adequate and necessary to ascertain the truth-value of singular existential statements and their logical conjunction, do not suffice alone—precisely because historical narratives possess a truth-value over and above that of their constituent facts. To turn a list of basic factual statements into a narrative account is to take a step "'beyond,' although not 'against,' such standards of scientificity," into a realm that is neither unscientific nor anti-scientific but rather "a-scientific."[80] In this realm of discourse, "there is no neutral intermediate space between narrative substances within which debate over them can be conducted," and the absence of shared epistemological criteria makes adjudicating among rival representations akin to "fighting a seventeenth-century naval battle after the wind has completely died down: clumsy, ineffective, and most often inconclusive."[81] Rather than ranked, competing accounts of the same phenomena can only be categorized as different but equally plausible images, and something more than Hempelian deductive logic is required for the process: tropologic or "'poetic logic,' which informs narrative discourse much more immediately than any version of syllogistic logic."[82]

The recognition of this problem is precisely what made White's *Metahistory* an instant albeit initially unnoticed game changer: in its opening chapter, White became the first theorist of history to introduce a full-fledged tropological framework for analysis of narrative historiography. In his definition,

> Tropology is the theoretical understanding of imaginative discourse, of all the ways by which various kinds of figurations ... produce ... images and connections among images capable of serving as tokens of a reality that can only be imagined rather than directly perceived. [These] connections ... are not logical ... but metaphorical in a general sense, i.e., based on the poetic techniques of condensation, displacement, symbolization, and revision.[83]

In developing the tropological lens, White ventured well beyond the narrow confines of the discipline of history to an eclectic mixture of thinkers from many other fields, including Vico, Ernst Gombrich, semiologists and literary theorists such as Erich Auerbach, Kenneth Burke, Northrop Frye,

Roman Jakobson, and Claude Lévi-Strauss, and sociologist Karl Mannheim. Their insights allowed him not only to detect the poetic dimension of historical writing but to dissect it into a number of fine layers and identify the different strategies available within each. The result is a sophisticated matrix for the classification of historiographical styles: "a way of tracking ... those 'swerves' from literality into figurative language by which the emplotment of real ... events is effected and, in the process, endowed with meanings far in excess of their significance as 'occurrences.'"[84]

The first and most fundamental stage at which these "swerves" take place is poetic prefiguration, during which the historian's mind initiates its engagement with the field of past phenomena by constituting it as an object of mental perception.

> In order to figure "what *really* happened" in the past ... the historian must first *pre*figure as a possible object of knowledge the whole set of events reported in the documents. This prefigurative act is *poetic* inasmuch as it is precognitive and precritical in the economy of the historian's own consciousness.[85]

It is guided by one of four archetypal master tropes intrinsic to all human language: Metaphor, Metonymy, Synecdoche, and Irony. Each generates specific literal relationships and figurative illuminations: Metaphor is representational, Metonymy reductionist, Synecdoche integrative, and Irony negational. Each also implies specific views concerning the representational capacity of language: whereas Metaphor, Metonymy, and Synecdoche communicate belief in the ability of language to grasp the nature of reality, Irony signals radical doubt, which makes this figure dialectical, relativizing, self-reflexive, and meta-tropological. Each master trope thus apprehends and constitutes the historical field in a distinctive manner. In doing so, it not only creates the historian's object of analysis, but simultaneously "predetermines the modality of the conceptual strategies he will use to explain it."[86] Subsequent poetic activity takes place within parameters imposed by the dominant trope during the primary phase.

The secondary stage may be subdivided into three levels, on which the historian invests the field of occurrences prefigured by a given master trope with concrete meaning: explanation by narrative emplotment, formal argument, and ideological implication. "Emplotment is the way by which a sequence of events fashioned into a story is gradually revealed to be a story of a particular kind."[87] The principal kinds are Romance, Tragedy, Comedy, and Satire. Analytically distinct from emplotment is formal or explicit argument, which generates sense by introducing specific principles governing the aggregation and classification of historical phenomena.[88] The main paradigms within this layer of poetic figuration are Formism, Organicism, Mechanism, and Contextualism. As an example, Formists emphasize the unique characteristics, variety, and color of objects inhabiting the historical

field in order to dispel their perceived similarities, whereas Organicists syn-
thesize them into sweeping teleological processes. As for the ideological
layer of historical narratives, it "reflect[s] the ethical element in the historian's assumption of a particular position on the question of ... the implications that can be drawn from the study of past events for the understanding
of present ones."[89] Each of the basic modalities—Conservatism, Liberalism, Radicalism, and Anarchism—resembles the others in masquerading
as the sole purveyor of rational and scientific historical knowledge and denouncing its competitors as ideological, but this is where their similarities
end. White follows Mannheim's sociology of knowledge in *Ideology and
Utopia* to argue that underneath their shared claim to realist representation
the four positions

> represent different attitudes with respect to the possibility of reducing
> the study of society to a science and the desirability of doing so; differ-
> ent notions of the lessons that the human sciences can teach; different
> conceptions of the desirability of maintaining or changing the social
> status quo; different conceptions of the direction that changes in the
> status quo ought to take and the means of effecting such changes; and,
> finally, different time orientations ... toward past, present, or future as
> the repository of ... society's ideal form.[90]

A particular combination of plot type, formal argument, and ideology
yields a distinctive historiographical style, although White stresses that
"the various modes of emplotment, argument, and ideological implication
cannot be indiscriminately combined in a given work."[91] Certain elective
affinities and structural homologies run across the different layers of secondary poetic composition, making a Comic plot, for example, incompatible with a Radical ideology. Similarly, the secondary stage as a whole tends
to correlate with the primary stage of prefiguration. Overall, White's matrix
for tropological analysis of narrative historical discourse comprises sixteen
categories within four different layers.[92]

White's relativism emerges from his notion that changes in historical imagination and narrative representational style proceed independently of the
factual historical record, which places no restrictions on them. "[T]here are
no apodictically certain theoretical grounds on which one can legitimately
claim an authority for any one of the modes [of historiography] over the others as being more 'realistic.'"[93] His general conclusions in *Metahistory* beg
to be reproduced at length:

> there can be no "proper history" which is not at the same time "philos-
> ophy of history"; the possible modes of historiography are ... *formaliza-
> tions* of poetic insights that analytically precede them and ... sanction
> the particular theories used to give historical accounts the aspect of
> an "explanation"; ... we are indentured to a *choice* among contending

interpretative strategies in any effort to reflect on history-in-general; ... the best grounds for choosing one perspective on history rather than another are ultimately aesthetic and moral rather than epistemological; and, finally, the demand for the scientization of history represents only ... a preference for a specific modality of historical representation, the grounds of which are either moral or aesthetic, but the epistemological justification of which still remains to be established.[94]

Even texts composed by historians and philosophers of history without any manifest political agendas, such as Burckhardt and Nietzsche, cannot avoid specific ideological implications. There is always "an irreducible ideological component in every historical account of reality,"[95] as White has never tired of repeating.

Every history has its myth. (...) There is no value-neutral mode of emplotment, explanation, or even description of any field of events. ... The very use of language itself implies ... a specific posture before the world which is ethical, ideological, or more generally political: not only all interpretation, but also all language is politically contaminated.[96]

The Emancipatory Politics of Narrative Theory

It may be tempting to infer from these conclusions that White considers history intellectually corrupt and calls for its abandonment or at least thorough purification, but such suppositions would amount to a fundamental misunderstanding of the larger project behind his analysis of the rhetorical dimension of modern historiography. Although his immediate objective, as Dominick LaCapra has summarized it, is to "make interpretive and explanatory strategies—which remain implicit in traditional historiography practiced as a craft—explicit, self-conscious, and subject to criticism,"[97] in exposing these strategies and the nonempirical content brought by them to story-like accounts about the past White does not demand to decontaminate historiography of ideology: "History was always ideological. (...) [I]t is impossible to go beyond ideology in the human sciences."[98] Much less does he propose to turn away from history altogether. Rather, his tropological framework serves him to denaturalize the currently dominant norms and protocols governing the production of historical knowledge, reveal their contingent status, and thereby empower marginalized individuals and collectivities to take full control of their pasts as a matter of taking full control of their presents and futures. In White's hands, in other words, narrative historical theory performs a distinctively emancipatory role: it facilitates human self-realization by dismantling artificial cognitive barriers in its path.

That White embraces history as essential to freedom even though he fully recognizes its inescapable ideological-justificatory function, indeed, precisely *because* of it, is abundantly clear from his reflections on the nature of historical systems. What distinguishes them from biological systems is that human individuals and collectivities have a unique capacity to constitute and reconstitute their ancestries in complete disregard of actual genetic connections: strictly on the basis of their dynamically evolving practical goals and interests. Unlike any other species, human beings choose who they are, and in significant part they "choose who they are by choosing who they *were*."[99] For this the historical past is eminently suitable by virtue of its essential absence, making it a *tabula rasa* ready for inscription and reinscription: "plastic in a way that the genetic past is not. Men range over it and select from it models of comportment for structuring their movement into the future."[100] In contrast to the biological past, "the *historical* past is not given; it has to be constructed in the same way and in the same extent ... [as] our sociocultural present."[101] It is in this sense that White celebrates history as a projection and locus of human freedom.

Unfortunately, the majority of people tend to approach history in the opposite manner: with the propensity to abdicate their unique capacity to constitute their origins. They routinely naturalize the historical past, forget their ownership of it and role in constructing it, and cast the present and the future as predetermined by what had gone on before. "They want to believe that what they have in fact created could not have been otherwise."[102] This desire drives them to turn a blind eye to the element of choice—and hence of ethics and politics—in historical narratives and instead (mis)conceptualize them as passive descriptions of objective developments inherent in the field of events themselves. Its plasticity and malleability forgotten, history as a repository of practical lessons teaching humans how to live thereby hardens into solid rock, ceases to express freedom, and becomes oppressive: a burden of platitudes whose dead weight stifles the mind until it loses sight of any alternative orders of existence and modes of behavior and begins imagining the future merely as a continuation of the past. The result is stasis: life imprisoned in the straitjacket of received ideas, norms, and institutions whose ethico-ideological foundations have receded from view so completely that those excluded, exploited, and otherwise disadvantaged by them are no longer even aware of their optional and political character, let alone capable of emancipatory action. As White describes the overall dynamic, "By constructing our present we assert our freedom, [but] by seeking retroactive justification for it in our past, we silently strip ourselves of the freedom that has allowed us to become who we are."[103]

During White's formative years immediately following World War II, mainstream Western historiography performed the conserving and homogenizing function in a particularly clever disguise: under a surface commitment to liberty, pluralism, and diversity. As celebrated by Popper in *Open Society and Its Enemies* (1945) and *The Poverty of Historicism* (1953), this historiography portrayed itself as a staunch defender of liberal democracy by eschewing the ideological presuppositions of the Marxist and fascist metanarratives invoked to sanction totalitarian dictatorship. White was not the first critic to point out that this program did not eliminate ideology from history but, on the contrary, fused them ever more completely and imperceptibly by concealing a highly partisan—Western, statist, gendered, racial—vision of society in the cloak of science, moving it beyond the reach of ethical contestability, and thus effectively narrowing rather than expanding the limits of political discourse. Already E. H. Carr, writing in the early 1960s under some of the same influences as would guide White's tropological investigations in *Metahistory* a decade later, notably Mannheim's sociology, stripped liberal empiricism of its scientific pretensions in his famous *What Is History?* (1961), drafted with the express intention of exploding the myths propounded by Popper and other leading members of the British liberal historical establishment, such as Herbert Butterfield.[104] But in a major advancement over Carr, who had failed to problematize the representational status of language, White informed his attack on empiricist historiography with rich insights from literary theory, which allowed him to appreciate the central role of narrative in constituting, rather than simply reproducing, historical reality. This gives extra depth to his position, discernible already in Carr's polemics, that historical knowledge is always ideologically motivated and that liberal empiricism is part of hegemonic consciousness serving the dominant strata: "In its claims to 'disinterestedness,'" the Rankean approach as "a monolithic interpretative 'consensus' ... manifests its 'interest' in the maintenance of the social status quo."[105]

The method and implications of White's critique of liberal empiricist historiography broadly resemble the method and implications of Thomas Kuhn's seminal critique of natural science in *The Structure of Scientific Revolutions* (1962). Originally trained as a physicist, Kuhn "brought ... all of science under history" and "opened the way to discussing science as a human and historical matter."[106] Similarly, White rose above his own native discipline, in this case history, and set out to historicize its standard approach to knowledge.[107] Notwithstanding its claims to truth and superiority over all its predecessors, this approach emerges out of his analyses as merely the currently accepted paradigm: a self-enclosed and self-referential matrix of conventions combining theory, methods, and criteria of evaluation. Based on an exemplary past achievement—Ranke's histories, analogous to Newton's laws of motion in physics—"that some particular scientific community acknowledges for a time as supplying the foundation for its further practice," this matrix ultimately rests on "the assent of the relevant community."[108] For Kuhn writing about natural science as for White writing about the science of history, in other words, evolution of knowledge is primarily a matter of cultural and sociological factors: the composition, beliefs, values, and practices of particular scientific communities embedded in particular historical contexts. Compared across time and place, these factors differ so radically as to make competing paradigms wholly incommensurable: "the choice ... between [them] proves to be a choice between incompatible modes of community life."[109] What paradigms do share in common is a conservative bias: resistance to rebellious modes of intellectual activity undermining the established foundations authorizing normal research. "Normal science ... suppresses fundamental novelties because these are necessarily subversive of its basic commitments."[110] The army of Newtonians dominating physics a century ago hardly welcomed the first proponents of quantum mechanics or even recognized them as fellow scientists. In the same vein, the legions of Rankean empiricists dominating contemporary historiography do not regard writers of historical novels as their peers, no matter that the latter, too, are in the business of crafting narratives out of facts.

The analogy between White's and Kuhn's analyses goes only so far, however, and breaks down over the issue of whether or not the chronological procession of paradigms displays any deeper motif. Whereas Kuhn views "scientific development as a succession of tradition-bound periods punctuated by non-cumulative breaks" and distances himself entirely from any notion of "a process of evolution *toward* anything,"[111] White postulates an intricate pattern of progress. In his *Metahistory*, charting the development of historical imagination in nineteenth-century Europe, the four master tropes governing the poetic construction of the past do not follow one another haphazardly, but along a dialectically unfolding upward spiral: a Vichian *corso* from a Metaphorical cast of mind through Metonymical and Synecdochic phases to an Ironic posture, presaging a *ricorso* back to the figure of Metaphor setting off a repetition of the sequence at a higher level of consciousness. This imbues White's metahistorical perspective with a distinctive utopian impulse, which several among his fellow narrativists have described as Kantian in essence.[112]

In illuminating the evolutionary trajectory of historical consciousness, White's tropology does not merely describe it but actively mediates its disclosure. Put differently, his narrative theory is fundamentally a theory of practice and a form of progressive political action, as befits a thinker who freely admitted, "I always regarded myself as a kind of Marxist."[113] Known among his intellectual acquaintances as a man of strong political convictions, White personified just about the exact opposite of an academic cloistered in the proverbial ivory tower, a stereotype for which traditional historians in particular bear disproportionate responsibility: rather than aloof to the political struggles of everyday life, he comprehended historical inquiry as a manner of direct participation in them and experiences his scholarship as an existential vocation. Perhaps nothing illustrates the politically engaged, practical dimension of his ideas more vividly than his legendary commitment to scores of future cultural historians and theorists from underrepresented groups under the auspices of the History of Consciousness Program. His pedagogical approach was emblematic of his counterhegemonic emancipatory philosophy: above all else, White held,

> students need ... demystification or learning to think critically about the clichés they have imbibed since infancy from a society that would

prefer them to be passive or apathetic in the exercise of their human rights than militantly vigilant about society's interest in depriving them of those rights.[114]

Such intellectually liberated historians will no longer function merely as clones regurgitating the methodological and epistemological mantras of their teachers from the senior ranks of the professional historical establishment but practice what White, drawing on Nietzsche's idea of critical history in *Untimely Meditations*, called progressive history. In sharp contrast to the mainstream approach, this alternative conception of inquiry into the past "means a history ... born of a concern for the future," whether the future of one's family, class, gender, political community, or the earth at large: "a history that goes to the past in order to find intimations of resources, intellectual, emotional, and spiritual, that might be useful for dealing with these concerns."[115] Unlike Rankean empiricists, progressive historians look back in time

> not in order to find out what really happened there or to provide a genealogy of and thereby legitimacy for the present, but find out what it takes to face a future we should like to inherit rather than one that we have been forced to endure.[116]

This attitude liberates the future from the prison of the past, "uses the past to imagine a future rather than to distract us from facing it,"[117] and thus restores the position of history as an expression of freedom: a practical guide chosen by individuals and collectivities in their quests for emancipation and self-realization. As an integral part of this process, the doors of the discipline will be flung wide open to a multiplicity of styles and methodologies, reflecting the plurality and variety of the goals of their proponents. "If historiography is to serve democratic rather than hegemonic ... ends," White had commented in this regard, "it would do well to work for diversity of interpretation rather than towards 'consensus' on what is the best interpretation of the past by professional scholars implicated in the social system as they find it."[118]

Not so much Kuhn, then, but rather the first generation of the Frankfurt School of critical social theory may be the most appropriate analogy for the purposes of grasping the politics of White's narrativist thesis. Whether their shared historicizing perspective, Marxist-inspired ideology critique, Kantian progressivism, focus on the role of hegemonic ideas and consciousness in obstructing human emancipation, or notion of theory as counterhegemonic political action, the parallels between them are deep and extensive, even if White had explicitly acknowledged only Mannheim among his intellectual inspirations, not Horkheimer or Adorno. The almost total neglect of White's affinities with the leading members of "Casa Marx" or "Red Castle," as the Frankfurt Institute for Social Research was dubbed in the Weimar Republic, represents a notable omission in the extensive secondary literature on him—and a promising avenue for future research.

Situating Narrative Theory: Between Modernism and Postmodernism

Due to its relativizing tendencies, the narrativist thesis has had a deeply polarizing impact and elicits sharply opposed responses across the humanities. On the one hand, reflexive thinkers and literary theorists such as Linda Hutcheon have eagerly welcomed White's intellectual contribution and promptly claimed his name for postmodernism in historical and literary studies.[119] On the other hand, professional historians working in the discipline's modernist empiricist mainstream, White's target audience, have reacted to his ideas with outrage—insofar as they have bothered to comment on them at all. Arguably, however, neither camp has done White justice: both overlook, for example, his consistent respect for singular existential statements as the factual building material for the poetic construction of historical narratives. This respect moderates his relativism and situates his narrativist theory of historical representation somewhere in between the extremes of naïve empiricism and hyper-reflexive deconstruction: as a subtle *via media* spanning the modernist and postmodernist approaches to historiography.

Among contemporary postmodernists, none has celebrated and appropriated White with more élan than Keith Jenkins, the *bête noire* of the British historical establishment. For Jenkins, White epitomizes the "radical historian" who, "unlike 'normal' ones, [doesn't] go to work to understand the past on its own terms and for its own sake" but rather engages in historical inquiry in order to formulate a practical guide to current and future problems, as a matter of "responding to a call that comes ... directly from ethics; from politics."[120] Normal historiography, by which Jenkins means Rankean empiricism, has failed to live up to its promises and suffers from terminal weaknesses. Where it posits disinterested observers, Jenkins sees scholars affected by ambitions, jealousies, careerism, institutionalization, duplicities, acts of gratitude, and all kinds of other suasive tendencies; where it casts their referent as hard factual evidence left over from the past and existing independently of their agendas, he finds "'nothing' but the product of their *inferences* based upon their existential (personal, ethical, public, ideological) condition"; and where it portrays itself as science, he perceives an imaginative literary-artistic discourse fulfilling all "the classic criteria for something to be of a rhetorical kind."[121] Superseding normal modernist historiography, radical historians not only raise its unacknowledged failures to the level of consciousness, but rejoice in them. They embrace the "essentially aesthetic nature of *all* histories" and revel in the acknowledgment that "rhetorical/aesthetic histories are the only game in town."[122]

For all these reasons, Jenkins has asserted that "the radical historian can subscribe ... *entirely* to White's decisionist/impositionist/relativistic position on narrativity"[123] and to the broader emancipatory project informing it:

> That the past is sublime in its "whole" and problematic in its parts; that at the level of meaning ... historical narratives are inexpungeably ...

relativistic; that skepticism about historical knowledge ... is a necessary counter to dogmas everywhere; that "the past" has no legitimate gate-keepers who can tell us what we can and cannot do with it (least of all academic historians); ... that the interminable openness of the past to countless readings should be celebrated and democratized in the hope that we might ... entertain those creative historical "distortions offered by minds capable of looking at the past with the same seriousness as ourselves but with different affective and intellectual orientations"; that this should alert us to the conserving nature of now pre-eminent narrations that tidily lock up events ... and ... absorb experimentation in the name of a fake pluralism; and that the essence of a radical history is its future-orientated politico/ethical thrust.[124]

These ideas have led Jenkins to openly declare White "an intellectual hero of mine" and *"the* point of departure for my thinking about history."[125] Insofar as radical historiography is concerned, White stands unsurpassed: "nobody does it better ...."[126]

Not to be outdone, traditional empiricists have reacted to White with equal enthusiasm, except in this case applied for denunciatory purposes. The most unscrupulous admonitions came from Arthur Marwick, who in the 1990s took it upon himself to defend respectable historiography from the postmodernist plague threatening to "consign ... history ... to the dust-bin of cultural practices."[127] In several highly public swipes at this program, Marwick identified White as its chief ideologue and portrayed him and his followers as neo-Marxist dilettantes "who have absorbed the shibboleths of post-structuralism"; never do actual historical research but only "sit on their backsides and conjure up utterly misleading accounts of what historians do, conventionally shaped to their political purposes (radical socialism ...)"; and "are hell-bent on change, not on the basis of hard-won knowledge, but in accordance with a few metaphysical speculations."[128] The literary techniques of deconstruction and discourse analysis developed by White and his aco-lytes such as Jenkins, whose *Rethinking History* (1991) struck Marwick "as the classic of postmodernist ineptitude," are of "no use to historians" and indeed represent "a menace to serious historical study."[129] It was imperative to guard against them, and the best way to do this, Marwick insisted, was to leave the study of history to professional historians. They alone possess the strict principles and methodological training necessary to discover the facts about the past, use clear and precise prose in their write-up, avoid im-aginative excess and "tricks of language," get the story told by the primary sources straight, and thereby achieve cumulative progress in the body of historical knowledge.[130]

Even Marwick's British empiricist colleagues instantly recognized his ef-forts for what they were: hollow *ad hominem* attacks that failed to engage with White's points and imploded the moment White responded. Embar-rassed, they quickly distanced themselves from Marwick's views.[131] As for

White's fellow narrativists, Ankersmit proclaimed Marwick's strictures as "mark[ing] an absolute low in the perennial battle of the historical discipline against the scourge of theory" and wondered how "a reasonably sensible person, such as Arthur Marwick undoubtedly is, could write such a perfectly inane and silly tirade ...."[132] But Marwick by no means exhausts the opposition that has gradually accrued in reaction to White's tropological relativism since *Metahistory* first came out over forty years ago; numerous other historians have chimed in.[133] And while a few more of them can be written off just as safely as Marwick—the conservative hysteria seeping through Gertrude Himmelfarb's condemnation of the postmodernist "flight from fact"[134] dwarfs even his paranoia—most cannot be dismissed so easily, or at all.

Carlo Ginzburg offers a case in point. Sharing with White roughly the same place at the left end of the ideological spectrum in historical studies—miles removed from the likes of Himmelfarb—and repeatedly praised by White for his cultural microhistory of sixteenth-century *mentalité* in *The Cheese and the Worms* (1976), he nonetheless excoriated White for collapsing historical truth into political effectiveness and flinging the door open to disturbing revisions or even denials of the twentieth century's most traumatic events on the basis of shifting pragmatic considerations.[135] This is what made Ginzburg's reproach—and other similar ones leveled by, for example, Dray and Chartier—so much more serious: the Holocaust, the event with a capital "E," the ultimate test case wheeled out by the historical profession each time an intruder pointing out the aesthetic dimension of historical representation just will not go away. Whether obliquely or in ruthlessly direct fashion, many voices confronted White with the same concern: that the

> tendency to conflate "historical" and "fictional" narrative and the ... emphasis on the "poetics" of history ... may be promoting a facile and irresponsible relativism which will leave many who espouse it defenseless before the most dangerous myths and ideologies, incapable of justifying any stand.[136]

Whereas Marwick fought White with a plastic water pistol, Ginzburg rolled out the Big Bertha, loaded it with genocide, and chained White to a lamppost in front of the barrel. "He thinks I am a fascist,"[137] White commented with dismay.

Such pitched interpretations of White's narrative theory certainly make for vibrant reading. They pinpoint unresolved tensions in his work, thresh out those of his arguments which he, perhaps fearing their implications, chose not to develop all the way to their logical conclusions, and in general place his ideas in a broader perspective. Given that White is not just a perceptive analyst of poetics but also a spell-binding poet, one of the masters of the academic essay form, this secondary literature plays an important role in enabling one to carve some distance from him. But there is a flipside: among the many excited commentaries by White's admirers and detractors, all of them motivated in part by their own agendas, it is quite easy to lose track of his own voice and become seduced into forgetting some of the subtler elements of his theory, which rather undermine his prevalent reception as a postmodernist relativist.

To begin with, throughout his long career White had consistently and repeatedly characterized himself as a modernist. "Gertrude Himmelfarb ... thinks I represent a *postmodernist* conception of history ... [and] Linda Hutcheon ... [too] always insists on it," he noticed, "But I see my own project as modernist. My whole intellectual formation, my own development took place within modernism."[138] By modernism, White means neither Rankean empiricist historiography, of course, nor Habermasian Enlightenment philosophy, but a specifically Western cultural and artistic movement exemplified by writers such as James Joyce, T. S. Eliot, Virginia Woolf, Marcel Proust, Gertrude Stein, and Ezra Pound. Their experimental works appeal to White because they recognize that the world has no underlying organizing essence, emphasize form as the locus of human efforts to endow the chaos of existence with meaning, and bring the whole aesthetics of style and taste into question.

> The modernist artist ... becomes interested in form itself. The form that is its own content. It turns out that human beings have a plastic power, a power of endowing with form. And thereby, meaning for modernist aesthetics is form itself. Wherever you find form or pattern ... there is human presence.[139]

White's narrativist theory applies the principles of cultural modernism to map the human fabrication of patterns of meaning out of the chaos of the historical past. "It falls to people who study history ... to endow it with meaning. And they do it by symbolization," which is to say that the meaning of history "depends upon ... the repertory of symbols they have available to them to produce their own version of it."[140]

In addition to White's self-understanding, another important consideration belying his postmodernist reputation stems from his fairly rigid formalism. It is worth recalling that according to his analytical framework in *Metahistory*, while the same set of facts can be troped in different ways, the number of tropes available for this process is limited. As historians colligate facts into proper historical accounts, they cannot narrativize them in just any way they would like; their poetic imagination and freedom are constrained by the preconceptual linguistic codes and structures of consciousness, of which there are only four basic types. White regards these archetypal tropes as stable, casts his theory based on them as "value free,"[141] and at times comes close to elevating it to the status of a universal phenomenology.[142] It is telling that many of the same critics who accused *Metahistory* of epistemological relativism simultaneously accused it of linguistic determinism.[143]

True, over the decades since the book's appearance White had gradually relaxed the categories making up his analytical framework. "To be quite frank," he admitted about *Metahistory* some twenty years after its publication, "it has a slightly tattered look about it even to my own eyes."[144] Another five years later he was even more candid: "That was a book of a certain 'structuralist' moment, and if I were writing it today, I would do it differently."[145] Nonetheless, and without abandoning the argument that historians exercise the same kind of creative freedom conventionally accorded to fiction writers, White had remained faithful to "the idea that the codes (linguistic and otherwise) circulating in a given culture *set limits* on what one can say ...."[146] The crafting of discourses therefore combines agency with determinism much in the way captured by Marx in his famous dictum, approvingly quoted by White, that "Men make their own history, but they do not make it just as they please; they do not make it under circumstances chosen by themselves, but under circumstances directly encountered, given, and transmitted from the past."[147]

Perhaps the clearest indication that White's postmodernist relativism has been overdrawn, however, is his respect for historical truth at the level of singular existential statements. His theory of historical representation "differentiates between the primary and secondary referent of historical writing. The former refers to the past events, the latter to the vision of reality upheld by the conceptual repertoire ... used to incorporate the facts into meaningful narratives."[148] It is certainly the case that for White proper "historical knowledge is always second-order knowledge,"[149] that he has systematically emphasized the secondary referent (the ethical-ideological perspective encapsulated in the narrative structure), and that this referent relies on poetic imagination, which endows it with inexpungible relativity limited only by the stock of available cultural and linguistic codes. But if in their compositional aspect historical narratives "have more in common with their counterparts in literature than they have with those in the sciences,"[150] the same cannot be said about the individual facts integrated by their representational frameworks: these are not a matter of poetic construction.

> Unlike literary fictions, such as the novel, historical works are made up of events that exist outside the consciousness of the writer. The events reported ... in a history ... cannot be ... invented in a way ... that they ... can ... in a novel.[151]

Stories about the past are told, but their building blocks are found—and can be classified as true or false based on empirical evidence.

Therefore, White "undercuts any traditional epistemology ... on the level of narrative structure" and argues that "the representational code is ... independent of the primary material," but when it comes to the primary material "he integrates ... independent epistemological categories according to which the factual accuracy of any given account can be measured."[152]

Historical narratives are incommensurable insofar as their secondary referents are concerned, each of these being equally valid within its own poetic frame, but in a nod to traditional empiricism White concedes that at the level of the singular existential statement, comparison among competing narratives is entirely possible: one can evaluate and rank histories according to their truth value, internal logical consistency, scope, and so on. Indeed, on at least one occasion, under the pressure of historians accusing him of aestheticizing the meaning of the Holocaust, White seems to have lost his nerve and accorded empirical evidence so much weight as to effectively undercut his tropological relativism—by asserting that the primary field of facts restricts the range of poetic structures for their emplotment, so that "the choice of a farcical style for the representation of some kinds of historical events would constitute ... a distortion of the truth about them."[153] It is not easy being chained to a lamppost in front of the Big Bertha.

In light of White's self-proclaimed cultural modernism, formalist and structuralist leanings, deference to basic facts at the research stage of historical inquiry, and also his aforementioned emancipatory political agenda reminiscent of the Frankfurt School, it is difficult to accept his predominant postmodernist classification: an image promulgated by the majority of his admirers and critics alike, from Hutcheon and Jenkins on the one side to Marwick and Himmelfarb on the other. A more nuanced and complex picture emerges: insofar as it is admissible to "fix" his theoretical position at all, White is neither a postmodernist nor, of course, a defender of traditional modernist historiography, but rather a rebel standing in no man's land between the two approaches. Unlike modernists with their scientific pretensions and blind worship of facts, he has reflected on the literary techniques of historical representation and is fully alert both to the role of artistic creativity in historical writing and to the ethical, political, and ideological fictions imparted to factual accounts of the past through their artificial narrativization. But if he rejects the notion of history as science, he does not reduce history to art, pure and simple, either. Unlike radical postmodernist literary theorists, who tend to view historical writing as a self-contained universe of symbols invented entirely for presentist purposes and devoid of any external referentiality, White stops well short of deconstructing historical narratives all the way down to the point of denying the existence of the past altogether. In a sense, an encounter with White is an encounter with a Janus-faced thinker: a *figural realist*, a mind at once too theoretical and linguistically reflexive for modernist empiricist historians and too historical and empirical for reflexive postmodernist theorists.

This reading aligns with White's Vichian predilection for comprehending fact and fiction, science and art, reason and imagination, subject and object, choice and necessity, and other binary pairings commonly deployed in the modern study of history and other fields of knowledge not as mutually exclusive opposites, but as terms continuous with one another.[154] This predilection ultimately propelled White to the recognition of writing in the middle voice as a literary strategy uniquely suited to the challenges confronting contemporary Western society in its efforts to represent the traumas of its recent past, "The Age of Extremes," as Eric Hobsbawm famously called the period 1914–1991.[155] In this distinctive verb form, unavailable in modern English but present in highly inflected languages such as Icelandic or ancient Greek, the subject acts on itself and thus cannot be categorized as either agent or patient but rather possesses elements of both.

In a universe celebrating the sublimity, contingency, opacity, and contradictions of human existence and pursuing holistic learning in an attempt to understand them, such a balanced and integrative perspective would enjoy widespread appreciation. But present-day Western, and particularly American, academe is a different world. Embedded in Cartesian rationalism rather than in the humanist legacy of Vico or Montaigne, it is engaged in a quest for certainty, anchored in the specific case of the American historical profession in the founding myth of value-free historical investigation— objectivity—symbolized by Ranke.[156] It dreams of dispelling all ambiguity, deals in static concepts and categories as a matter of course, and makes them the basis for ever-increasing specialization and fragmentation of inquiry along zealously guarded disciplinary boundaries. In such a world, stepping across separate fields of knowledge and epistemological presuppositions legitimating their division amounts to criminal trespassing, and a rebel discovered standing in no man's land between them is bound to be greeted, not as a mutual friend, but as a shared enemy: with two shots, one in the chest and one in the back. White's overall impact has therefore been quite minimal.

Beyond Historiography: Narrative Theory and Academic International Relations

If White, Ankersmit, and others associated with narrative historical theory have failed to make a big splash in professional historiography, their standing in academic international relations is worse still: near total obscurity. This is not surprising, given that since its inception after World War I the field has been fixated on policy issues and evinces a strong ahistorical bias: "A dominant attitude, partly against history, partly just indifferent to it," which "has been reinforced, especially in the U.S., by ... an economistic, natural science based understanding of the social world."[157] Only a few international relations scholars attuned to the politics of language and representation and located at the margins of the discipline, miles away from its positivist core, have noticed White and incorporated him in their work: Campbell in his analysis of the ways US national security discourse constitutes American national identity, or Elizabeth Shakman Hurd in her argument about the key role of depictions of Islam in producing the myth of Western secularist political authority.[158] Even these exceptional cases, however, employ White's arguments tangentially at best, confine his name to a few references in the margins, and leave the depths of his theory untapped.

As for the overwhelming majority of specialists making up the disciplinary community, his *Tropics* will evoke only rainforests and iguanas.

It would amount to a stunning lapse of critical acumen to fall for the ahistorical pretensions and accept them at face value. That most international relations scholars treat the arena of world politics in static terms, as a preformed reality independent of their wishes and readily available for policy-oriented scientific analysis, does not mean that history is absent from their thought, only that they implicitly narrate it in a particular way: one combining Tragic emplotment with Mechanistic argumentation and Conservative ideological implication, to put it in terms of White's tropology. Nowhere in mainstream academic international relations discourse do these poetic choices show up more conspicuously than in the notion of anarchy: widely used throughout the field to describe the essential structure of the international system. Insofar as this notion represents the starting point for the scientific study of world politics—the field's *sine qua non*, justifying among other things its autonomy from other areas of intellectual inquiry—it may be regarded as the very core of serious international relations research. Insofar as it encapsulates an elaborate story, this core is a complex rhetorical artifact.

The purpose of the next chapter is precisely to lay out the story of anarchy and flesh out its fictions: isolate and bring to light the nonfactual content brought by international relations scholars to their ostensibly factual image of the international arena. By doing so, the chapter commences this book's overarching project: blurring the line between fact and fiction in stories about world politics.

Notes

1 See Paul Ricoeur, *Time and Narrative*, vol. 1, trans. Kathleen McLaughlin and David Pellauer (Chicago and London: University of Chicago Press, 1984), 31–51.
2 George Whalley, Commentary on Aristotle, *Poetics*, trans. George Whalley, ed. John Baxter and Patrick Atherton (Montreal, QC, and Kingston, ON: McGill-Queen's University Press, 1997), 44 n. 1. Similarly, Ricoeur (*Time and Narrative*, 48) observes that "From the beginning the term *poiēsis* puts the imprint of dynamism on all the concepts in the *Poetics* and makes them concepts about operations."
3 George Whalley, "On Translating Aristotle's *Poetics*," in Aristotle, *Poetics*, 11.
4 Aristotle, *Poetics*, §20.
5 Gerald F. Else, *Plato and Aristotle on Poetry* (Chapel Hill, NC: University of North Carolina Press, 1986), 75.
6 Cf. Ricoeur's emphatic rejection of "any interpretation of Aristotle's *mimēsis* in terms of a copy or identical replica. Imitating or representing is a mimetic activity inasmuch as it produces something. (...) If we continue to translate *mimēsis* by 'imitation,' we have to understand something completely contrary to a copy of some preexisting reality and speak instead of a creative imitation. And if we translate *mimēsis* by 'representation,' ... we must not understand by this word some redoubling of presence, as we could ... do for Platonic *mimēsis*, but rather the break that opens the space for fiction." (*Time and Narrative*, 34, 45.)

7 Aristotle, *Poetics*, §58.
8 William Shakespeare, *Hamlet, Prince of Denmark*, ed. Philip Edwards (Cambridge and New York: Cambridge University Press, 2003), III. i. 56–60.
9 Mircea Eliade, *The Myth of the Eternal Return, Or, Cosmos and History*, trans. Willard R. Trask (Princeton, NJ: Princeton University Press, 1991 [1954]).
10 Whalley, Commentary on Aristotle, *Poetics*, 126 n. 227. [Emphasis original.]
11 Ibid., 82 n. 79.
12 Ricoeur, *Time and Narrative*, 41.
13 Aristotle, *Poetics*, §23.
14 Ibid., §28.
15 Ibid., §39.
16 Ibid., §27.
17 Ibid.
18 Ibid., §35. [Emphasis original.]
19 Ricoeur, *Time and Narrative*, 43.
20 Aristotle, *Poetics*, §34. "The accent, in [Aristotle's] analysis of this idea of a 'whole,' is ... put on the absence of chance." (Ricoeur, *Time and Narrative*, 39.)
21 Nancy Partner, "The Fundamental Things Apply: Aristotle's Narrative Theory and the Classical Origins of Postmodern History," in Nancy Partner and Sarah Foot, eds., *The SAGE Handbook of Historical Theory* (London: SAGE, 2013), 504.
22 Ibid.
23 Ricoeur, *Time and Narrative*, 48.
24 Gerald F. Else, *Aristotle's Poetics: The Argument* (Cambridge, MA: Harvard University Press, 1963), 449. See also Ricoeur, *Time and Narrative*, 50.
25 Else, *Aristotle's Poetics*, 300.
26 Aristotle, *Poetics*, §30. [Emphasis original.]
27 Ibid., §29.
28 Ibid., §31. [Emphasis original.]
29 Ibid.
30 Ibid., §33. [Emphasis original.]
31 Else, *Aristotle's Poetics*, 321–322. [Emphasis original.]
32 See especially Ranke's preface to his *History of Latin and Teutonic Nations, 1494–1514* (London: George Bell and Sons, 1887), originally published as *Geschichten der romanischen und germanischen Völker von 1494 bis 1514*, vol. 1 (Leipzig and Berlin: Reimer, 1824). "Henceforth, history and fiction were never to be mixed, even though the historians continued to favor the narrative mode of representation characteristic of myth, fable, epic, romance, novel, and drama." (Hayden White, "Historical Fiction, Fictional History, and Historical Reality," *Rethinking History* 9, nos. 2/3 [2005]: 150.)
33 Partner, "Aristotle and Postmodern History," 495–496, 498.
34 Jean-François Lyotard, *The Postmodern Condition: A Report on Knowledge*, trans. Geoff Bennington and Brian Massumi (Minneapolis: University of Minnesota Press, 1984), xxiv.
35 Arthur C. Danto quoted in Ewa Domańska, *Encounters: Philosophy of History After Postmodernism* (Charlottesville and London: University Press of Virginia, 1998), 167.
36 Literature on White's life and thought is extensive and multilingual. For a convenient entry point, see the excellent bibliography in the *Festschrift* published on the occasion of his eightieth birthday: Frank Ankersmit, Ewa Domańska, and Hans Kellner, eds., *Re-Figuring Hayden White* (Stanford: Stanford University Press, 2009), 351–366. Additional materials include Hayden White, "The Aim of Interpretation Is to Create Perplexity in the Face of the Real: Hayden

White in Conversation with Erlend Rogne," interview by Erlend Rogne, *History and Theory* 48, no. 1 (2009): 63–75; Robert Doran, "The Work of Hayden White I: Mimesis, Figuration and the Writing of History," in Partner and Foot, eds., *SAGE Handbook of Historical Theory*; Robert Doran, "Humanism, Formalism, and the Discourse of History," introduction to Hayden White, *The Fiction of Narrative: Essays on History, Literature, and Theory, 1957–2007*, ed. Robert Doran (Baltimore, MD: Johns Hopkins University Press, 2010); and Herman Paul, *Hayden White* (London: Polity, 2011).

37 Hayden White, "Human Face of Scientific Mind: An Interview with Hayden White," interview by Ewa Domańska, *Storia della Storiografia* no. 24 (1993): 14. "Barthes," White stated explicitly, "is ... definitely ... the thinker dearest to me...." (Ibid., 19.)

38 Ibid., 6.

39 Dan Stone, "Paul Ricoeur, Hayden White, and Holocaust Historiography," in Jörn Stückrath and Jürg Zbinden, eds., *Metageschichte: Hayden White und Paul Ricoeur: Dargestellte Wirklichkeit in der europäischen Kultur im Kontext von Husserl, Weber, Auerbach und Gombrich* (Baden-Baden: Nomos, 1997), 268.

40 Patrick Finney, "Hayden White, International History and Questions Too Seldom Posed," *Rethinking History* 12, no. 1 (2008): 104.

41 Doran, "Humanism, Formalism, and Discourse of History," xiii.

42 Hayden White, *Figural Realism: Studies in the Mimesis Effect* (Baltimore, MD, and London: Johns Hopkins University Press, 1999), 9.

43 See White, "Human Face," 9.

44 White, "Aim of Interpretation," 74.

45 Louis O. Mink, "Narrative as a Cognitive Instrument," paper presented at the Midwest MLA meeting, Chicago, 1974, 3, quoted in idem, *Historical Understanding*, ed. Brian Fay, Eugene O. Golob, and Richard T. Vann (Ithaca, NY: Cornell University Press, 1987), 20 n. 17.

46 Hayden White, *Metahistory: The Historical Imagination in Nineteenth-Century Europe* (Baltimore, MD, and London: Johns Hopkins University Press, 1973), 6.

47 Ibid., 6–7.

48 Mink, *Historical Understanding*, 60.

49 Walter Bryce Gallie, *Philosophy and the Historical Understanding* (New York: Schocken, 1964), 66.

50 Mink, *Historical Understanding*, 60.

51 White, *Metahistory*, ix–x. [Emphasis original.]

52 Hayden White, "The Politics of Contemporary Philosophy of History," *Clio* 3, no. 1 (1973): 36.

53 Hayden White, *Tropics of Discourse: Essays in Cultural Criticism* (Baltimore, MD, and London: Johns Hopkins University Press, 1978), 121–122.

54 Hayden White, *The Content of the Form: Narrative Discourse and Historical Representation* (Baltimore, MD, and London: Johns Hopkins University Press, 1987), 45.

55 White, *Fiction of Narrative*, 202. [Emphasis original.]

56 White, *Tropics*, 125. See also Hayden White, "An Old Question Raised Again: Is Historiography Art or Science?" *Rethinking History* 4, no. 3 (2000): 405: "any representation of reality in the form of a narrativization necessarily fictionalizes its subject matter, however much it may be based on facts."

57 Frank R. Ankersmit, *Narrative Logic: A Semantic Analysis of the Historian's Language* (The Hague: Nijhoff, 1983), 1. [Emphasis original.] Cf. Louis O. Mink, "Narrative Form as a Cognitive Instrument," in Robert H. Canary and Henry Kozicki eds., *The Writing of History: Literary Form and Historical Understanding*, (Madison: University of Wisconsin Press, 1978), 148: "very little

48   *Narrative Theory*

attention has been paid to the form of historical narratives, as distinguished from the individual statements comprised by that form, as communicating its own unique kind of understanding and explanation. Most often the form of historical narratives has been taken for granted as merely a more or less arbitrary way of setting out the constituent statements which alone make truth claims."

58 Hayden White, "Response to Arthur Marwick," *Journal of Contemporary History* 30, no. 2 (1995): 245.
59 Frank R. Ankersmit, "Reply to Professor Zagorin," *History and Theory* 29, no. 3 (1990): 278. [Emphasis original.]
60 Ibid. Cf. Ankersmit, *Narrative Logic*, 98: "It is no exaggeration to say that the purpose of nearly all historical writing, the only exception being some pieces of historical 'research'..., is to create such 'images' or 'pictures.'" According to William H. Dray, "On the Nature and Role of Narrativity in Historiography," *History and Theory* 10, no. 2 (1971): 156–157, the "claim that all history ... narrates ... [is] untenable," but nonetheless "the construction of narratives is ... a prominent ... aspect of historiography."
61 Ankersmit, *Narrative Logic*, 1.
62 Frank R. Ankersmit, "Historiography and Postmodernism," *History and Theory* 28, no. 2 (1989): 144. [Emphasis original.]
63 White, *Tropics*, 126–127. [Emphasis original.]
64 White, *Figural Realism*, 28.
65 Hayden White, "A Conversation with Hayden White," interview by Ewa Domańska, *Rethinking History* 12, no. 1 (2008): 8.
66 Mink, "Narrative Form as Cognitive Instrument," 144.
67 Mink, *Historical Understanding*, 82–87.
68 Ibid., 79. [Emphasis original.]
69 Mink, "Narrative Form as Cognitive Instrument," 143.
70 Mink, "Narrative as Cognitive Instrument," 3. [Emphasis original.]
71 Ankersmit, *Narrative Logic*, 96–104. Ankersmit adopts "colligation" and "colligatory concepts" from William H. Walsh, "Colligatory Concepts in History," in W. H. Burston and D. Thompson, eds. *Studies in the Nature and Teaching of History* (New York: Humanities Press, 1967), and aligns them with Mink's notions of configurational comprehension and synoptic judgment. See Ankersmit, "Reply to Zagorin," 280.
72 Ankersmit, "Reply to Zagorin," 281.
73 Hayden White, "Hayden White on 'Facts, Fictions and Metahistory': II. A Discussion with Hayden White," interview by Richard J. Murphy, *Sources: Revue d'études anglophones* 2 (Spring 1997): 14.
74 Arthur C. Danto, *Narration and Knowledge* (New York: Columbia University Press, 1985), 115.
75 Ibid., 114.
76 David Carr, "Narrative and the Real World: An Argument for Continuity," *History and Theory* 25, no. 2 (1986): 117.
77 Chris Lorenz, "Historical Knowledge and Historical Reality: A Plea for 'Internal Realism,'" *History and Theory* 33, no. 3 (1994): 315.
78 Ankersmit, *Narrative Logic*, 19.
79 Ankersmit, "Reply to Zagorin," 282.
80 Ibid., 287.
81 Ibid., 293.
82 Hayden White, "A Response to Professor Chartier's Four Questions," *Storia della Storiografia* no. 27 (1995): 64. See also Ewa Domańska, "Hayden White: Beyond Irony," *History and Theory* 37, no. 2 (1998): 177.
83 White, "Is Historiography Art or Science?" 392–393.
84 White, "Response to Chartier," 70.

85 White, *Metahistory*, 30–31. [Emphasis original.]

86 Ibid., 31.

87 Ibid., 7.

88 Ibid., 11.

89 Ibid., 22.

90 Ibid., 24.

91 Ibid., 29.

92 Detailed discussions of White's tropological grid include Hans Kellner, "A Bedrock of Order: Hayden White's Linguistic Humanism," *History and Theory* 19, no. 4 (1980): 1–29; David Konstant, "The Function of Narrative in Hayden White's *Metahistory*," *Clio* 11, no. 1 (1981): 65–78; and Juraj Šuch, "Niekoľko poznámok k dielu Haydena Whita," *Filozofia* 55, no. 10 (2000): 809–819. Alternative conceptualizations of the layers of poetic activity in historical composition are possible, of course. See, for example, the model developed by Jerzy Topolski, "Historical Narrative: Towards a Coherent Structure," *History and Theory* 26, no. 4 (1987): 75–86.

93 White, *Metahistory*, xii.

94 Ibid. [Emphasis original.]

95 White, *Metahistory*, 21.

96 White, *Tropics*, 129.

97 Dominick LaCapra, *Rethinking Intellectual History: Texts, Contexts, Language* (Ithaca, NY: Cornell University Press, 1983), 75.

98 White, "Conversation with White," 20–21.

99 Kellner, "White's Linguistic Humanism," 4. [Emphasis added.] See also idem, "A Distinctively Human Life," in Ankersmit, Domańska, and Kellner, eds., *Re-Figuring White*, 3–6.

100 White, *Fiction of Narrative*, 132.

101 Ibid., 135. [Emphasis original.]

102 Ibid.

103 Ibid.

104 See E.H. Carr to R.W. Davies, December 9, 1959, quoted in R. W. Davies, "Edward Hallett Carr, 1892–1982," *Proceedings of the British Academy* 69 (1983): 504.

105 White, "Is Historiography Art or Science?" 402.

106 Danto, *Narration and Knowledge*, xi–xii.

107 Cf. White, "Conversation with Hayden White," 16: "I historicize historical learning itself and this is what most historians do not do. ... They do not realize that 'history' is not only *about* change but is itself—whether understood as a process or as accounts of a process—constantly changing; they do not historicize their own operations." [Emphasis original.]

108 Thomas S. Kuhn, *The Structure of Scientific Revolutions*, 2nd ed. (Chicago: University of Chicago Press, 1970), 10, 94.

109 Ibid., 94.

110 Ibid., 5.

111 Ibid., 170–171, 208. [Emphasis original.]

112 See, for example, Hans Kellner, "Hayden White and the Kantian Discourse: Tropology, Narrative, and Freedom," in Chip Sills and George H. Jensen eds., *The Philosophy of Discourse: The Rhetorical Turn in Twentieth-Century Thought*, vol. 1 (Portsmouth, NH: Boynton/Cook Publishers, 1992); and Frank Ankersmit, "White's 'New Neo-Kantianism,'" in Ankersmit, Domańska, and Kellner, eds., *Re-Figuring White*.

113 White, "Human Face," 9. In this connection, Wulf Kansteiner has observed that "*Metahistory* displays a strong didactic agenda" in that White, by "mak[ing] historians aware of their ... preconceptual prefigurations of their subject matter,"

encourages them to "rethink their representational choices in light of their political and aesthetic commitments." ("Hayden White's Critique of the Writing of History," *History and Theory* 32, no. 3 [1993]: 278.)

114   White, "Conversation with White," 13.

115   Ibid., 18–19.

116   Ibid.

117   Ibid.

118   White, "Is Historiography Art or Science?" 402.

119   Linda Hutcheon, *A Poetics of Postmodernism: History, Theory, Fiction* (New York and London: Routledge, 1988), 15, 96, 121, 143.

120   Keith Jenkins, "'Nobody Does It Better': Radical History and Hayden White," *Rethinking History* 12, no. 1 (2008): 64.

121   Ibid., 65–68. [Emphasis original.]

122   Ibid., 69.

123   Ibid.

124   Ibid., 70.

125   Ibid., 72, 73. [Emphasis original.]

126   Ibid., 73. See also Keith Jenkins, *On "What Is History?": From Carr and Elton to Rorty and White* (London: Routledge, 1995); idem, "A Conversation with Hayden White," *Literature and History* 7, no. 1 (1998): 68–82; and idem, "On Hayden White," in *Why History? Ethics and Postmodernity* (London: Routledge, 1999).

127   Arthur Marwick, "History's Men at War," *Times Higher Education Supplement*, no. 1281, 23 May 1997, 13.

128   Arthur Marwick, "Age-Old Problems: The Empiricist," *Times Higher Education Supplement*, no. 1151, 25 November 1994, 17.

129   Arthur Marwick, "Two Approaches to Historical Study: The Metaphysical (Including 'Postmodernism') and the Historical," *Journal of Contemporary History* 30, no. 1 (1995): 20, 26, 29.

130   Ibid., 6–11, 22–23.

131   See, for example, Richard Evans, "Truth Lost in Vain Views," *Times Higher Education Supplement*, no. 1297, 12 September 1997, 18. For White's responses, see Hayden White, "Age-Old Problems: The Theorist," *Times Higher Education Supplement*, no. 1151, 25 November 1994, 17, and idem, "Response to Marwick."

132   Frank R. Ankersmit, *Historical Representation* (Stanford: Stanford University Press, 2001), 252.

133   See especially Roger Chartier, "Quatre questions à Hayden White," *Storia della Storiografia* no. 24 (1993): 133–142; Georg Iggers, "Historiography between Scholarship and Poetry: Reflections on Hayden White's Approach to Historiography," *Rethinking History* 4, no. 3 (2000): 373–390; Arnaldo Momigliano, "The Rhetoric of History and the History of Rhetoric: On Hayden White's Tropes," *Comparative Criticism* 3 (1981): 259–268; and William H. Dray, review of *The Content of the Form*, by Hayden White, *History and Theory* 27, no. 3 (1988): 282–287. White's replies include "Response to Chartier" and "Is Historiography Art or Science?"

134   Gertrude Himmelfarb, "Telling It as You Like It: Post-modernist History and the Flight from Fact," *Times Literary Supplement*, 16 October 1992, 12–15.

135   Carlo Ginzburg, "Just One Witness," in Saul Friedländer, ed., *Probing the Limits of Representation: Nazism and the "Final Solution"* (Cambridge, MA: Harvard University Press, 1992).

136   Lionel Gossman, *Between History and Literature* (Cambridge, MA: Harvard University Press, 1990), 303. Cf. Dray, review of *Content of Form*, 287, and Chartier, "Quatre questions," 140–142.

137 White, "Human Face," 7.

138 Ibid., 14. [Emphasis original.]

139 White, "Aim of Interpretation," 70.

140 Ibid., 71.

141 White, *Metahistory*, 431.

142 White, *Tropics*, 6, 12–13, 19, 22, 117. Cf. White, *Fiction of Narrative*, 163, calling for "a general theory of language ... [as] a formal criterion for assigning significance to different literary works" in literary history. Kellner ("White's Linguistic Humanism," 23) thus sees White's analytical apparatus in *Metahistory* as encapsulating "an existential paradox": "If language is irreducible ... then human freedom is sacrificed. If men are free to choose their linguistic protocols, then some deeper, prior, force must be posited. White asserts ... [both] that men *are* free, and that language *is* irreducible." [Emphasis original.]

143 See for example Chartier, "Quatre questions," 133–136, and Iggers, "Historiography between Scholarship and Poetry," 377.

144 White, "Response to Chartier," 67.

145 White, "Is Historiography Art or Science?" 391.

146 White, "Response to Chartier," 63. [Emphasis original.]

147 Ibid.

148 Kansteiner, "White's Critique," 282.

149 White, "Is Historiography Art or Science?" 398.

150 White, *Tropics*, 82.

151 White, *Metahistory*, 6 n. 5.

152 Kansteiner, "White's Critique," 281.

153 White, *Figural Realism*, 12.

154 See especially White, *Metahistory*, 31 n. 13, and idem, *Tropics*, 143, where White praises Vico's "genius to perceive the fallacies contained in such oppositions." Cf. Domańska, "White: Beyond Irony," 177.

155 See, for instance, White, *Fiction of Narrative*, 255–262, and idem, *Figural Realism*, 37–42, arguing for the superiority of literary modernism—including intransitive writing and the middle voice—in representations of the Holocaust, with Primo Levi as an illustrative example.

156 Peter Novick, *That Noble Dream: The "Objectivity Question" and the American Historical Profession* (Cambridge: Cambridge University Press, 1988), 3–4. For a critical genealogy of the rationalist "quest for certainty," see Stephen Toulmin, *Cosmopolis: The Hidden Agenda of Modernity* (New York: Free Press, 1990).

157 Barry Buzan and Richard Little, "Why International Relations Has Failed as an Intellectual Project and What to Do about It," *Millennium: Journal of International Studies* 30, no. 1 (2001): 24–25.

158 David Campbell, *Writing Security: United States Foreign Policy and the Politics of Identity* (Minneapolis: University of Minnesota Press, 1992); Elizabeth Shakman Hurd, *The Politics of Secularism in International Relations* (Princeton, NJ: Princeton University Press, 2008). See also Finney, "White, International History and Questions Too Seldom Posed," and Richard Devetak, "After the Event: Don DeLillo's *White Noise* and September 11 Narratives," *Review of International Studies* 35, no. 4 (2009): 795–815.

2 The Story of Anarchy
The Poetic Core of Scientific International Relations

That Reg Presley, the lyricist behind the 1960s hit song "Love Is All Around," got things terribly wrong, for the world is full of power, not love, is not the only news awaiting undergraduate students in their initial courses at top American international relations departments. Simultaneously, they will make another discovery: that the discipline is brimming with anarchists. These are not the ordinary sort of anarchists exemplified by Bakunin and other nineteenth-century Russian and French subversives; typically clad in pressed button-down shirts and khaki pants, most Ivy League professors of international relations harbor no radical tendencies and would not know what to do with a Molotov cocktail except drink it in the faculty lounge. But the term "anarchists" is highly apt for them anyway, for a different reason: it captures a deeply entrenched belief, one espoused more or less by everyone in the discipline's mainstream, that the international realm is best and most accurately described as anarchy.

The fictions of this particular factual representation of reality are most apparent precisely to those whom the disciplinary community deems least qualified to pass any judgment on it: outsiders and newcomers such as the hapless college freshmen about to be exposed to the subject for the first time. It is especially in the opening lectures of introductory international relations courses that the enrolled participants, confronted for the first time with the discipline's foundational assumptions, conceptual toolkit, and specialist vocabulary, experience their artificiality most keenly and intensively, for there is nothing natural, intuitive, or commonsensical about narrating the world in terms of anarchy. The radical strangeness of this framing of the international arena comprises perhaps the best index of anarchy's nature as a *poiēma*: a linguistic fabrication and a rhetorical performance backed by power, in this case power bestowed by academic authority.

Unfortunately, the experience of this strangeness is fleeting: it evaporates with every next lecture and reading assignment. After all, what is the objective of introductory courses if not to initiate aspiring international relations students in the technical language of the field so that it becomes their own tongue? By the end of term, they—or at any rate those of them who wish to pass—will have completely absorbed the notion of anarchy, become fluent in its usage, and lost any sense of its artificiality. Of the once ample cognitive detachment enabling them to react to it with frank puzzlement, question it as an odd representation of reality, perceive its nonfactual elements, and thus recognize its poetic construction, nothing will have remained. Just at that moment, their professors will start applauding them for mastering the basic intellectual machinery necessary for serious *critical* inquiry into world affairs: what distinguishes legitimate social scientists from mere amateur observers among the reading public.

This chapter seeks to defamiliarize anarchy again. Its purpose is to flesh out its concealed poetic dimension—its "content of the form" (White), "narrative substance" (Ankersmit), or "synoptic judgment" (Mink)—by analyzing this representation of the international arena through the lens of narrative theory introduced earlier. It is tempting to cast this project as an effort to decolonize the intellects of international relations academics and restore them to the lost innocence of young undergraduates yet to attend their first lecture in the discipline. But this characterization would be deceptive. Once exposed to the anarchy narrative, one cannot simply erase it from consciousness—much as Murray Siskind, once exposed to "THE MOST PHOTOGRAPHED BARN IN AMERICA" signs along the path guiding him to the tourist attraction in Don DeLillo's novel *White Noise*, cannot simply delete them from his mind when he finally arrives at the destination. Glancing at the barn, he realizes their result:

> No one sees the barn. ... Once you've seen the signs about the barn, it becomes impossible to see the barn. ... What was the barn like before it was photographed? ... What did it look like...? We can't answer these questions because we've read the signs.[1]

The countless references to anarchy lining the academic path to bona fide knowledge about international relations arrest imagination in a similar manner, except twice as powerfully. For unlike the barn, which at least presents itself to the eyes as a discrete physical object, the international arena is unobservable: *entirely* a matter of its linguistic signification.

The most that can be achieved, then, is not emancipation in the sense of regaining some pure or innocent mental state from which to perceive the international stage *wie es eigentlich ist*. Rather, it is emancipation in the sense of becoming aware of the image as image: realizing that anarchy is just one of many possible constructions of the space of world affairs, that it rests on specific presuppositions, that it comes with important implications, and that its prevalence in serious international relations literature is a matter of poetic, ethical, ideological, and political choices.

Anarchy as the Foundation of Contemporary International Relations Scholarship

Just as it is difficult to conceive of Paris without the Eiffel Tower, which despite its relative novelty has come to symbolize the French capital, so the notion of anarchy, although not systematically elaborated until the second half of the twentieth century, defines the landscape of contemporary international relations theory. Proponent or opponent, one cannot hide from its long shadow. It is by no means the only representation of the international environment available in the field; many other images have been proposed in the last fifty years, such as the "cobweb" model of complex interdependence or the core-periphery model of world-systems analysis.[2] But these alternatives are just that: alternatives. None of them has achieved more than a fraction of the recognition accorded to anarchy, whose status as a bedrock concept underpinning practically all post-1945 mainstream research has led one scholar to call it the "Rosetta stone of International Relations"[3] and prompted the *Oxford Handbook of International Relations* to place it at the top of its list of the discipline's ontological "Founding Givens."[4] In less articulated forms, anarchy structured the discourse about international relations already during the field's formative years spanning the middle of the nineteenth century and World War II.[5] It may very well lurk in the background of every perspective on world affairs developed within the field since its inception.[6]

Among thinkers employing the image of anarchy as a core foundation in their theories, scientifically minded realist and neorealist scholars—many of them with prominent government advisory and policy planning positions on their resumes—have stood at the forefront. In his first contribution to the discipline in the late 1950s, Kenneth Waltz narrated the international stage as "anarchy" composed of "many sovereign states, with no system of law enforceable among them, [and] with each state judging its grievances and ambitions according to the dictates of its own reason or desire...."[7] Twenty years later, in a treatise instantly declared canonical by the rest of the field, he repeated this representation of the international arena: "International systems are decentralized and anarchic."[8] Around the same time, Robert Gilpin introduced his own realist analysis of international relations by depicting the international environment in similar terms: "independent actors in a state of anarchy."[9] Robert Art and Robert Jervis took the notion of anarchy even a step further: whereas Waltz was careful to use it merely as a simplifying *assumption* made for the sake of constructing a theory capable of explaining otherwise obscured causal chains, they declared that "anarchy is the fundamental *fact* of international relations."[10]

In more recent times, John Mearsheimer listed anarchy as the chief presupposition underpinning his so-called "offensive realist" theory of international relations: his "first assumption is that the international system is anarchic."[11] Echoing Waltz, he cast "the realist notion of anarchy ... [as] an ordering principle, which says that the system comprises independent states that have no central authority above them."[12] For Mearsheimer the image of anarchy is warranted not only by virtue of its explanatory power, but also due to its descriptive precision: "Sound theories are based on sound assumptions," and the assumption of anarchy struck him as "a reasonably accurate representation of an important aspect of life in the international system."[13] In the immediate aftermath of the Cold War, to the extent that the end of communism in Europe and the demise of the Soviet Union in 1989–1991 did nothing to alter the anarchical structure of the international system, Mearsheimer used his theory to reject the rosy predictions by Western statesmen and academics that future international relations would be qualitatively different from what had gone on before the fall of the Berlin Wall and that peace and cooperation would replace great power conflict and competition.[14] On the contrary, he argued, things would remain more or less the same.

The narrative of anarchy is not unique to realists and neorealists. With smaller or greater qualifications, it has been embraced by scholars of other theoretical persuasions as well, including neoliberalism, the English School, and constructivism. Laying out his neoliberal institutionalist account of international relations, Robert Keohane made it explicit that his differences with neorealism do not include anarchy. He agreed with Waltz's representation of the international stage and adopted it as his own foundational assumption, merely relaxing it somewhat by noting examples of interdependence among self-interested sovereign states in a system without any centralized authority.[15] In neoliberalism, therefore, "Anarchy, defined as lack of common government, remains a constant."[16] The same holds for the English School: nowhere in his most famous study does its principal proponent, Hedley Bull, dispute "the fact of anarchy, in the sense of the absence of government or rule. It is obvious that sovereign states ... are not subject to a common government, and that ... there is ... an 'international anarchy.'"[17] He merely objects to the claim "that, as a consequence of this anarchy, states do not form together any kind of society."[18] Instead, Bull invokes certain shared interests, norms, and institutions—mutual respect for sovereignty, for instance, or the expectation that agreements will be kept—to argue "that modern states have formed, and continue to form, not only a system of states but also an international society."[19]

In the constructivist approach developed by Alexander Wendt, a similar insight is part of a broader thesis that *"Anarchy is what states make of it"*[20] and that they can make different things of it: from a Hobbesian arena of endemic zero-sum competition and war of all against all at the one end of the spectrum, to a Kantian pluralistic community characterized by collective security interests and durable peace at the other, with a Lockean modality resembling Bull's "anarchical society" somewhere in between.[21] There are, in other words, several possible cultures of anarchy depending on the history of prior interaction. But underneath Wendt's widely praised revision of neorealist theory to account for the neglected role of ideas and sociohistorical processes in constituting international actors, their behavior, and their mutual relations, the assumption persists that the relevant actors are sovereign states in a system without centralized authority. A much more reflexive thinker than Waltz, Mearsheimer, or Keohane, Wendt admits frankly that "no one can 'see' the state or international system," that "international politics does not present itself directly to the senses," and that the "'observation' of unobservables is always theory-laden."[22] But he is just as unequivocal that part of his project is to "provide the foundation for the realist claim that states and the states system are real ... and knowable ..., despite being unobservable."[23] In its representation of the international environment, his constructivist approach thus remains committed to the narrative of anarchy.

Finally, the centrality of this narrative to contemporary academic international relations discourse is evident not just from the many texts employing it as their starting point, but also from those opposed to it. In American academic circles, critics of anarchy comprise an endangered species: they work at obscure departments and lack the seniority, prestige, and influence of the field's superstars. But they have been busy at work, even if none of them has yet attempted to unravel the fictions of the anarchy representation by analyzing it through the lens of Whitean narrative theory. Some of them have engaged with the narrative in a fairly innocuous manner, merely pointing out its ambiguities in order to replace it with a different image of the world of international politics.[24] Others have dug deeper and acted more ruthlessly, excavating anarchy's hidden normative and ideological presuppositions without bothering to propose any alternatives.[25] Either way, their voices of dissent are perhaps even more indicative of anarchy's standing in the discipline than are the voices of the proponents. So powerful is the pull of the concept that even those rejecting it feel compelled to discuss it.

Anarchy thus may be declared a "black hole," as Ankersmit described the nonempirical substance of narrative representations of reality, even before the following pages flesh out this substance. Ankersmit used the term to highlight the purely aesthetic nature of narrative substances as semantic objects which, like black holes in the physical universe, can be referred to but do not refer to anything other than or outside themselves.[26] But in the galaxy of contemporary international relations theory, the analogy also works for another reason: such is anarchy's position and gravity that, again like a black hole, it pulls everything and everyone in its vicinity into its orbit.

> [It] offers a simple, arresting, and elegant image ... [which] orders the minds of policymakers ..., [serves as] an analytic assumption for neorealism and neoliberal institutionalism..., [and] is an empirical reality for various sociological and constructivist theories of international politics.[27]

Theorists and approaches at the center of the disciplinary galaxy revolve around it as a matter of course, without so much as thinking about it. A little further out, doubt and questions emerge, but not enough for scholars to break out of the narrow paths of research delineated by the anarchy assumption, merely alter them somewhat.

Only in the remote regions does the attraction of anarchy finally begin to weaken until, in the outermost reaches of the galaxy, it drops to zero: viewed from critical distance, insofar as it appears in literature produced by scholars at the margins of the field at all, anarchy figures only as a target of censure. What happens beyond, in the vast expanses of the intellectual universe where the anarchy narrative receives neither support nor opprobrium but is simply ignored, commanding no influence whatever? These are properly a realm of aliens, no longer part of the galaxy of academic international relations.

The Disciplinary Meaning and Implications of Anarchy

Before subjecting the anarchy narrative to tropological analysis, it is necessary to unpack its meaning in depth, get a better idea of the story it tells about the international arena, and point out some of the implications it generates. As is about to become clear, anarchy not only shapes the research agenda of academic international relations in decisive ways, but is essential to the field's very standing as an autonomous area of inquiry in the first place.

In keeping with its popular definition, it may be tempting to assume that what international relations scholars mean by "anarchy" is simply chaos, but as the above passages clearly indicate this would be a mistake. In the specialist language of the field, "To say that world politics is anarchic does not imply that it entirely lacks organization."[28] In other words, "[anarchy] does not mean that [the international system] is chaotic or riven by disorder."[29] Rather, it means the lack of central authority: the international stage is anarchic in the sense that it features "no higher ruling body [above sovereign states],"[30] that there is no "government over government,"[31] and that politics there takes place "in the absence of government."[32] The point is frequently brought out by analogizing the international arena to the state of nature described by Thomas Hobbes in his *Leviathan*, in which individual human beings dwell prior to the establishment of supreme authority capable of overawing them.[33] Sovereign states exist in a similar environment: "anarchy—a multiplicity of powers without a government."[34]

Besides detailing the technical meaning of the anarchy narrative in academic international relations, these definitions reveal that leading scholars widely articulate the concept via a specific linguistic strategy: by contrast to a different—less visible yet no less foundational—narrative permeating their discourse, namely that of hierarchy as the default representation of the domestic arena. Simply put, anarchy is whatever and wherever hierarchy is not, and vice versa. To this extent, the two narratives are indeed unintelligible except in relation to one another: as a binary system where each of the opposites simultaneously presupposes and enables the other. Waltz's canonical account of the anarchic structure of international politics is illustrative: it fundamentally depends on a juxtaposition with the domestic sphere rendered in hierarchic terms, which receives the same amount of attention and performs an integral function as a mirror concept. "The parts of domestic political systems," Waltz opens his famous discussion, "stand in relations of super- and subordination. Some are entitled to command; others are required to obey. The parts of international political systems," he goes on, "stand in relations of coordination. Formally, each is the equal of all the others. None is entitled to command; none is required to obey."[35] It is in this manner, against the backdrop of "domestic systems [which] are centralized and hierarchic," that he ultimately arrives at the assertion that "International systems are decentralized and anarchic."[36]

The story of anarchy thus has to be understood within a larger narrative constituting *all* political space, not just the portion of it which has been the traditional concern of academic international relations: the international arena, whose boundaries and separation from the national arena(s) rely on the narrative to begin with. Critics have called this larger narrative "The Great Divide"[37] or "Inside/Outside"[38] on account of its core organizing dichotomy, which bifurcates the political realm into two mutually exclusive and exhaustive domains and counterposes the one within states to the one without, with the Janus-faced principle of sovereignty as the line of demarcation. Waltz gave this dichotomy its clearest expression when he wrote that "The ordering principles of the two structures are distinctly different, indeed, contrary to each other,"[39] but it is by no means specific to him. Rather, the division "between the internal and the external, or between the domestic and the international," where "the state is thought to embody the internal," saturates the entire field and "provides a pervasive framework for theorizing within [it]."[40] There is, in other words, not one black hole at the center of the disciplinary galaxy of international relations, but two in tight orbit around each other: anarchy *and* hierarchy. As one member of the disciplinary community acknowledged, the duality "drives our thinking, often in ways not explicitly recognized," and expresses established common sense: every serious international relations scholar knows that "Domestic society and the international system are demonstrably different."[41]

If this is the case, a tropological analysis exposing the fictions of anarchy's putatively factual representation of the international arena is bound to have ramifications extending beyond the image of anarchy itself. Because the anarchy representation co-constitutes the Great Divide, which in turn governs the field and its knowledge protocols, deconstructing the "fact" of anarchy to a poetic performance cannot avoid destabilizing the whole cluster of scholarship revolving around it, including the "fact" of the sovereign state. To get a sense of the extent and seriousness of the consequences, one only needs to trace the manifestations of the Great Divide in the disciplinary discourse. Where, in what shapes and forms, does the anarchy/hierarchy binary surface in academic international relations?

A few examples will suffice, beginning with the very identity of international relations as a discrete field of inquiry apart from others within political science, not to mention beyond political science. The claim to autonomy springs precisely from the assumption that the international environment differs from the domestic sphere. "A political structure is akin to a field of forces in physics: Interactions within a field have properties different from those they would have if they occurred outside of it,"[42] and since the international structure is anarchy whereas the domestic structure is hierarchy, it follows that separate conceptual and methodological toolkits are needed for the study of each. This argument is discernible already in early discussions about the scope of academic international relations just after World War II, when the field was coalescing. "The technical knowledge of IR," wrote one of the field's leading American proponents at the time,

> is not merely the extension to a wider geographical scale of knowledge of social relations inside the national community, but has unique elements of its own. (...) The distinguishing characteristic of IR as a separate branch of learning is ... [its concern] with the questions that arise in the relations between autonomous political groups in a world system in which power is not centered at one point.[43]

Three decades later, Waltz used the same argument from anarchy to narrow the field's focus to a specific task, namely the production of systemic theories: "theories that explain how the organization of a realm [anarchy] acts as a constraining and disposing force on the interacting units [states] within it."[44] To engage in unit-level theorizing instead or even just in part would be, according to Waltz, erroneous and reductionist: "Propositions at the unit level do not account for the phenomena observed at the systems level."[45] The whole cannot be comprehended through the study of the parts, and international relations scholars should refrain from "try[ing] to explain international politics in terms of (...) the behavior, the strategies, and the interactions of states."[46]

Not everyone in the field's contemporary mainstream divorces the international and domestic arenas and their attendant methods of analysis as categorically as Waltz, whose framework may be considered the strongest variant of the Great Divide. Especially Wendt's constructivism bridges the Inside/Outside dichotomy in significant ways by casting the sovereign state and the international system as "mutually constitutive ... entities. Each is in some sense an effect of the other; they are 'co-determined.'"[47] Insofar as even Wendt persists in seeing the state and the international system as "ontologically distinct,"[48] however, the distance between international relations scholarship and other fields of political science does not vanish, only shrinks.

A related expression of the Great Divide concerns prospects for qualitative change in world politics: whereas the Inside is comprehended as a domain of possibility and progress, the Outside is viewed as a domain of necessity and stasis in the sense that its dynamics are thought to preclude the pursuit of any goals beyond bare self-preservation. The Hobbesian analogy frequently invoked to augment the anarchy narrative of the international arena is telling in its bleakness: "it is manifest," Hobbes wrote in passages dear to mainstream international relations scholars,

> that during the time men live without a common power to keep them all in awe, they are in that condition which is called war ... of every man against every man. (...) In such condition there is no place for industry, ... no culture of the earth, ... no arts, no letters, no society, ... [only] continual fear and danger of violent death, and the life of man, solitary, poor, nasty, brutish, and short.[49]

Especially neorealists argue that anarchy—combined with other assumptions such as that states are rational actors, want to preserve their sovereignty, and cannot be certain about each other's intentions—thus inevitably generates a pattern of fear, self-help, and power competition.[50] States can opt out of this pattern, but not without jeopardizing their long-term survival. Insofar as they follow it, there is no functional differentiation among them: regardless of their internal differences, each does the same thing as all the others in the international arena, namely pursues national security as its overriding foreign policy concern.[51]

These behavioral dispositions dictated by anarchy are deemed self-perpetuating and self-reinforcing, since measures taken by one state to increase its security tend to diminish the security of its competitors, leading them to adopt similar measures generating similar consequences in turn: a paradox captured by John Herz in the notion of a "security dilemma."[52] In this vein, Waltz's neorealist account of the international system, as one of his critics deftly pointed out,

> contains only a reproductive logic, but not transformational logic. (...) [I]n any social system, structural change itself ultimately has no source *other than* unit-level processes. By banishing these from the domain of systemic theory, Waltz ... exogenizes the ultimate source of systemic change.[53]

The Great Divide surfaces as a dichotomy between cyclical recurrence in the international arena, terminally locked into a zero-sum contest, and linear progress inside sovereign communities, where quests for better tomorrows can be articulated, implemented, and enforced under centralized authority.[54]

A third manifestation of the Great Divide concerns the type of knowledge which, in the discipline's mainstream, genuine international relations scholarship must aspire to if it wants to escape mere amateurism and dilettantism: scientific analysis as opposed to moral inquiry. Since the Outside is not amenable to progressive change, serious students must waste no time pondering ethical questions about what the international arena *should* be and instead dedicate themselves wholly to analyzing it as it *is*. Even before Waltz positioned anarchy as the ostensibly immutable, rock-solid starting point for anyone seeking to explain international relations, Martin Wight unpacked its implication for the nature of disciplinary knowledge: if "political theory" denotes "speculation about the State" conducted in "the language appropriate to man's control of his social life," and if "international theory" denotes "a tradition of speculation about relations between States, a tradition imagined as the twin of speculation about the State," then "international theory ... does not ... exist."[55] It is a misnomer, since international relations scholars do not theorize, but only codify practice, whose essential invariability across time and space *a priori* rules out the sort of normative inquiry that philosophers concerned with the Inside have pursued as a matter of course since the days of Plato's *Republic*: political theory as "the theory of the good life."[56]

The reason why the Outside evinces stubborn "recalcitrance ... to being theorized about," according to Wight, is precisely because it is "the realm of recurrence and repetition," "the field in which political action is most regularly necessitous," and the stage on which "the same old melodrama" of power politics is being replayed over and over again: "If Sir Thomas More or Henry IV ... were to return to England and France in 1960 ... [and] contemplated the international scene, ... they would be struck by resemblances to what they remembered...."[57] Compared to the rich body of Western political theory replete with countless visions of progress, international theory is, Wight stated, remarkable only by virtue of its paucity. Today the belief that the static anarchic nature of the international environment precludes any kind of thinking over and above instrumental knowledge and clinical analysis of the mechanics of self-preservation is written into the very name of the discipline: international *relations*, as opposed to international *politics* or international *political theory*, which contain unwelcome connotations of potential for moral choice and normatively driven transformation. Particularly in the United States, academic international relations discourse has become so rabidly anti-theoretical—both in its self-understanding and in its attitudes toward competing perspectives—as to turn "theory" into a term of opprobrium.

The broader result is a stunted, narrow intellectual agenda: international relations scholarship as a technology of survival and control within anarchy as the strategic environment of sovereign state interaction, where outcomes of one's moves depend on moves by others. Not surprisingly, rational choice and game theory loom large on the minds of the discipline's leading lights. Robert Axelrod's classic *Evolution of Cooperation* is representative of this trend:

> Today, the most important problems facing humanity are in the area of international relations, where independent, egoistic nations face each other in a state of near anarchy. (...) Under what conditions will cooperation emerge in a world of egoists without central authority? (...) Many of the problems take the form of an iterated Prisoner's Dilemma.[58]

In the best of circumstances, this intellectual agenda yields graduate training programs light on humanities and heavy on mathematics and statistics, whose mastery separates the wheat from the chaff: the discipline's most successful entrants are, above all else, computer programming whizzes able to reduce even the most stubborn and sprawling datasets to crisp, clean outputs in the blink of an eye—and happy to submit to a job market that increasingly treats them in a similar fashion, as nothing more than a name attached to a journal citation count and impact factor number. At worst, the obsession with empirical methods turns in on itself and transforms computation into its own target of investigation, with application to politics as only a peripheral exercise. Gary King, the highly decorated current director of the Institute for Quantitative Social Science at Harvard, personifies this phenomenon in his capacity as government professor-*qua*-software developer in hot pursuit of computerized coding, text analysis automation, algorithms compensating for missing dataset information, and unified statistical analysis. Generalists who, whether out of blissful ignorance or youthful rebellion, have somehow managed to evade the disciplining process and insist on approaching the study of international relations in a holistic perspective informed by philosophy, literature, sociology, and history are systematically shut out.

The discipline's neorealist-neoliberal mainstream in this sense epitomizes the problem-solving approach to international thought outlined by Robert W. Cox: it is as analytically sophisticated in its efforts to explain and harmonize relations within anarchy as it is blind to anarchy's contingent historical, social, discursive, and ethical construction.[59] The latter considerations do not keep it awake at night. It protects itself from them in a manner typical of all paradigms, by being circular and self-referential: the fact of anarchy mandates positivist inquiry, which in turn rules out exactly the sort of critical-constitutive theorizing required to deconstruct anarchy's facticity.

> [As] positivists, we are methodologically predisposed to look for precisely the kind of model [of the international system] they [neorealists] 'reveal' ... [and] we join them in excluding from the realm of proper scientific discourse precisely those modes of criticism that would allow us to unmask the move for what it is. At the very moment we begin to question this [model], we are given to feel that we have stumbled beyond the legitimate grounds of science, into the realm of personal ethics, values, loyalties, or ends. We are given to feel that our complaints have no scientific standing. And so as scientists, we swallow our questions.[60]

As part of the Great Divide, the concept of anarchy generates many other dichotomies beyond the domestic versus the international, progress versus stasis, international relations versus political theory, and positivist problem-solving versus critical-normative inquiry.[61] But instead of reciting them all, it is more important to conclude the discussion of anarchy's implications with a key caveat: namely that the noun "implications" requires qualification, for it unduly simplifies the complex question of what drives what in disciplinary international relations. Does the field's autonomy stem from the anarchic nature of the international environment, or does the notion of anarchy stem from the desire of a segment of the scholarly community to set itself apart from others, lay exclusive claim to unique expertise in certain matters, and thereby guarantee itself departmental funding, professorships, research grants, and access to corridors of power? Is the discipline dominated by positivist problem-solvers because anarchy does not permit normative theorizing, or is anarchy in the spotlight because the discipline is dominated by positivist problem-solvers? Which is the factor, which the consequence? The answer is by no means straightforward. Only an outsider thoroughly oblivious to the sociology of the discipline and to the day-to-day life of its members—their egos, ambitions, jealousies, insecurities, pet projects, rank-climbing, brow-beating, gate-keeping, maneuvering now to form an alliance, now to stage an attack—would fail to notice that anarchy is not just a foundation, but also a symptom. It not only holds the various elements making up the galaxy of the disciplinary discourse in their proper orbits, but is also held by them in place in turn.

Anarchy as a Mechanistic Argument

Bearing this qualification in mind, a tropologist starts from the assumption that reality, in this case the reality of the international environment, is chaotic and does not come ready-made in intelligible patterns awaiting discovery. Whatever else they might portend to be or do, accounts and concepts of international relations are most patently and immediately literary artifacts, and insofar as they depict events in meaningful wholes, these are actively fabricated, not simply found. Where there is pattern, there is human life, language, purpose, and politics. Already simple data collection and coding, procedures elemental to the empirical research protocols privileged by the disciplinary mainstream, comprise micro-exercises in Aristotelian *poiēsis*: guided by historically contingent and largely precognitive criteria of relevance, similarity, and difference, scholars select some phenomena while omitting others, group like with like and unlike with unlike, and in this manner begin to carve order and meaning out of the essentially meaningless.

The same applies to anarchy, except in a far more profound sense, for as an image of reality it is much more patterned, narrativized, and story-like than a bare dataset. Its highly articulated form indicates the presence of extensive nonempirical content: multiple fictions of anarchy's factual representation of the world. These fictions are a result of figurative-imaginative processes which, using the tropological framework developed by Hayden White, may be broken down into and analyzed on at least three different levels: formal argument, narrative emplotment, and ideological implication.

On the level of formal argument, the observer conceptualizes the unprocessed historical field "by invoking principles of combination which serve as putative laws of historical explanation"[62] and produces meaning by constructing a deductive-nomological model relating historical entities to each other and to larger wholes. This model may be understood as a syllogism whose major premise consists of some ostensibly universal law of causal relationships, minor premise specifies the boundary conditions of the law's application, and conclusion deduces the events that actually occurred from the premises by logical necessity. In some cases the purportedly universal law is stated explicitly and after philosophical reflection, such as when Heraclitus proclaimed that no man ever steps into the same river twice or Marx set out his thesis about the relationship between the base and superstructure. On other occasions, the major premise may be unstated and amount to no more than a banal observation, such as "what goes around, comes around," employed to guide, say, a representation of the rise and fall of an empire. Whether implicit or explicit, nebulous or philosophically rich, however, a formal argument is present in every historical narrative as one of the poetic steps necessary to render reality intelligible, and it is possible to distinguish four paradigmatic modes: Formist, Organicist, Mechanistic, and Contextualist.[63] Each encapsulates different metahistorical presuppositions about the nature of the historical field and consequently espouses different criteria as to what counts as a properly historical explanation of any given set of events. Side by side, the four archetypes thus display "congenital disagreement" over the question of "the appropriate form that a historical account, considered as a formal argument, ought to take."[64]

The Formist paradigm emphasizes the rich diversity, texture, and vividness of reality. Accounts written in this mode of explanation aim to identify and differentiate the minute attributes of entities inhabiting the historical field so as to illuminate the uniqueness and autonomy of each individual agent, agency, or action and undermine any appearance of shared commonalities. Formist representations thus tend to be dispersive, broad in scope, and conceptually imprecise in their generalizations (insofar as they offer any at all).

By comparison, Organicism is integrative: it views the discrete particulars populating the historical field as components of abstract wholes which are greater than and qualitatively different from the sum of their parts. The thrust of Organicist representations is to trace the crystallization of these larger entities out of the vast universe of dispersed microscopic occurrences, and the crystallizing processes themselves are cast as suggestive of a gradual unfolding and disclosure of a still more synthetic movement: that of the totality of human existence—history with a capital "H"—toward its ultimate *telos*.

The Mechanistic paradigm evinces similar tendencies toward abstraction and integration, but unlike Organicism it is reductive rather than synthetic in that it imagines the larger trends it sees at play in the historical field as invariant causal relationships: universal "laws" of history. Akin to laws of natural science, these impose strict limits on the movement of historical entities, much as Newtonian gravity imposes strict limits on the movement of physical bodies. As White notes, "Mechanism is inclined to view the 'acts' of the 'agents' inhabiting the historical field as manifestations of extrahistorical 'agencies' that have their origins in the 'scene' within which the 'action' depicted in the narrative unfolds."[65]

In the Contextualist mode, historical explanation involves situating events in their proper circumstances and mapping their intricate interrelationships with other events occupying the historical field at a given time. In this sense, Contextualism combines the dispersive inclinations of Formism and the integrative impulses of Mechanism and Organicism. Relative to the impressionistic nature of Formist representations, it displays larger patterns, but these reach neither the level of abstraction typical of Organicist principles of grand historical progress nor the timeless quality of Mechanistic laws.

The anarchy representation advanced by mainstream international relations scholars is heavily rooted in the Mechanistic mode of historical explanation. Especially in the neorealist rendition of anarchy, the Mechanistic commitments are so pronounced as to be unmistakable. They are on display already in Waltz's preliminary discussion of the nature and purpose of theoretical knowledge in the initial pages of his seminal *Theory of International Politics*. Waltz opens this discussion with a distinction between theory and reality and stresses that the former is neither "an edifice of truth" nor a complete "reproduction of reality," but rather a human creation: an artificial "picture, mentally formed, of a bounded realm or domain of activity," which is to be judged not according to its descriptive accuracy but according to its explanatory and predictive power.[66] To generate this power, "simplification is required" so as to "lay bare the essential elements in play and indicate the necessary relations of cause and interdependency,"[67] and this simplification

> is achieved mainly in the following four ways: (1) by isolation, which requires viewing the actions and interactions of a small number of actors and forces as though in the meantime others things remain equal; (2) by abstraction, which requires leaving some things aside in order to concentrate on others; (3) by aggregation, which involves lumping disparate elements together according to criteria derived from a theoretical purpose; (4) by idealization, which requires proceeding as though perfection were attained or a limit reached even though neither can be.[68]

Tropologically, this list comprises practically the full menu of the integrative and reductive strategies typical of Mechanistic poetics. Instead of calling on scholars to pay attention to each particle populating the field of international reality, celebrate their infinite diversity, and dispel any appearance of larger unifying patterns, Waltz demands exactly the opposite: "to find the central tendency among a confusion of tendencies, to single out the propelling principle even though other principles operate, to seek the essential factors when innumerable factors are present."[69] In his view, theory must carve up the totality of events and occurrences into smaller domains, restrict scope to only one of them, treat the microscopic entities within as components of bigger wholes, abstract the general from the particular, and thereby seek to expose the fundamental cause-and-effect chains at work.

Waltz's Mechanistic frame of mind is not, however, apparent only from his definition of theory. Above all, it surfaces in his discussion of what theory is supposed to explain and predict in the first place: the actual reality of international relations, which he considers to be pre-theoretical in that he calls it simple "facts of observation" visible to anyone and everyone who cares to look.[70] This reality, Waltz's asserts, manifests intrinsic trends whose regularity approaches timeless laws. Although he is aware that diversity, change, and accidents abound in the fine grain of international relations, he notes them only to turn around and, as befits a proper Mechanist following his integrative and reductive instincts, dissolve them through abstraction and aggregation, which immediately reveal fundamental similarity and continuity on the macroscopic level of the global whole: a "striking sameness in the quality of international life through the millennia."[71] Flux and variations across time and space merely obscure the central motif of existence: that nothing new takes place under the sun and that the world essentially stands still. "The texture of international politics remains highly constant, patterns recur, and events repeat themselves endlessly. The relations that prevail internationally seldom shift rapidly in type or in quality. They are marked instead by dismaying persistence..."[72] Martin Wight opined that this persistence would have made the Cold War readily comprehensible to Sir Thomas More. Waltz similarly alleged that it would have made World War I familiar to the ancient author of the *First Book of Maccabees*.

Waltz subsequently develops his theory of international relations in faithful compliance with his Mechanistic conception of international reality and presuppositions about the purpose and nature of theoretical knowledge. The putative "fact" that "the similarity and repetition of international outcomes persist despite ... variations in ... the agents [states and leaders] that supposedly cause them" serves him as a springboard for the central question motivating his inquiry: "How can one account for the disjunction of observed causes and effects?"[73] His answer is straightforward: by using the four means of simplification to combine, integrate, and reduce diverse international actors into a larger whole, the anarchic system of sovereign states, which amounts to more than the sum of its parts, is qualitatively different from them, and subjects all of them to the same type of pressure.

> If the same effects follow from different causes, then constraints must be operating on the independent variables in ways that affect outcomes. (...)

Since the variety of actors and the variations in their actions are not matched by the variety of outcomes, we know that systemic causes are at play.[74]

Anarchy is this systemic cause, and it explains international relations precisely in the manner typical of Mechanistic narratives: the "acts" (foreign policies) of the "agents" (states) populating the historical field are presented as expressions of extrahistorical "agencies" (*Realpolitik*) that have their origins in the "scene" (anarchy) within which the "action" (international relations) unfolds. In Waltz's words, "Agents ... act; systems as wholes do not. But the actions of agents ... are affected by the system's structure," which "designates a set of constraining conditions" that "limit and mold agents ... and point them in ways that tend toward a common quality of outcomes even though the efforts and aims of agents ... vary."[75] The reason why international relations remain static across history is because of their enduring anarchic structure.

Although Waltz announces that this conclusion is "a statement that will meet with wide assent,"[76] a tropologist cannot help but disagree. Within the Mechanistic paradigm of narrative historiography, Waltz's findings may indeed enjoy consensus, but outside it his confidence is misplaced: mere wishful thinking. To observers working from the Formist, Contextualist, or Organicist perspectives, both his conception of the nature and purposes of international relations theory and his characterization of international reality will be alien to the point of unintelligible.

Far more attuned to the particular and microscopic, Formists and Contextualists will dismiss Waltz's obsession with aggregation, generalization, and macroscopic trends as a project to filter out the rich color and texture of international life. Theory, they will counter, should strive to disperse any appearances of likeness; it ought to illuminate the full diversity of discrete phenomena, not obscure this diversity in the name of abstract similarities and causal explanatory power. Where Waltz comprehends the international arena as a force field manifesting timeless empirical laws, a Heraclitean Formist will comprehend it as a river in which ever-new waters flow and say that it is impossible to step into the same world of international relations twice. Even if the river of time somehow ceased to move, one would still be left with variation across place. Here Formist and Contextualist critiques would draw attention to how the image of anarchy at once unduly standardizes political communities horizontally, in relation to one another, and vertically, homogenizing political space within each.

Concerning horizontal standardization, the anarchy narrative implicitly treats all states as formally like by virtue of their sovereignty, but this glosses over the oftentimes stunning differences among them. Whereas Waltz sees the United States and Somalia, for example, as two pieces of fruit, a Formist will see an apple and an orange—and quickly add not just grapes, peaches, or strawberries to the spread, but also bread, wine, cheese, and chocolate, since international relations involve many other types of actors besides sovereign states, much as food involves many other types of edibles besides fruit. Concerning homogenization of domestic space, a Formist would disperse the international arena not only in the horizontal plane, but also vertically: by smashing the American apple, as it were, to reveal the miscellany of entities within. Some of these will be empty air pockets: the remote, inhospitable, and inaccessible regions of Alaskan wilderness, although physically inside US sovereign territory, are for all practical purposes "off the grid" of politics, unorganized either hierarchically or anarchically. Others might incidentally look an awful lot like scaled-down versions of the Somalian orange: the rival gangs, chronic turf warfare, absent law enforcement, shooting death rates, poverty, and stagnation in the urban area of South Central Los Angeles delineated by Washington Boulevard, Slauson Avenue, South Main Street, and Long Beach Boulevard might just make a refugee from conflict-torn Mogadishu feel right at home in California ZIP code 90011. Regardless, to zoom in on each of the microcosms and appreciate the myriad of contrasts setting it apart from all the others is to quickly lose sense of any overarching category: the notion of sovereign states as unitary rational actors vanishes.

Organicists will be just as unhappy with the anarchy representation of international relations, albeit for different reasons. They will not fault Waltz, Mearsheimer, or Keohane for eliding the individuating characteristics of particular historical agents, objects, and occurrences, since Organicism shares the same predisposition toward sweeping trends and general categories. But Organicists will refuse to join them in regarding these trends and categories as resistant to change and impermeable to human wishes. "Organicist strategies of explanation ... eschew the search for the *laws* of historical process, when the term 'laws' is construed in the sense of universal and invariant causal relationships, after the manner of Newtonian physics...."[77] Whereas Waltz casts anarchy as a straitjacket confining sovereign states to a narrow range of behavioral patterns in endless cyclical recurrence, Organicists will conceive of the structure and its manifestations as a specific *phase* in the teleological unfolding of the totality of world affairs through time. In the Organicist paradigm, the ideas and principles guiding the movement of particles in the historical field "function not as restrictions on the human capacity to realize a distinctively human goal in history, as the 'laws' of history ... do in the thought of the Mechanist, but as guarantors of an essential human freedom."[78] From this angle, the error committed by neorealists and neoliberals consists of reifying the transient. Their static conception of anarchy and the sovereign state mistakes a stopover for a final destination and sees a terminus where Organicists see a preface introducing the next stage in the progressive transformation of political reality.

Taken together, the contrasts of Formism, Contextualism, and Organicism throw the poetic choices underpinning the anarchy representation on the level of formal argument into sharp relief. The "fact" of anarchy emerges as a linguistic creation whose substance involves specific nonempirical presuppositions—the fictions of Mechanism—about how to properly organize the historical field and combine its elements. Waltz's account of the international arena does not, of course, exhaust the anarchy discourse in contemporary international relations literature; although disproportionately influential, his narrative is only one among others, some of which depart from his views in significant ways. Especially Wendt's recent rereading of anarchy as a dynamic social structure capable of various manifestations depending on the history of prior interactions among states introduces differences that are more than simply cosmetic—and may have very well eclipsed Waltz's statement in impact in recent times. With appropriate qualifications to account for these differences, however, the conclusions of a tropological analysis of the deductive-nomological layer of Waltz's representation remain intact. Wendt's efforts to disperse anarchy into a spectrum of more concrete, distinctive, and localized cultures may be regarded as a nod in the direction of Contextualism and Formism, but insofar as the dispersion is limited and does not do away with the unifying concept, Mechanism remains the dominant mode of formal argument even in his instance.

Anarchy as a Tragic Plot

Next to formal argument, another level on which narrative representations of reality figure forth its meaning is emplotment, whereby a succession of events making up a given story is gradually unveiled as a narrative of a distinctive type: Romance, Satire, Comedy, or Tragedy.[79] Each of these options adds another layer of tropological sense to the chaos of unprocessed historical occurrences and, working together with rhetorical strategies on the deductive-nomological and ideological levels, allows one to answer the all-important question: what message do the occurrences display?

The distinguishing theme of Romance is human triumph over the world. Exemplified by the biblical tale about the resurrection of Christ or, more recently, by Leni Riefenstahl's cinematic story of Hitler's impending redemption of Germany in *Triumph des Willens* (1935), Romantic plots depict protagonists emerging from, conquering, and ultimately transcending temporal existence, whose various obstacles are thus shown to be no match for the awesome liberating power of the human spirit. Good prevails over evil, virtue over vice, and happiness over suffering. Satire communicates the opposite message: defeat under the burden of trials and tribulations implicitly recognized to be insurmountable. Rather than masters of existence, human beings are its foredoomed victims, whose lives and achievements are bound to be relentlessly battered, compromised, and in the end obliterated by the forces of death and decay. Satirical authors often experience the sense of human inadequacy so intensively that their works problematize their own ability to act as images of reality and concede their inevitable failure in this regard. Compared to Romance's heroic motifs and naïve use of language,

Satire thus stands apart by virtue of its metalinguistic reflexivity and ironic detachment culminating in "the theatre of the absurd."[80]

Unlike Romance and Satire, Comedy and Tragedy portray neither total triumphs nor total defeats but "partial liberation ... and provisional escape from the divided state in which men find themselves in this world."[81] Their plots build up to tentative settlements rather than absolute closures and may be regarded as "*qualifications* of the Romantic apprehension of the world ... in the interest of taking seriously the forces which *oppose* the effort at human redemption naïvely held up as a possibility ... in Romance."[82] Not nearly as sanguine as their Romantic counterparts, Comic and Tragic writers recognize the presence of adversity in the world, but without following Satirists all the way to ascribing it the kind of overwhelming magnitude and nihilistic implications which make the preservation of sanity conditional on flight into ironic laughter and self-ridicule. The main difference between Comedy and Tragedy lies in their respective conceptions of man's provisional victories. In Comedy, they take the shape of "the prospect of occasional *reconciliations* of the forces at play in the social and natural worlds."[83] Comic plots thus often begin with seemingly irresolvable discords and subsequently depict their transformation into eventual harmony, typically symbolized by festivities in the concluding act. Tragedy does not believe in such resolutions. Instead of merry celebrations of unity, it shows the demise of the protagonist which shakes the world and exacts a heavy toll on society. Nevertheless, the dramatic downfall is never totally lethal; plentiful survivors are spared in order to ponder, together with the audience, what went wrong. The somber ending hints at the answer: it signals that human knowledge and endeavors are subject to firm limits, warns that overstepping them means courting disaster, and intimates that far more terrible conflicts and divisions are in store should the warning be ignored. Whereas Comedy "eventuates in a vision of the ultimate *reconciliation* of opposed forces," then, Tragedy yields "a *revelation* of the nature of the forces opposing man"[84] and lets members of the audience achieve provisional liberation from the ordeals of life by heightening their consciousness through "the epiphany of the law governing human existence which the protagonist's exertions against the world have brought to pass."[85]

In academic international relations as it has evolved since its formal inception in 1919, both the anarchy representation of the international arena and the broader realist and neorealist theoretical perspectives in which it is rooted express a Tragic sensibility informed by the violence of the twentieth century, a century of war, including from the late 1940s the threat of nuclear omnicide. This sensibility did not permeate the field at the outset. During its formative years in the immediate wake of World War I, the discipline exuded a mentality more suggestive of the Romantic or Comic paradigms: one radiating with optimism, idealism, and confidence in humankind's impending redemption from the evils of armed interstate conflict. It was dominated by Anglophone liberal progressivists, whose academic and practical efforts to come to grips with the Great War relied heavily on the assumption of a fundamental harmony of interests in the world.

This assumption was especially pronounced in the case of Woodrow Wilson, the principal architect of the postwar order and the leading liberal internationalist of the era, in whose honor the world's first chair in international relations was endowed at University College of Wales, Aberystwyth. Wilson prefaced his famous list of America's World War I objectives by stating that "What we demand in this war ... is nothing peculiar to ourselves," that "our programme ... is ... the programme of the world's peace," and that "All the peoples of the world are in effect partners in this interest."[86] As he saw it, US war aims merely channeled heretofore suppressed universal goals and aspirations, in whose light all international quarrels and discords emerged as unnecessary and contrived—products of capricious leaders, bad or missing institutions, and general lack of enlightenment. Whatever divisions plagued the family of nations were reconcilable. Through proper reforms including democratization at the domestic level and institutional transformation of the international order to the League of Nations based on collective security, national self-determination, free commerce, open diplomacy, and judicial settlement of disputes, humanity could be united, escape its long history of war, transcend it, and achieve lasting peace. Early twentieth-century liberal international relations thinkers such as Wilson, then, were not mired in Tragic consciousness, but espoused a Romantic or, in more pragmatic cases, Comic view of the world and human possibility. In Wilson's instance, this view was directly inspired by the biblical story of salvation and represented a secularized expression of his Presbyterian millennialist beliefs, which led him to declare the November 11, 1918, armistice "the final triumph of civilization over savagery."[87]

Such self-assured proclamations, of course, proved premature as the Versailles peace settlement began eroding practically from the moment of its ratification and then rapidly collapsed in the 1930s. Instead of becoming heaven on earth, Europe morphed into hell riven by economic crises, totalitarian dictators, waves of terror unleashed by their regimes against enemies both internal and foreign, and finally World War II. In Nazi and Soviet concentration camps, the siege of Stalingrad, and the firebombing of Dresden, savagery returned in abundance, and it was under its sobering impact that self-proclaimed realists such as Hans Morgenthau, Reinhold Niebuhr, and George F. Kennan countered liberal internationalism with a much darker outlook on international relations: one evocative of the Tragic plot archetype.

They arrived at it via different paths. Morgenthau's commenced with international law: before fleeing his native Germany for the United States, where he eventually gained distinction as the preeminent realist international relations theorist of his generation, he spent the late 1920s and early 1930s immersed in critical sociological reflections on the nature and limits of international legal norms.[88] Kennan's perspective grew out of his rich diplomatic experience at American embassies around Europe, in whose course he witnessed international conflict firsthand: he walked the streets of Prague the day after the Munich Agreement, spent months in Nazi internment after Germany declared war on the United States, and flew over the bombed-out ruins of Stalingrad en route to Moscow to facilitate America's grand alliance with the Soviet Union against the Third Reich.[89] As for Niebuhr, his realism emanated from his Augustinian conception of man as a sinful creature "inclin[ed] to transmute his partial and finite self and ... values into the infinite good,"[90] which led Niebuhr to denounce all political visions of redemption—whether the "soft utopianism" of American liberals or the "hard utopianism" of Soviet Bolsheviks—as expressions of human pride and desire to dominate others.[91] But regardless of their divergent backgrounds, Morgenthau, Kennan, and Niebuhr all shared a number of typically Tragic presuppositions: that strife was inevitable in the world; that divisions pitting nations against each other could never be fully bridged, only carefully managed; that leaders vowing to unify humanity were bound only to magnify them; that the advent of the nuclear age had made such leaders far more dangerous than at any previous time in history; and that international relations scholars had ethical responsibility to constantly remind statesmen about the limits of foreign policy.

Kennan's geopolitical vision illustrates this Tragic perspective on world affairs well. As he and his fellow State Department officials struggled to define the parameters of the post-World War II order and America's strategy of response to Soviet expansionism, Kennan broke with liberal internationalism on multiple counts. He assumed neither any underlying universal harmony of interests capable of bringing nations together in a global community of peace, nor the myth of America as a special country providentially appointed to exemplify these interests and shine their light across the seas, nor again the idea that US national security depended on this task—on enlightening states and the international system as a whole with America's democratic principles and institutions. For Kennan "the most notable feature of the international environment was its diversity, not its uniformity,"[92] and within this environment the United States was no better and no worse than other countries. Unlike Wilson, who proclaimed America a "spirit among the nations of the world,"[93] Kennan categorically "reject[ed] ... the image of ourselves [Americans] as teachers and redeemers to the rest of humanity, ... the illusions of unique superiority and virtue on our part, the prattle about Manifest Destiny or the 'American Century.'"[94] As an approach to US national security, the Wilsonian project to democratize states and the international system under the umbrella of shared American-inspired procedures and institutions was ill-conceived: blithely ignorant of the plurality of the world beyond America's borders. This plurality could not be simply brushed aside; from Kennan's Tragic perspective, it was not just a fog of misunderstandings bound to dissipate amidst celebrations of human triumph and global accord at the end of the drama of history, as Wilson interpreted it in his Romantic mode of comprehension. On the contrary, it was existentially real and impossible to overcome, making conflict inevitable and generating the imperative to work with it rather than against it.[95]

In this vein, Kennan conceptualized the international arena not as a *single* household whose members are in principle united and merely need to be reminded of this at the dinner table with a stern Wilsonian sermon, lest their infantile quarrels bring the roof down, but as a *fragmented* space occupied by scores of independent units, among whom five military-industrial power centers predominated and constantly vied against each other: the United States, Great Britain, *Mitteleuropa* (Germany and Central Europe), the Soviet Union, and Japan. The key to US national security was to maintain their colliding interests in equilibrium so that no one of them could rise to oppress or conquer the rest. As Kennan stated in late 1948, just as the Soviets were about to end America's nuclear monopoly and acquire their own atom bomb, "Our safety depends on our ability to establish a balance among the hostile ... forces of the world: To put them ... one against the other; to see that they ... are thus compelled to cancel each other out."[96] American statesmen had to abandon the assumption—tropologically Romantic or Comic—that American and Soviet postwar interests coincided, frankly state their differences with Stalin, and pursue "a long-term, patient but firm and vigilant containment of Russian expansive tendencies...."[97]

The ultimate objective of this strategy was to dissuade the Soviets from trying to convert the world to Marxism-Leninism while refraining from attempts to convert them, or anyone else, to American liberal democracy in turn. Kennan in this sense acted as a Tragic poet warning audiences in *both* Washington and Moscow that neither knew what was best for others around the world, that universalist foreign policy ambitions—whether American liberal or Soviet communist—were too dangerous in the context of a diverse and divided international arena armed with nuclear weapons, and that a failure to curb them could trigger a conflict yet far more catastrophic than either of the two World Wars just past.[98] His overall standpoint may be characterized as Tragic precisely because it combined "a pessimistic view of the international order ... [with] a degree of measured optimism as to the possibilities for restraining rivalries within it."[99]

The anarchy representation of the international stage formulated by neorealist scholars in more recent decades encapsulates the same Tragic judgment of the world and human possibilities in it as underpins Kennan's pentagonal concept of the geopolitical environment. Indeed, the neorealist version of the anarchy narrative does little else than formalize and generalize this concept in accordance with standards and protocols appropriate to social-scientific inquiry. Instead of working with five specific military-industrial centers in the immediate aftermath of World War II, for instance, it introduces the broader and more modular category of "great powers"[100] in order to expand its range of applicability beyond a particular historical context. But this does nothing to the underlying presuppositions about the plurality of interests, insurmountability of differences, and inevitability of conflict. The anarchy narrative retains all of them and uses them to communicate the same wisdom about relations among nations as Tragedy communicates about relations among its protagonists: the only kind of reconciliations they can attain is

> in the nature of resignations ... to the conditions under which they must labor in the world. These conditions ... are asserted to be inalterable and eternal, and the implication is that man cannot change them but must work within them. They set the limits on what may be aspired to ... and legitimately aimed at in the quest for security and sanity in the world.[101]

It is precisely for these reasons that critical international relations theorists have classified Waltz's neorealism as an example of "problem-solving theory," whose distinguishing characteristics are that it "takes the world as it finds it ... as the given framework for action," accepts prevailing social and power relations and institutions without asking whether or how they might be changed, and operates within the fixed confines imposed by their parameters.[102]

To the extent that the neoliberal and constructivist statements of the anarchy narrative depart from the neorealist one in according the international environment greater room for cooperation, the conclusion that the anarchy narrative expresses a Tragic mode of emplotment requires some qualification. Wendt, for example, admits the possibility of international relations metamorphosing from Hobbesian zero-sum conflict to Kantian harmony, and so he tropes the international arena in much less unambiguously Tragic terms. According to his constructivist theory, oppositional identities and antagonisms dividing sovereign states are not immutable and over time may resolve themselves into shared interests and happy friendships, undergoing the sort of transformation indicative of a Comic plot type.

But instead of working out all such qualifications in full, it is worth stressing the relentless disguising and burying, especially pronounced in neorealist literature, of the rhetorical foundations of the anarchy narrative under a language of rationality, objectivity, and empiricism deemed to be the only kind of language suitable for social science, conceived in turn as a mode of intellectual activity free of and apart from ethics. This move is on prime display in the false dichotomy with which Mearsheimer introduces his *Tragedy of Great Power Politics*: "it behooves us to see the world as it is, not as we would like it to be."[103] What this Rankean exhortation and its underlying dichotomy of reality and fantasy miss is the whole bulk of narrative theory: that the factual world, in order to make any sense at all, must be rendered in story form, that this form involves nonfactual substance and corresponding poetic choices on several different levels, and that Tragedy is but *one* of the choices available on but *one* of these levels, that of emplotment. Claiming to see the world as it is, in other words, Mearsheimer nonetheless and necessarily sees it exactly as he would like it to be, only he fails to admit it and understand why it cannot be otherwise. Just as Waltz, other neorealists, neoliberals, and the vast majority of scholars in the discipline's social-scientific mainstream, he lacks any theory of language beyond the naïve assumption that verbal expressions are perfectly transparent windows granting the mind undistorted access to a preformed reality on the outside: an assumption scores of thinkers in other corners of the modern academic universe have been problematizing for over half a century, often to reject it out of hand.

Not that earlier realists such as Niebuhr, Morgenthau, and Kennan enriched their international thought with sophisticated tropological reflections allowing them to fully grasp the poetic nature of political reality and the role of narrative language in its constitution. But at least they were keenly attuned to the power of words—the political nature of political concepts—in academic international relations and foreign policy discourse, instinctively understood the moral-political sources and implications of international relations theory, and certainly did not see themselves as scientists. After his exit from the State Department Kennan retired to the Institute for Advanced Study in Princeton, where he spent the next half-century writing award-winning histories and memoirs; Niebuhr's international thought was nothing if not applied theology; Morgenthau considered it scandalous that post-World War II American political science turned to natural-scientific methodology; and all three harbored deep distrust of scientific rationalism. They comprehended international relations scholarship in decidedly normative terms: as an ethical project.[104]

To a tropologist analyzing mainstream academic international relations discourse today, in the wake of the Whitean revolution in narrative historiography and equipped with its intellectual achievements, this classical realist self-understanding feels remarkably refreshing. Whether or not he shares its Tragic inclinations, its sincerity elicits respect and even admiration. That contemporary neorealists and neoliberals have failed to retain so much as a speck of it in their writings is an achievement only in the ironic sense of the term: a genuine fiasco.

Anarchy as a Conservative Ideology

Intertwined with formal argument and plot type, a third nonfactual element embedded in narrative accounts of reality is ideology: "a set of prescriptions for taking a position in the present world of social praxis and acting upon it…."[105] At least four basic options may be identified within this tropological layer: Conservatism, Liberalism, Radicalism, and Anarchism. Each of them expresses specific views on a number of fundamental questions, including whether society can and should be studied scientifically, whether the social status quo should be preserved or changed, in what direction any potential changes should proceed, through what means, and in which part of the temporal sequence—whether the past, present, or future—lies society's ideal form.[106]

The main contrast among the competing outlooks lies in their attitude toward existing society: from social transcendence at the one end of the ideological spectrum to social congruence at the other. Anarchism is the most socially transcendent in that it denounces present society as corrupt and alienated, postulates a remote mythical past of innocence and purity, and projects it onto the nontemporal plane as a utopia achievable through a conscious return to the original human essence buried underneath the corrosive sediment of civilization. Radicalism is somewhat less socially transcendent (or, equivalently, more socially congruent) in that it views the utopia in immanent terms, as a possibility nascent within the established order and already looming on the horizon, and focuses on the elaboration of the revolutionary means to trigger its onset. Liberalism is less transcendent and more congruent still, since it moves the utopia from the immediate future off to a more distant one—in part to protect existing society from any Anarchist or Radical attempts at revolutionary transformation. Finally, Conservatism is the least socially transcendent of all. This is by virtue of its inclination to "regard as a 'utopia'—that is, the best form of society that men can 'realistically' hope for, or legitimately aspire to," precisely "the institutional structure that *currently* prevails."[107]

It hardly needs to be said that the different attitudes toward established society go hand in hand with different valorizations of social change: what Radicalism or Liberalism welcome as progress, for instance, Conservatism is liable to decry as regress. What may not be so obvious, however, is that the ideological implication of a given narrative of historical reality is not necessarily permanently stuck under one or the other of the four competing headings; its classification may shift over time. The reason is that Conservatism, Liberalism, Radicalism, and Anarchism all stake out their claims relative to their sociohistorical circumstances, and these are dynamic. Therefore, representations that are socially transcendent at one point in time might, by virtue of changes in sociohistorical context, become socially congruent at another, and vice versa. In the context of a universal world-state, for example, a factual narrative depicting geopolitical space as an arena fragmented among diverse communities recognizing no shared authority could be categorized as either Liberal, Radical, or Anarchist, depending on additional considerations such as whether it situates this arena in a forgotten past worth resurrecting or in a more or less imminent future, but in any case it would be a socially transcendent narrative: one at odds with the status quo and at least tacitly subversive of it. In a world so fragmented, however, the same narrative would be socially congruent and Conservative.

Incidentally, the evolution of the ideological implications of the anarchy narrative in twentieth-century Anglophone international relations scholarship may be understood precisely in these terms: as a development from Liberal or even Radical impulses of classical realism, articulated in the first half of the century to combat the reigning universalist theoretical orthodoxies, foreign policy initiatives, and international institutional designs of the day, to the Conservative overtones of neorealist and neoliberal accounts, produced from the late 1970s onward and doing little else than codifying the Cold War order. The socially affirmative character of the latter literature has not escaped its critics, who have pointed out that the assumption of anarchy's permanence "is not merely a convenience of method, but also an ideological bias"[108] reflecting dominant interests content within the established order. This Conservative bias flows naturally out of the combination of Tragic and Mechanistic commitments pervading the neorealist, neoliberal, and to a somewhat lesser degree also constructivist literature on the levels of plot type and formal argument. "Where a set of events emplotted as a Tragedy ... [is] explained 'scientifically' (or 'realistically') by appeal to strict laws of causal determination," White has noted in this regard, inadvertently furnishing an apt characterization of Waltz's and Mearsheimer's theories, "the implication is that men are indentured to an ineluctable fate," and "the ideological thrust of histories fashioned in [this way] is generally 'Conservative'...."[109]

The congruence of traditional international relations theory with the Cold War order is especially tight in the instance of Waltz's neorealism, as evidenced by his discussion of the ideal number of great powers in the international system in his *Theory of International Politics*. After copious inferences and analogies, he eventually concludes that the best of all possible worlds is precisely the one in existence at the time of his writing: a bipolar form of anarchy. "Problems of national security ... clearly show the advantages of having two great powers, and only two, in the system."[110] Ideologically, Waltz's influential treatise thus functions to vindicate superpower management of international relations by the United States and Soviet Russia to the exclusion of everyone else.

However, the Conservatism of the neorealist image of the international arena became most visible not in Waltz's America during the Cold War, but *after* the Cold War and in places where its passing induced the greatest amount of change: places such as the former Soviet satellites in Central Europe. The transformation of Czechoslovakia's relationship with the outside world, for example, was so rapid, all-encompassing, and thoroughgoing in its internal effects that those who came of age in that country in the decade following 1989 often experience cognitive dissonance when looking back at their childhood today. Within just a couple of years of the Velvet Revolution, the Red Army withdrew, its barracks were razed, and the statues of Stalin and Lenin disappeared from town squares. Children who used to look at them from windows of neighboring public schools had Russian struck from their required curricula and could now elect English, German, or French as their foreign language instead. Universal military service was abolished. Borders opened up, direct coach service to London's Victoria Station started departing from Prague several times a week, and the national airline introduced nonstop flights to destinations as far west as its new planes—purchased from Boeing and Airbus rather than Tupolev, the traditional supplier—could reach without refueling: all the way to New York. European Union (EU) membership brought new highways, railways, and other large-scale public works courtesy of the European Regional Development Fund and sent university students abroad on Erasmus exchanges. In short, whereas in the United States the end of the Cold War did not affect average Americans in any significant way and, to the extent that they had noticed it at all, was experienced as a distant event, a matter of newspaper headlines and television reports, in places such as Czechoslovakia it induced a massive, all-encompassing, and keenly felt earthquake. This earthquake altered, often beyond all recognition, both the physical landscape within which ordinary Czechs live their daily lives and the very identity of each and every citizen: by, for example, placing new passports and driver's licenses in their pockets and new license plates on their cars, all imprinted with EU insignia.

Against the backdrop of these profound and fast-paced changes, ongoing neorealist assertions throughout the 1990s about the *permanence* of anarchy and its various implications—that international relations remained divided among competing sovereign states, that the promise of international institutions was false, and that instability in Europe was actually likely to increase with the demise of Cold War bipolarity—took on a distinctive sound: that of crying dinosaurs desperately clinging to a bygone era in hopes of prolonging it for at least a little while longer. The new international and domestic political environment in Central Europe exposed the anarchy narrative as a Conservative relic from the world of yesterday, a world that fell together with the Berlin Wall and, like most of that notorious structure, was either pulverized by wrecking balls, hauled off to museums, or simply left to rust away on its own.

This is not to say that the anarchy representation of the international arena is bound to remain Conservative in its ideological implications forever. It is not difficult to imagine scenarios in which it would express socially transcendent rather than congruent attitudes. One might be brewing within the EU today. Since the end of the Cold War, the project of European integration initiated by Robert Schuman, Jean Monnet, Paul-Henri Spaak, and other statesmen in the 1950s has progressed so far that in several respects Winston Churchill's famous call for a United States of Europe has been realized, but the community in place is not immune to internal rifts. Particularly the recent euro currency crisis triggered by Greece's enormous sovereign debt has proven quite divisive: austerity measures stipulated in the bailout packages prepared by the troika of the European Commission, European Central Bank, and International Monetary Fund met with fierce popular opposition in the already depressed Greek economy, provoked violent uprisings in Athens, brought an anti-austerity government into power, made the country's exit from the eurozone a real possibility, and threatened to spread the crisis to other debt-ridden nations such as Spain, Italy, and Portugal. The European Monetary Union—one of the cornerstones of the EU—was thereby shaken in its very foundations. Compounding these difficulties, the dramatic surge in numbers of Syrian, Afghan, and Iraqi asylum seekers since April 2015 has destabilized the EU further. As even the most affluent and welcoming member countries such as Germany and Sweden slowly but surely run out of capacity to absorb the immigrants, begin experiencing internal tensions, and encounter rising xenophobia, populism, and nationalism, calls for abolishing the free movement of persons and reinstating border controls in the Schengen Area appear destined to proliferate—and could, in due time, confine the brunt of Europe's worst refugee crisis since World War II to the EU's southern perimeter. This would effectively turn member countries most exposed to the migrant flow into a protective buffer.

In such circumstances, it would be a miracle if in Greece, to point out the most obvious candidate, no angry voices rose up proposing to extricate the country from the increasingly unfavorable status quo in part by rereading the political economy of the EU through the state-centric optic of the anarchy narrative of international relations: as a set of ideas, norms, and institutions serving a handful of rich and powerful nations in the core of Europe at the expense of the periphery. Used in this manner and context, the anarchy narrative would adopt a distinctly Radical ideological thrust of the sort exemplified by, for instance, the subversive Marxist economist Yanis Varoufakis: Greece's finance minister and parliamentarian for the Coalition of the Radical Left (SYRIZA) prior to resigning both positions in protest against the government's capitulation to EU-imposed austerity conditions in summer 2015.

Were it to take on such a role, the anarchy narrative would in many ways resume the emancipatory function performed by classical realism in the 1930s and 1940s, when its leading proponents similarly sought to challenge, negate, and transcend prevalent international relations wisdoms and practices of the day. Kennan proposed his "particularized" geopolitical framework for US national security strategy as a critical counter to the appallingly naïve traditional universalist assumptions guiding American statecraft at a time when these assumptions threatened to facilitate the expansion of America's main adversary after World War II: Stalin's Soviet Union.[111] Morgenthau conceived of political realism in contradistinction to utopianism, whose Wilsonian liberal strand codified in the Treaty of Versailles he held directly responsible for the smothering of the Weimar Republic and the rise of Nazism in the 1920s and 1930s. The transcendent implications were most pronounced in the case of E. H. Carr. His famous realist attack on post-World War I liberal internationalism in *The Twenty Years' Crisis* and subsequent works such as *The New Society*, as the next chapter is about to show, may be read as an expression of a Radical progressive agenda inspired by Marxist ideology critique: a counterhegemonic project to transform and move beyond the sovereign state and anarchy as the established forms of, respectively, domestic and international political community. To this extent, it was a very far cry indeed from any sort of Conservatism.

Toward a Genealogy of Anarchy's Facticity

White's tropological framework for analysis of narrative representations of reality has its peculiarities and limitations. Aside from its relativizing tendencies discussed in the previous chapter, one may object to its neat division of the poetic dimension into three separate layers, to its identification of exactly four master options within each, and to the resulting implication that there is a finite number of combinations. Such a lens may be too rigidly structuralist: too disciplining of the dynamic variety of narrative styles and too eager to arrest them in a handful of inflexible categories. Another issue arises from the framework's application. White formulated the tropological optic as part of a specific project, for the purpose of deconstructing the works of major nineteenth-century European historians and laying bare their nonempirical content, which begs an obvious question: can the optic be divorced from its original target and redirected at twentieth-century international relations scholarship? Even if yes, a third concern may be voiced about the scope of the new target: insofar as the anarchy narrative cannot be separated from the narrative of state sovereignty, which it at once presupposes and implies, a tropological investigation of the former would seem to necessitate a simultaneous excavation of the poetics of the latter. The analysis performed here, in other words, may be incomplete, treating only one side of the coin.

But even with such gaps and limitations, many of which result strictly from constraints of space, White's tropological lens offers a solid and well-developed springboard for at least a preliminary exposition of the rhetorical moves and choices behind the dominant representation of the international arena in international relations scholarship today. This exposition reveals that the anarchy narrative installed at the center of the disciplinary discourse by Waltz and embraced by the neorealist, neoliberal, and Wendtian constructivist mainstream is no more realistic than any other renditions of the international stage are in the eyes of their respective proponents. All of them involve some nonempirical content simply by virtue of their narrative form.

Through this discovery, tropological analysis paves the road to a number of new and important questions. Why and how has the anarchy representation come to predominate over and suppress the various alternatives, frequently to the point of completely silencing them? Why and how, in the way most contemporary international relations scholars (not to mention the ordinary public) imagine the space of international politics, has the highly charged root morpheme "real" and its derivatives such as "reality," "realistic," and "realism" become associated precisely with a tale combining Mechanistic, Tragic, and Conservative commitments instead of another story? Why do these powerful words not designate, for example, a Satirical narrative: one mordantly laughing its head off at the anarchy representation by juxtaposing its blithe assertion of sovereign states' *de jure* equality with their ever-growing *de facto* inequality? Why does the narrative currently designated by them not go by another name?

Giving complete and definitive answers, if such exist at all, is beyond the present scope. But at least one reason enabling today's proponents of the anarchy representation to claim that they describe the international arena as it really is has to do with the history of international relations thought, specifically with their ability to invent this history in a manner sympathetic to their perspective: as a fable in which they inherit, protect, and transmit heroic discoveries made about the natural constitution and rhythms of the international arena by their intellectual predecessors. The reality of anarchy and other mainstream disciplinary constructs, in other words, depends in part on conjuring up a lineage tracing them back to a suitable army of favorably disposed dead intellectual giants, who in turn are worth remembering and celebrating precisely to the extent that they foreshadow and introduce these constructs.

Among these giants of yesteryear, E. H. Carr stands as one of the most prominent. It is now time to turn to his disciplinary legacy and show that, insofar as it cannot display any message unless rendered in narrative form, it is no less saturated with poetic fictions than the fact of anarchy itself.

Notes

1 Don DeLillo, *White Noise* (New York: Viking, 1985), 12–13.
2 For the cobweb model, see Robert O. Keohane and Joseph S. Nye, Jr., eds., *Transnational Relations and World Politics* (Cambridge, MA: Harvard University Press, 1972), and Keohane and Nye, *Power and Interdependence: World Politics in Transition* (Boston, MA: Little, Brown, 1977). For the core-periphery model, see Immanuel Wallerstein, *The Modern World-System*, vol. 3 (New York: Academic Press, 1974–1989).
3 Charles Lipson, "International Cooperation in Economic and Security Affairs," *World Politics* 37, no. 1 (1984): 22.
4 Christian Reus-Smit and Duncan Snidal, eds., *The Oxford Handbook of International Relations* (Oxford and New York: Oxford University Press, 2008), 364.
5 See Brian C. Schmidt, *The Political Discourse of Anarchy: A Disciplinary History of International Relations* (Albany: State University of New York Press, 1998). A notable example from the period is G. Lowes Dickinson, *The European Anarchy* (New York: Macmillan, 1916).
6 Such is the claim of Martin Hollis and Steve Smith, *Explaining and Understanding International Relations* (Oxford: Clarendon Press, 1990), 7.
7 Kenneth N. Waltz, *Man, the State and War: A Theoretical Analysis* (New York: Columbia University Press, 1959), 159.
8 Kenneth N. Waltz, *Theory of International Politics* (Reading, MA: Addison-Wesley, 1979), 88.

9   Robert Gilpin, *War and Change in World Politics* (Cambridge and New York: Cambridge University Press, 1981), 7.

10 Robert J. Art and Robert Jervis, *International Politics*, 2nd ed. (Boston, MA: Little, Brown, 1986), 7. [Emphasis added.] First published in 1976 and currently in its 12th edition, this volume surely holds some kind of record for textbook longevity.

11 John J. Mearsheimer, *The Tragedy of Great Power Politics* (New York and London: Norton, 2001), 30.

12 Ibid.

13 Ibid.

14 See John J. Mearsheimer, "Back to the Future: Instability in Europe after the Cold War," *International Security* 15, no. 1 (1990): 5–56, and idem, "The False Promise of International Institutions," *International Security* 19, no. 3 (1994/95): 5–49, whose discussion of realism and anarchy (pp. 9–12) reappears in the subsequent *Tragedy of Great Power Politics* practically verbatim.

15 Robert O. Keohane, *After Hegemony: Cooperation and Discord in the World Political Economy* (Princeton, NJ: Princeton University Press, 1984), 73, 85, 88, 122–23.

16 Robert Axelrod and Robert O. Keohane, "Achieving Cooperation under Anarchy: Strategies and Institutions," in David A. Baldwin, ed., *Neorealism and Neoliberalism: The Contemporary Debate* (New York: Columbia University Press, 1993), 86. This has engendered the view that under the surface neoliberalism and neorealism do not express competing approaches so much as the same perspective: a "neo-neo synthesis." See Ole Wæver, "The Rise and Fall of the Inter-Paradigm Debate," in Steve Smith, Ken Booth, and Marysia Zalewski, eds., *International Theory: Positivism and Beyond* (Cambridge and New York: Cambridge University Press, 1996), 163–7, 172–3. Cf. Kenneth N. Waltz, "Structural Realism after the Cold War," *International Security* 25, no. 1 (2000): 25: "[neoliberal institutionalism] never was an alternative to realism. Institutional theory … has as its core structural realism."

17 Hedley Bull, *The Anarchical Society: A Study of Order in World Politics*, 2nd ed. (Basingstoke: Macmillan, 1995), 44.

18 Ibid.

19 Ibid., 22–23. See also Barry Buzan, "From International System to International Society: Structural Realism and Regime Theory Meet the English School," *International Organization* 47, no. 3 (1993): 327–352.

20 Alexander Wendt, "Anarchy Is What States Make of It: The Social Construction of Power Politics," *International Organization* 46, no. 2 (1992): 395. [Emphasis original.]

21 Alexander Wendt, *Social Theory of International Politics* (Cambridge: Cambridge University Press, 1999), 264–266, 299–302, 283–285.

22 Ibid., 5.

23 Ibid., 48.

24 See Helen Milner, "The Assumption of Anarchy in International Relations: A Critique," *Review of International Studies* 17, no. 1 (1991): 67–85, rejecting anarchy in favor of interdependence.

25 See especially Richard K. Ashley, "Untying the Sovereign State: A Double Reading of the Anarchy Problematique," *Millennium: Journal of International Studies* 17, no. 2 (1988): 227–262, and Aaron Beers Sampson, "Tropical Anarchy: Waltz, Wendt, and the Way We Imagine International Politics," *Alternatives* 27, no. 4 (2002): 429–457. Examples from outside American international relations include Beate Jahn, *The Cultural Construction of International Relations: The Invention of the State of Nature* (London: Palgrave, 2000).

26 See Frank R. Ankersmit, *Narrative Logic: A Semantic Analysis of the Historian's Language* (The Hague: Nijhoff, 1983), 96–104, and idem, "Reply to Professor Zagorin," *History and Theory* 29, no. 3 (1990): 281.

27 Stephen D. Krasner, "Compromising Westphalia," *International Security* 20, no. 3 (1995/1996): 115. Strictly speaking, Krasner is not referring directly to anarchy but to the so-called Westphalian model, reflecting the shared understanding among today's international relations scholars that the Peace of Westphalia (1648) marks "the beginning of the modern international system as a universe composed of sovereign states, each with exclusive authority within its own geographic boundaries." (Ibid.)

28 Axelrod and Keohane, "Achieving Cooperation under Anarchy," 86.

29 Mearsheimer, *Tragedy*, 30.

30 Ibid.

31 Inis L. Claude, *Swords into Plowshares: The Problems and Progress of International Institutions*, 4th ed. (New York: Random House, 1971), 14.

32 William T. R. Fox, "The Uses of International Relations Theory," in idem, ed., *Theoretical Aspects of International Relations* (Notre Dame, IN: University of Notre Dame Press, 1959), 35, quoted in Waltz, *Theory*, 88.

33 The analogy is helpfully outlined in Jack Donnelly, "Realism," in Scott Burchill and Andrew Linklater, eds., *Theories of International Relations*, 5th ed. (Basingstoke: Palgrave Macmillan, 2013), 34–36.

34 Martin Wight, *Power Politics*, ed. Hedley Bull and Carsten Holbraad (Leicester: Leicester University Press, 1978), 101.

35 Waltz, *Theory*, 88.

36 Ibid.

37 Ian Clark, *Globalization and International Relations Theory* (Oxford and New York: Oxford University Press, 1999), 15–32.

38 R. B. J. Walker, *Inside/Outside: International Relations as Political Theory* (Cambridge and New York: Cambridge University Press, 1993).

39 Waltz, *Theory*, 88.

40 Clark, *Globalization*, 12, 15.

41 James A. Caporaso, "Across the Great Divide: Integrating Comparative and International Politics," *International Studies Quarterly* 41, no. 4 (1997): 564.

42 Waltz, *Theory*, 73.

43 Frederick S. Dunn, "The Scope of International Relations," *World Politics* 1, no. 1 (1948): 144.

44 Waltz, *Theory*, 69, 71.

45 Ibid., 69.

46 Ibid.

47 Alexander E. Wendt, "The Agent-Structure Problem in International Relations Theory," *International Organization* 41, no. 3 (1987): 360.

48 Ibid.

49 Thomas Hobbes, *Leviathan*, ed. Edwin Curley (Indianapolis, IN, and Cambridge: Hackett, 1994), chap. 13, §8–9.

50 See, for example, Mearsheimer, *Tragedy*, 30–32. As Caporaso, "Across the Great Divide," 564, puts it, without necessarily subscribing to the view, "[the international system] is competitive anarchy where formally similar states rely on self-help and power bargaining to resolve conflict. Domestic society (not system) is, by contrast, rule-based."

51 Waltz, *Theory*, 96–97. Cf. Donnelly, "Realism," 37.

52 John H. Herz, "Idealist Internationalism and the Security Dilemma," *World Politics* 2, no. 2 (1950): 157–180. Cf. Mearsheimer, *Tragedy*, 37–38.

53 John Gerard Ruggie, "Continuity and Transformation in the World Polity: Toward a Neorealist Synthesis," review of *Theory of International Politics*, by Kenneth N. Waltz, *World Politics* 35, no. 2 (1983): 285. [Emphasis original.]

54 Again, where the Great Divide is less sharply drawn, as in Wendt's constructivist approach restoring unit-level variables and processes to systemic analysis, endogenizing the sources of international systemic change, and thus

incorporating a logic of transformation, the stasis/progress opposition softens accordingly: states *can* advance from, for instance, Hobbesian to Lockean anarchy. Since anarchy remains ontologically distinct from the domestic environment, however, there are limits to collapsing the stasis/progress binary: transformative change can occur Outside, but not nearly to the same breadth and depth as Inside.

55　Martin Wight, "Why Is There No International Theory?" *International Relations* 2, no. 1 (1960): 35, 48.

56　Ibid., 48.

57　Ibid., 42–43, 48.

58　Robert Axelrod, *The Evolution of Cooperation* (New York: Basic Books, 1984), 3, 190. Game-theoretic treatments of international relations are too numerous to list. Classic studies include Thomas C. Schelling, *Strategy of Conflict* (Cambridge, MA: Harvard University Press, 1960). Notable examples of more recent literature include Robert Jervis, "Cooperation under the Security Dilemma," *World Politics* 30, no. 2 (1978): 167–214; Bruce Bueno de Mesquita, *The War Trap* (New Haven, CT: Yale University Press, 1981); Duncan Snidal, "The Game Theory of International Politics," *World Politics* 38, no. 1 (1985): 25–57; Kenneth A. Oye, "Explaining Cooperation under Anarchy: Hypotheses and Strategies," *World Politics* 38, no. 1 (1985): 1–24; idem, ed., *Cooperation under Anarchy* (Princeton, NJ: Princeton University Press, 1986); and Baldwin, ed., *Neorealism and Neoliberalism*.

59　Cf. Robert W. Cox, "Social Forces, States and World Orders: Beyond International Relations Theory," in Robert O. Keohane, ed., *Neorealism and Its Critics* (New York: Columbia University Press, 1986), 207–210.

60　Richard K. Ashley, "The Poverty of Neorealism," in Robert O. Keohane, ed., *Neorealism and Its Critics* (New York: Columbia University Press, 1986), 285–286. The circular nature of paradigm-based arguments is discussed in Thomas S. Kuhn, *The Structure of Scientific Revolutions*, 2nd ed. (Chicago: University of Chicago Press, 1970), 109–110.

61　They include the world of states versus the world of people, communitarianism versus cosmopolitanism, thick versus thin morality, and more. See Clark, *Globalization*, 15–26.

62　Hayden White, *Metahistory: The Historical Imagination in Nineteenth-Century Europe* (Baltimore, MD, and London: Johns Hopkins University Press, 1973), 11.

63　Ibid., 13.

64　Ibid.

65　Ibid., 17.

66　Waltz, *Theory*, 8.

67　Ibid., 10.

68　Ibid.

69　Ibid.

70　Ibid., 6.

71　Ibid., 66.

72　Ibid.

73　Ibid., 67.

74　Ibid., 68–69.

75　Ibid., 73–74.

76　Ibid., 66.

77　White, *Metahistory*, 16. [Emphasis original.]

78　Ibid.

79　Ibid., 7. Cf. Northrop Frye, *Anatomy of Criticism: Four Essays* (Princeton, NJ: Princeton University Press, 1957).

80 The term was coined by Martin Esslin, *The Theatre of the Absurd* (Garden City, NJ: Doubleday, 1961), in reference to authors such as Samuel Beckett, Eugène Ionesco, Harold Pinter, Edward Albee, and Václav Havel.

81 White, *Metahistory*, 10.

82 Ibid. [Emphasis original.]

83 Ibid., 9. [Emphasis original.]

84 Ibid., 10. [Emphasis original.]

85 Ibid., 9.

86 Woodrow Wilson, Address to a Joint Session of Congress, 8 January 1918, in Arthur S. Link et al., eds., *The Papers of Woodrow Wilson*, vol. 69 (Princeton, NJ: Princeton University Press, 1966–1994), 45: 536.

87 Woodrow Wilson, Remarks at a Stag Dinner, 28 December 1918, in Link et al., eds., *Papers of Wilson*, 64: 491. For a detailed analysis of the religious sources of Wilson's international thought and practice, see Milan Babík, "George D. Herron and the Eschatological Foundations of Woodrow Wilson's Foreign Policy, 1917–1919," *Diplomatic History* 35, no. 5 (2011): 837–857, and idem, *Statecraft and Salvation: Wilsonian Liberal Internationalism as Secularized Eschatology* (Waco, TX: Baylor University Press, 2013).

88 See Christoph Frei, *Hans J. Morgenthau: An Intellectual Biography* (Baton Rouge: Louisiana State University Press, 2001), especially chaps. 5–7, and also William E. Scheuerman, "Realism and the Left: The Case of Hans J. Morgenthau," *Review of International Studies* 34, no. 1 (2008): 29–51.

89 These experiences are documented in George F. Kennan, *The Kennan Diaries*, ed. Frank Costigliola (New York and London: Norton, 2014), and also John Lewis Gaddis, *George F. Kennan: An American Life* (New York: Penguin, 2011).

90 Reinhold Niebuhr, *The Nature and Destiny of Man: A Christian Interpretation*, vol. 2 (New York: Scribner's Sons, 1941, 1943), 1: 122.

91 See Reinhold Niebuhr, "Two Forms of Utopianism," *Christianity and Society* 12, no. 4 (1947): 6–7, and idem, "Augustine's Political Realism," in *The Essential Reinhold Niebuhr: Selected Essays and Addresses*, ed. Robert McAfee Brown (New Haven, CT, and London: Yale University Press, 1986). The best summary of Niebuhr's Christian conception of man and its implications for his international relations thought remains Michael Joseph Smith, "The Prophetic Realism of Reinhold Niebuhr," in *Realist Thought from Weber to Kissinger* (Baton Rouge and London: Louisiana State University Press, 1986).

92 John Lewis Gaddis, *Strategies of Containment: A Critical Appraisal of American National Security Policy during the Cold War*, revised ed. (Oxford and New York: Oxford University Press, 2005), 27.

93 Woodrow Wilson, Address on the American Spirit, 13 July 1916, in Link et al., eds., *Papers of Wilson*, 37: 415.

94 George F. Kennan, *Around the Cragged Hill: A Statement of Personal and Political Philosophy* (New York: Norton, 1993), 182–183.

95 The same Tragic perspective underlies Morgenthau's realist theory of international relations, which he introduced in his most famous work by stating that the world is "inherently a world of opposing interests and of conflict among them" and that "to improve the world one must work with those forces, not against them." (*Politics among Nations: The Struggle for Power and Peace*, 5th ed. (New York: Knopf, 1973), 3.

96 George F. Kennan, Lecture at the National War College, Washington, DC, 21 December 1948, George F. Kennan Papers, Box 17, Seeley Mudd Manuscript Library, Princeton University.

97 George F. Kennan ["X," pseud.], "The Sources of Soviet Conduct," *Foreign Affairs* 25, no. 4 (1947): 575.

98 Cf. Milan Babík, "'X' Ten Years On: The Fictions of George F. Kennan's Recent Factual Representations," *Review of International Studies* 42, no. 1 (2016): 74–94.

99 Gaddis, *Strategies of Containment*, 31.

100 Waltz, *Theory*, 72–73; Mearsheimer, *Tragedy*, 5.

101 White, *Metahistory*, 9.

102 Cox, "Social Forces," 208.

103 Mearsheimer, *Tragedy*, 3–4.

104 Much of the credit for the recovery of the ethical and rhetorical dimension belongs to the recent critical reassessment of the nature and legacy of classical realism spearheaded by scholars such as Murielle Cozette, Seán Molloy, William E. Scheuerman, Michael C. Williams, and Vibeke Schou Tjalve. Examples of this exciting literature include Cozette, "Reclaiming the Critical Dimension of Realism: Hans J. Morgenthau on the Ethics of Scholarship," *Review of International Studies* 34, no. 1 (2008): 5–27; Molloy, "Truth, Power, Theory: Hans Morgenthau's Formulation of Realism," *Diplomacy and Statecraft* 15, no. 1 (2004): 1–34; Scheuerman, "A Theoretical Missed Opportunity? Hans J. Morgenthau as Critical Realist," in Duncan Bell, ed., *Political Thought and International Relations* (Oxford: Oxford University Press, 2009); Tjalve and Williams, "Reviving the Rhetoric of Realism: Politics and Responsibility in Grand Strategy," *Security Studies* 24, no. 1 (2015): 37–60; and Williams, *The Realist Tradition and the Limits of International Relations* (Cambridge: Cambridge University Press, 2005). See also Babík, "'X' Ten Years On"; William Bain, "Deconfusing Morgenthau: Moral Inquiry and Classical Realism Reconsidered," *Review of International Studies* 26, no. 3 (2000): 445–464; and Daniel F. Rice, *Reinhold Niebuhr and His Circle of Influence* (New York: Cambridge University Press, 2012).

105 White, *Metahistory*, 22.

106 Ibid., 24.

107 Ibid., 25. [Emphasis original.]

108 Cox, "Social Forces," 209.

109 White, *Metahistory*.

110 Waltz, *Theory*, 161.

111 Cf. Gaddis, *Strategies of Containment*, 26–28, and Babík, "'X' Ten Years On," 82–84.

3 The Fictions of
E. H. Carr's Realism

Dead Theorist as a
Literary Artifact

Contemporary American international relations scholars do not spend their careers talking only about war and peace, power and security, or conflict and cooperation among sovereign states in an anarchic system. The stuff of world politics is not their sole obsession. As any insider familiar with the discipline knows, they also dedicate serious time and energy to talking about each other: praising, quarreling, labeling, pigeonholing, and gossiping. This behavior not only infuses the annual meeting of the American Political Science Association with the unmistakable feel of a high school cafeteria but has been institutionalized in a wide array of disciplinary practices and procedures. Among these, perhaps the most illustrative and time-honored example is the confidential reference letter, without which no application for a faculty position, tenure, or major research grant is complete. It contains one scholar's opinions of another, is accorded great weight by search and promotion committees, and often triggers heated discussions—occasionally even a fistfight—among their members.

Such practices are neither accidental nor peripheral to research proper. Rather, they are inherent features of a discipline which at its core, regardless of its adamant pretensions to science, is a branch of rhetoric. The problem of self-legitimation plaguing the field within the broader economy of knowledge, namely how to persuade the public at large to accept it as the exclusive purveyor of true learning about world politics, also plagues every scholar within the narrower confines of the disciplinary community: how to persuade it to listen exactly to him or her? In the absence of universal evaluative procedures and standards of judgment, without any firm grounds defining the subject matter, best theory, or even just criteria for adjudication, solving this problem and achieving professional success depends on extrascientific factors, above all on mastering the politics of pedigree and reputation.

For newcomers, this translates into the imperative to forge close links with well-established senior scholars, preferably the discipline's reigning heavyweights. This is why at top American departments many graduate students in their final years coauthor their first publications with their supervisors: in hopes of piggybacking into the profession on the prestige of their teachers. That for the senior scholars this sort of "coauthoring" might involve nothing beyond hastily scribbling their name on the cover of a manuscript laboriously prepared entirely by someone else must not bother the young researchers queuing up to join the guild; looking the other way is a small price to pay for a shot at one of the scarce tenure-track positions harboring access to wealth, status, and leisure. Be that as it may, in the American branch of the discipline today publication endorsements and reference letters from the likes of Gary King or John Mearsheimer are worth their weight in gold. Much as Ali Baba's magic "Open Sesame!" they unlock doors that would remain firmly shut otherwise.

For the heavyweights the problem of self-legitimation is not as acute as for aspiring scholars without established reputations. Entrenched in tenured positions and endowed chairs, they wield sufficient professional status and job security to act as the discipline's arbiters and gate-keepers. Their control of various professional perks and vetting procedures—not only letters of recommendation, but also graduate teaching and research assistantships, dissertation examination verdicts, hiring committee decisions, and so on—lets them promote sympathizers, demote dissenters, and in this manner cultivate a base of support for their intellectual positions.

Still, not all dissenters can be chased away, and even sympathizers often turn out to be mere sycophants who desert their masters the moment the latter have ceased to be useful. Therefore, even the heaviest of the heavyweights have to resort to additional measures in an effort to lend authority to their teachings.

Among these measures, none is as simple, reliable, and effective as crafting and disseminating a particular narrative of the discipline's past in which today's top scholars appear as guardians of exemplary intellectual achievements performed by the discipline's "gods" *in illo tempore*: during the creation of scientific international relations, at the sacred dawn of the discipline's origins. Orwell's dictum, "whoever controls the present controls the past," does not summarize only the politics of historical representation through which the Inner Party of Oceania legitimates its regime in *Nineteen Eighty-Four*; as Kuhn hinted, it also captures the way dominant paradigms justify their rule within disciplinary communities.[1] Much like Oceania's Ministry of Truth, leading international relations academics constantly (re)produce the past so that it vindicates them: the credibility of their work presupposes and relies on an entire fabric of sympathetic portrayals of earlier thinkers. Unlike pesky graduate students and fickle junior faculty, these have the immense advantage of being dead and therefore perfectly obedient; one can make them say anything. For "the past is a place of fantasy. It does not exist anymore. One can only study it by way of things that have been left as effects,"[2] and these effects can be assembled to yield practically an unlimited number of stories and meanings, satisfying the needs of even the most demanding customers. Through it all, the fundamentally ideological function of historical narratives shines bright and clear.

Edward Hallett Carr (1892–1982)

Nobody demonstrates this more vividly than E. H. Carr, or more precisely his disciplinary images, since Carr died in 1982 after an exceptionally fruitful academic, journalistic, and diplomatic career spanning nearly seventy years. Born to a middle-class family in London in the final decade of the Victorian era and growing up in Edwardian England, Carr won a scholarship to study Classics at Cambridge and was recruited by the Foreign and Commonwealth Office during World War I. As a junior diplomat he was part of the British delegation to the Paris Peace Conference in 1919, where he assisted with the drafting of the Versailles Treaty. His subsequent assignments included a posting at the British Embassy in Riga, Latvia, in the late 1920s, during which time he became deeply interested in Russian culture. This pastime quickly blossomed into a full-fledged passion yielding Carr's first book, a biography of Fyodor Dostoevsky, followed by three more in quick succession, each dealing with a prominent nineteenth-century Russian figure: Alexander Herzen, Karl Marx, and Mikhail Bakunin.[3]

In 1936 Carr's ambitions, his dissatisfaction with the direction of postwar British and American statecraft, and tensions within the Foreign Office prompted him to quit diplomatic service and become, rather ironically, the Woodrow Wilson Professor of International Politics at the University College of Wales, Aberystwyth. Already a major figure in British public intellectual circles thanks to his frequent commentary on Russian and international affairs in magazines such as the *Fortnightly Review, The Spectator,* and *The Times Literary Supplement,* Carr reached new audiences through the prestigious appointment—the world's first chair in international relations at the time of its inception in 1919. The publication of *The Twenty Years' Crisis* in 1939, mounting a scathing attack on interwar Anglo-American liberal internationalism and advocating accommodation of Nazi Germany, earned him widespread notoriety.[4] After the outbreak of World War II and Hitler's assault on Europe, Carr quickly renounced his support for appeasement, quietly deleted it from subsequent editions of the book, and instead became one of Britain's leading patriotic voices. His countless editorials in *The Times,* on whose staff he spent much of the war, rivaled Churchill's speeches as some of the nation's most spirited battle cries against the Third Reich. Unlike the Prime Minister, however, Carr displayed strong left-wing tendencies and propounded an Anglo-Soviet alliance not just as a strategic measure for the purpose of winning the conflict, but as a durable relationship for the purpose of shaping the postwar order. He spelled out his views on the postwar organization of Europe in a series of books published between 1941 and 1951, including *The Future of Nations, Conditions of Peace, Nationalism and After,* and *The New Society,* all of which channel his enthusiastic support for welfare socialism and deep antipathies toward liberal democracy, capitalism, and national self-determination.[5]

With the onset of the Cold War, dismayed by the split with the Soviet Union, Carr lost interest in international relations and turned all his attention to history, especially the history of Russian communism, whose study would preoccupy him for the rest of his life—over three decades of uninterrupted effort. The result, his massive *History of Soviet Russia*, remains a classic in Soviet studies to this day.[6] While working on it, Carr forged lasting friendships with leading western Marxist thinkers including Isaac and Tamara Deutscher and Herbert Marcuse. His historical writing was informed by keen philosophical reflections on the nature of history and historiography. He discussed them especially in his Trevelyan Lectures at Cambridge, later published under the title *What Is History?* which has sold over one quarter of a million copies to date: more than any other of his books.[7] In light of these achievements, it is no surprise that Carr's death from cancer at the age of ninety was mourned not as a departure of a famous diplomat or international relations scholar, but as the passing away of a distinguished historian. His obituary in *The Times* bore the title: "Mr. E. H. Carr: Eminent Historian of Soviet Russia."[8]

This has not, however, detained contemporary international relations experts from claiming Carr as one of their own and appropriating—*disciplining*—his legacy for their purposes. If not so much in his native Britain, where his intellectual breadth and versatility across different fields of learning enjoy relative recognition, then certainly in the United States the vast majority of international relations scholars has not the faintest suspicion of his achievements as a diplomat, journalist, or historian; they regard him exclusively as a fellow specialist. In this capacity, Carr outranks even the discipline's current heavyweights and belongs to the ultimate class of thinkers: the saintly apostles of academic international relations, a veritable pantheon accorded periodic worship and commemoration in the temple of the undergraduate textbook. The extent of his posthumous presence in contemporary academic international relations discourse makes it practically impossible for anyone in the discipline, whether a novice or a veteran scholar, not to encounter him somewhere along the way. Carr's bequest has given rise to an entire "cottage industry of articles and books about [him] and his ideas,"[9] whose list of contributors reads like a "Who's Who" of current international relations theory: from John Mearsheimer, Robert Gilpin, and Hedley Bull via Michael Cox, Andrew Linklater, and Robert W. Cox to a legion of younger scholars such as Seán Molloy and William Scheuerman. The origins of this "cottage industry" go as far back as 1948, when Hans Morgenthau, nowadays a fellow divinity rubbing shoulders with Carr in the discipline's hollowed shrines, published a review of Carr's international political thought.[10]

Not even all this noise about Carr, however, can move his gravestone and alter the fundamental fact that he is physically absent and no longer around. Insofar as he remains alive in international relations theory today, it is solely as an Aristotelian *poiēma*: a product of poetic discourse and imagination driven by the objective of displaying a specific message, teaching the audience a certain lesson, and thereby shaping the life of the polis both disciplinary and general. His presence has to be actively fashioned out of the effects he had left behind. Crucially, none of the fabrications ever employs the complete record of everything Carr had written, for such a representation would be cognitively unintelligible and didactically and rhetorically useless. Rather, they all necessarily select some portions of Carr's extant oeuvre while ignoring others, and the choices vary dramatically from scholar to scholar—to the point of not intersecting at all. As is about to emerge, even where his interpreters work with identical passages drawn from the same source, such as *The Twenty Years' Crisis*, the data can be put together in divergent ways yielding divergent stories. This illustrates well the central point of Whitean narrative theory: namely that historical meaning is not found but emerges through storytelling, as a matter of rhetorical and configurational moves on several tropological levels.

There is consequently not just one Carr in contemporary international relations literature but several. What they all share in common is that they are results of *poiēsis*, which endows representations of the past with an element of fiction precisely by virtue of giving them the form of a coherent, well-ordered plot: in this case a legendary thinker one can picture, understand to have espoused a particular theory of international relations, and revere or revile for that reason. Thanks to this nonempirical element, the Carr industry is not unlike the car industry: each model is a vehicle assembled to reflect the unique purposes, interests, and styles of its owners. Two representations currently overshadow all others and are worth scrutinizing in detail: Carr as a classical realist, the dominant reading popular above all in American universities, where it enjoys a near monopoly, and Carr as an early critical theorist, an alternative image developed over the last quarter century primarily in British circles. Although each constituency champions its rendition of Carr as the sole accurate portrait and rejects the other, a narrative theorist knows differently, especially if he adopts Ankersmit's argument about narrative substances as semantic black holes referring to nothing other than or outside themselves.[11] In that case, the choice between competing Carrs boils down to nothing but aesthetics.

Carr as a Classical Realist

Among Carr's disciplinary readings, the one with the longest pedigree and broadest recognition—the standard image, in other words—is the one casting him as a realist: Carr is widely regarded as one of the founders of classical realism as a modern social-scientific approach to international relations theory. Propounded especially though not only by American realist scholars, this portrayal is the staple of all introductory literature and predominates in advanced scholarship as well, with "The nursery, chief residence, and now rest-home of Carr the unambiguous Realist [being] the IR textbook."[12]

While never entirely uncontested or able to stamp out dissenting interpretations, this representation enjoys near hegemony within the domain of Carr's disciplinary renditions—much like the realist tradition within international relations theory at large. Both constitute part of the discipline's common sense, with many students and scholars not even aware of any other options.

Few contemporary international relations thinkers have gone to greater lengths propounding the standard image of Carr than John Mearsheimer, whose framing of Carr's legacy is at once detailed and emblematic of the mainstream consensus. Mearsheimer placed Carr among realism's main representatives already in *The Tragedy of Great Power Politics*, where he referred to *The Twenty Years' Crisis* as a "seminal realist tract"[13] and characterized it as one of the principal foundations of the realist paradigm. Together with Morgenthau's *Politics among Nations* and Waltz's *Theory of International Politics*, Carr's study encompassed "the three most influential realist works of the twentieth century."[14] But because Mearsheimer's main project in *The Tragedy* was to lay out his own brand of realist theory, "offensive realism," he confined his remarks about Carr to only a few peripheral passages. His representation of the British thinker thus remained relatively nebulous.

A few years later, however, it took center stage and surfaced in full when Mearsheimer was invited to deliver the prestigious E. H. Carr Memorial Lecture at the University College of Wales at Aberystwyth, Carr's one-time home institution. Mearsheimer dedicated the entire talk and ensuing essay to asserting Carr's realist identity. Drawing almost exclusively on *The Twenty Years' Crisis*, he declared resolutely that "Carr is a realist" and repeated that the volume constituted a "classic realist tract."[15] As grounds for this assessment, Mearsheimer singled out two features of Carr's argument above all others: his view of sovereign states as primary international actors and his emphasis on power as the key element in their relations.

Both of these features indeed figure in *The Twenty Years' Crisis*, as Mearsheimer demonstrated with abundant references. As Carr wrote in the preface to the second edition,

> in the first place, [the book] was written with the deliberate aim of counteracting the glaring and dangerous defect of nearly all thinking, both academic and popular, about international politics in English-speaking countries from 1919 to 1939—the almost total neglect of the factor of power.[16]

He spent an entire chapter on the concept of power in international affairs and concluded it by stating that "International politics are always power politics; for it is impossible to eliminate power from them."[17] Carr was careful to note that international politics was not only about power; state behavior was motivated by other factors as well, including morality. But he added that even if "politics cannot be satisfactorily defined exclusively in terms of power, it is safe to say that power is always an essential element of politics."[18] Carr consequently paid the factor of power close attention, coming up with a sophisticated analysis of its different facets: military, economic, and ideological. Among these, he regarded the military component as supreme to the others by virtue of "the fact that the ultima ratio of power in international relations is war."[19]

Mearsheimer argued that it was precisely these repeated claims about the fundamental role of power that "earned Carr his realist spurs," adding that Carr's state- and power-centric "perspective, of course, is what makes [him] a realist."[20] As ultimate proof of Carr's realism, Mearsheimer pointed out Carr's bleak assessment of international law and morality as merely products and vehicles of power, an assessment at the dead center of his assault on interwar liberal internationalism in *The Twenty Years' Crisis*:

> The exposure of the real basis of [its] professedly abstract principles is the most damning and most convincing part of the realist indictment of utopianism.... [T]hese supposedly absolute and universal principles were ... but the unconscious reflections of national policy based on a particular interpretation of national interest at a particular time.[21]

In this biting analysis of ostensibly universal liberal norms, ideals, and institutions, "Carr's realism comes shining through" for Mearsheimer.[22] Lest it be thought that the realist attitude had been falsely misread into *The Twenty Years' Crisis* by Carr's realist followers and that Carr would not have endorsed or even recognized it, Mearsheimer observed that in a brief autobiographical sketch composed for Tamara Deutscher at the end of his life the British thinker himself had retrospectively characterized the book as a hard-hitting realist work.[23]

Carr's state-centric focus, emphasis on power, and discounting of international law and morality in *The Twenty Years' Crisis* are not the only affinities running between him and contemporary realists, who consequently consider him one of their chief forerunners. Other parallels are present, such as Carr's desire to transform academic international relations from wishful thinking akin to medieval alchemy into serious science. As he explained right at the outset of *The Twenty Years' Crisis*, "purpose ... is a condition of thought,"[24] and this maxim applied not least to the birth and formative stages of academic international relations, accounting for the discipline's early utopian tendencies manifest in Woodrow Wilson's rosy vision of durable peace under the auspices of the League of Nations. "The science of international politics," Carr elaborated,

> has ... come into being in response to a popular demand. It has been created to serve a purpose.... It took its rise from a great and disastrous war [World War I]; and the overwhelming purpose which dominated and inspired the pioneers of the new science was to obviate a recurrence

of this disease of the international body politic. The passionate desire to prevent war determined the whole initial course and direction of the study. Like other infant sciences, the science of international politics has been markedly and frankly utopian.[25]

The goal of world peace entirely overshadowed observation and analysis. The role of realism, Carr proposed, was to reverse the imbalance: stop day-dreaming about happy tomorrows, turn to the present, investigate actual facts and processes of world politics, and thereby make international relations scholarship scientifically respectable. "No science deserves the name until it has acquired sufficient humility ... to distinguish the analysis of what is from aspiration about what should be."[26] Carr therefore invited students of international relations "to embark on that hard ruthless analysis of reality which is the hallmark of science."[27] Without this analysis the centrality of sovereign states and power in world politics would remain obscured to them.

In result, contemporary realists claim Carr as one of their precursors not only because of his specific recommendations about *what* academic international relations should study—states and power—but also because of his suggestions about *how* the discipline should study it in the first place: using the scientific method and, at an even more basic level, rationalist epistemology. In the opening chapter of his *Tragedy of Great Power Politics*, Mearsheimer thus discussed the virtues and functions of realist theory in part by referring to Carr's methodological exhortations about the need to analyze hard reality. These serve Mearsheimer to anchor his own definition of academic international relations as a social science modeling itself on natural science, employing dispassionate observation and rational analysis to detect cause-and-effect patterns in world politics, and using these patterns to predict and control the future.[28] Similarly Robert Gilpin, whose stature among contemporary American realists approaches Mearsheimer's, has praised Carr's methodological remarks in *The Twenty Years' Crisis* as a demand for a modern positivist science of international politics.[29] Even Hedley Bull, whose realism was couched in a more historical rather than social-scientific perspective, saw Carr as an unvarnished positivist.[30]

These, then, are some of the key features of the realist representation of E. H. Carr, his dominant image in international relations scholarship. His head is where his feet are: planted firmly in the present rather than soaring high above it in the thin air of tomorrow's intoxicating possibilities. Surveying his environs, he finds a world permanent in its essence, independent of his perceptions, and impervious to his wishes and actions: a world where sovereign states eclipse all other forms of political organization and vie for power as they always have and always will. He harbors no hopes for any kind of progressive transformation of this order. Instead, he exudes a spirit of resignation typical of all realists, who, in Mearsheimer's neat summary of their outlook, "are pessimists when it comes to international politics ... (and) see no easy way to escape the harsh world of security competition and war."[31]

Carr as an Early Critical Theorist in *The Twenty Years' Crisis*

Articulated on the basis of a publicly available and verifiable factual record consisting of his preserved writings, the realist image of Carr seems beyond reproach: solid like a rock. Many in the discipline consider it self-evident that among ghosts making up the field's grand history, who so often put undergraduates to sleep in broad daylight during theory lectures at the semester's beginning only to keep them awake long into the night during review sessions at the semester's end, just before finals, Carr personifies the realist view of international relations.

Nevertheless, since the early 1990s a small but growing number of international relations scholars has steadfastly advanced a different reading: Carr as an early proponent of critical theory. Since critical theory is conventionally regarded as the opposite of realism, this alternative Carr is just about everything the dominant Carr is not. Had he been Chinese, the duality would have suggested the serenity of the *yin* and the *yang* in perfect balance, but since he was English and a Londoner at that, one barely resists shrieking out in horror: apparently the deity rubbing shoulders with Morgenthau in the pantheon of academic international relations is none other than Dr. Jekyll and Mr. Hyde. If American scholars have not yet run for cover, it is only because they do not see one of Carr's two faces: unlike the realist tradition, critical theory is mired in obscurity in the United States. Thus they carry on repeating the fairy tale about Carr's realism with Daoist tranquility—without so much as suspecting the dangerous critical theorist hidden within.

Much as in the case of Carr's realist image, scholars responsible for his rendition as an early critical theorist are no obscure thinkers, but some of the discipline's leading lights, except this time predominantly British rather than American. They include such prominent members of British academic international relations royalty as Ken Booth and Andrew Linklater. Booth discussed Carr's legacy during his inaugural lecture as E. H. Carr Professor at Aberystwyth. He used the occasion to offer a compelling account of the normative elements permeating *The Twenty Years' Crisis* with the intention to tone down the book's mainstream realist interpretation and "restore the balance in favor of utopianism."[32] A few years later Linklater made an even more explicit attempt to "release Carr from the grip of the Realists"[33] and portray him as a representative of the critical perspective. Carr's international thought struck Linklater as highly dynamic, transformative, and emancipatory: moving beyond the sovereign state and anarchy as, respectively, the prevalent type of political community and the established form of the international arena. In this vein, Linklater jettisoned his initial perception of Carr as an "unadulterated realist" and recast him as a visionary thinker far ahead of his times: a pioneer of critical international theory who "set out the case for post-exclusionary forms of political organization" and whose "writings contain a striking analysis of the changing nature of the modern state and the possibility of new forms of political association."[34]

Carr's critical perspective can be detected already in his opening discussion of the nature of international political thought in *The Twenty Years' Crisis*. The chief assumption anchoring this discussion—"purpose ... is a condition of thought; and thinking for thinking's sake is as abnormal and barren as the miser's accumulation of money for its own sake"[35]—foreshadows Robert W. Cox's later essay on critical international theory to such an extent that one wonders whether Cox had perhaps simply recycled Carr's carbon copy.[36] Much like Cox but four decades earlier, Carr held that international relations theory is inherently goal driven, infused with aims of its proponents. Unlike in natural sciences, where facts exist independently of their observers' purpose, in political science "the purpose is not irrelevant ... to the investigation and separable from it: it is itself one of the facts. ... Purpose and analysis [are] part and parcel of the single process."[37] To this extent, Carr espoused a distinctly anti- or post-positivist epistemology typical of critical theory, insisting unequivocally that "Political science is the science not only of what is, but of what ought to be" and that "Political thought is itself a form of political action."[38]

In his ensuing realist attack on "utopianism," which made *The Twenty Years' Crisis* so famous and endearing to today's realist thinkers such as Gilpin and Mearsheimer, Carr merely applied his anti-positivist epistemology to the hegemonic international relations doctrine of the day. Carr identified this doctrine mainly with liberal rationalist thinkers, their presupposition of a hidden fundamental harmony among nations, and their proposals—epitomized by Woodrow Wilson's post-World War I "New Diplomacy"—to achieve this harmony through national self-determination, democratization, *laissez-faire* trade, international law, and collective security under the auspices of the League of Nations.[39] In the 1920s, these measures were widely anticipated to make the world safe for democracy and do away with the old balance-of-power system, which hindered peace by leaving each state to fend for itself through power politics. In the new system, the sovereignty of each country would be publicly guaranteed by the collective will of the League, serving as a deterrent to aggression and making power politics obsolete: no longer necessary as an instrument of foreign policy.

From Carr's critical perspective, however, the liberal internationalist project was not only wooly-headed alchemy but something much darker and more sinister. Underneath its noble and allegedly universal goals, a set of more pragmatic motivations lurked in the silent background. In *The Twenty Years' Crisis* Carr took it upon himself to peel back the surface rhetoric and expose these hidden mainsprings. His realist critique cuts to the very heart of liberal internationalism: the concept of the harmony of interests, viewed by Carr as the bedrock of the whole utopian structure.[40] "Carr's central point is that ... [this concept] glosses over the real conflict that is to be found in international relations, which is between the 'haves' and the 'have-nots.'"[41] In a world of scarcity, conflict is inevitable, and any attempt to obscure this by preaching a harmony of interests must be understood in the context of the essential dynamic of struggle, as an ideology constructed by the dominant nations to maintain their position:

> If theories are revealed as a reflexion of practice and principles of political needs, this discovery will apply to the fundamental theories and principles of the utopian creed, and not the least to the harmony of interests which is its essential postulate. (...) [T]he utopian, when he preaches the doctrine of the harmony of interests, is ... clothing his own interest in the guise of a universal interest for the purpose of imposing it on the rest of the world.[42]

The ostensibly absolute and universal principles of law and morality espoused by leading liberal internationalists such as Wilson in his famous Fourteen Points were, insofar as Carr was concerned, thinly veiled manifestations of narrow national power interests.[43] What allowed him to reach this insight was precisely his anti-positivist conception of political thought as a form of political action reflecting the goals of its advocates.

Proponents of Carr's representation as a critical theorist therefore stress that the thrust of his realist assault on liberal internationalism in *The Twenty Years' Crisis* was to historicize and relativize the dominant international relations theory, not to posit realism as the new paradigm to supersede the old "utopian" one. In advancing his realist analysis, Carr did not seek to pronounce the final word on international politics, for no such final words were possible from his anti-positivist perspective. "The realism of *The Twenty Years' Crisis* is not a theoretical construct," as Tim Dunne has warned, "but a critical weapon which Carr turned against 'utopianism.' (...) It is of paramount importance to make a formal distinction between 'realism' as a theory of international politics, and Carr's version of realism as an epistemic 'tool' or 'weapon.'"[44]

This weapon did not have a single fixed target, but one dynamically evolving out of the historical process. It was applicable not only to Wilsonian liberal internationalism, but also to any other subsequent international relations theory erected on allegedly absolute and universal foundations. In this sense, Carr's approach

> was not based on particular values but unfolded in the mere negation of the leading ideology of the day: at times it required a critique of Utopianism, as during the inter-war period [1919–1939], and at others a critique of the stasis of Realpolitik, as during the heyday of the Cold War.[45]

His realism in *The Twenty Years' Crisis* represented a specific phase of his general impulse to critical negation, marking the book as an eminently counterhegemonic text: "indeed the most successful counterhegemonic text."[46]

Lending further credence to the reading of Carr's realism as "a necessary corrective to the prevailing utopianism rather than an alternative to it"[47] are the intellectual inspirations of *The Twenty Years' Crisis*, discernible from the context of Carr's prior writings. These reveal the powerful influence of, among others, Fyodor Dostoevsky. Carr discovered his novels during his diplomatic posting in Riga in the late 1920s. The Russian writer's awareness of human irrationality, displayed through his characters' anarchistic tendencies and relativization of all traditional values, had a profound transformative impact on Carr. On the one hand, it liberated him from the easy rationalist worldview of his native Victorian England: "intellectually Carr had stepped out into a parallel universe."[48] To this extent, it was precisely Dostoevsky, as Carr interpreted him in his eponymous 1931 biography, who had prefigured Carr's relativizing realist assault on liberal internationalism in *The Twenty Years' Crisis*, a book that grew out of *Dostoevsky* and may be viewed as its sequel in Carr's intellectual development.[49]

But Dostoevsky also highlighted the perilous consequences of skeptical relativism and anti-rationalism taken all the way to their logical extreme: chaos and the loss of all meaning. Carr understood this point as well: in *The Twenty Years' Crisis*, "the substance of modern realism was the same as pessimistic nihilism in Dostoevsky."[50] Encapsulating pure negation, realism "fail[ed] to provide any ground for purposive or meaningful action"[51] and as such posed a threat of total stasis; for society and civilization to survive, an overarching goal and a sense of direction toward its fulfillment were necessary. In this vein, Carr recognized that "any sound political thought must be based on elements of both utopia and reality. … Having demolished the current utopia with the weapons of realism, we still need to build a new utopia of our own …"[52] Realism could not be more than a fleeting phenomenon: "a transitory exception."[53]

The role performed by this intermittent phenomenon in the *longue durée* of history was decidedly transformative: at critical junctures, realism functioned as a dialectical catalyst for social and political progress—another key consideration making it possible to interpret Carr's analysis as a form critical international theory. As his longtime friends and collaborators have noted time and again, "[Carr] was ever the optimist"[54] who "always believed in progress"[55] and "carried with him to the end of his life the … confidence in the future which was a notable feature of [his native] late-Victorian and Edwardian England."[56] Although he composed *The Twenty Years' Crisis* during the darkest moments of the interwar era, with World War II already discernible on the horizon, his faith in progress did not break down in the book. Rather, it merely "transformed into a radical criticism of Western society."[57] Through his realist negation of utopianism, Carr sought to liberate the theory and practice of international politics from the dead weight of defunct ideas and institutions and to open up space for subsequent intellectual and political progress. He sketched out the potential direction of this progress in numerous works immediately following *The Twenty Years' Crisis*, such as *Nationalism and After* and especially *The New Society*, which constitutes Carr's most systematic outline of his ideal future: a vision of welfare society characterized by, among other things, central economic planning.

This fundamentally emancipatory agenda was shaped by western Marxism, whose impact on Carr surpassed Dostoevsky's and gives the clearest indication of the critical wellsprings of Carr's analysis of liberal internationalism in *The Twenty Years' Crisis*. Although Jonathan Haslam, who spent several years working with Carr in the late 1970s and early 1980s, has suggested that "Carr could never truly be called a Marxist,"[58] Carr merely rejected the determinist current of Marxist philosophy. As for the rest, above all Marxist ideology critique, he acknowledged his admiration and intellectual debt openly, repeatedly, and without hesitation. Already in 1933, in an article commemorating the fiftieth anniversary of Marx's death, Carr praised Marx "as the most far-seeing genius of the nineteenth century and one of the most successful prophets in history."[59] Much later, near the end of his life, Carr explained that in the 1930s he "did a lot of reading and thinking on Marxist lines," and he described *The Twenty Years' Crisis*, the product of this activity, as "not exactly a Marxist work, but strongly impregnated with Marxist ways of thinking, applied to international affairs."[60]

This Marxist impregnation is visible in the text even without Carr's acknowledgment. His critical analysis of liberal internationalism often utilizes the language of class conflict and relies heavily on a domestic analogy to the liberal-capitalist state, whose values and institutional machinery Carr regards as instruments of bourgeois hegemony. Domestic laws and morality, ostensibly impartial, serve the interests of the powerful, and the same holds at the international level:

> Just as the ruling class in a community prays for domestic peace, which guarantees its own security and predominance, and denounces class-war, which might threaten them, so international peace becomes a special vested interest of predominant Powers. (...) Politically, the alleged community of interest in the maintenance of peace ... is capitalized ... by a dominant nation or group of nations.[61]

Just as the liberal state represents a tool used by the bourgeoisie to promote its interests domestically, so the League of Nations, the flagship institution of liberal internationalism, represents a tool used by the Great War victors to maintain a favorable status quo in the international arena. In the same vein, "*laissez-faire*, in international relations as in those [domestic ones] between capital and labor, is the paradise of the economically strong."[62]

What Carr took from Marxism in the 1930s, then, was precisely what contemporary critical international theorists take from it today: not its deterministic conception of history, but its critical sociology as a means of uncovering veiled foundations of political ideas and as a tool for mapping the full extent of hegemonic consciousness blocking emancipatory progress. "I've always been more interested in Marxism as a method of revealing the hidden springs of thought and action, and debunking the logical and moralistic façade generally erected around them," Carr told Tamara Deutscher, "than in the Marxist analysis of the decline of capitalism."[63]

He had absorbed much of the Marxist sociology of knowledge through Karl Mannheim.[64] Carr's notion that international political ideas always reflect the standpoint of their proponents—the principle guiding his negation of liberal utopianism—flowed from Mannheim's critical analysis of sociohistorical foundations of knowledge in *Ideology and Utopia* (1936), first published in English just as Carr was commencing to write *The Twenty Years' Crisis*.[65] Mannheim, according to Carr,

> believed that the essence of reality is dynamic, and that to seek any static point within it from which to deliver "timeless" judgments is a fundamental error. The individual's apprehension of this ever-changing reality is necessarily partial and relative. He can see it only from the perspective of time and place in which he finds himself.[66]

It was this position that endowed Carr's international relations thought with post-positivist and historicizing tendencies. On the one hand, these earned him dismissive comments from those of his disciplinary colleagues wedded to a more traditional social-scientific conception of world politics as a realm governed by timeless laws. Hans Morgenthau, for instance, found much to like in *The Twenty Years' Crisis*, enough to list the text among the ten books that had had the most influence on his intellectual development.[67] But he recoiled at the extent of Carr's historicism: in a review essay published the same year as *Politics among Nations*, where Morgenthau defined realism as a theory based on objective principles rooted in human nature, the German émigré scolded Carr for being a relativist "observer ... unfortified by a transcendent standard of ethics."[68]

By the same token, however, Carr's rejection of any such transcendent standards in favor of an epistemology stressing their perspectival and historically conditioned character makes it possible to view his analysis of "utopianism" in *The Twenty Years' Crisis* as an early precursor to contemporary critical international thought.

> If [Carr's] insistence on a historical, interpretive orientation towards knowledge about international relations is viewed as fundamental to [his] approach, then despite [his] own obliviousness about "critical theory" it ... [is] appropriate to regard [him] as [a] critical realist of the early, non-self-conscious variety.[69]

Robert W. Cox certainly recognized a kindred spirit in Carr. In the very essay introducing critical theory to academic international relations, Cox noted that the British scholar espoused a "historical mode of thought" and consistently sought to "understand institutions, theories and events within their historical contexts,"[70] as reflections of particular configurations of social forces.

Beyond *The Twenty Years' Crisis*: Further Evidence of Carr's Critical Leanings

Although the anti-positivist epistemology, historicizing tendencies, counterhegemonic drive, progressive-emancipatory agenda, and western Marxist inspirations of Carr's realist analysis of liberal internationalism in *The Twenty Years' Crisis* provide plentiful empirical support for his alternative representation as an early critical theorist, additional evidence abounds. Indeed, Carr's anti-positivism and commitment to emancipatory progress may be most visible elsewhere in his oeuvre: in his Trevelyan Lectures on the nature of history and historiography, which became his bestselling *What Is History?*

Already Carr's initial response to the title of his study is indicative: "When we attempt to answer the question, What is history?" he wrote in the opening passages, "our answer ... reflects our own position in time."[71] Amplifying his emphasis on the purpose-driven and historically relative character of thought in *The Twenty Years' Crisis*, Carr distanced himself from the twin notions that facts exist independently of the historian's consciousness and that historiography amounts to nothing more than a passive recovery of the past. In his perspective, "historians interpret and their interpretations are as historically situated as they are themselves."[72] The objectivist "cult of facts," as Carr pejoratively called it, pervasive in scientific positivism, British empiricism from Locke to Russell, and liberal historical imagination in general, was utterly foreign to him. The banner of this cult, Ranke's exhortation to write history *wie es eigentlich gewesen*, struck Carr as fraudulent: "an incantation designed ... to save [historians] from the tiresome obligation to think for themselves."[73] Destroying this cult was one of Carr's main objectives in *What Is History?* whose preparation he described to a friend as "an opportunity to deliver a broadside on history in general and on some of the nonsense ... talked about it by Popper and others."[74]

Carr did not reject the existence of facts altogether; he freely granted that historical knowledge involves basic factual statements which can be checked for their fidelity and accuracy. This is not the historian's main task, however, only a preliminary one. As he argued in passages strikingly similar to some of the key insights of today's narrative theory of historiography, "[accuracy] is a necessary condition of his work, but not its essential function. (...) The duty of the historian to respect his facts is not exhausted by the obligation to see that his facts are accurate."[75] The essential task is to decide which facts to include, which ones to exclude, and how to organize the ones included: poetics, in a word.

> The facts speak only when the historian calls on them: it is he who decides to which facts to give the floor, and in what order or context. (...) They are like fish swimming about in a vast and sometimes inaccessible ocean; and what the historian catches will depend partly on chance, but

> mainly on what part of the ocean he chooses to fish in and what tackle
> he chooses to use—these two factors being, of course, determined by
> the kind of fish he wants to catch.[76]

Historical knowledge necessarily involves selection and interpretation,
through which values, goals, interests, and social standpoints of historians
seep in, enabling them to discern what is worth knowing about the past in
the first place. To this extent, Carr appears to have been clearly cognizant of,
in White's terminology, the "fictions of factual representation": the nonempirical content brought by historians to their accounts of past events by virtue of endowing them with well-ordered plots. Carr would have agreed with
White that insofar as histories have the shape of comprehensible stories,
they "are told or written, not found,"[77] and that "[19th-century historians]
did not realize that facts do not speak for themselves, but that the historian
speaks for them, speaks on their behalf."[78]

According to Carr, purpose and analysis therefore cannot be separated in
the formation of historical knowledge any more than in international relations theory; they are fused, imperceptibly shading into each other. If in *The
Twenty Years' Crisis* the relativistic implications of this insight were already
strong enough to alarm Morgenthau, in *What Is History?* Carr worked them
out to an even fuller extent, drawing fierce indignation from the likes of
Geoffrey Elton, the positivist historian of Tudor England and Carr's col-
league at Cambridge.[79] Insofar as "The point of view of the historian enters
irrevocably into every observation which he makes," Carr noted, "history
is shot through and through with relativity."[80] This doubled the value of
historical accounts for Carr; they illuminated not only the past, but also and
especially the social standpoint from which they had been composed.[81] The
unavoidable presence of this standpoint in historical narratives led Carr to
flatly reject the notion of positive historical reality: "The belief in a hard
core of historical facts existing objectively and independently of the interpretation of the historian is a preposterous fallacy."[82] More sweepingly, and
repeating a point made in *The Twenty Years' Crisis*, Carr concluded that
not just historiography, but "Social sciences as a whole, since they involve
man as ... both investigator and thing investigated, are incompatible with
any theory of knowledge which pronounces a rigid divorce between subject
and object."[83]

Based on this anti-positivist epistemology, one would expect Carr to reso-
nate with current postmodernist historians and literary theorists—a reception that Carr, were he alive today, would probably appreciate. According
to Haslam, "He would have found himself amused rather than threatened
by post-modernists."[84] However, at least one prominent contemporary an-
tifoundationalist, Keith Jenkins, has given Carr a cold shoulder, rebuffing
him as a "modernist" and a "certainist" who believed in firm foundations of
historical knowledge, in objective historical truth, and in the possibility of
its recovery and representation in the present.[85] These predilections make

Carr "just too mystifying ... to be reflexive enough [a guide] to the question of what is history today."[86] Jenkins has consequently distanced himself and those he regards as his fellow postmodernists, including White and Rorty, from Carr's views. To what extent does this assessment undercut efforts to interpret Carr as a critical theorist?

Jenkins could be taken to task on a number of counts, notably for downplaying Carr's anti-positivist leanings while simultaneously exaggerating those of some of the postmodernists.[87] But he is right in the sense that throughout *What Is History?* Carr constantly tempered his relativism with a firm belief in reason as a common element underpinning all historical thinking. Just as during his preceding realist analysis of "utopianism" in *The Twenty Years' Crisis*, influenced by Dostoevsky's warnings about the dangers of growing irrationality in Europe, Carr remained fully conscious of the treacherous consequences of full-fledged relativization of knowledge. For this reason, merely "broadsiding" the objectivist "cult of facts" would not do. As Haslam put it, Carr foresaw that pure deconstruction would result "in intellectual paralysis through denying the possibility of writing genuine history and might ... ultimately be a reactionary force—for all its claims to radicalism—because it is less subversive than nihilistic in its message."[88] Like his realist assault on liberal internationalism, Carr's critical negation of liberal empiricist historiography in *What Is History?* therefore constituted only a passing, transient phase. It was as exceptional as the slim volume itself viewed against the broader backdrop of Carr's monumental *History of Soviet Russia*, to which he dedicated the entire second half of his productive life and from whose composition *What Is History?* represented merely a short break. This was Carr's true obsession: not the destructive task of negating liberal historiography, but the constructive task of mapping the Bolshevik Revolution and the Soviet system as the initial stages of a new society and sources of key lessons for Western capitalism.[89]

Carr's aims in *What Is History?* thus extended beyond merely attacking liberal empiricism. His ultimate goal was "to carve out a space between simple empiricism on the one hand and total anarchy on the other."[90] In this space, Carr inserted a conception of history as an open-ended process of emancipation based on the universal foundation of human rationality. While different historians might very well select different facts and organize them in different ways when studying a given period, each "distils from the experience of the past ... that part which is amenable to rational explanation."[91] The construction of historical plots is always guided by and in turn expresses reason. In this vein, Carr suggested that "history is a 'selective system' ... of causal orientations to reality."[92] Narratives of the same historical event may diverge dramatically based on the subjective standpoints of their authors, but all of them display cause-and-effect patterns and rationality, which is always exercised for some purpose. Subjectivism in this sense coexists, however precariously, with rationalism and foundationalism in Carr's philosophy of history.

Lending further credence to Jenkins' view of Carr as a "modernist," the change these purposes undergo in the *longue durée* is not haphazard and chaotic according to Carr, but follows an evolutionary trajectory. Carr's enduring optimism and belief in historical progress manifested themselves in *What Is History?* as much as in the earlier *Twenty Years' Crisis*. "While 'situating' the production of facts and historical interpretation, [Carr] also ... wants to confirm the cumulative, progressive character of history itself. ... History moves forward, if not in a straight line."[93] Notably, progress was not teleology for him; Carr firmly rejected the notion of inevitable movement of temporal affairs toward a final state of perfection as an expression of Judeo-Christian salvationism.[94] "The presumption of an end of history," he stressed, "has an eschatological ring more appropriate to the theologian than to the historian."[95] Instead, he espoused an idea of progress as an open-ended process. "I profess no belief in the perfectibility of man, or in a future paradise on earth," Carr declared, "but I shall be content with the possibility of unlimited progress ... towards goals which can be defined only as we advance towards them."[96] In perhaps the most succinct formulation, he defined his idea of historical change in terms of "the progressive development of human potentialities."[97]

This formulation makes it patent that Carr's idea of rational progress, though it constrained his anti-positivism and reflexivity, does not do any damage to his representation as a critical theorist, but rather tends to underscore it. The notion of evolutionary rationality—progressive rational emancipation of human beings from self-imposed limits to their potential and autonomy—stands at the very center of critical international theory, concerned precisely with "securing freedom from unacknowledged constrains, relations of domination, and conditions of distorted communication and understanding that deny humans the capacity to make their future through full will and consciousness."[98] The radically transformative and even utopian tendencies embedded in this project, which Robert W. Cox acknowledged as part and parcel of the critical perspective, permeated Carr's philosophy of history also. They were so pronounced that "the charge Carr directed at the interwar idealists ... could be turned against him: his view of the future relied more on aspiration than analysis."[99] His developmental and progressive understanding of the historical process was certainly diametrically opposed to the traditional realist skepticism that history essentially stands still, rooted in an unchanging human nature (as for Morgenthau) or in permanent structural features of international politics (as for Waltz and Mearsheimer).[100]

What Is History? thus may be invoked as powerful additional evidence of the critical moorings of Carr's analysis of interwar international relations thought formulated earlier in *The Twenty Years' Crisis*. Carr's views on historical knowledge and the shape of the historical process display a striking fit with critical international theory as laid out by Cox and others. The overlap includes not only a conception of history as progress toward emancipation, but also the emphasis on the historically relative and inescapably normative character of all knowledge. Carr was adamant that any abstract and universal values and standards of judgment inevitably involve the specific substance of their proponents' historical situations and aspirations:

> When we examine these supposedly absolute and extra-historical values, we find that they ... are in fact rooted in history. The emergence of a particular value or ideal at a given time or place is explained by historical conditions of place and time. The practical content of hypothetical absolutes like equality, liberty, justice, or natural law varies from period to period, or from continent to continent. Every group has its own values which are rooted in history.[101]

This view was not new, but merely generalized an old argument made already in *The Twenty Years' Crisis* with respect to interwar English-speaking international relations scholars and statesmen such as Woodrow Wilson, their liberal internationalist doctrine of universal harmony of interests, and their position at the helm of victorious nations seeking to retain power, dominance, and hegemony in the aftermath of World War I. In *What Is History?* Carr only repeated the charge on a larger canvas, launching "the second blistering attack on the liberal establishment, this time ... on the liberal historical establishment, as opposed to the liberal establishment ... in the field of international relations."[102] In the process, Carr's critical sociology of knowledge and reality, unmistakable already in his negation of liberal internationalism two decades earlier, received its fullest expression.

Dr. Jekyll and Mr. Hyde: a Tropological Analysis of Carr's Representations

Which representation of Carr is true, which false? Which ghost embodies his actual spirit: the realist or the critical? Not that they have no other siblings. If one stares at certain portions of *The Future of Nations* just long enough, one might catch a glimpse of a third Carr: neither a realist nor a critical theorist, but an early adherent of functionalism, a strand of international relations thought arguing that certain tasks performed by sovereign states would be better served by other actors and institutions, whose forms should follow the tasks (or "functions") in question.[103] But this third Carr, along with whatever others might be spooking around the discipline's pantheon, is merely a little brother to the two discussed above, who together overshadow the rest. Which one of them is real? And how is it possible that there are two of them in the first place—polar opposites, no less?

For a narrative theorist, these questions are not difficult to answer. From the perspective of White's framework for analysis of factual narrative discourse, each image of Carr amounts to a *poiēma* which is skillfully crafted rather than passively found, possesses intelligibility precisely to the extent that it selects some parts of the empirical record while omitting others, figures the selected information using specific strategies on several distinct but related tropological levels (formal argumentation, emplotment, ideological implication), and is just as true within its poetic frame of reference as any other competing representation is within its own. More than one representation of Carr can be true at the same time, including when they dramatically disagree; just because the realist *poiēma* relies on facts does not automatically mean that the critical *poiēma* is false, and vice versa. Narrative theory does not equate *verum* with *factum*. It regards the former as a broader category: one encompassing not only hard facts conveyed in singular existential statements, but also additional nonempirical "content of the form" generated by colligating them into synoptic wholes. Narrative truth, in other words, has an irreducible moral-aesthetic dimension.

Realists trope Carr using the same rhetorical moves as underpin the concept of anarchy, their representation of the international arena. On the level of formal argument, these moves are Mechanistic insofar as they reduce the sprawling record of Carr's writings to a few passages from *The Twenty Years' Crisis*, which are lifted out of their circumambient space, read in almost total disregard of Carr's other works and sociohistorical context, and regarded as the fundamental insights informing all his thought. A diligent researcher, it is presumed, could find them in his earlier and later writings also, even if perhaps less clearly articulated and buried under thick sediments of other ideas. This treatment of the historical field faithfully reflects the Mechanistic conception of explanation typical of mainstream (social-scientific) international relations thought exemplified by neorealists such as Waltz and Mearsheimer: explanation as a process of stripping away all confusing details and variety in order to lay bare the essential principles and central tendencies operating in the background.[104] Among the thousands of pages of Carr's extant texts, this essential tendency is *The Twenty Years' Crisis*, more precisely those of his utterances in the book's early chapters calling for a science of international relations based on the axiom that sovereign states pursue national interest defined in terms of power—the discipline's equivalent of Newton's first law of physics.

Mearsheimer's 2004 Carr Memorial Lecture is emblematic of the Mechanistic disposition inherent in the realist image of Carr. Although Mearsheimer's treatment comprises just about the most detailed account of Carr's realist legacy, it relies almost exclusively on *The Twenty Years' Crisis*: out of twenty-one primary text references to Carr's writings, Mearsheimer makes nineteen to this book alone, one apiece to *Nationalism and After* and Carr's autobiography for Tamara Deutscher, and none at all to anything else in Carr's vast body of work. He does not hide the reductive orientation: "when I define Carr as a realist, I am describing him as such on the basis of the arguments he made in *The Twenty Years' Crisis*."[105] Like fine Moravian *slivovice*, the essence of Carr's intellectual achievement is revealed via relentless distillation purging away obscuring impurities—all ninety-nine percent of them. The ghost figured forth out of Carr's oeuvre by the realist *poiēma* is therefore a bare-bones skeleton, incidentally what a human being looks like to Moravians stumbling out of their secret distilleries after a morning of drinking, equipped with a sort of alcoholic X-ray vision.

The situation is analogous on the levels of emplotment and ideology. The realist *poiēma* is not only a product of Mechanists diving into the bottomless well of the past and climbing back out with a corpse of a fellow Mechanist. It is also a Tragedy in that it casts Carr's message about the primacy of sovereign states, inevitability of conflict, and signal role of power in international relations as a profound lesson unheeded in its day and vindicated only in retrospect, after a nearly terminal global disaster caused by statesmen espousing alternative conceptions of world affairs. Carr's realist analysis emerges as an act of clairvoyant insight, whose ignorance by post-World War I liberal idealists led to the shattering of the universe during World War II and whose mastery by the survivors of that conflict, down to the present generation, is imperative in order to preclude yet worse catastrophes. The ideological substance of this insight is Conservative to the point of deterministic. Concerning his attitude toward the status quo, the realist narrative frames Carr as a thinker who denies any scope for progressive change through free will, "emphasize[s] the irresistible strength of existing forces and the inevitable character of existing tendencies," and "insist[s] that the highest wisdom lies in accepting, and adapting oneself to, these forces and these tendencies."[106]

The poetic style of the realist representation of Carr—its unique combination of Mechanistic, Tragic, and Conservative tropological commitments—explains why this representation focuses almost exclusively on *The Twenty Years' Crisis* in the first place. After all, Carr's intellectual legacy can be distilled in any number of ways, to any one of his countless extant texts. In principle, no obstacle exists to narrowing his main achievement solely to *What Is History?*; to a 1977 letter to Stanley Hoffmann in which Carr proclaimed that "No science of international relations exists" and that "The study of international relations in English speaking countries is simply a study of the best way to run the world from positions of strength;"[107] or, for that matter, to writings that have nothing to do with international affairs, political theory, history, or any other academic subject at all, such as Carr's family correspondence. But the realist image finds the core of his contribution in *The Twenty Years' Crisis* precisely because, of all Carr's texts, it is this book, particularly its first half, that offers the most material for sculpting his realist monument. The book's conceptual language is replete with terms dear to neorealists today, such as "science," "state," "power," and "realism" itself, and the subtitle, *An Introduction to the Study of International Relations*, can be read as indicating that Carr—again like contemporary neorealists—considered international relations a specialist field apart from others. In *What Is History?* or Carr's family correspondence, by contrast, no such language or suppositions can be found, and his letter to Stanley Hoffmann reads more like a frontal assault on one of neorealism's most cherished possessions: its scientific status. On the basis of these writings, one could narrate Carr as an anti-positivist historian or a private person (a father, a husband, and so on), but not as a realist international relations theorist, indeed not as an international relations theorist of any kind.

The rhetorical strategies governing critical international theory's engagement with the unprocessed historical field diverge significantly from those underpinning neorealism. On the level of formal argument, the critical perspective is holistic and synthetic rather than reductive and also pays far more attention to sociohistorical circumstances: it treats individual ideas in their proper settings and as way stations in the progressive unfolding of general consciousness toward emancipation, not as manifestations of timeless principles limiting human freedom.[108] Instead of Mechanism, in other words, it employs Organicist and Contextualist modes of explanation. On the level of emplotment, it tropes the drama of history in much more optimistic terms: as a story whose conflicts and antagonisms are real but nevertheless resolvable in the long run, which is to say, as a Comedy rather than Tragedy. The corresponding ideological implication is Liberal or Radical, certainly not Conservative. Critical theorists deem existing society to be alienated from its ideal form, whose immanent possibility is yet to be actualized in the more or less distant future via more or less revolutionary means, including via critical theory as a form of emancipatory political action.

Consequently, the critical *poiēma* tropes forth a very different Carr. On the level of formal argument, it does not emaciate the body of his intellectual bequest to the first few chapters of *The Twenty Years' Crisis* but integrates and synthesizes them with the rest of the book and with Carr's other texts, all of which it interprets not only in relation to each other, but also in relation to their proper historical context, as at once its reflections and catalysts. Unlike the realist skeleton, the critical Carr is therefore a voluptuous figure with at least as much meat on its bones as Rubens' Three Graces. He spans disciplinary divides and defies easy classification, as illustrated by Peter Wilson's artful description of Carr as "sort-of-Realist/Functionalist/Keynesian/Marxist-influenced/proto-IR-Critical Theorist."[109] From the critical perspective, understanding what Carr was truly up to in *The Twenty Years' Crisis* involves also knowing something about his fears of modern European nihilism in *Dostoevsky*; his inspirations by Marx and Mannheim; his unceasing personal optimism; his disgust with positivism in *What Is History?*; and the impact on his mind of World War I and especially the Bolshevik Revolution and the Soviet experiment with central planning.

Intertwined with the move to Contextualist and Organicist modes of historical explanation are shifts in plot type and ideological implication. Considered in isolation, the passages in *The Twenty Years' Crisis* calling for a science of international relations centered on sovereign states as the currently prevalent type of political community, on the factor of power as the essential guide to their mutual relations, and on the inevitability of conflict among them indeed make it possible to regard Carr as a Tragic Conservative. But placed in their circumambient environment, as particular phases in the broader arc of Carr's overall intellectual trajectory instantiated in the specific context of the interwar era, the same passages surface as exercises in Marxist-inspired sociology of knowledge and ideology critique indicative of a Comic-Liberal or Comic-Radical mindset. In the late 1930s, it was exactly by adopting a state- and power-centric optic that Carr was able to counter the hegemonic discourse of Wilsonian liberalism, see through its universal pretenses, and expose it as an expression of narrow national interests of a few Great War victors, all in order to stimulate progressive transformation of international relations toward his utopian vision of a more rational, harmonious, and just world order. This vision was post-statist and post-Westphalian insofar as it moved beyond the territorially bounded sovereign community and called for more inclusive and collectivist forms of political association. Carr hinted at it already in the final chapters of *The Twenty Years' Crisis* and fully unveiled it soon thereafter in texts such as *The Future of Nations* and *Nationalism and After*.

To set the realist Carr next to the critical Carr, then, is to discover an abyss without a bottom. Not only do the two representations diverge in their substantive content almost to the point of being mutually exclusive, whereby the realist reading tends to marginalize those parts of Carr's oeuvre emphasized by his critical portrait and vice versa. They are also embedded in discrepant tropological perspectives governing the initial conceptualization of the raw empirical record, the purpose of historical narratives crafted out of it, and everything in between: including judgments on what is worth knowing in the first place, how individual data are to be combined, what is the scope of human possibility, whether the past was better or worse than the present, what the future ought to look like, and, if it ought to look different from the present, what means of change should be adopted. Indeed, the differences in substantive content are largely derivative, flowing from the differences in tropological form: *who* Carr is, whether an early realist or proto-critical theorist, depends on *how* his extant work has been troped. Each representation is compelling if judged by its own poetic criteria, but between them very little if any meeting ground exists.

In this the two images faithfully mirror the equally strained inter-paradigm debate—or, more accurately, standoff—between the dominant social-scientific neorealist-neoliberal consensus and critical theory in academic international relations today. Like competing tropological lenses, competing paradigms are incompatible and incommensurable: "The differences between [them] are ... irreconcilable."[110] This is because "paradigms provide scientists not only with a map but also with some of the directions essential for map-making."[111] As such they combine "theory, methods, and standards together, usually in an inextricable mixture," which means that the choice between rival paradigms "cannot be determined ... by the evaluative procedures ... of normal science, for these depend ... upon a particular paradigm, and that paradigm is at issue."[112] As one of the battle fronts in the ongoing civil war between critical and mainstream international relations scholarship, the discourse about Carr's legacy evinces the same dynamics: the image propagated as true by the one faction is dismissed as deluded by the other.[113] After all, the unique alcoholic X-ray vision cherished by fat Moravian *bon vivants* in their home distilleries as a type of divine *illuminatio* under the banner of *in vino veritas* will be decried by obsessively dieting and exercising American fitness experts as ethanol-induced coma bordering on clinical death.

Given the lack of shared standards of judgment, the answer to the question of which representation of Carr is right depends on extrascientific factors. It is a matter of rhetoric: the art and politics of persuasion through language. Many attacks on each of Carr's images are possible, but not without being self-referential—and for that reason largely invisible to its intended recipients. A critical theorist might accuse Carr's realist interpreters of failing to notice that their rendition of his past achievements is partial and relative to their current goals and purposes, but this argument presupposes critical theory's conception of purpose-driven knowledge in the first place. To the extent that this conception is alien to today's mainstream realists, who instead espouse a more traditional social-scientific notion of truth as independent of its observers, the charge is inevitably going to fall on deaf ears. In this vein, guardians of Carr's realist reputation and guardians of his legacy as a critical theorist are bound to talk more or less through each other when debating the relative merits of their respective representations, with each faction producing circular arguments satisfying the epistemological, methodological, and substantive criteria that it sets for itself.[114]

Elevating any particular reading of Carr over the others then boils down to its proponents' ability to convert as many students as possible to their point of view and to shout down, suppress, exclude, and otherwise silence advocates of alternative representations. The truth about Carr's legacy is indeed a matter of headcounts and cannot be grasped without understanding the sociology of academic international relations: the whole intricate machinery of production of specialist knowledge about international politics and about Carr as one of the discipline's alleged founders. Who gets to write textbooks introducing him to masses of impressionable undergraduates during their initial contact with the "serious" study of international relations, which will set the terms of their subsequent engagement with, among other things, Carr's accomplishments? Who gets to lecture on him to packed auditoriums, anonymously referee book and journal article manuscripts discussing him, and vote on hiring or promotion files of junior academics portraying Carr in this or that fashion? Were all of these functions performed by neorealists of Mearsheimer's persuasion, a scholar narrating Carr as a proto-critical theorist would be brushed aside and his academic credentials questioned. No matter how scrupulous in weaving his narrative strictly out of verifiable facts, and no matter how convinced on that ground of the fundamental truth of his position and of the fundamental blindness of those surrounding him, he would come under severe pressure to alter his views or else leave the disciplinary community.

Such a scholar—whether a critical heretic in the church of realists or a realist dissident in the kingdom of critical theory—would find himself in a situation not unlike the one encountered by the main protagonist in H. G. Wells' short story "The Country of the Blind": an explorer named Nuñez.[115] During a trek deep in the Andes, Nuñez accidentally falls off a steep mountainside into an uncharted valley completely isolated from the outside world, where he quickly realizes that all its inhabitants are blind. When he attempts to take advantage of his healthy eyes to teach and rule them, however, he fails. Instead of following his various advices, the villagers, fully adapted to only four senses and having no concept of sight whatsoever, diagnose his obsession with "seeing" as a form of illness. The cure they prescribe is simple: gouging his eyes out.

Carr as a Poetic Creation

If the two images of Carr share anything in common, it is only this: both are poetic-literary artifacts. The very notion of Carr as a thinking subject depends on turning what survives of his work into a comprehensible story intended to display and teach this or that lesson. A complete record of his writings, one commencing with his earliest toddler scribbles, ending with words and sentences penned on or shortly before the day of his death, and encompassing everything he had committed to paper in between, would display no meaning whatsoever aside from bare chronology, assuming one would take the great pains to order all the constituent pieces according to their date.[116] Carr's books, essays, reviews, editorials, and Foreign Office memos would be subsumed in a vast amorphous sea of, among other things, his restaurant bill signatures, grocery shopping lists, job application cover letters, appointments diary entries, vacation postcard greetings, marriage and divorce settlement papers, newspaper annotations, crude words hastily drawn on a street wall during a grammar school prank, perhaps, or doodles completed during his lengthy train commutes between London and Aberystwyth in the late 1930s and early 1940s—maybe depicting Stalin, Hitler, an attractive woman sitting across the isle, or all three together atop a white unicorn, since even an individual as supremely intelligent, focused, driven, and put-together as Carr surely lapsed into occasional whimsy. "Reality," to recall Hayden White's remark, "is highly complex. You can't tell a simple story about it. ... [T]he more information you get, the less comprehension you can have of a situation."[117] The full reality of Carr's bequest would be ungraspable.

Comprehending Carr's legacy is therefore predicated on taking the bewildering mass of his achievements and chiseling a compelling tale out of it, discarding large portions of the record in the process. Not that card-carrying neorealists are oblivious to the necessity of selection and simplification in studying reality, as evidenced by Mearsheimer's frank admission that "we could not make sense of the complex world around us without simplifying theories."[118] Waltz actually reflected on this necessity in detail in his *Theory of International Politics*, going so far as to distinguish several different ways of simplifying.[119] But what he failed to notice is that all of these ways are poetic in nature: his masterpiece, much like Mearsheimer's *Tragedy of Great Power Politics*, is entirely oblivious to the constitutive role of narrative language and tropes in depictions of reality. For Waltz and Mearsheimer, as for neorealist and neoliberal international relations theorists at large, simplification is about *finding* the logic of reality deemed to inhere in the material world, independent of its observers and immune to their wishes, not about actively *fashioning* it through poetics. The human-made fictions of Carr's realism—and more broadly the nonempirical content brought to factual representations of reality by virtue of narrativization, which White has done so much to excavate and map—therefore remain obscured to them.

Carr is not the only academic international relations deity whose standard realist reputation has recently come in doubt. Similar revisionist historiography has engulfed the legacy of Hans Morgenthau, widely considered the founding father of modern American realism. The last fifteen years have witnessed "a remarkable turnabout in ... [Morgenthau's] scholarly fortunes."[120] Far from a rationalist scientist unconcerned with ethics and skeptical about any possibility of progress in world affairs, the German emigré displayed powerful inclinations toward critical theory according to a number of younger scholars today.[121] In the words of one of them, Morganthau's "realist theory of international politics ... [was always] also, fundamentally, a normative and *critical* project which questions the existing status quo."[122] His mind was not nearly as wedded to the standing order as is commonly believed but contained a subversive, counterhegemonic dimension: a "supple political ethics" anchored in the resolve to speak truth to power.[123] Epistemologically, Morgenthau "reject[ed] ... the rational as a basis for truth in the late 1960s and 1970s"[124] and comprehended realism in reflexive terms: as a body of knowledge limited by its situation in a specific time and place. Although his famous principle that "politics, like society in general, is governed by objective laws ... impervious to our preferences"[125] seems to signal positivism and scientific rationalism, digging a little bit deeper dramatically alters the picture, similar to how proceeding beyond *The Twenty Years' Crisis* alters the realist image of Carr.[126] For all these and other reasons, Morgenthau may be regarded as an early critical international theorist: a thinker whose "realist project is ... best understood as a critique of the powers-that-be."[127]

For the vast majority of international relations students in the United States today, however, the mere possibility that Carr or Morgenthau could have been anything other than realists is foreign, indeed inconceivable. The problem-solving character of mainstream research in the field, whose scientific aspirations lead it to focus on the surrounding world rather than the eye of the beholder, and moreover on the surrounding world in the present moment rather than the past or the future, has devastated the field's capacity to think historically, let alone ponder deeper questions about the nature and purpose of historical narratives. Critical analysis of the poetic production and ideological function of Carr's or Morgenthau's dominant representations—and of disciplinary history in general, which they make up—is a remote province populated by a handful of misfits and troublemakers.

This state of affairs is both comic, given the massive amount of attention accorded to history and philosophy of history by Carr himself, and tragic. As Milan Kundera famously observed in one of his novels, "The struggle of man against power is the struggle of memory against forgetting."[128] Insofar as many international relations students not only forgot the wealth of facts missing from Carr's stereotypical representation as a realist, but never even noticed them to begin with, and thus are not aware that any forgetting took place at all, they have lost this struggle without putting up a fight: a stunning act of capitulation to the inertia of received wisdom and its vested interests.

Notes

1 See Thomas S. Kuhn, *The Structure of Scientific Revolutions*, 2nd ed. (Chicago: University of Chicago Press, 1970), 167.
2 Hayden White, "Human Face of Scientific Mind: An Interview with Hayden White," interview by Ewa Domańska, *Storia della Storiografia* no. 24 (1993): 7.
3 Edward Hallett Carr, *Dostoevsky, 1821–1881: A New Biography* (London: Allen & Unwin, 1931); idem, *The Romantic Exiles: A Nineteenth-Century Portrait Gallery* (London: Victor Gollancz, 1933); idem, *Karl Marx: A Study in Fanaticism* (London: Dent, 1934); idem, *Michael Bakunin* (London: Macmillan, 1937).
4 Edward Hallett Carr, *The Twenty Years' Crisis, 1919–1939: An Introduction to the Study of International Relations* (London: Macmillan, 1939).
5 Edward Hallett Carr, *The Future of Nations: Independence or Interdependence?* (London: Kegan Paul, 1941); idem, *Conditions of Peace* (London: Macmillan, 1942); idem, *Nationalism and After* (London: Macmillan, 1945); idem, *The New Society* (London: Macmillan, 1951).
6 Edward Hallett Carr, *A History of Soviet Russia*, vol. 14 (London: Macmillan, 1950–1978).
7 Edward Hallett Carr, *What Is History?* (New York: Vintage, 1961).
8 Edward Hallett Carr, "Eminent Historian of Soviet Russia." *The Times*, 5 November 1982.
9 John J. Mearsheimer, "E. H. Carr vs. Idealism: The Battle Rages On," *International Relations* 19, no. 2 (2005): 147.
10 Hans J. Morgenthau, "The Political Science of E. H. Carr," *World Politics* 1, no. 1 (1948): 127–134.
11 See especially Frank R. Ankersmit, *Narrative Logic: A Semantic Analysis of the Historian's Language* (The Hague: Nijhoff, 1983), 96–104.
12 Peter Wilson, "Radicalism for a Conservative Purpose: The Peculiar Realism of E. H. Carr," *Millennium: Journal of International Studies* 30, no. 1 (2001): 130.
13 John J. Mearsheimer, *The Tragedy of Great Power Politics* (New York and London: Norton, 2001), 18.

14 Ibid., 14.
15 Mearsheimer, "Carr vs. Idealism," 139–140.
16 Edward Hallett Carr, *The Twenty Years' Crisis, 1919–1939: An Introduction to the Study of International Relations*, 2nd ed. (New York: Harper & Row, 1946), vii. All subsequent references are to this edition.
17 Ibid., 145.
18 Ibid., 102.
19 Ibid., 109.
20 Ibid., 139, 141.
21 Carr, *Twenty Years' Crisis*, 80.
22 Mearsheimer, "Carr vs. Idealism," 141.
23 Ibid., 151, n. 22. Mearsheimer was referring to E. H. Carr, "An Autobiography," in Michael Cox, ed., *E. H. Carr: A Critical Appraisal* (New York: Palgrave, 2000), xix, where Carr noted that soon after publishing *The Twenty Years' Crisis* he "began to be a bit ashamed of [its] harsh 'realism.'"
24 Carr, *Twenty Years' Crisis*, 3.
25 Ibid., 8.
26 Ibid., 9.
27 Ibid., 10.
28 See Mearsheimer, *Tragedy*, 4–12, where he describes the world as "a laboratory to decide which theories best explain international politics" (p. 8) and casts his "offensive realism"—distilled out of empirical evidence—as a tool to "to peer into the future" (p. 8) working "like a powerful flashlight in a dark room: even though it cannot illuminate every nook and cranny, most of the time it is ... excellent ... for navigating through the darkness" (p. 11).
29 Robert Gilpin, "The Richness of the Tradition of Political Realism," in Robert O. Keohane, ed., *Neorealism and Its Critics* (New York: Columbia University Press, 1986), 305.
30 Hedley Bull, "*The Twenty Years' Crisis* Thirty Years On," *International Journal* 24, no. 4 (1969): 628–630.
31 Mearsheimer, *Tragedy*, 17.
32 Ken Booth, "Security in Anarchy: Utopian Realism in Theory and Practice," *International Affairs* 67, no. 3 (1991): 528.
33 Andrew Linklater, "The Transformation of Political Community: E. H. Carr, Critical Theory and International Relations," *Review of International Studies* 23, no. 3 (1997): 324.
34 Ibid., 321–322. Booth and Linklater have not been alone in striving to revise Carr's standard disciplinary reputation; other notable scholars involved in the effort include Peter Wilson, Charles Jones, Michael Cox, Seán Molloy, and Jonathan Haslam, Carr's onetime research assistant. See Wilson, "Radicalism for Conservative Purpose;" idem, "E. H. Carr's *The Twenty Years' Crisis*: Appearance and Reality in World Politics," *Politik: Danish Journal of Political Science* 12, no. 4 (2009): 21–25; Jones, "E. H. Carr: Ambivalent Realist," in Francis A. Beer and Robert Hariman, eds., *Post-Realism: The Rhetorical Turn in International Relations* (East Lansing: Michigan State University, 1997); idem, *E. H. Carr and International Relations: A Duty to Lie* (Cambridge and New York: Cambridge University Press, 1998); Cox, ed., *Carr: Critical Appraisal*; Seán Molloy, "Dialectics and Transformation: Exploring the International Theory of E. H. Carr," *International Journal of Politics, Culture, and Society* 17, no. 2 (2003): 279–306; idem, *The Hidden History of Realism: A Genealogy of Power Politics* (New York: Palgrave Macmillan, 2006); and Haslam, *The Vices of Integrity: E. H. Carr, 1892–1982* (London and New York: Verso, 1999). See also Paul Howe, "The Utopian Realism of E. H. Carr," *Review of International Studies* 20, no. 3 (1994): 277–297. As an example, Molloy ("Dialectics

and Transformation," 280) insists on "Carr's standing as a progenitor of critical or post-positivist approaches to international relations."

35 Carr, *Twenty Years' Crisis*, 3.

36 Cf. Robert W. Cox, "Social Forces, States and World Orders: Beyond International Relations Theory," in Robert O. Keohane, ed., *Neorealism and Its Critics* (New York: Columbia University Press, 1986), 207: "Theory is always *for* someone and *for* some purpose. (...) There is ... no such thing as theory in itself...." [Emphasis original.]

37 Carr, *Twenty Years' Crisis*, 4.

38 Ibid., 5.

39 Not that the "utopians" would have necessarily recognized themselves as such; indeed, Carr seems to have concocted the category out of heterogeneous thinkers and elements, as persuasively demonstrated by Brian C. Schmidt, *The Political Discourse of Anarchy: A Disciplinary History of International Relations* (Albany, NY: State University of New York Press, 1998), 219. See also Tim Dunne, "Theories as Weapons: E. H. Carr and International Relations," in Cox, ed., *Carr: Critical Appraisal*, 221–222.

40 See Carr, *Twenty Years' Crisis*, 62.

41 Chris Brown, *Understanding International Relations*, 2nd ed. (Basingstoke: Palgrave, 2001), 28.

42 Carr, *Twenty Years' Crisis*, 75. As one of Carr's later collaborators summarized the central argument, "the common assumption that every nation has an identical interest in peace masked the conflict of interest between nations desirous of maintaining the status quo and nations desirous of changing it." (R. W. Davies, "Edward Hallett Carr, 1892–1982," *Proceedings of the British Academy* 69 [1983]: 486.)

43 See Carr, *Twenty Years' Crisis*, 83.

44 Dunne, "Theories as Weapons," 218, 224. As Carr himself pointed out, "realism is liable to assume a critical ... aspect." (*Twenty Years' Crisis*, 10.)

45 Stefano Guzzini, *Realism in International Relations and International Political Economy: The Continuing Story of a Death Foretold* (London: Routledge, 1998), 23. Cf. Jonathan Haslam's poignant remark that "[Carr] loved to spit at orthodoxy." ("E. H. Carr's Search for Meaning, 1892–1982," in Cox, ed., *Carr: Critical Appraisal*, 33.)

46 Wilson, "*Twenty Years' Crisis*: Appearance and Reality," 22–23.

47 Davies, "Carr," 486.

48 Haslam, "Carr's Search for Meaning," 24. See also idem, *Vices of Integrity*, 44–46.

49 Kuniyuki Nishimura, "E. H. Carr, Dostoevsky, and the Problem of Irrationality in Modern Europe," *International Relations* 25, no. 1 (2011): 48.

50 Ibid., 55.

51 Carr, *Twenty Years' Crisis*, 92.

52 Ibid., 93. Cf. Dunne, "Theories as Weapons," 218: "[Carr] was dissatisfied with a non-utopian realism, privileging in the final analysis a complex relationship between the two constructs. This tension has been lost in the orthodox interpretation of the work as a founding text in the realist canon."

53 Nishimura, "Carr, Dostoevsky, and Irrationality," 57.

54 Haslam, "Carr's Search for Meaning," 34.

55 Haslam, *Vices of Integrity*, 193.

56 Davies, "Carr," 475.

57 Ibid.

58 Haslam, *Vices of Integrity*, 54.

59 John Hallett [E. H. Carr], "Karl Marx: Fifty Years Later," *Fortnightly Review*, no. 319 (March 1933): 625–638.

60 Carr, "Autobiography," xx.

61 Carr, *Twenty Years' Crisis*, 82.

62 Ibid., 60.

63 Carr, "Autobiography," xviii.

64 For Mannheim's influence on Carr, see Jones, *Duty to Lie*, chap. 6.

65 Karl Mannheim, *Ideology and Utopia* (London: Routledge & Kegan Paul, 1936), originally published in German as *Ideologie und Utopie* (Bonn: F. Cohen, 1929).

66 Edward Hallett Carr, "Karl Mannheim," in *From Napoleon to Stalin, and Other Essays* (Basingstoke: Macmillan, 1980), 180.

67 Christoph Frei, *Hans J. Morgenthau: An Intellectual Biography* (Baton Rouge: Louisiana State University Press, 2001), 113. Other entries on the list included works by Friedrich Nietzsche, Max Weber, Hannah Arendt, Reinhold Niebuhr, Charles Norris Cochrane, Alexander Hamilton, Blaise Pascal, Plato, and Aristotle.

68 Morgenthau, "Political Science of E. H. Carr," 134. See also Morgenthau, "The Surrender to the Immanence of Power: E. H. Carr," in *Dilemmas of Politics* (Chicago: University of Chicago Press, 1962), 350–357.

69 Richard Falk, "The Critical Realist Tradition and the Demystification of Inter-state Power: E. H. Carr, Hedley Bull and Robert W. Cox," in Stephen Gill and James Mittelman, eds., *Innovation and Transformation in International Studies* (Cambridge: Cambridge University Press, 1997), 40.

70 Cox, "Social Forces," 211. Cox added that this critical-historical mode of thought distinguished Carr from later realists such as Waltz, who "have transformed realism into a ... problem-solving theory" and "tended to adopt [its] fixed ahistorical view of the framework for action." (Ibid.)

71 Carr, *What Is History?*, 5.

72 Anders Stephanson, "The Lessons of *What Is History?*" in Cox, ed., *Carr: Critical Appraisal*, 285.

73 Carr, *What Is History?*, 5.

74 E. H. Carr to R. W. Davies, 9 December 1959, quoted in Davies, "Carr," 504.

75 Carr, *What Is History?*, 8, 32.

76 Ibid., 9–10, 26.

77 Hayden White, "Figuring the Nature of the Times Deceased: Literary Theory and Historical Writing," in Ralph Cohen, ed., *The Future of Literary Theory* (London: Routledge, 1989), 27.

78 Hayden White, *Tropics of Discourse: Essays in Cultural Criticism* (Baltimore, MD, and London: Johns Hopkins University Press, 1978), 125.

79 See especially Geoffrey Elton, *The Practice of History* (London: Methuen, 1967). The controversy is discussed in Haslam, *Vices of Integrity*, 204.

80 Carr, *What Is History?*, 89–90.

81 "There is no more significant pointer to the character of a society than the kind of history it writes." (Carr, *What Is History?*, 53.)

82 Ibid., 10.

83 Ibid., 94.

84 Haslam, *Vices of Integrity*, 216.

85 Keith Jenkins, *On "What Is History?": From Carr and Elton to Rorty and White* (London: Routledge, 1995), 43–64.

86 Ibid., 10. See also Keith Jenkins, "An English Myth? Rethinking the Contemporary Value of E. H. Carr's *What Is History?*," in Cox, ed., *Carr: Critical Appraisal*, 304–321.

87 After all, recall that White went on record to say that "I am a modernist ... [whose] whole intellectual formation ... [and] development took place within modernism," a self-definition seconded by Hans Kellner's observation that "[White] emphasizes that he in no way belongs to the poststructuralist camp of those who deny the reality of evidence and historical facts." See Hayden White,

"Interview: The Image of Self-Presentation," interview by Hans Kellner and Ewa Domańska, *Diacritics* 24, no. 1 (1994): 92.

88 Haslam, *Vices of Integrity*, 216–217.
89 Davies, "Carr," 492, 499.
90 Stephanson, "Lessons of *What Is History?*," 286. Cf. Davies, "Carr," 504: "[Carr] equally argued that history is not entirely relative or subjective."
91 Carr, *What Is History?*, 136.
92 Ibid., 138.
93 Stephanson, "Lessons of *What Is History?*," 286.
94 Cf. Wilson, "*Twenty Years' Crisis*: Appearance and Reality," 23–24.
95 Carr, *What Is History?*, 152.
96 Ibid., 158.
97 Ibid., 157.
98 Richard K. Ashley, "Political Realism and Human Interests," *International Studies Quarterly* 25, no. 2 (1981): 227. For evolutionary rationality, see Mark Hoffman, "Conversations on Critical International Relations Theory," *Millennium: Journal of International Studies* 17, no. 1 (1988): 91–95. Cf. Scott Burchill et al., *Theories of International Relations*, 2nd ed. (Basingstoke: Palgrave, 2001), 163–164.
99 Howe, "Utopian Realism," 295.
100 Randall Germain, "E. H. Carr and the Historical Mode of Thought," in Cox, ed., *Carr: Critical Appraisal*, 329.
101 Carr, *What Is History?*, 108.
102 Wilson, "Radicalism for Conservative Purpose," 124. The two establishments intersected, of course, as illustrated by Woodrow Wilson: not only the leading liberal internationalist statesman and president of the United States, but also an internationally acclaimed historian and president of the American Historical Association. In the latter capacity he was invited by Lord Acton to contribute to *The Cambridge Modern History*, a project intended to provide a complete and definitive record of the past—and for that reason denounced by Carr (*What Is History?*, 3) as a prime example of the nineteenth-century liberal empiricist "cult of facts." Wilson obliged, and his chapter on Lincoln and state rights now appears in *The Cambridge Modern History*, vol. 7 (New York: Macmillan, 1902). For Acton's request, see his letter to Wilson dated May 10, 1899, in Arthur S. Link et al., eds., *The Papers of Woodrow Wilson*, vol. 11 (Princeton, NJ: Princeton University Press, 1971), 117–118.
103 Note Carr's comment that "In Europe, the present need is to build up larger military and economic units while retaining existing or smaller units for other purposes." (*Future of Nations*, 56.)
104 Cf. Kenneth N. Waltz, *Theory of International Politics* (Reading, MA: Addison-Wesley, 1979), 10.
105 Mearsheimer, "Carr vs. Idealism," 151, n. 22.
106 Carr, *Twenty Years' Crisis*, 10. Cf. Mearsheimer, *Tragedy*, 17.
107 E. H. Carr to Stanley Hoffmann, 30 September 1977, quoted in Davies, "Carr," 487. Hoffmann agreed with this assessment. Indeed, nowadays the argument that traditional international relations scholarship amounts to little else than a systematic rationalization of American power and predominance in world affairs, although also espoused by Cox ("Social Forces," 248), tends to be associated primarily with Hoffmann's name. See Stanley Hoffmann, "An American Social Science: International Relations," *Daedalus* 106, no. 3 (1977): 41–60.
108 Cf. Cox, "Social Forces," 208–209: whereas neorealism (as a type of problem-solving theory) fragments reality into multiple discrete spheres, studies any given issue only in relation to the specialized area of activity in which it arises, and assumes that all the other aspects of action are fixed, in effect ignoring them, "Critical theory is directed to the social and political complex as a

whole ... (and) leads toward the construction of a larger picture ... of which the initially contemplated part is just one component...."

109 Wilson, "Radicalism for Conservative Purpose," 130.

110 Kuhn, *Structure of Scientific Revolutions*, 103.

111 Ibid., 109.

112 Ibid., 94, 109.

113 Cf. Mearsheimer's pointed remark during his 2004 Carr Memorial Lecture at Aberystwyth, presumably to a room full of critical theorists including Linklater and Booth, that although "Some idealists might argue that ... [Carr] is not a realist but a closet idealist, this is not a serious argument" (Mearsheimer, "Carr vs. Idealism," 144).

114 Cf. Kuhn, *Structure of Scientific Revolutions*, 109–110.

115 Herbert George Wells, "The Country of the Blind," *The Strand Magazine* 27, no. 160 (April 1904): 401–415.

116 Not even the minimal meaning of a purely chronological sequence would be universally intelligible, however; "it is itself relative to the culture because there are different chronologies and different chronological conventions." Hayden White, "Hayden White on 'Facts, Fictions and Metahistory': II. A Discussion with Hayden White," interview by Richard J. Murphy, *Sources: Revue D'Etudes Anglophones* 2 (Spring 1997): 14.

117 Hayden White, "The Aim of Interpretation Is to Create Perplexity in the Face of the Real: Hayden White in Conversation with Erlend Rogne," *History and Theory* 48, no. 1 (2009): 74.

118 Mearsheimer, *Tragedy*, 9.

119 Waltz, *Theory*, 10.

120 Daniel J. Levine, "Why Hans Morgenthau Was Not a Critical Theorist (and Why Contemporary IR Realists Should Care)," *International Relations* 27, no. 1 (2012): 95.

121 Morgenthau's hegemonic image has been perpetuated not only by contemporary realists, but often also by critical theorists: as a handy straw man serving their arguments. An example is Jim George, *Discourses of Global Politics: A Critical (Re)Introduction to International Relations* (Boulder, CO: Lynne Rienner, 1994), dismissing Morgenthau as a scientific positivist adhering to a spectator theory of knowledge. According to William Bain, George's representation is a myth which "does more to 'discipline' and 'marginalize' Morgenthau than to invite earnest debate and ... serious reflection"; among other things, it entirely misses that Morgenthau's "realism is representative of a rich moral tradition" which "emphasizes ... the need to locate statecraft in historical, social, and political context." (Bain, "Deconfusing Morgenthau: Moral Inquiry and Classical Realism Reconsidered," *Review of International Studies* 26, no. 3 [2000]: 445–446.) Similarly, Murielle Cozette has commented scathingly that "[realism's] critical side is consistently—and conveniently—forgotten ... by the more recent, self-named 'critical' approaches," adding that "[these approaches] tend to rely on a truncated and misleading picture of what realism stands for and ... never properly engage with realists' arguments." (Cozette, "Reclaiming the Critical Dimension of Realism: Hans J. Morgenthau on the Ethics of Scholarship," *Review of International Studies* 34, no. 1 [2008]:6, 8.)

122 Cozette, "Critical Dimension of Realism," 6. [Emphasis original.]

123 William E. Scheuerman, "Was Morgenthau a Realist? Revisiting *Scientific Man vs. Power Politics*," *Constellations* 14, no. 4 (2007): 526. See also idem, "Realism and the Left: The Case of Hans J. Morgenthau," *Review of International Studies* 34, no. 1 (2008): 29–51, and idem, "A Theoretical Missed Opportunity? Hans J. Morgenthau as Critical Realist," in Duncan Bell, ed., *Political Thought and International Relations* (Oxford: Oxford University Press, 2009).

124 Seán Molloy, "Truth, Power, Theory: Hans Morgenthau's Formulation of Realism," *Diplomacy and Statecraft* 15, no. 1 (2004): 2.
125 Hans J. Morgenthau, *Politics among Nations: The Struggle for Power and Peace*, 5th ed. (New York: Knopf, 1973 [1948]), 4.
126 Morgenthau's under-researched conversations with Reinhold Niebuhr, for example, suggest that "For both men, American political thought was betrayed by the false notion that the methods appropriate to the natural sciences were applicable to understanding the much more complicated realities of human nature." (Daniel F. Rice, *Reinhold Niebuhr and His Circle of Influence* [New York: Cambridge University Press, 2012], 10.)
127 Cozette, "Critical Dimension of Realism," 8.
128 Milan Kundera, *The Book of Laughter and Forgetting*, trans. Aaron Asher (New York: Harper, 1996), 4.

4 Bin Laden Meets Bill Lawton

The Politics of Don DeLillo's Poetic Representation of 9/11

Preceding chapters have exposed the fictions of factual literature on international relations: the nonempirical content brought by professional academics to their accounts by virtue of narrativizing them. But showing that the ostensibly factual discourse of academic international relations is saturated with unacknowledged poetic elements, on whose account it may be regarded as a type of rhetoric, the art and politics of persuasion through language, is not the only goal of this book. There is another: to demonstrate that fictional depictions of world affairs often draw on real political events and have real political implications, a claim in the spirit of Aristotle's teachings that poets are no less poets for constructing their plots out of actual happenings and that their stories actively shape society's consciousness of political reality. Just as it is possible to speak about the poetics of international politics, in other words, it is possible to speak about the politics of international poetics: the factual basis and consequences of fictional narrative representations of world affairs.

That fiction often works with real historical events should be common sense, and to nobody more so than to international relations scholars. This is for the simple reason that ever since Homer's *Iliad* generations upon generations of Western poets have been crafting their stories exactly out of the same material as preoccupies academic international relations: war.[1] Just like the discipline's history, the history of the art of the novel is in significant extent the history of writing about armed conflict. It starts with a warrior, after all, or at any rate a protagonist pretending to be one: Don Quixote, the aspiring knight errant at the heart of Miguel de Cervantes's eponymous masterpiece inaugurating the genre. The list of famous novels dealing with war goes on and on: *War and Peace* by Leo Tolstoy, *All Quiet on the Western Front* by Erich Maria Remarque, *The Good Soldier Švejk* by Jaroslav Hašek, *For Whom the Bell Tolls* by Ernest Hemingway, *Catch-22* by Joseph Heller, *Slaughterhouse-Five* by Kurt Vonnegut, *The Things They Carried* by Tim O'Brien, to name just a few. Some probe a specific episode, such as the infamous 1945 Allied firebombing of Dresden, while others offer a more synoptic view of war and its impact on society, whether during the Napoleonic era, World War I, World War II, or Vietnam. Structure and language vary just as much: from Hemingway's somber athletic prose to the dark humor of Hašek's absurd comedy, from Remarque's linear plot to Vonnegut's chaotic flashbacks and time travel. But all use as their building blocks actual war occurrences, ones that are publicly documented, empirically verifiable, and frequently part of their authors' direct personal experiences.[2]

It should be just as obvious that fictional narratives, even ones made up entirely of imaginary persons and events, have real political implications. In the history of the novel, this point, too, appears already at inception: Don Quixote embarks on his knightly adventures after excessive reading of old chivalric romances, meaning that Cervantes tells a story not just about an aspiring warrior but also about the power of literature to transform real life. Precisely because they wield this power, writers can easily find themselves persecuted by the state. After publishing *The Joke* (1967), novelist Milan Kundera, whose work is the subject of the next chapter, was expelled from the Communist Party of Czechoslovakia, forced into exile, and stripped of his Czechoslovak citizenship. Salman Rushdie suffered an even grimmer ordeal after his *Satanic Verses* (1988) came out: Ayatollah Khomeini, Supreme Leader of Iran at the time, charged him with blasphemy against Islam and issued a *fatwa* calling for his death. Thanks to heavy police protection Rushdie managed to escape the ensuing spate of assassination attempts, but his associates were less fortunate. William Nygaard, his Norwegian publisher, was shot three times outside his home in Oslo, and Hitoshi Igarashi, his Japanese translator, paid the ultimate price after being stabbed to death in his office at the University of Tsukuba. The most recent report by the Writers in Prison Committee of PEN International lists over two hundred attacks against writers across the globe in 2017, from long-term imprisonment to temporary detentions, from threats to murders.[3]

This chapter demonstrates the international political inspirations and implications of fiction using Don DeLillo's *Falling Man*, a novel about the September 11, 2001, terrorist attacks in New York City.[4] No international relations scholar would deny 9/11 the status of a watershed event in contemporary American society, politics, foreign relations, and international affairs at large. Newspaper columnist Ellen Goodman was speaking for all: "Tuesday morning, our world changed," she wrote three days after the attacks in a piece reprinted in major domestic and international broadsheets under headings such as "Shattering the Luxury of Our Charmed Life," "Our Reality Show: We No Longer Have the Luxury of Feeling Safe," and "Our Charmed Life Has Gone Forever."[5] The event claimed three thousand civilian lives, instantly ended America's post-Cold War euphoria, and transformed the country into a hyper-paranoid security state. It immersed it in a permanent "war on terror" involving an all-out assault on civil liberties at home and two invasions abroad, which brought chaos to the Middle East and cost thousands American and tens of thousands Afghan and Iraqi lives, not to mentions trillions of taxpayer dollars. The attacks now figure in every US history textbook and also, alongside the American Revolution,

George Washington, or Martin Luther King, Jr., among the one hundred civics lessons whose mastery is required of all immigrants applying for American citizenship.[6] Clearly, 9/11 has etched itself indelibly in the country's collective memory and identity.

DeLillo's *Falling Man* is the preeminent literary representation of the traumatic event in contemporary American fiction. Novels dealing with 9/11 are relatively rare; during the first six years following their occurrence, the attacks had inspired only thirty of them, compared to over a thousand non-fiction titles.[7] But the small quantity does not necessarily mean low quality: Frédéric Beigbeder's *Windows on the World* (2003), Jonathan Safran Foer's *Extremely Loud and Incredibly Close* (2005), Ken Kalfus's *Disorder Peculiar to the Country* (2006), John Updike's *Terrorist* (2006), and Mohsin Hamid's *Reluctant Fundamentalist* (2007) have all garnered considerable critical acclaim.[8] Even amidst such distinguished company, however, DeLillo stands in a league of his own. When on the tenth anniversary of the attacks the journal *Modern Fiction Studies* ran a special issue on 9/11 fiction, fourteen of the seventy essays submitted for consideration focused solely on *Falling Man*, leading the editors to proclaim DeLillo's work "hypercanonical" and remark that "we could have almost produced an issue devoted exclusively to this novel."[9]

The political message of *Falling Man*, as is about to emerge, springs from its critique of the official 9/11 discourse: DeLillo draws attention to the centrality of visual media in shaping mass perceptions of the event, relativizes the widespread distinction between benevolent America and its malevolent Islamic Other, and suggests, against the dominant narrative propagated by the White House, that the memory of those killed in the Twin Towers should be honored not with a military crusade aimed at exacting revenge but with a reflection on the terror latent in the global spread of American corporate capitalism and consumer culture. This argument takes shape against the backdrop of DeLillo's longstanding belief that art should serve a distinctive function in society: opposing and negating received ideas backed by state and corporate power and emancipating human individuals from their oppressive weight.

DeLillo: Hiding in Plain Sight

Born in the Bronx neighborhood of New York City in 1936, Don DeLillo is an American novelist, dramatist, essayist, and short story writer with over a dozen novels to his name. His parents immigrated to the United States from Abruzzo, Italy, and raised him in the working-class Italian-American community near Arthur Avenue, although his stories are devoid of any ethnic focus of the sort animating, for example, Philip Roth's fiction, much of which chronicles the Jewish experience of America.[10] DeLillo spent his childhood living in a large, tightly knit Catholic family whose eldest members never learned English, playing in the streets with a football made out of old newspapers, and dreaming of becoming a baseball radio announcer. He attended Cardinal Hayes High School, where (by his admission) he mainly slept, and subsequently enrolled at Fordham University, where he studied Communication Arts with about as much enthusiasm.[11] His real education took place elsewhere: in the cinema, during cheap afternoon matinee screenings of European New Wave films by Jean-Luc Godard, Michelangelo Antonioni, Federico Fellini, and Ingmar Bergman.[12]

After college graduation in 1958, DeLillo went to work as a copywriter for the advertising agency of Ogilvy, Benson & Mather and simultaneously began publishing his first short stories in literary magazines such as *Epoch* and *The Kenyon Review*. In the mid-1960s, he quit the advertising job in order to pursue his literary aspirations full-time—despite facing uncertain prospects and material hardship, thanks to which he spent much of this period living in a closet-sized apartment with a fridge in the bathroom. The violent death of President John F. Kennedy in Dallas, Texas, on November 22, 1963, had a profound impact on DeLillo's literary development: "It was a great shock, the kind that resonates through the years,"[13] he later commented. "Maybe it invented me. ... [I]t's possible I wouldn't have become the kind of writer I am if it weren't for the assassination."[14] His first novel, *Americana*, came out in 1971, and two more quickly followed by 1973. DeLillo's literary reputation was thereby established.

Since then, DeLillo has become a living legend: a towering presence in modern American literature. His accomplishments include two Pulitzer Prize nominations, the National Book Award, the PEN/Faulkner Award, and the inaugural Library of Congress Prize for American Fiction. When in 2006 the *New York Times Book Review* organized an informal poll asking some 125 prominent writers, editors, and literary critics to identify the single best work of American fiction published in the last quarter-century, DeLillo's *Underworld* finished second only to Toni Morrison's *Beloved*, and the top twenty selections included two more of his works.[15] His recognition extends worldwide, as evidenced by the Jerusalem Prize. Its jury awarded it to DeLillo in 1999, praising his work for its "unrelenting struggle against even the most sophisticated forms of repression of individual and public freedom during the last half century."[16] DeLillo thus became the award's first American recipient, joining Bertrand Russell, Max Frisch, Simone de Beauvoir, Jorge Luis Borges, Milan Kundera, Eugene Ionesco, J. M. Coetzee, and other distinguished laureates.

Despite all this, chances are that save for a handful of exceptions international relations scholars have no familiarity with DeLillo. The general educated public, from which they come, has largely abandoned novels, and most of those who persist in reading them no longer do so out of thirst for socially and politically engaged commentary coupled with formal invention. Instead, they look for entertainment: escapist fantasies and fetishistic distractions packaged in predictable, easy-to-consume plots such as the voyeuristic *Fifty Shades* trilogy full of taboo sex, the *Twilight* saga about vampires, or *The Lord of the Rings* installments teeming with wizards, orcs, and elves. Compared to these rousing page-turners generating record sales figures, DeLillo's novels are dull tomes that hit bookstore shelves mainly to stay on them. As an observer commented in 1982, "[DeLillo] has not had large commercial success," and "few readers ... clamor for [his] work."[17] Things have changed since then, but not by much.

Part of DeLillo's obscurity is due to the author himself: one of the most reclusive American novelists alive and also one of the most indifferent to mass market reception. In the first decades of his writing career, his elusiveness approached that of J. D. Salinger, who had disappeared from public life in the 1960s and resurfaced only in 1988, against his will, when journalists sniffed him out on his farm in Cornish, New Hampshire, took his photograph, and published it on the front page of *The New York Post* under a headline screaming "Catcher Caught!" DeLillo does not acknowledge his reputation for hiding: "I've been called 'reclusive' a hundred times and I'm not even remotely in that category."[18] But his behavior and closest associates testify to the contrary. "DeLillo's a monk," in the words of Gerald Howard, his editor at Viking in the late 1980s.[19] When a literary critic tracked him down in Athens in 1979, DeLillo handed him a business card engraved only with his name and the words: "I don't want to talk about it."[20] He does not appear on radio or TV, teach creative writing seminars, deliver commencement speeches, collect honorary degrees, or even review works by other authors, and he rarely gives any interviews or public readings. He lets his novels do all the talking and relishes dwelling in their shadows, out of sight. "With every book," he explained, "I get a little smaller. In the end there'll be nothing left."[21] International relations scholars, then, may be excused for not noticing him.

Alone in a Room: The Writer's Classic Condition

DeLillo's desire for obscurity is no accident. Nor is it a publicity stunt or a quirk of his personality, although he does admit that he is "just not a public man" and lacks the "necessary self-importance."[22] Rather, his anonymity reflects his carefully thought-out conception of the novelist's proper place in society. DeLillo has articulated this conception on many different occasions, and comprehending it is the first prerequisite for grasping the full political import of his literary works, including those dealing with key international events and phenomena such as terrorism and 9/11.

Central to DeLillo's artistic ethics is the notion of retreat from society: fiction writers should work "alone in a room," to use a figure recurring throughout his reflections on the subject. "People in rooms have always seemed important to me,"[23] he stated already in his first public interview. Years later, in an address delivered at New York Public Library during a stand-in for the imprisoned Chinese writer Wei Jingsheng in May 1997, DeLillo referred to "be[ing] alone in a room" as "the writer's classic condition."[24] He intimated the same idea privately to fellow novelist David Foster Wallace, whose struggle with depression frequently paralyzed his ability to work and who asked DeLillo for encouragement. DeLillo's response illustrates his ideal of artistic withdrawal: "We die indoors," he assured Wallace in his pep talk, "and alone."[25] Serious fiction writing requires cognitive and physical detachment. "A novel is a mystery, which a writer keeps to himself sometimes for years before letting it out of his room. He works in solitude. (...) [He] is the person somewhere out there, anonymous, a fool in his room...."[26]

DeLillo's ethics of seclusion is not discernible only from his extranovelistic commentary and personal work habits. It is also visible in his favorite pastime in his early writing days: mid-week matinee movie screenings, which usually boil down to sitting alone in a dark room. Above all, however, it is evident from his fiction: "Most of my novels," DeLillo recognized, "seem to turn on a character ... alone in a small room."[27]

Examples abound. In *Great Jones Street*, rock music superstar Bucky Wunderlick vanishes from his band mid-tour into a tiny unfurnished apartment in order to prepare the release of his "Mountain Tapes": an experimental album composed in his soundproof studio in the mountains in pursuit of "silence endowed with acoustical properties"[28] as a revolutionary art form liberated from the deafening "tropics of fame"[29] of the commercial media culture. Similarly in *Libra*, which deals with the Kennedy assassination, DeLillo tells a story of

> a *real* character who spent a significant amount of time in a room alone. Of course that was [Lee Harvey] Oswald himself, who planned the murder of General Walker in a room only slightly larger than a closet, who spent time in the brig [in the Marines], who lived in ... Dallas in a room about the size of a jail cell, and who finally ended up in a real jail cell, before he himself was killed.[30]

In *Cosmopolis*, the entire plot of the novel takes place in a small room, this time one on wheels: a luxurious stretch limousine. Sitting inside, a 28-year-old billionaire currency trader and investment asset manager named Eric Packer traverses Manhattan on his way to death from a gunshot wound inflicted by his stalker, Benno Levin: a disgruntled former employee squatting in a vacant tenement near Eleventh Avenue as yet another case of a man alone in a room. Setting these examples side by side, one cannot fail to notice a distinctive "pattern of withdrawal"[31] running through DeLillo's works.

The protagonist who best embodies this pattern shares more than a dash of resemblance with DeLillo himself: Bill Gray, the character at the center of *Mao II*. A world famous novelist, Bill leads a hermit's existence somewhere in upstate New York. When he reemerges from it after thirty years, his editor exclaims: "You have a twisted sense of the writer's place in society.

You think the writer belongs to the far margin, doing dangerous things."[32] The editor subsequently reveals that a Swiss poet named Jean-Claude Julien has been abducted by terrorists in the Middle East, where he is currently "chained to a wall in a bare room in Beirut,"[33] and he asks Bill to facilitate Julien's release by giving a reading from his poetry at a news conference in London: a media event demanded by the terrorists to generate exposure for their cause. Bill's response eventually leads to his second disappearance: he embarks on a one-man journey in search of the poet-hostage, a quest motivated as much by his fraternal desire to rescue Julien as by his artistic wish to assume Julien's place in the cell. As he nears Lebanon via Athens and Cyprus, Bill suffers internal injuries in a hit-and-run car accident and ends up succumbing to them aboard a ferry in the Mediterranean without ever reaching his destination. Since robbers promptly strip his dead corpse of his passport and all other forms of identification, this time around his disappearance becomes absolute: the ultimate exile of anonymous death.

Automatically conflating novelistic characters with their authors is, of course, one of the cardinal sins of literary criticism. DeLillo himself warned against it: "No, Bill Gray is not modeled on my life or work,"[34] he replied to a question whether the protagonist was autobiographical. Nevertheless, this has not detained him from making deeply suggestive assertions to the opposite effect. "I called him Bill Gray just as a provisional name," he revealed the genesis of the character in a 1991 interview, frankly admitting that "I used to say to friends, 'I want to change my name to Bill Gray and disappear.' I've been saying it for ten years. But he began to fit himself into that name, and I decided to leave it."[35] Clear traces of Gray also appear elsewhere in DeLillo's nonfiction, such as his pamphlet coauthored with Paul Auster in defense of Salman Rushdie, whose ordeal after Khomeini's *fatwa* greatly upset DeLillo and informs the plot of *Mao II*.

The conclusion is thus hard to escape: "Gray and DeLillo speak the same language—often verbatim."[36] In certain key respects, the fictional protagonist of *Mao II* indeed does appear to be a stand-in for his maker. Above all, "Bill Gray can be said to personify DeLillo's desire to escape,"[37] even if DeLillo has declined to follow his character to the place where this desire finds its ultimate consummation: the unmarked grave.

Bad Citizenship: The Novel as a Vehicle of Individual Emancipation

The wish to flee to the fringes of society broaches a broader theme in DeLillo's conception of the art of the novel: his view of the novel's social purpose. His insistence that serious fiction writing presupposes a position of "Silence, exile, cunning, and so on,"[38] as he once explained his reclusiveness referencing Stephen Dedalus from James Joyce's *Portrait of an Artist as a Young Man*, stems from his idea of how the novelist should function in society in the first place. Understanding this idea, which may be classified as an expression of modernism in contemporary fiction, is the second prerequisite for appreciating the full political import of DeLillo's work on 9/11.

According to DeLillo, the novelist's fundamental role, the duty without which no fiction writer deserves the name, is to oppose the existing sociopolitical order. In his novels, this belief is thematized most explicitly through Bill Gray. In a meditation serving yet another indication of Gray's likely status as DeLillo's alter ego, the protagonist of *Mao II* reflects that "a writer creates a character as a way to reveal consciousness, increase the flow of meaning. This is how we [novelists] reply to power and beat back our fear."[39] Gray's editor in the story certainly sees him precisely in those terms: as a novelist convinced that the art of the novel is fundamentally subversive and that "The state should want to kill all writers. Every government, every group that holds power or aspires to power should feel so threatened by writers that they hunt them down, everywhere."[40]

DeLillo has also stepped out from behind his characters to express these convictions directly. In a much-quoted 1988 interview with Ann Arensberg, he tied them to his emphasis on exile and seclusion:

> The writer is the person who stands outside society, independent of affiliation and independent of influence. The writer is the man or woman who automatically takes a stance against his or her government. There are so many temptations for American writers to become part of the system and part of the structure that now, more than ever, we have to resist. American writers ought to stand and live in the margins, and be more dangerous.[41]

Ten years later, DeLillo repeated his definition of the writer as an oppositional figure in order to capture the essence of Wei Jingsheng's plight inside his Chinese jail cell. "[Wei's] art," DeLillo said at the 1997 stand-in for the dissident, "is to be still—not silent but still. ... And whirling around this stillness, there is something continuous and ponderous and vast—the perennial frenzy of the state," in whose context Wei's defiant struggle represented "the artist's enduring effort to realize his role—a writer in opposition to the state."[42]

DeLillo's assertions about authorial responsibility and the novel's fundamental role as an instrument of resistance emanating from the fringes of society have not escaped notice by literary critics. Philip Nel has characterized DeLillo's fiction as an "actively adversarial art" striving to destabilize American culture and society through "small incisive shocks."[43] "DeLillo's work," Nel added, "is a continuation of the modernist avant-garde, applying its critical potential to contemporary American life."[44] Similarly, François Happe has described DeLillo's novels as "fiction against systems" driven by a deep-seated impulse to resist what it portrays.[45] According to John Duvall, DeLillo seeks "to construct an opposition to the forces of consumer culture ... [and uses] the novel as a counterforce to the image manipulation of capital,"[46] a project reflecting "a long tradition of American novelists from Hermann Melville and Mark Twain to Morrison and Pynchon who are critical of home as found."[47] In perhaps the most elegant summary, Frank Lentricchia simply placed DeLillo among "writers who conceive their vocation as an act of cultural criticism."[48] Only the conservative pundit George Will has managed to be more succinct when he denounced DeLillo's *Libra* as "an act of literary vandalism and bad citizenship,"[49] unwittingly producing "the best backhanded testimony ... in a long time on behalf of the social power of literature...."[50] DeLillo welcomed Will's verdict as a badge of honor:

> Being called a "bad citizen" is a compliment to a novelist.... That's exactly what we ought to do. We ought to be bad citizens ... in the sense that we're writing against what power represents, and often what government represents, and what the corporation dictates, and what consumer consciousness has come to mean. In that sense, if we're bad citizens, we're doing our job.[51]

Notably, in DeLillo's instance the oppositional performance that is fiction writing does not express any impulse to forge a new society. "[A novelist] does not write on behalf of a better world,"[52] DeLillo stated bluntly. "Norman Mailer wanted ... to change the consciousness of our times," he elaborated, "But I? No, no, I never wanted anything like this. ... I never wanted to change the world."[53] Rather, the resistance and dissent inherent in the art of the novel serve something else for DeLillo: individual emancipation and autonomy.

> Writing is a form of personal freedom. It frees us from the mass identity we see in the making all around us. In the end, writers will write not to be outlaw heroes of some underculture but mainly to save themselves, to survive as individuals. ... If serious reading dwindles to near nothingness, ... the thing we're talking about when we use the word 'identity' has reached an end."[54]

The novel fulfills its role precisely to the extent that it liberates the individual from the homogenizing thrust of the surrounding culture and hegemonic consciousness.

World as Words: The Narrative Fabric of Reality

This emancipatory role cannot be carried out without accomplishing a more basic task first: exposing the fundamental plasticity of existence. One of DeLillo's principal objectives thus has been to denaturalize and problematize the world, strip it of its appearance of timelessness and inevitability, and reveal its tentative status as a product of history, social forces, and symbolic discourse. Just as Whitean narrativists in critical historiography, DeLillo strives to move his readers to the view that reality is poetically constructed rather than simply found and "that the shape ... of their culture dictates the shape ... of the self."[55]

Emphasis on the constitutive role of narrative language in the human consciousness of reality has been a central feature of DeLillo's work since the very beginning. "Naming things helps us hold the world together, almost literally," he explained, adding that "Names are the sub-atomic glue of the human world."[56] Without them, meaningful reality disintegrates into unintelligible chaos. Already in the 1970s, at the outset of his literary career, he "began to suspect that language was a subject as well as an instrument in [his] work."[57] Thirty years later, he was certain: "Before history and politics, there is language."[58]

Consequently, crafting precise, authentic, and beautiful prose has been DeLillo's overriding concern. His writing method has not only an aural dimension but also visual and tactile ones: DeLillo needs to see the letters on the page, hear the hammer of his manual typewriter, and feel the paper and pencil with his fingers when making corrections. Words are, quite literally, the physical world in all its multisensory complexity for him. "When I work," he described the process, "I have a sculptor's sense of the shape of the words I am making."[59] His ability to render the seemingly stable present a constantly evolving textual artifact emanating from within a dynamic historical process may be DeLillo's foremost distinction:

> What makes [him] one of the most important American novelists since 1970 is his fiction's repeated invitation to think historically. (...) DeLillo ... has a rare gift for historicizing our present, a gift that empowers engaged readers to think historically themselves. ... [He] teases out the ways in which our contemporary world bears the traces of such crucial events from the mid twentieth century as the rise of Adolf Hitler's fascism, the assassination of President John F. Kennedy, and Cold War brinkmanship. In his most important novels ... DeLillo explores the ways in which contemporary American personal identity ... is related to larger social and cultural forces forged over time.[60]

To the extent that denaturalizing reality means picturing the world as other than it is, the freedom encapsulated in the art of the novel is synonymous with imagination. Exercising this freedom—avoiding merely perpetuating conventional wisdoms and frameworks of meaning—is not easy: serious writers must dare to take artistic risks and turn their backs on lucrative book deals. "I think this is why ... some of us ... write long, complicated, challenging novels," DeLillo has noted in this regard: "As a way of stating our opposition to the requirements of the market."[61] For their part, serious readers must be ready to accept the challenge, venture out of their comfort zones, and, worst of all in today's gratification-driven consumer society, engage with literature not necessarily designed for entertainment purposes, at least not primarily. "The best reader is one who is most open to human possibility, to understanding the great range of plausibility in human actions."[62]

DeLillo's ability to subvert received knowledge, render necessity contingent, illuminate previously unsuspected constraints on individual autonomy, and thereby carve out space for alternative paths toward individual self-realization manifests itself in all his works and represents the main reason behind his Jerusalem Prize. It also earns him a firm place in the history of the novel: the great literary tradition born the moment Miguel de Cervantes, sitting at his writing desk in early seventeenth-century Spain, made Alonzo Quijano, a poor village gentleman, steal a copper shaving basin from a barber, proclaim it a helmet, put it on his head, and set off in pursuit of knightly glory as Don Quixote de la Mancha. Prior to this quest, "A magic curtain, woven of legends, hung before the world," for

> the world, when it rushes toward us at the moment of our birth, is already made-up, masked, *reinterpreted.* ... Cervantes sent Don Quixote journeying and tore through the curtain. The world opened before the knight errant in all the comical nakedness of its prose. ... [It] is by tearing through the curtain of pre-interpretation that Cervantes set the new art going; his destructive act echoes and extends to every novel worthy of the name; it is *the identifying sign of the art of the novel.*[63]

DeLillo's fiction is shot through and through with this identifying sign, and it is on account of its presence that his novels must be regarded as fundamentally political. This is not in the narrow partisan definition of the term, of course: DeLillo has gone on record repeatedly that his works do not express any particular ideology. "I don't have a political theory or doctrine that I'm espousing,"[64] he stated in 1988, when the publication of *Libra*, his fictional account of the Kennedy assassination, prompted accusations that he was a paranoid leftist; "I ... don't have any political program. Not only for my books, but for my life or for the life of my country."[65] But to conceive of politics in the broader sense of a struggle against hegemonic power and stasis, whether the status quo be dominated by the right or the left, is to realize that DeLillo's novels—any novels possessing the identifying sign of the art—are political automatically, by virtue of their oppositionality.

And when they adopt as their subject matter objects, events, and phenomena symbolizing not only American society but the world order, such as the Twin Towers of New York's World Trade Center in the case of *Falling Man*, the reach of this oppositionality expands accordingly. Such fiction is no longer merely political but international-political: a vehicle facilitating global, not just local or individual, emancipation.

The Hypnotic Power and All-Encompassing Reach of Late Capitalist Culture

Unfortunately, regardless of DeLillo's determination to resist American culture and its global aspirations, there is no escaping the integrative pressures of contemporary consumer society. In the context of advanced corporate capitalism with its mass media, entertainment, and advertising industries, whose networks and devices have spread across the entire planet and penetrated the innermost realms of private life, all the way into the bedrooms, the modernist ideal of a writer secluded from the established order is no longer an option. This severely circumscribes or even obliterates the emancipatory potential of the art of the novel. Explaining how DeLillo addresses the problem of fiction's limits in a world wholly dedicated to the commandment, "Consume or die,"[66] is the third and final prerequisite for understanding the political import of his novelistic work.

That industrial capitalism has fundamentally altered the social function of art is old news, of course. The Frankfurt School and its various offshoots have been mapping the transformation of aesthetic expression from a subversive force into a commodity sustaining the economic, political, and ideological goals of the modern state since the 1930s. Writing in the early years of the Third Reich with its spectacular Nuremberg rallies and propaganda films such as Riefenstahl's *Triumph des Willens*, Walter Benjamin argued that the same technological processes that liberated art from its original religious basis were responsible for reconstituting its cultic and ritual forms around new content, turning aesthetics into a vehicle of "covert control" exercised by the modern state in its evolution toward fascism.[67] The fate of modern art—from an instrument of liberation to an instrument of domination—was in this sense emblematic of the dialectic of the Enlightenment, during which emancipatory reason turned into totalitarian utopias and eventually Auschwitz. As Horkheimer and Adorno remarked in 1947, "mankind, instead of entering a truly human condition, is sinking into a new kind of barbarism. ... There is no longer any available form of linguistic expression which has not tended toward accommodation to dominant currents of thought."[68]

After World War II, Herbert Marcuse ascribed capitalism's ability to not only survive the cataclysm but boom in its wake precisely to bourgeois "affirmative culture."[69] Epitomized by life in postwar America, its capacity to conceal the antagonisms at the heart of modern consumer society and coopt even the most radical cultural elements threatening to undermine its hegemony was second to none. Adorno described this capacity using terms such as "tolerated negativity" and "negatively useful" and grew convinced that it had stifled the emancipatory impulse of Western modernity beyond recovery.[70] More recently, Fredric Jameson has echoed Adorno's pessimism with his view that the logic of late capitalism commodifies all aesthetic production, instantly turns every new art form into an advertising vehicle, and as such completely divests art of its ability to establish a critical-oppositional vantage on the existing social order.[71]

DeLillo and other novelists who persist in viewing their art as a form of protest experience the suffocating weight of consumer culture keenly and acutely. Its pressure is palpable in DeLillo's voice. "We [Americans] have a rich literature," he stated,

> But sometimes it's ... too ready to be neutralized, to be incorporated into the ambient noise. This is why we need ... the novelist who writes

against power, ... against the corporation or the state or the whole apparatus of assimilation. We're all one beat away from becoming elevator music.[72]

Jonathan Franzen made the same point, except more scathingly, when he exposed the world of American fiction writing as a cesspool swarming with novelists composing their works to film producer specifications and prostituting their literary talents to anyone willing to promise lucrative contracts, glossy magazine cover shoots, and limousine rides to celebrity parties.

> The institution of writing and reading serious novels is like a grand old Middle American city gutted and drained by superhighways. Ringing the depressed inner city of serious work are prosperous clonal suburbs of mass entertainments: techno and legal thrillers, novels of sex and vampires, of murder and mysticism. The last fifty years have seen a lot of white male flight to the suburbs and to the coastal power centers of television, journalism, and film. (...) American publishing is now a subsidiary of Hollywood, and the blockbuster novel is a mass-marketable commodity, a portable substitute for TV.[73]

The pervasiveness and irresistibility of the profit-driven industry practices, leaving dissident novelists embattled and with no place to hide, led Franzen to a particularly savage verdict: "The American writer today faces a totalitarianism analogous to the one with which two generations of Eastern bloc writers had to contend."[74] Interestingly, one of these Eastern bloc novelists, indeed perhaps the most accomplished of them, drew exactly the same comparison, and well before Franzen: Milan Kundera. "My experience with Communism," Kundera reflected on his life in Czechoslovakia from his subsequent French exile, "strikes me as an outstanding introduction to the modern world in general."[75] It prepared him well for Western liberal-capitalist society, which, as the next chapter will reveal, he found to be no less oppressive than the pre-1989 totalitarian system in his native country. The only difference was the source of the dictate: the Communist Party in the one, free market in the other.

DeLillo acknowledges the totalizing force of capitalist culture throughout all his novels and in several ways. One is his choice of subjects: his fiction is about rock music (*Great Jones Street*), high finance (*Cosmopolis*), college football (*End Zone*), waste generated by planned obsolescence (*Underworld*), mass media images and television as an "electronic form of packaging"[76] (*Americana, White Noise, Libra, Mao II*), and other typical symbols of American consumerism. Another is the eventual fates he gives his artist heroes: despite their best efforts to vanish into anonymity in order to forge authentic lives apart from the alienating effects of mass market society, indeed often precisely *because* of these efforts, they end up serving the impersonal logic of consumption, which repeatedly demonstrates its limitless capacity to integrate even the most reluctant oppositional elements. In *Mao II*, Bill Gray's three decades of hiding in upstate New York merely fuel his popularity, so that when he comes out of his self-imposed exile "[he] is at the height of his fame."[77] When he vanishes again en route to Beirut, this time permanently, the outcome is no different: Scott Martineau, his market-savvy assistant, decides to withhold his unpublished personal papers precisely so that Bill's public aura can grow even further, enabling Scott to forge a profitable writing career of his own as the exclusive apostle-exegete of the departed legend.[78] The message DeLillo drives home is clear: such is the nature of the glare of consumer culture that attempts to flee it only magnify it, making artists even more iconic and marketable, for nothing sells better than enigma and mystery. This message applies as much to Bill Gray as it did to real-life J. D. Salinger or, for that matter, as it does to DeLillo himself.

The ultimate symbol in DeLillo's fiction of the sway of consumerism over the American mind is the character of Steffie in *White Noise*: a young girl whose father catches her chanting "Toyota Celica" in sleep.[79] This image evokes hypnopaedia in Huxley's *Brave New World*, "The greatest moralizing and socializing force of all time," whereby infants in nurseries are standardized into perfectly obedient vestiges of the state by being subjected to repetitive whispers of easy-to-follow directives, "Till at last the child's mind *is* these suggestions, and the sum of these suggestions *is* the child's mind."[80] But unlike in Huxley's dystopian novel, where the hypnopaedia enslavement takes place at night, in Steffie's case it occurs in broad daylight—and is so thorough that it colonizes even her dreams. With this, the conquest of human imagination and cognitive space by the rampant forces of the market becomes complete.

Writing and Terror: Resisting Capitalist Culture

In such circumstances, the modernist conception of fiction as a tool of emancipatory critique undertaken by an avant-garde standing outside society ceases to make any sense, for there is no outside remaining: no island of refuge short of death. "In the West," DeLillo eventually conceded, "every writer is absorbed...."[81] This bleak concession all but erases the youthful optimism of his early career, when in the first sentence of his first public interview he defined his artistic ethos in terms of fostering individual autonomy from a Joycean position of "silence, exile, and cunning." In his mature novels, DeLillo "demonstrates the limits of silence, exile, and cunning."[82] Protagonists such as Bill Gray serve him to reveal "the inadequacies of ... [the] Joycean model of authorship by dramatizing how it does not elude the 'nets' of politics and celebrity, but actually makes [the author] more exploitable...."[83]

None of this means, however, that DeLillo has concluded that resistance to capitalist society is impossible. On the contrary, in eerily prescient passages written more than a decade before 9/11, he began associating emancipatory action with a new vanguard: terrorists. Speaking through characters such as Bill Gray, DeLillo suggested that these share a special connection—"a curious knot"—with writers in that they, too, "make raids on human consciousness. What writers used to do before [they] were all incorporated."[84] But only terrorists take bad citizenship to a level appropriate to late capitalist culture and its curtain of mass media images, whose ambient noise and glow only a spectacular bomb blast—not a hermit scribe working alone in a small room—is loud and bright enough to tear. "There's too much everything, more things and messages and meanings than we can use in ten thousand lifetimes," and in a society "reduced to blur and glut, terror is the only meaningful act."[85] The changing of the guards occurred with Beckett: "the last writer to shape the way we think and see. After him, the major work involves midair explosions and crumbled buildings."[86] This is what it takes to disrupt the status quo, prevent hegemonic stasis, and unlock potential for transformation. "Terror makes new future possible," as one of the terrorists boasts in *Mao II*; "We do history in the morning and change it after lunch."[87]

Where does this leave novelists such as DeLillo? In the dust, one may be tempted to surmise. After all, that is precisely what Bill Gray and another intellectual named George Haddad admit to each other in *Mao II*:

> Years ago I used to think it was possible for a novelist to alter the inner life of the culture. Now bomb-makers and gunmen have taken that territory. ... What terrorists gain, novelists lose. The degree to which they [terrorists] influence mass consciousness is the extent of our decline as shapers of sensibility and thought. The danger they represent equals our own failure to be dangerous.[88]

On at least one occasion, DeLillo stepped forth from behind his characters and made the point directly: "There once was a time when the writer had influence on how his contemporaries thought, how they saw the world, how they lived. ... Does literature still have this power today? No, I think it has lost this power."[89]

In light of such comments, it appears that DeLillo's ultimate answer to the question of the novelists' status in a thoroughly commercialized world is quite simple: irrelevance. By his mature phase, he seems to have entirely abandoned his initial modernist view of fiction as a form of emancipatory action. Although this action remains possible, it requires the methods of gunmen rather than writers. As one of the latter, DeLillo has thus resigned himself to social impotence symptomatic of the capture of art by markets in postmodern America. By implication, if his late novels such as *Falling Man* have any political thrust at all, it is strictly conservative: supporting rather than challenging the current order.

This conclusion, however, would be too pessimistic, much as its mirror image—DeLillo as a heroic outsider entirely oblivious to postmodernity's ability to absorb dissent—would be too naïve. DeLillo's awareness of the integrative power of consumer culture has not led him to discard the idea of fiction as a bastion of individual freedom. Even in *Mao II*, which probes the status of novelists in late capitalism most explicitly, the argument about the loss of their social and political influence to terrorists receives a number of powerful rebuttals. For one, the notion of terrorism as a phenomenon unassimilated by the logic of late capitalism eventually surfaces as a myth: DeLillo reveals that the Lebanese Maoists are just as dependent on market exchange and global mass media as everyone else is. They turn their Swiss hostage into a commodity, sell him to another fundamentalist faction "like a Rolex or a BMW,"[90] and further their cause by participating in a global publicity photo shoot.[91] But above all, DeLillo points out that only novelists resist Western consumer society without simultaneously striving to replace it with other forms of repressive order. Terrorist groups, by stark contrast, "are perfect little totalitarian states. (...) Even if I could see the need for absolute authority," Bill Gray states,

> my work would draw me away. The experience of my consciousness tells me how autocracy fails, how total control wrecks the spirit, how my characters deny my efforts to own them completely, how I need internal dissent, self-argument.... Do you know why I believe in the novel? It's a democratic shout.[92]

In the final verdict, therefore, DeLillo's mature conception of the novelist's place and function in society fits neither the modernist nor the postmodernist paradigm but rather combines both. It embodies modernism in that it continues to envision fiction as a vehicle of emancipatory critique, and it embodies postmodernism in that it formulates this critique immanently, by utilizing and participating in the web of cultural symbols it seeks to negate, thereby acknowledging their inescapability. In this mixed perspective, "Politically and aesthetically potent works ... issue not from a solitary island but cunningly from within the culture itself."[93] DeLillo is not the only American novelist to have arrived at this destination; Franzen is another. Among other things, it has led them to relax their reclusiveness and slowly start coming out of the woodwork and into the limelight: "belatedly following my books out of the house," as Franzen put it, "and even hitting a few parties."[94]

Whether this idea of authorship should be celebrated as a carefully negotiated compromise between the modernist and postmodernist views or decried as a sellout of the former to the latter is a good question. Die-hard proponents of the modernist ideal of literature's social and political obligations might very well reject out of hand any talk of fiction accommodating itself to the demands of today's celebrity-driven media culture. Even more moderate voices, those willing to concede that the ideal's survival depends on such accommodation, may recoil at the casual ease with which compromise often morphs into treason. Franzen illustrated this ease when he showed up on *Oprah*. For his part, DeLillo trotted out on the red carpet at the 2012 Cannes Film Festival in the company of such purveyors of fine acting as Robert Pattinson, the teen heartthrob who rose to worldwide fame as vampire Edward Cullen in the box office record-breaking *Twilight* movie series and, after wiping blood off his chin, portrayed Eric Packer in the Hollywood adaptation of DeLillo's *Cosmopolis*. Such appearances are difficult to interpret other than as acts of capitulation: to the film industry, publicists, sales figures, and coffers of cash. Considered in their light, DeLillo's and Franzen's suave literary ruminations against capitalism and consumerism surface as plain hypocrisy.

But there are reasons to have more faith, and DeLillo's *Falling Man* supplies one of them. In this novel, DeLillo exposes and appropriates the protocols of symbolic representation governing the flow of information in America's thoroughly medialized, spectacle-driven society, uses them to liberate the reader from the official 9/11 narrative propounded by the White House, and thereby reasserts the power of literature to shape mass consciousness against both the state and its terrorist foes. As such, *Falling Man* constitutes a prime example of historiographic metafiction: a type of novel whose "theoretical self-awareness of history and fiction as human constructs ... is made the grounds for its rethinking and reworking of the forms and contents of the past."[95] On the one hand, this species of literature is so self-reflective and auto-referential as to smack of narcissism: it explicitly draws attention to its status as fiction, thematizes its human production, and includes it among the events of the story being told.[96] It is "process made visible."[97] But at the same time the concern with the poetic activity is far from introverted: "not simply the case of novels metafictionally reveling in their own narrativity or fabulation."[98] Rather, it is applied to actual historical occurrences in order to denaturalize their received meanings and definitions.[99] In overall result, therefore, historiographic metafiction is both fundamentally contradictory in that "it always works *within* conventions in order to subvert them" and, by the very same token, "resolutely historical and inescapably political."[100]

Falling Man in Initial Reception: A Politically Tone-Deaf Trauma Novel?

Chronologically, *Falling Man* is not DeLillo's first post-9/11 novel; this attribute belongs to *Cosmopolis*, which came out in 2003 but does not deal with the attacks since its manuscript was nearly complete when they took place. Nor was it his first piece of prose about the event. Stunned by what had happened, DeLillo instantly suspended his novelistic work in order to pen a rare nonfiction feature for the December 2001 issue of *Harper's*.[101] His immediate response to 9/11 thus resembled that of many other prominent novelists including Salman Rushdie, Ian McEwan, Martin Amis, Jay McInerney, and

Zadie Smith. All of them saw their "so-called work in progress ... reduced, overnight, to a blue streak of autistic bubble"[102] and temporarily fled fiction for essays and journalism.

Soon, however, DeLillo resumed his craft. He commenced writing *Falling Man*, his first novel about 9/11, in November 2004. "I still know the precise date," he made the point of recalling later: "It was the day after the reelection of [President] George W. Bush."[103] The inspiration for the book came to him suddenly in the form of a powerful mental image: a man walking through the streets of Manhattan after the attacks covered in dust and ashes and carrying someone else's briefcase. To his surprise, when DeLillo started researching 9/11 in preparation for composing the manuscript, the image cropped up in many newspapers as part of the actual historical record. He gave the anonymous businessman a name and identity—Keith Neudecker, a real estate lawyer employed at the World Trade Center—and turned him into the main character of *Falling Man*.

The novel is written in the third person and illuminates the intersecting lives of several other figures: Lianne, Keith's estranged wife; Nina Bartos, Lianne's mother and a retired art historian; Martin Ridnour, a German-born international art dealer and Nina's lover; and Hammad, one of the plane hijackers. The narrative is broken up and scattered, full of sudden gaps and leaps between characters, places, and situations, but it opens and ends at the same site and in the same moment: the apocalypse at Ground Zero minutes after the aircraft have struck. This moment is focalized through Keith:

> It was not a street anymore but a world, a time and space of falling ash and near night. (...) They came out onto the street, looking back, both towers burning, and soon they heard a high drumming rumble and saw smoke rolling down from the top of one tower, billowing out and down, methodically, floor to floor, and the tower falling, the south tower diving into the smoke.... The windblast sent people to the ground. (...) He was walking north through rubble and mud and there were people running past holding towels to their faces or jackets over their heads. (...) The roar was still in the air, the buckling rumble of the fall. This was the world now. (...) He wore a suit and carried a briefcase. There was glass in his hair and face, marbled bolls of blood and light.[104]

Within the space bookended by this catastrophic image of suffering, loss, and destruction, one of the novel's many plot lines follows Keith's attempts to cope with the event. He tries to process the dreadful experience in a number of ways, such as by returning to Lianne and their son Justin, but his efforts ultimately prove fruitless and he winds up losing himself in endless sessions of high-stakes poker. What prevents his healing is a particularly harrowing memory: the sight of people leaping to their deaths from the windows atop the burning towers. As Keith stumbles out of the World Trade Center at the beginning of the novel,

> There was something else then, outside all this, not belonging to this,
> aloft. He watched it coming down. A shirt came down out of the high
> smoke, a shirt lifted and drifting in the scant light and then falling
> again, down toward the river.[105]

This occurrence is so intolerably painful that Keith's mind rejects it, choosing to remember only a garment instead of a fellow human being, and his
inability to come to terms with it persists throughout the book right up to
the final sentences, which find Keith exactly where he was at the beginning:
watching "a shirt come down out of the sky. He walked and saw it fall, arms
waving like nothing in this life."[106] The falling man remains unassimilated
and unassimilable: a site of terror beyond the reach of comprehension, language, and representation.

Literary critics responded in a peculiar fashion. DeLillo's attention to
the inner lives of a few individuals such as Keith, coupled with the novel's
nonlinear structure full of disorienting temporal shifts, silences, repetition,
and chaotic subject positioning, engendered the impression that *Falling
Man* was no more than a typical "psychic trauma novel that reproduces
fragmented traumatic memory and ... follows many of the conventions of
the genre."[107] Based on this reading, many reviewers attacked DeLillo for
entirely missing—or even deliberately obscuring—the larger cultural and
political significance of 9/11. Richard Gray stated that DeLillo's concerns
with domesticity and familiality "dissolve public crisis in the comforts of
the personal" and that *Falling Man* "adds next to nothing to our understanding of the trauma at the heart of the action. In fact, it evades that
trauma...."[108] Michiko Kakutani similarly rejected the character of Keith
Neudecker as "a pathetic, adolescent-minded creature ... playing stupid
card games in the Nevada desert," excoriated DeLillo for failing to convey
either "the zeitgeist in which 9/11 occurred or the shell-shocked world it left
in its wake," and dismissed *Falling Man* as "a terrible disappointment."[109]
Perhaps most devastatingly, Sven Cvek argued that insofar as *Falling Man*
deals in private relationships and individual pathologies instead of global
socioeconomic forces and issues, it effectively depoliticizes the attacks and
conceals more than it reveals.[110] "We need a fiction of international relations and extraterritorial citizenship," but American 9/11 literature including *Falling Man* offers no such thing, manifesting an abysmal "failure of the
imagination."[111]

It is undeniable, of course, that *Falling Man* functions as trauma therapy:
an attempt to come to grips with the shock of 9/11. After all, this was precisely one of the goals articulated by DeLillo in his initial public reaction to
the event: "the world narrative belongs to terrorists (...), and it is left to us
to create the counter-narrative."[112] In his *Harper's* piece he confessed that
"When the second tower fell, my heart fell with it," and he revealed the full
extent of his own psychological injury by adding that the collapse of the

buildings "was so vast and terrible that it was outside imagining even as it happened" and that "the massive spectacle ... continues to seem unmanageable, too powerful a thing to set into our frame of practiced response."[113] The terrorists left both a gaping hole in New York City's skyline and "a void in one's soul."[114] In these circumstances, one of the writer's tasks was "to understand what this day has done to us" and "to give memory, tenderness, and meaning to all that howling space."[115] Several years later, DeLillo set out to do just that in *Falling Man*: try to humanize the unspeakable terror of 9/11 by telling a story about it. Given his highly tactile, multisensory experience of the writing process, the novel may be regarded as an exercise not only in mental healing but also in physical reconstruction: a response to both emotional and urban trauma. "I felt like an architect designing a building,"[116] DeLillo recounted his work on *Falling Man*.

But in addition to trauma therapy, *Falling Man* is and does a lot more, as Gray and Kakutani would have noticed had they borne in mind DeLillo's artistic ethics, his minute attention to language as the fundamental fabric of reality, his modernist ideal of fiction as a vehicle of emancipation engaged in an insurgency against the all-encompassing logic of postmodern mass media culture, and his formulation of the relationship between literature and terror. Read in the context of these broader trends guiding DeLillo's novelistic career, *Falling Man* instantly blossoms from a tone-deaf book about a handful of damaged individuals into exactly what many of its initial critics were calling for: fiction with its finger on the pulse of contemporary international relations, a piece of literature rendering 9/11 in terms of larger socioeconomic forces and provocatively casting the event as an act of resistance to the global hegemony of Western liberalism. The first step in this project, a deconstruction exposing 9/11 as a seeming stable ontological effect of dynamic discursive performances, is hidden, much like DeLillo himself, in plain sight: right on the cover of *Falling Man*, in its very title.

Reading the Title: *Falling Man* as a Meditation on the Poetics of Political Reality

Deceptively simple, this title is in fact a gateway to a complex reflection about the constitutive role of poetics and symbolic representation in figuring forth political reality. Contrary to what one might expect, the two words do not refer to the 9/11 jumpers at the World Trade Center, at least not directly, but rather to the character of David Janiak: a fictional street artist who in the story stuns New York City inhabitants by unexpectedly appearing suspended from a thin wire around various places in Manhattan in the weeks following the attacks. Lianne first encounters him at Grand Central Station, where she finds him "upside down, wearing a suit, a tie and dress shoes."[117] When she accidentally stumbles upon him a second time and again observes the "jolt, the sort of midair impact and bounce, the re-coil, and now the stillness, arms at his sides, one leg bent at the knee,"[118] the sight engenders a powerful recollection in her mind:

> It hit her hard when she first saw it, the day after, in the newspaper. The man headlong, the towers behind him. The mass of the towers filled the frame of the picture. The man falling, the towers contiguous ... behind him. The enormous soaring lines, the vertical column stripes. The man with blood on his shirt, ... or burn marks, and the effects of the columns behind him, the composition, ... darker stripes for the nearer tower, the north, lighter for the other, and the mass, the immensity of it, and the man set almost precisely between rows of darker and lighter stripes. Headlong, free fall, ... and this picture burned a hole in her mind and heart, dear God, he was a falling angel, and his beauty was horrific.[119]

DeLillo does not identify the newspaper image in further detail anywhere in the novel, but the description leaves no doubt about what he has in mind, Janiak reenacts, and Lianne sees in Janiak's stylized pose: the notorious picture of one of the World Trade Center jumpers taken by Associated Press photographer Richard Drew near the North Tower at 9:41:15 a.m. EST on September 11, 2001. It appeared on page A7 of the *New York Times* and in dozens of other dailies worldwide the next morning, immediately sparked a fierce public outcry across the United States, and was promptly withdrawn from coverage by all domestic media outlets.

Even a brief inquiry into the referential basis of the title of DeLillo's novel thus yields a major insight: *Falling Man* is a representation of a representation of a representation of 9/11. DeLillo portrays Janiak's performance, which acts out Drew's photograph, which in turn depicts a particular occurrence that took place at Ground Zero during the attacks. Whatever else it does in its capacity as a trauma novel, in other words, *Falling Man* is also and above all a metafictional meditation on the symbolic nature of postmodern reality, in which images of events and objects proliferate exponentially, displace them, and become events and objects in their own right, gradually compressing life into an ever-smaller echo chamber. In this kind of reality, the distinction between fact and fiction evaporates: all is artifice generated through mimetic processes, especially print and visual media, which lie at the heart of post-modern life. *Falling Man* foregrounds their constitutive role specifically with respect to 9/11. These processes are not incidental to the novel but stand on a par with its protagonists as part and parcel of the story. Indeed, personified by Janiak, they *are* one of the protagonists.

The force of DeLillo's metafictional commentary on postmodern simula-cra doubles when one notices that underneath the thick sediment of alien-ated reproductions, which include the novel itself, there is no original. The falling man captured in Drew's photograph is absent. This is not only for the obvious reason that he had physically perished in the attacks, leaving behind only his visual, theatrical, and literary images, but also because to this day he has not been identified, meaning that these images—chronologically starting with Drew's photograph—have no indexical value. There has been no shortage of efforts to ascertain the jumper's name. In perhaps the most famous example, investigative journalist Tom Junod approached the task with the single-mindedness of a bomb dog sniffing for clues even in awkward, morally questionable places.[120] Along the way, he uncovered a massive amount of suppressed or little-known information: that the total number of jumpers most likely exceeded two hundred, that some tried parachuting using drapes and tablecloths, that at least one of them struck and instantly killed a firefighter on the ground, that the New York Medical Examiner's Office categorically denied that anyone actually jumped (insisting instead that all were blown out), and that the man in question might be Jonathan Briley, an employee at the Windows on the World restaurant atop the North Tower. But in the final analysis Junod had to concede that although

> Briley might be the Falling Man (...) the only certainty we have is the certainty we had at the start: ... Richard Drew took a picture of a man falling through the sky—falling through time as well as through space. The picture went all around the world, and then disappeared, as if we willed it away. One of the most famous photographs in human history became an unmarked grave, and the man buried inside its frame—the Falling Man—became the Unknown Soldier in a war whose end we have not yet seen. Richard Drew's photograph is all we know of him.[121]

Even if the jumper's identity were known, it would be deeply problematic to characterize Drew's image as a direct eyewitness record of an event *wie es eigentlich geschehen ist*. Strictly speaking, Drew never witnessed the original occurrence with his own eyes. His equipment got in the way:

> Due to the motion blur of the towers, the artificial proximity attributed to the 200 mm zoom lens, and the closure of the shutter that obfuscates the image at the very moment of exposure, Drew could not see the moment as it flit past.[122]

The event was well beyond his or anyone else's sensory capacities: humanly invisible. It emerged to him only subsequently, after he had returned to the AP headquarters later that morning and inserted his digital camera disk with material acquired at Ground Zero—between ten and fifteen photo sequences of up to twelve frames each—into his laptop. This is when the perfectly inverted figure suspended in front of the Twin Towers appeared for the first time, thanks entirely to Drew's professional-grade camera, above all its high-speed continuous frame-advance mechanism capable of spreading action lasting only a fraction of a second over half a dozen shots or more: a feat no human eye or brain can achieve.

Advanced visual imaging technology thus not only separated Drew from the event but literally produced it. If his famous photograph—and all subsequent reproductions based on it, whether visual, stage, or prosaic—can be said to represent historical reality at all, then only in the Aristotelian definition of *mimēsis* as a process of active fabrication, not in the Platonic notion of passive copying. The image's journey from Drew's laptop to the AP server and into the pages of the *New York Times*, where it came to embody the reality of 9/11 for millions of viewers across America and around the world, further underscores the inventive dimension of the mimetic process: Drew *chose* the photo from among all the others he had taken, and he did so on the basis of aesthetic criteria. "That picture," he recalled later, "just jumped off the screen because of its verticality and symmetry."[123]

Falling Man, then, is and deals in representations *only*, with no ultimate referent. These do not imitate some preestablished historical field but precede it and constitute it for the audience. DeLillo suggests that aesthetic depictions of the falling man as the proxy for 9/11—his novel, Janiak's street performance, Drew's photo—are all there is. In this vein, "the novel forces us to acknowledge the entropic nature of our postmodern condition."[124] It may be read as a culmination of DeLillo's argument, running like a silver thread through all his prior work, about the penetrative power and reach of late capitalist media culture, where photographic images saturate everyone's phenomenal field to the point of occluding what they depict, in effect becoming new reality. The blue halo of this culture does not leave even a novelist of DeLillo's critical-oppositional acumen any other option than to weave his prose out of spectacular visuals exemplified by Drew's picture. Artistic representations of 9/11 in this sense presuppose the totalizing mass media culture and are impossible without it.

The same applies to 9/11 itself. Declared on its first anniversary "the most documented event in human history,"[125] it became real precisely to the extent that it lent itself to domestic and international media coverage, which is why al-Qaeda targeted architectural landmarks designed for the camera lens to begin with: the Twin Towers, world's tallest buildings at the time of their completion and the icons stamped on just about every postcard and travel guide of America from the early 1970s right until September 11, 2001. This was the true genius of Osama bin Laden and Khalid Sheikh Mohammed: discerning that in the context of the West's thoroughly medialized experience of reality the impact of the attacks depended primarily on their cinematic shock value, not their human and material toll. The audience responded as expected: among the many objects damaged or destroyed, including the Pentagon or the wreckage of Flight 93 in rural Pennsylvania, the collapse of the World Trade Center almost completely overshadowed the rest on newspaper and magazine covers, for in public consciousness the structure not only symbolized American society, in all its narcissistic global aspirations, but *was* this society. The Twin Towers expressed "technology's irresistible will to realize in solid form whatever becomes theoretically allowable," and technology, DeLillo acknowledged on behalf of his nation, is our fate, our truth. It is what we mean when we call ourselves the only superpower on the planet. ... We don't have to depend on God or the prophets or other astonishments. We are the astonishment. The miracle is what we ourselves produce....[126]

In staging and directing the awesome movie thriller that was the destruction of the Twin Towers, al-Qaeda's operatives pitted the cultural logic of American capitalism against itself to decisively alter the inner life of post-Cold War American society. They thereby manifested their role as radical shapers of consciousness: a role DeLillo had ascribed to Middle Eastern terrorists already a decade prior in *Mao II*, when his fellow citizens were celebrating the triumph of American liberalism as the culmination of humankind's ideological evolution and nobody had yet heard of Osama bin Laden.

Countering the Hegemonic 9/11 Discourse

DeLillo's self-reflective foregrounding of the central role of symbolic representations in the constitution of 9/11 is not the end of his engagement with the event in *Falling Man* but only the beginning. It merely prefaces his main goal: to counter the hegemonic 9/11 discourse backed by state power with different narratives of what transpired that morning.

Today 9/11 carries so many burdens—of interpretation, of sentimentality, of politics, of war—that sometimes it's hard to find the rubble of the actual event beneath the layers of edifice we've built on top of it. ... In [*Falling Man*] DeLillo shoves us back into the day itself....[127]

In its metafictional aspect, the novel illuminates the textual fabric of this edifice and reveals that, like the human world at large, 9/11 is glued out of words. Once this has been accomplished, it is time to perform the principal—historiographic—task: melt the glue, rearrange the words in new constellations, ones based on alternative "synoptic judgment" (Mink), "narrative substance" (Ankersmit), or "tropological style" (White), and in this manner rework the past as part of a practical effort to stimulate sociopolitical change in the present.

The dominant interpretation of 9/11 was disproportionately shaped by those in power at the time: above all the neoconservative Republican administration under the executive leadership of President George W. Bush and Vice President Dick Cheney. Its members immediately set out to "fix the exact nature and meaning of the events,"[128] weaving them into an official discourse which structured the country's subsequent linguistic, cognitive, and policy responses. This discourse reduced the universe of the event's representations to roughly five interconnected stories: 9/11 as trauma, as a world-changing event, as an act of terrorism, as an act of war, and as an act of evil.[129] The criterion guiding the narrativization was political serviceability:

each of the constructions "should be seen as performative rather than con-stative" in that its truthfulness and seriousness were determined by "the purpose of justifying neoconservative policies articulated both within and without the White House."[130] Between 2001 and 2003 alone, Bush used the term "evil" in at least three hundred and nineteen speeches, including as part of the notorious "Axis of Evil" catchphrase introduced during his first State of the Union address on January 29, 2002.[131] The political reality fab-ricated out of this language was utterly dark and dangerous: full of insidious mortal enemies lurking at America everywhere, both within and without its borders, preparing to strike it again. In this ominous world of permanent national emergency, the country's survival required radical measures, many of them extralegal. They included invasions of Iraq and Afghanistan, mas-sive defense spending, indefinite detention of terrorist suspects without trial, and the use of torture, rendition, and domestic surveillance, to name a few. The hegemonic 9/11 discourse in this sense served as a rhetorical warrant authorizing egregious breaches of the US Constitution and Bill of Rights, of principles of sound national economic stewardship and fiscal responsibility, and of international law, norms, and trust.

Although there are hardly any traces of this discourse in *Falling Man*, it is indisputably DeLillo's chief target: the magic curtain of official legends and pre-interpretation he wants to tear through. On the one hand, as all his other works, this novel, too, refuses to propound any partisan ideology or worldview; to this extent it may be regarded as non- or apolitical. But on the other hand, again as the rest of his fiction, *Falling Man* nonetheless mani-fests a trenchant act of bad citizenship flowing from DeLillo's lifelong re-solve to write against the state: a resolve at the heart of his beliefs about the novelist's proper role in society. In a rare interview accompanying the nov-el's release, DeLillo conveyed his disenchantment with post-9/11 American society, politics, and statecraft quite frankly:

> We find ourselves in a strange situation. After 9/11, Americans stood behind their government, there were no protests against the operation in Afghanistan, and at first also no criticism of the Iraq war. And even today, although opinion polls have tipped over, one senses no public attitude of protest even remotely reminiscent of the Vietnam era. As one of the characters in *Falling Man* expresses it: I don't know America anymore. I feel this way too.[132]

That DeLillo commenced writing the novel the day after Bush's presiden-tial reelection was no coincidence but an expression of fierce indignation. So was another important new beginning in DeLillo's life around this time: his decision to register as a voter.[133] The events of 9/11 and their appropriation by the White House for the purposes of assaulting American citizens and foreign nations greatly alarmed him and intensified his political involve-ment. For someone equating opposition to the state with fiction writing, this entailed above all taking to the typewriter.

Falling Man amply demonstrates that DeLillo knows how to handle his weapon of choice. Throughout the book, he subjects the official 9/11 discourse to small incisive shocks, which, much like machine gunfire on the battlefield, come out of the novel's woodwork at unexpected moments and punch out gaping holes revealing radically different representations of the event. Witness the nameless medic who briefly appears on the scene to remove glass from Keith's face after the attacks. "Where there are suicide bombings," he quips while working with tweezers,

> the survivors, the people nearby who are injured, sometimes, months later, they develop bumps, for lack of a better term, and it turns out this is caused by small fragments, tiny fragments of the suicide bomber's body. The bomber is blown to bits, literally bits and pieces, and fragments of flesh and bone come flying outward with such force and velocity that they get wedged, they get trapped in the body of anyone who's in striking range. ... They call this organic shrapnel.[134]

This small talk is in fact a big invitation: to imagine 9/11 at the molecular scale, as a story of microscopic physical and chemical objects and processes. At this level there are no Twin Towers, jetliners, or human beings, let alone globalization, capitalism, inequality, religious fundamentalism, or transnational terrorism, still less victimhood and retribution, right and wrong. There are only tiny particles of matter behaving according to impersonal forces. Compared to the official 9/11 discourse, such a representation is no less factual for being strange and unfamiliar. Gesturing at it helps *Falling Man* flesh out the aesthetic dimension of historical truth, strip the White House depiction of 9/11 of its appearance of necessity, reveal its contrived quality, and render it but one of the event's many potential narratives.

The domain of these narratives is in principle boundless: the cognitive space DeLillo unlocks through his metafictional deconstruction of 9/11 combined with such piercing suggestions of the event's other histories has no limits. Once the reader's mind is released into it, there is no stopping it from coming up with new readings of its own, ones beyond those offered either by the Bush cabinet or by *Falling Man*. An example might be a purely arithmetic interpretation where $9/11 = 0.81$. Their respective truths are not logical and mutually exclusive but tropological and concurrent: each valid within its own poetic frame of reference. In this manner, the novel engenders the awareness that the history of 9/11 is actively produced, not discovered, and resides in the sphere of ethics and rhetoric: the art and politics of persuasion through language.

Bin Laden and Bill Lawton: Twin Brothers Meet at Twin Towers

Where in the tropics of 9/11 historiography stands DeLillo himself? Given that *Falling Man* issues from a spirit of opposition to the state, it may be tempting to assume that his sympathies therefore reside with the terrorists.

But jumping to such easy conclusions would merely demonstrate the lingering sway of the 9/11 narrative articulated by the Bush administration, which simplified the world into a Manichean battleground between good and evil and asserted that "Either you are with us, or you are with the terrorists,"[135] insinuating that whoever did not support the neoconservative White House automatically belonged among America's lethal foes.

DeLillo's position is much subtler. It expresses the same ethos staked out by his fictional alter ego, novelist Bill Gray, in *Mao II*: counterhegemonic dissent aligned with terrorists by virtue of resisting the same adversary, America's totalizing capitalist culture, yet irreconcilably separated from them insofar as their ideological vision is no less repressive. Indeed, in *Falling Man* DeLillo intimates that Islamic fundamentalism, personified by bin Laden, constitutes not so much an antithesis to American consumerism, personified by a made-up character named Bill Lawton, as its twin. This is the ultimate and most subversive message embedded in DeLillo's 9/11 writings: that behind the spectacular mass media images of their violent collision over Lower Manhattan, the transnational forces of radical jihad and global capitalism hold hands and possess common features. Chief among them is the obliteration of personal autonomy, judgment, empathy, and responsibility by religious orthodoxy in the one case and by secular neoliberal dogma in the other. Neither system is acceptable to DeLillo, who negates both by revealing just how much each resembles the other.

DeLillo distances himself from al-Qaeda's worldview both in the *Harper's* essay and in *Falling Man*. The organization "ha[s] gone beyond the bounds of passionate payback" and encapsulates a return "to medieval expedience, to the old slow furies of cutthroat religion."[136] He rejects this worldview because it is, like all comprehensive accounts of existence, subtractive and anti-humanist: blind to the diversity, contingency, and ambiguity of individual lives.

> Plots reduce the world. (...) Does the sight of a woman pushing a stroller soften the [terrorist] to her humanity and vulnerability, and her child's as well, and all the people he is here to kill? This is the edge, that he does not see her. ... [T]here is no defenseless human at the end of his gaze.[137]

When Hammad, one of the al-Qaeda operatives readying themselves for the attacks in *Falling Man*, briefly manages to stretch that gaze in a rare moment of reflection, the glimpse of fellow human beings among his targets immediately subjects him to troubling doubts: "does a man have to kill himself in order to accomplish something in the world?" he asks Amir, leader of his Florida-based sleeper cell, and "What about the lives of the others he takes with him?"[138] But his misgivings promptly subside once Amir reminds him of the fundamentalist teachings, from whose perspective "there are no others. The others exist only to the degree that they fill the role we have designed for them."[139] Through this exchange, DeLillo simultaneously humanizes Hammad against the stereotypical demonization of Islamic fighters in the official 9/11 discourse and shows the devastating consequences of Hammad's immersion in a similarly reductive doctrine for his own ability to think independently and relate to other human beings. This doctrine "closed the world to the slenderest line of sight, where everything converges to a point."[140]

DeLillo's attitude toward capitalist globalization spearheaded by the United States is just as critical. The relentless pressure of the neoliberal world economy on foreign cultures is every bit as aggressive as global jihad. "The sense of disarticulation we hear in the term 'Us and Them' has never been so striking, at either end,"[141] DeLillo notes the polarization of the relationship between American society and the Arab Muslim world, but the distinction is false. It is not the case that 9/11 signifies an encounter between sane Western democratic values on the one hand and "a virus"[142] of misguided zealotry on the other, as Nina condescendingly dismisses Islamic extremism in *Falling Man*; such a framing, typical of the Bush administration, betrays a stunning failure of introspection. It leaves out the long history of injustice, exploitation, and violence perpetrated by the United States abroad and says nothing "about lost lands, failed states, foreign intervention, money, empire, oil, the narcissistic heart of the West."[143] DeLillo restores this unsavory underbelly of American capitalism to public awareness. Although the terrorists

> use the language of religion, ... this is not what drives them. (...) Forget God. These are matters of history. This is politics and economics. (...) One side has the capital, the labor, the technology, the armies, the agencies, the cities, the laws, the police and the prisons. The other side has a few men willing to die. (...) They strike a blow to this country's dominance ... to show how a great power can be vulnerable. A power that interferes, that occupies.[144]

DeLillo thus alerts his fellow American citizens that the "bitterness, distrust, and rancor" lashing out at them from the Arab Muslim world are not gratuitous but provoked by "the thrust of our technology," "the blunt force of our foreign policy," and the unstoppable "power of American culture to penetrate every wall, home, life, and mind."[145] Instead of chalking up the 9/11 attacks to simple religious fanaticism, they must be seen as carefully calibrated political acts expressing a strategy of resistance to America's global hegemony. Hammad, Amir, and their al-Qaeda comrades take a stand against "being crowded out by other cultures, other futures, the all-enfolding will of capital markets and foreign policies."[146] Unlike the collapse of the World Trade Center, this crowding out has unfolded in a gradual and diffuse fashion, over several decades, and as such does not lend itself to photography (which erases time and context); therefore, it may be invisible and incomprehensible to the photographic consciousness of postmodern American society. But this does not make its terror any less real than the terror of Islamic fundamentalism. In this sense, "DeLillo contrasts al-Qaeda with America; medieval vengeance with advanced technology; [and] a brotherhood of martyrs with global markets," but in doing this "he deconstructs the very dichotomies others reinforce."[147]

The critique of American capitalism in *Falling Man* culminates when DeLillo tacitly charges the United States with fascism. This accusation is carefully concealed in the character of Martin Ridnour and emerges only in extranovelistic context. Martin's real name, as the plot reveals, is Ernst Hechinger, and he has a secret history of left-wing radicalism: in the 1960s he was a member of Kommune One, a collective "demonstrating against the [West] German state, the fascist state,"[148] and also may have been involved with the Red Brigades in Italy. Nina, his lover, tells her daughter Lianne about a curious item in his Berlin apartment: "A wanted poster. German terrorists of the early seventies. Nineteen names and faces. ... Wanted for murder, bombings, bank robberies."[149] She then adds that in Martin's view the 9/11 hijackers share an important link with the men and women in the poster: "He thinks ... these jihadists ... have something in common with the radicals of the sixties and seventies. He thinks they're all part of the same classical pattern."[150]

As with Richard Drew's iconic photograph of the World Trade Center jumper, which is central to *Falling Man* but anonymous throughout the novel, DeLillo never specifies the poster directly, but in this case, too, its identity can be established unequivocally from the abundant clues: it is the West German police leaflet depicting members of the Red Army Faction (RAF). More commonly known as the Baader-Meinhof Group, this urban guerrilla organization appeared in the Federal Republic in 1970 as a militant wing of the country's student protest movement, whose milder offshoots also included Kommune One. It took up armed struggle against the West German state and staged violent kidnappings and assassinations of its bureaucratic and corporate elites, many of whom were former Nazi Party members.[151] The government dealt with the protest movement in an increasingly heavy-handed fashion: by arresting its leaders and supporters, barring them from employment, and amending the country's *Grundgesetz* (Basic Law) with broad peacetime emergency provisions strengthening law enforcement, telecommunications surveillance, and executive power—all in the name of national security. When Ulrike Meinhof was found hanged in her jail cell in 1976 and Andreas Baader, Gudrun Ensslin, and Jan-Carl Raspe, her fellow RAF members and Stammheim prison inmates, met the same fate a year later, with all three discovered dead on the morning of October 18, 1977, the highly dubious circumstances of their perishing raised instant and lasting suspicions that their suicides were no suicides but extralegal executions carried out by the authorities. The Federal Republic appeared to have morphed into what it was trying to extirpate: a terrorist entity.

Against the background of this historical information, the silent implication of Martin's argument surfaces in full: by analogizing al-Qaeda to
the Baader-Meinhof Group, he simultaneously draws a link between contemporary American democracy and the reactionary West German state,
highlighting how the Bush cabinet's response to 9/11—whether the Patriot
Act, concentration of executive power, or systematic resort to extrajudicial
measures including rendition and torture—resembles the quasi-fascist emergency policies of the Federal Republic in the 1960s and 1970s. "The parallels
between German and American state repression are seldom explicit ... in
Falling Man ... but they are never far from mind."[152] Appropriately for a
writer fully alert to the essential role of visuals in American society today,
DeLillo cues his readers into these parallels through a skillful manipulation of photographic images: Martin's RAF wanted poster circulated by
the West German police in the early 1970s, on the one hand, and the 9/11
hijackers list released by the FBI a few days after the World Trade Center
attacks, on the other. Their layout is virtually identical and depicts exactly
the same number of faces, which DeLillo's characters repeat several times,
conspicuously, for effect: "Nineteen."[153]

The most direct equation of American capitalism with Islamic fundamentalism in *Falling Man* involves the picture of Osama bin Laden. Next
to Drew's *New York Times* photograph and the Baader-Meinhof poster,
this is a third key image operationalized by DeLillo in his metafictional
historiographic effort to subvert what he reluctantly partakes in: America's
commercial mass media culture as an organ of state power and official
9/11 propaganda. In television and newspaper coverage of the attacks, bin
Laden's image gradually displaced all others, including those of the Twin
Towers and the hijackers; his bearded face came to personify the evil whose
eradication supplied the Bush administration with the moral foundation for
America's "War on Terror." It is no surprise, then, to encounter the al-Qaeda
leader in *Falling Man*. But DeLillo introduces him with a crucial twist: in
disguise, filtered through the minds of the novel's few children characters,
specifically Keith and Lianne's nine-year-old son Justin and his two best
friends, Robert and Katie. Like everyone else, the three preadolescents see
and hear about bin Laden daily following the attacks, but because his foreign
name is too difficult for them to spell correctly, it registers in their imagination—
and is initially presented to the novel's unsuspecting audience—in its simpler
English phonetic equivalent: "Bill Lawton." Lianne is at a complete loss trying
to figure out who this man might be, but Keith eventually grasps his true identity, explains it to her, and thereby also unveils it to the audience:

> Together [the children] developed the myth of Bill Lawton. ... Robert
> thought, from television or school or somewhere, that he was hearing
> a certain name. ... He was hearing Bill Lawton. They were saying bin
> Laden. ... In other words he never adjusted his original sense of what
> he was hearing.[154]

Astonished by the revelation, Lianne experiences a vague sense of "some important meaning ... located in the soundings of the boy's small error."[155]

Just what this "important meaning" might be, neither Lianne nor any other of DeLillo's characters ever clarifies in the pages of *Falling Man*. But outside the text, from the perspective of literary theory, "the soundings of the boy's small error" constitute a classic example of metonomasia: a poetic technique involving transposition of proper names to illuminate obscured aspects of their bearers' identities. In their default significations, "bin Laden" stands for religious fanaticism, aggression, lawlessness, terror, and mass murder arriving from faraway lands, whereas "Bill Lawton"—a name distinct only by its ordinariness—evokes America's small-town everyman: a local used car dealer, drive-thru bank teller, middle school teacher, or perhaps Elks Lodge member, at any rate a honest, tolerant, hardworking, peace-loving, and law-abiding fellow citizen. In metonomasia, however, "the familiar name is transposed on the mass murderer ... [and] in return the attributes of the mass murderer are transposed on one very much like us [Americans]."[156]

One way to interpret the figure of Bill Lawton in *Falling Man*, then, is along the lines of Hannah Arendt's thesis about the banality of evil: there is a terrorist in every ordinary American. Whether they sell used Buicks or teach children algebra, most US citizens live and work at a considerable remove from the point where the cudgel of American foreign policy, corporate interests, and consumer culture strikes and crushes hapless foreign peoples, and they may harbor no feelings good or ill toward them. But they are nonetheless complicit, if only by virtue of mindlessly accepting and periodically regurgitating all the myriad clichés—about America's exceptional destiny in the world, the universal appeal of her founding ideals, the righteousness of private property and free markets, and so on—which are at once essential to their proud patriotic identity and marvelously adept at disguising even the most blatant acts of international aggression as campaigns of rescue and liberation. In this vein, *Falling Man* "subtly reveals as much about the presumptuousness of American culture as ... about the nefariousness of the hijackers' suicidal plot" and forces the audience to acknowledge that "the American Bill Lawton, and those who toil in his name, have likewise visited death and destruction on third-world cultures with impunity."[157]

Historiographic Metafiction and the Politics of Narrating 9/11

What transpired in New York City on September 11, 2001, is widely regarded as a turning point in contemporary American society, politics, foreign relations, and international affairs at large. But on critical reflection facilitated by Don DeLillo's novelistic work, this historical event, much like the international arena or the figure of E. H. Carr in the pantheon of legendary international relations theorists discussed in preceding chapters, has no inherent meaning. It can be represented in innumerable ways, all of which involve some nonempirical content in that they express strategic choices about which facts to emphasize, which to leave out, and how to trope the former. "Stories are told or written, not found," to recall Hayden White's narrativist thesis, whose kernels go all the way back to Aristotle's *Poetics*, and as such "All stories are fictions."[158] The (hi)story of 9/11 is no exception.

Insofar as one of the event's narrative configurations has managed to overshadow others and achieve the appearance of pure factuality, this is because the state and commercial mass media successfully repressed and concealed the nonempirical—poetic, moral, and political—dimension of the 9/11 discourse. By restoring this element, DeLillo's works negate and undermine this campaign and serve as an emancipatory counter to it.

> Representations are apparatuses of capture that assign sense to an event in accordance with the type of forces that produce these representations. Consequently ... the critical task is to render visible the acts of seeing that generate specific representations. (...) [DeLillo's] most significant intervention in the post-9/11 discourse ... is that present-day attempts to image a (traumatic) event's sense cannot operate exclusively at the level of the event's content ... without attending to the *rhetorical* mode of presentation, the ethical how.[159]

In *Falling Man*, a textbook example of historiographic metafiction, the process of historical representation takes center stage as an integral part of the story proper. Whether through the character of David Janiak reenacting the World Trade Center jumpers, references to photographic images such as Richard Drew's "Falling Man," or sketches of radically different yet equally factual ways of seeing 9/11 such as at the molecular scale, DeLillo deliberately and self-reflectively zeroes in on the techniques of (re)constructing the past. His novel is thus political not only in the obvious sense of being inspired by a real political event, but above all by virtue of charting the poetic-rhetorical moves necessary to invest the event with meaning and by virtue of deploying them against the state to destabilize the event's hegemonic interpretation. If George Will saw *Libra* as bad citizenship, *Falling Man* would strike him and other conservative pundits as outright literary terrorism: an assessment DeLillo would doubtless consider an honor trumping even the Jerusalem Prize.

Few international relations scholars, hardly any of them American, have grasped that "September 11, like all political events, did not speak for itself. It required interpretation, and it did not have to lead to a War on Terror."[160] Fewer still have informed their investigations of the politics of the event's narrativization with insights from novels, let alone DeLillo's *Falling Man*, never mind its status as the preeminent literary treatment of 9/11 in contemporary American fiction.[161] At best, this neglect amounts to a missed opportunity to observe and examine the operation of political power at the most basic level: that of language used to give phenomena their initial description. At worst, it blinds international relations specialists to the extent to which this power inevitably infiltrates their own thought and writings, rendering them unwitting pawns of hegemonic interests and the status quo. Either way, scholarly analyses of international relations oblivious to the politics of language start too late: on the curtain of pre-interpretation, in Kundera's elegant expression, as if there were no vibrant political life unfolding backstage, as if there were no curtain and backstage to begin with. Insofar as tearing down this curtain constitutes the identifying sign of the art of the novel, fiction such as DeLillo's *Falling Man* is of inestimable value to the critical study of international relations and political power, including the academic discourse of international relations as one of the power's many channels.

Notes

1   Christopher Coker appears to be the only contemporary senior international relations scholar to have noticed this and taken the pains to analyze the main archetypes of war characters in literature for the benefit of fellow scholars. See his *Men at War: What Fiction Tells Us About Conflict, from The Illiad to Catch-22* (New York: Oxford University Press, 2014).

2   Of the novelists listed here, all except Tolstoy saw combat in wars subsequently recounted in their works: Remarque, Hašek, Heller, Vonnegut, and O'Brien as soldiers, Hemingway as a Red Cross ambulance driver and later newspaper correspondent present at, among other events, the Battle of the Ebro (1938) and D-Day Normandy landings (1944). In some war novels, such as O'Brien's, the degree to which these actual experiences inform the story practically abolishes the line between fiction and reality.

3   See the Committee's 2017 Case List at https://pen-international.org/app/uploads/PEN-CaseList_2017-FULL-v2-1UP.pdf [accessed 25 May 2018].

4   Don DeLillo, *Falling Man: A Novel* (New York: Scribner, 2007).

5   Ellen Goodman, "Shattering the Luxury of Our Charmed Life," *Seattle Times*, 14 September 2001, n.p.; idem, "Our Reality Show: We No Longer Have the Luxury of Feeling Safe," *Pittsburgh Post-Gazette*, 14 September 2001, A15; and idem, "Our Charmed Life Has Gone Forever," *Guardian Weekly*, 20 September 2001, 31.

6   See US Department of Homeland Security, Citizenship and Immigration Services, *Learn About the United States: Quick Civics Lessons for the Naturalization Test* (Washington, DC: GPO, 2013), 23.

7   Bob Minzesheimer, "Novels About 9/11 Can't Stack up to Non-fiction," *USA Today*, 11 September 2011, D1.

8   Other notable examples of 9/11 fiction include Lynne Sharon Schwartz's *Writing on the Wall* (2004), Claire Messud's *Emperor's Children* (2006), Jay McInerney's *Good Life* (2006), Jess Walter's *Zero* (2006), Deborah Eisenberg's *Twilight of the Superheroes* (2007), and Andre Dubus's *Garden of the Last Days* (2008).

9   John N. Duvall and Robert P. Marzec, "Narrating 9/11," *Modern Fiction Studies* 57, no. 3 (2011): 394.

10 Cf. Daniel Aaron, "How to Read Don DeLillo," in Frank Lentricchia, ed., *Introducing Don DeLillo* (Durham, NC: Duke University Press, 1991), 67–68: "nothing in [DeLillo's] novels suggests a suppressed 'Italian foundation'; hardly a vibration betrays an ethnic consciousness."

11 David Remnick, "Exile on Main Street: Don DeLillo's Undisclosed Under-world," *New Yorker*, 15 September 1997, 45.

12 Don DeLillo, "An Interview with Don DeLillo," interview by Kevin Connolly, in Thomas DePietro, ed., *Conversations with Don DeLillo* (Jackson: University Press of Mississippi, 2005), 39. Among his other influences, DeLillo has repeat-edly acknowledged abstract expressionist paintings in the Museum of Modern Art and the music at the Jazz Gallery and the Village Vanguard. See Robert R. Harris, "A Talk with Don DeLillo," *New York Times Book Review*, 10 October 1982, BR26; Gerald Howard, "The American Strangeness: An Interview with Don DeLillo," in DePietro, ed., *Conversations*, 128; and DeLillo, "'Writing as a Deeper Form of Concentration': An Interview with Don DeLillo," interview by Maria Moss, in DePietro, ed., *Conversations*, 155–168.

13 DeLillo, "Seven Seconds," interview by Ann Arensberg, *Vogue*, August 1988, 338.

14 DeLillo, "'An Outsider in This Society': An Interview with Don DeLillo," inter-view by Anthony DeCurtis, *South Atlantic Quarterly* 89, no. 2 (1990): 285–286. See also DeCurtis, "Matters of Fact and Fiction," *Rolling Stone*, 17 November 1988, 113–121, 164. In 1993, DeLillo reaffirmed this assessment: "I don't think my books could have been written in the world that existed before the Kennedy assassination. ... It's conceivable that ... the confusion and psychic chaos and the sense of randomness that ensued from that moment in Dallas ... made me the writer I am—for better or worse." (Quoted in Vince Passaro, "Dangerous Don DeLillo," in DePietro, ed., *Conversations*, 77–78.)

15 See A. O. Scott, "In Search of the Best," *New York Times Book Review*, 21 May 2006, 16–19, and the poll results in the same issue. Judges included Harold Bloom, Carlos Fuentes, Mario Vargas Llosa, Ian McEwan, Cynthia Ozick, and Richard Russo. DeLillo was one of only three writers to have more than one of his novels receive multiple nominations.

16 "Jerusalem Prize for Don DeLillo," *Publishers Weekly* 245, no. 18 (3 May 1999): 17. See also the official homepage of The Jerusalem International Book Fair: www.jerusalembookfair.com.

17 Harris, "Talk with DeLillo," 26.

18 Quoted in David Streitfeld, "Don DeLillo's Gloomy Muse," *Washington Post*, 14 May 1992, C1.

19 Quoted in Passaro, "Dangerous DeLillo," 82.

20 See Don DeLillo, "An Interview with Don DeLillo," interview by Thomas LeClair, *Contemporary Literature* 23, no. 1 (1982): 19.

21 DeLillo, "An Interview with Don DeLillo," interview by Maria Nadotti, trans. Peggy Boyers, ed. Don DeLillo, *Salmagundi* no. 100 (Fall 1993): 87.

22 DeLillo, "Outsider in This Society," 284.

23 DeLillo, "Interview with DeLillo," by LeClair, 30.

24 Don DeLillo, "The Artist Naked in a Cage," *New Yorker*, 26 May 1997, 7. In the form of Wei's jail cell, DeLillo added, this classic condition "has been cru-elly extended..." Note the motif of solitude in the title of Wei's autobiography, whose publication occasioned the stand-in: Wei Jingsheng, *The Outrage to Stand Alone: Letters from Prison and Other Writings*, ed. and trans. Kristina M. Torgeson (New York: Viking Penguin, 1997).

25 Quoted in D. T. Max, "Final Destination," *New Yorker*, 11 and 18 June 2007, 68. Unbeknownst to either of the two men, Wallace would become a tragic case in point on September 12, 2008, when he hanged himself in the garage of his home in Claremont, California, next to a neatly stacked unfinished manuscript of his new novel, *The Pale King*. For details of his suicide, see D. T. Max, *Every Love Story Is a Ghost Story: A Life of David Foster Wallace* (New York: Viking, 2012), 301.

26 Don DeLillo, "Der Narr in seinem Zimmer," *Die Zeit*, no. 14, 29 March 2001, n.p. [Translation mine.] The vision of the novelist as an individual forging ahead in

isolation from society is not unique to DeLillo, of course. Jonathan Franzen, for example, voiced a similar notion when he said that "Solitary work—the work of writing, the work of reading—is the essence of fiction." ("Perchance to Dream: In the Age of Images, a Reason to Write Novels," *Harper's*, 1 April 1996, 41.)

27 DeLillo, "Interview with DeLillo," by Connolly, 29.

28 Don DeLillo, *Great Jones Street* (Boston: Houghton Mifflin, 1973), 166.

29 Ibid., 4.

30 DeLillo, "Interview with DeLillo," by Connolly, 30. [Emphasis original.]

31 Mark Osteen, *American Magic and Dread: Don DeLillo's Dialogue with Culture* (Philadelphia: University of Pennsylvania Press, 2000), 450.

32 Don DeLillo, *Mao II* (New York: Vintage, 1991), 97.

33 Ibid., 98.

34 DeLillo, "Interview with DeLillo," by Nadotti, 89.

35 Quoted in Passaro, "Dangerous DeLillo," 79.

36 Philip Nel, "DeLillo and Modernism," in John N. Duvall, ed., *The Cambridge Companion to Don DeLillo* (Cambridge: Cambridge University Press, 2008), 24.

37 Paula Martín Salván, "'The Writer at the Far Margin': The Rhetoric of Artistic Ethics in Don DeLillo's Novels," *European Journal of American Studies* 1 (2007): 9. For the argument that Bill Gray may be seen as DeLillo's mouthpiece, see also Mark Edmundson, "Not Flat, Not Round, Not There: Don DeLillo's Novel Characters," *Yale Review* 83, no. 2 (1995): 123.

38 DeLillo, "Interview with DeLillo," by LeClair, 20.

39 DeLillo, *Mao II*, 200.

40 Ibid., 97.

41 DeLillo, "Seven Seconds," 390.

42 DeLillo, "Artist Naked in Cage," 6–7.

43 Philip Nel, *The Avant-Garde and American Postmodernity: Small Incisive Shocks* (Jackson: University Press of Mississippi, 2002), 96, 113.

44 Philip Nel, "'A Small Incisive Shock': Modern Forms, Postmodern Politics, and the Role of the Avant-Garde in *Underworld*," *Modern Fiction Studies* 45, no. 3 (1999): 738 n.14.

45 François Happe, *Don DeLillo: La fiction contre les systèmes* (Paris: Belin, 2000).

46 John N. Duvall, "Introduction: From Valparaiso to Jerusalem: Don DeLillo and the Moment of Canonization," *Modern Fiction Studies* 45, no. 3 (1999): 561.

47 John N. Duvall, "The Power of History and the Persistence of Mystery," introduction to Duvall, ed., *Cambridge Companion to DeLillo*, 3.

48 Frank Lentricchia, "The American Writer as Bad Citizen," in Lentricchia, ed., *Introducing DeLillo*, 2.

49 George F. Will, "Shallow Look at the Mind of an Assassin," *Washington Post*, 22 September 1988, A25.

50 Lentricchia, "American Writer as Bad Citizen," 5.

51 Quoted in Remnick, "Exile on Main Street," 48.

52 DeLillo, "Narr in seinem Zimmer," n.p.

53 DeLillo, "'Ich kenne Amerika nicht mehr,'" interview by Christoph Amend, *ZEITMagazin Leben*, no. 42, 10 October 2007, n.p. [Translation mine.]

54 DeLillo quoted in Franzen, "Perchance to Dream," 54. Cf. DeLillo, "Narr in seinem Zimmer," n.p.: "[The novelist] finds identity in sentences. He writes in order to be free, to survive as an individual."

55 Lentricchia, "American Writer as Bad Citizen," 2. DeLillo endorsed this interpretation. See Adam Begley, "The Art of Fiction CXXXV: Don DeLillo," in DePietro, ed., *Conversations*, 105.

56 DeLillo, "Interview with DeLillo," by Connolly, 37.

57 DeLillo, "Interview with DeLillo," by LeClair, 21. As David Cowart has noted, "One cannot ... overemphasize the centrality of the language theme in any and

all of DeLillo's novels, stories, plays, and essays." ("DeLillo and the Power of Language," in Duvall, ed., *Cambridge Companion to DeLillo*, 151.)

58 DeLillo, "Narr in seinem Zimmer," n.p.

59 DeLillo, "Interview with DeLillo," by Nadotti, 96.

60 Duvall, "Power of History," 2. In a similar vein, Lentricchia ("American Writer as Bad Citizen," 6) sees the hallmark feature of DeLillo's novels in "their historical rigor ...: the unprecedented degree to which they prevent their readers from gliding off into the comfortable sentiment that the real problems of the human race have always been what they are today."

61 DeLillo, "Interview with DeLillo," by Moss, 165.

62 DeLillo quoted in Harris, "Talk with DeLillo," 26.

63 Milan Kundera, *The Curtain: An Essay in Seven Parts*, trans. Linda Asher (New York: Harper, 2007), 92. [Emphasis original.]

64 DeLillo, "Outsider in This Society," 303.

65 DeLillo, "Interview with DeLillo," by Connolly, 38. See also DeLillo, "'Ich kenne Amerika nicht mehr,'" where DeLillo declared himself politically independent and refused to discuss the subject any further. When asked by his interviewer why, he responded in the language of his native Bronx: "Because it's none of your fucking business."

66 DeLillo, *Underworld* (New York: Scribner, 1997), 287.

67 Walter Benjamin, "The Work of Art in the Age of Mechanical Reproduction," in *Illuminations*, ed. Hannah Arendt, trans. Harry Zohn (New York: Schocken, 1969), 224, 239–241.

68 Max Horkheimer and Theodor W. Adorno, *Dialectic of Enlightenment*, trans. John Cumming (New York: Herder and Herder, 1972), xii.

69 Herbert Marcuse, "The Affirmative Character of Culture," in *Negations: Essays in Critical Theory*, trans. Jeremy J. Shapiro (Boston: Beacon Press, 1968).

70 Theodor W. Adorno, "Culture and Administration" (1960), *Telos*, no. 37 (1978): 93–111.

71 Fredric Jameson, *Postmodernism, or, The Cultural Logic of Late Capitalism* (Durham, NC: Duke University Press, 1991).

72 Quoted in Begley, "Art of Fiction: DeLillo," 96–97. See also DeLillo, "Narr in seinem Zimmer," n.p.: "The writer knows that if he ... has some luck, then he'll become a t-shirt, a coffee cup or a shopping bag. A sort of punishment, which he half fears, half desires. To become part of the all-encompassing image mill. Absorbed and incorporated and reproduced, rendered harmless and surreal."

73 Franzen, "Perchance to Dream," 38–39.

74 Ibid., 43.

75 Quoted in Guy Scarpetta, "Politický Kundera," in Bohumil Fořt, Jiří Kudrnáč, and Petr Kyloušek, eds., *Milan Kundera aneb Co zmůže literatura? Soubor statí o díle Milana Kundery* (Brno: Host, 2012), 167. [Translation mine.]

76 DeLillo, *Americana* (Boston: Houghton Mifflin, 1971), 270.

77 DeLillo, *Mao II*, 52.

78 Similarly, in *Great Jones Street* the revolutionary "acoustic silence" of Bucky Wunderlick's "Mountain Tapes" ultimately decays into yet another rock music industry product under the shrewd management of his handler, Globke, who uses it to secure Bucky's return on tour.

79 DeLillo, *White Noise* (New York: Viking, 1985), 154–155.

80 Aldous Huxley, *Brave New World* (Scranton, PA: Harper Perennial, 1989 [1946]), 28. [Emphasis original.]

81 DeLillo, "Artist Naked in Cage," 6.

82 Mark Osteen, "DeLillo's Dedalian Artists," in Duvall, ed., *Cambridge Companion to DeLillo*, 138.

83 Mark Osteen, "Becoming Incorporated: Spectacular Authorship and DeLillo's *Mao II*," *Modern Fiction Studies* 45, no. 3 (1999): 644. See also Joseph Tabbi, *Postmodern Sublime: Technology and American Writing from Mailer to Cyberpunk* (Ithaca, NY: Cornell University Press, 1995), 173, arguing similarly that in *Mao II* DeLillo reveals the "impossibility of achieving a wholly literary opposition" to consumer culture.

84 DeLillo, *Mao II*, 41. Critics immediately took to headlining their reviews of *Mao II* with titles such as "Look for a Writer and Find a Terrorist," and the controversy surrounding DeLillo's argument only increased after September 11, 2001. DeLillo responded that "If he was writing the book today ... he would be more diplomatic about linking the artist and the terrorist," but he did not alter his fundamental conception of the relationship between the two. See, respectively, Lorrie Moore, "Look for a Writer and Find a Terrorist," *New York Times*, 9 June 1991, n.p., and Emma Brockes, "View from the Bridge," *Guardian*, 23 May 2003, sec. Features & Reviews, 20.

85 DeLillo, *Mao II*, 157.

86 Ibid., 156. Unsurprisingly, after 9/11 some of DeLillo's followers started mythologizing him as a "Medusa" of our time: a writer producing novels full of "clairvoyant characters and prophetic foreknowledge" enabling readers to experience "a kind of reverse déjà vu." See, respectively, Adam Thurschwell, "Writing and Terror: Don DeLillo on the Task of Literature after 9/11," *Law and Literature* 19, no. 2 (2007): 280, and Peter Boxall, *Don DeLillo: The Possibility of Fiction* (New York: Routledge, 2006), 157–158. Cf. also John Carlos Rowe, "*Mao II* and the War on Terrorism," *South Atlantic Quarterly* 103, no. 1 (2004): 21–43. Recall, however, that the decade preceding the publication of *Mao II* suffered from no shortage of terrorist acts, including the bombing of Pan Am Flight 103 over Lockerbie, Scotland, on December 21, 1988, and the attack on US Marine Corps barracks in Beirut on October 23, 1983, killing 241 American servicemen.

87 DeLillo, *Mao II*, 235.

88 Ibid., 156.

89 DeLillo, "'Ich kenne Amerika nicht mehr,'" n.p.

90 DeLillo, *Mao II*, 235.

91 Cf. Osteen's interpretation of *Mao II* as a novel "showing how terrorism ... is irretrievably mediated by the journalistic and photographic gatekeepers who record and comment upon terrorist actions." ("Becoming Incorporated," 644.)

92 DeLillo, *Mao II*, 158–159.

93 Osteen, "DeLillo's Dedalian Artists," 145. See also idem, "Becoming Incorporated," 644.

94 Franzen, "Perchance to Dream," 51.

95 Linda Hutcheon, *A Poetics of Postmodernism: History, Theory, Fiction* (New York and London: Routledge, 1988), 5.

96 Linda Hutcheon, *Narcissistic Narrative: The Metafictional Paradox* (London and New York: Routledge, 1984 [1980]), 6, 12.

97 Ibid., 6.

98 Linda Hutcheon, *The Politics of Postmodernism*, 2nd ed. (London and New York: Routledge, 2002), 48.

99 Hutcheon, *Poetics of Postmodernism*, 4–5, 21.

100 Ibid., 4–5. [Emphasis original.]

101 DeLillo, "In the Ruins of the Future: Reflections on Terror and Loss in the Shadow of September," *Harper's*, December 2001, 33–40.

102 Martin Amis, *The Second Plane: September 11: Terror and Boredom* (New York and Toronto: Knopf, 2008), 12.

103 DeLillo, "'Ich kenne Amerika nicht mehr,'" n.p.

104 DeLillo, *Falling Man*, 3, 246.

105 Ibid., 4.

106 Ibid., 246.

107 Sonia Baelo-Allué, "9/11 and the Psychic Trauma Novel: Don DeLillo's *Falling Man*," *Atlantis: Journal of the Spanish Association of Anglo-American Studies* 34, no. 1 (2012): 76.

108 Richard Gray, *After the Fall: American Literature Since 9/11* (Chichester: Wiley-Blackwell, 2011): 17, 28. See also idem, "Open Doors, Closed Minds: American Prose Writing at a Time of Crisis," *American Literary History* 21, no. 1 (2009): 128–151. Cf. Pankaj Mishra's complaint that American 9/11 fiction has confined itself "to the domestic life" and its authors have struggled "to define [the] cultural otherness of Islam." ("The End of Innocence," *Guardian*, 19 May 2007, n.p.)

109 Michiko Kakutani, "A Man, a Woman and a Day of Terror," *New York Times*, 9 May 2007, n.p.

110 Sven Cvek, *Towering Figures: Reading the 9/11 Archive* (Amsterdam and London: Rodopi, 2011), 197.

111 Michael Rothberg, "A Failure of the Imagination: Diagnosing the Post-9/11 Novel: A Response to Richard Gray," *American Literary History* 21, no. 1 (2009): 153.

112 DeLillo, "Ruins of Future," 33, 34.

113 Ibid., 35, 37, 39.

114 Ibid., 39.

115 Ibid.

116 DeLillo, "Ich kenne Amerika nicht mehr," n.p.

117 DeLillo, *Falling Man*, 33.

118 Ibid., 168.

119 Ibid., 221–222.

120 Tom Junod, "The Falling Man," *Esquire*, September 2003, 177–181, 198–199.

121 Ibid., 198.

122 Aaron Mauro, "The Languishing of the Falling Man: Don DeLillo and Jonathan Safran Foer's Photographic History of 9/11," *Modern Fiction Studies* 57, no. 3 (2011): 588.

123 Quoted in Junod, "Falling Man," 178. This perfectly illustrates Susan Sontag's remark that "Despite the presumption of veracity that gives all photographs authority, ... the work that photographers do is no generic exception to the usually shady commerce between art and truth. Even when photographers are most concerned with mirroring reality, they are still haunted by tacit imperatives of taste and conscience." (*On Photography* [New York: Farrar, Straus and Giroux, 1977], 6.)

124 Gary Walton, "The Triune Trope of the 'Falling Man' in Don DeLillo's *Falling Man*: The Commodification of 9/11 Trauma," *Kentucky Philological Review* 24 (2009): 48.

125 Sarah Boxer, "One Camera, Then Thousands, Indelibly Etching a Day of Loss," *New York Times*, 11 September 2002, n.p.

126 DeLillo, "Ruins of Future," 37.

127 Frank Rich, "The Clear Blue Sky," *New York Times Sunday Book Review*, 27 May 2007, n.p.

128 Richard Jackson, *Writing the War on Terror: Language, Politics and Counter-Terrorism* (Manchester: Manchester University Press, 2005), 38.

129 Richard Devetak, "After the Event: Don DeLillo's *White Noise* and September 11 Narratives," *Review of International Studies* 35, no. 4 (2009): 804–805.

130 Ibid., 805.

131 This is the count arrived at by Peter Singer cited in Renee Jeffery, "Beyond Banality? Ethical Responses to Evil in Post-September 11 International Relations," *International Affairs* 81, no. 4 (2005): 180. Singer consequently bestowed on Bush the dubious honor of calling him the "President of Good and Evil." See Singer, *The President of Good and Evil: The Ethics of George W. Bush* (Melbourne: Text Publishing, 2004).

132 DeLillo, "Ich kenne Amerika nicht mehr," n.p.

133 Ibid.

134 DeLillo, *Falling Man*, 16.

135 George W. Bush, Address Before a Joint Session of the Congress on the United States Response to the Terrorist Attacks of September 11 (September 20, 2001), in *Public Papers of the Presidents of the United States: George W. Bush, 2001*, vol. 2 (Washington, DC: GPO, 2003), 1142.

136 DeLillo, "Ruins of Future," 34, 37.

137 Ibid., 34.

138 DeLillo, *Falling Man*, 174, 176.

139 Ibid., 176.

140 Ibid., 174.

141 DeLillo, "Ruins of Future," 34.

142 DeLillo, *Falling Man*, 46–47.

143 Ibid., 113.

144 Ibid., 46–47.

145 DeLillo, "Ruins of Future," 33, 34.

146 DeLillo, *Falling Man*, 80.

147 Linda S. Kauffman, "The Wake of Terror: Don DeLillo's 'In the Ruins of the Future,' 'Baader-Meinhof,' and *Falling Man*," *Modern Fiction Studies* 54, no. 2 (2008): 356.

148 DeLillo, *Falling Man*, 146.

149 Ibid., 147.

150 Ibid.

151 See especially Stefan Aust, *Baader-Meinhof: The Inside Story of the R.A.F.*, trans. Anthea Bell (Oxford and New York: Oxford University Press, 2009), and also Jeremy Varon, *Bringing the War Home: The Weather Underground, the Red Army Faction, and Revolutionary Violence in the Sixties and Seventies* (Berkeley: University of California Press, 2004).

152 Kauffman, "Wake of Terror," 362.

153 DeLillo, *Falling Man*, 147.

154 Ibid., 73–74.

155 Ibid.

156 Joseph M. Conte, "Don DeLillo's *Falling Man* and the Age of Terror," *Modern Fiction Studies* 57, no. 3 (2011): 570.

157 Ibid.

158 Hayden White, *Figural Realism: Studies in the Mimesis Effect* (Baltimore, MD, and London: Johns Hopkins University Press, 1999), 9.

159 Marco Abel, "Don DeLillo's 'In the Ruins of the Future': Literature, Images, and the Rhetoric of Seeing 9/11," *PMLA* 118, no. 5 (2003): 1236, 1239. [Emphasis original.]

160 Ronald Krebs and Jennifer Lobasz, "Fixing the Meaning of 9/11: Hegemony, Coercion, and the Road to War in Iraq," *Security Studies* 16, no. 3 (2007): 413.

161 Richard Devetak appears to be the only one to have analyzed the politics of 9/11 historiography with reference to DeLillo but, alas, without noticing *Falling Man* at all. See Devetak, "After Event," which relies solely on *White Noise*.

5 The End of History as an April Fool's Joke

Milan Kundera's Literary Critique of Western Liberalism after 1989

The Soviet-led invasion of Czechoslovakia in the summer of 1968, one of the defining moments of the Cold War, shook the international stage. In the wee hours of August 21, windowpanes around the small Central European country began rattling with the noise of tanks and military aircraft bringing in over two hundred thousand Warsaw Pact troops. The orders from Moscow were clear: to crush Czechoslovakia's democratic socialist reformist movement led by Alexander Dubček. Many Czechoslovak citizens displayed extraordinary courage resisting the aggression: during medal ceremonies at the Olympic Games in Mexico City, legendary gymnast Věra Čáslavská defiantly turned her eyes down and away during the Soviet national anthem right in front of TV cameras broadcasting her gesture worldwide. But the protests were to no avail. Dubček was deposed and the Prague Spring morphed into a long winter of hardline normalization under Soviet occupation and Brezhnev's doctrine of limited sovereignty that would last until the fall of Communism in Europe in 1989.

From the perspective of today's mainstream international relations theory, the invasion is not difficult to explain: leading American neorealist and neoliberal scholars such as Mearsheimer or Keohane would argue that its principal cause was the anarchical structure of the international system. Without world government to protect them, great powers live in perpetual fear of each other, have no choice but to take matters of national security and survival into their own hands, and safeguard their sovereignty by maintaining or increasing their strength relative to their rivals. Since Dubček's policies and other developments in Czechoslovakia in early 1968 threatened to weaken the internal cohesion of the Soviet empire in its contest against the West, Brezhnev made a rational decision to reverse them.

Back in the 1960s, however, Antonín Novotný, General Secretary of the Communist Party of Czechoslovakia (KSČ) and Moscow's loyal puppet prior to being ousted by Dubček in the run-up to the Prague Spring, thought about the situation very differently. When he was pondering the potential triggers that could cause the Soviets to intervene in his country's internal affairs, anarchy was nowhere on his mind. Instead, speaking some months before the invasion, he saw the main trouble elsewhere: in the Czechoslovak

Writers' Union, whose reformist faction was getting increasingly audacious in its demands for democratization. In June 1968 it even dared to publish them, to the severe irritation of Party officials in Prague and Moscow alike, in an open manifesto "Two Thousand Words."[1] Within this faction, one rabble-rouser stood out in particular: "I consider [him] the main cad," Novotný told his fellow Stalinists in the KSČ leadership, "Let's not kid ourselves. [He is] one of the main ideological creators of the whole opposition front which has emerged in the Writers' Union."[2] The choice spirit was novelist and essayist Milan Kundera.

Novotný's words alone earn Kundera a firm place in this book, part of whose goal is precisely to demonstrate the real international political implications of fiction writing. If not in North America, certainly in Central Europe it has long been common sense that a typewriter is more powerful than a machine gun and can, if put to work in the right manner and circumstances, provoke a major international crisis: in Kundera's case, a full-out military conquest of a sovereign state by the combined armies of four different countries, including one superpower. Indeed, to Kundera's name ordinary Czechs would quickly add a whole list of other poets, novelists, dramatists, and essayists if asked about the role of writers in the Prague Spring, such as Václav Havel, Ludvík Vaculík, Josef Škvorecký, Ivan Klíma, and Pavel Kohout. Each of them could just as easily be the subject of this chapter.

To justify the focus on Kundera, then, the following pages will do more than simply regurgitate his well-known reputation, certified by Novotný from the very top of the Czechoslovak government in the 1960s, as a dissident political novelist capable of moving Warsaw Pact tank battalions with the tip of his pen. In addition, they will reveal that the traditional image of Kundera as an anti-Communist pamphleteer is untenably narrow: a myth. It is a Cold War relic fabricated as much by his Stalinist censors in the Eastern Bloc as by his audiences in the West: the former anxious to get rid of him, the latter eager to appropriate him in a self-serving effort to enlist one of the most acclaimed writers from behind the Iron Curtain as a champion of liberal democracy in the ideological fight against socialism. This orthodox representation of Kundera ignores his intellectual moorings in socialist humanism, not to mention his youthful support of the 1948 Communist Party takeover in Czechoslovakia, and dramatically exaggerates his affection for Western liberalism and market capitalism. Above all, it fails to notice that the Stalinist setting of Kundera's pre-1989 novels is incidental to them, serving merely to raise far more fundamental questions which lie at the core of his fiction: questions about the meaning of history and about the ability of human beings to control the consequences of their actions, to name a few. What Kundera has to say about these themes applies beyond the narrow context of Czechoslovak Stalinism. Indeed, his ironic critique of modern rationality and visions of universal harmony, although originally aimed at the Marxist-Leninist utopia, is equally pertinent to the liberal-capitalist end of history proclaimed in the West in 1989. In Kundera's recent novels, it surfaces in his assault on "imagology": the totalizing dictatorship of empty mass media images.

Milan Kundera: an Anti-Stalinist Knight Battling for Western Liberalism?

Kundera was born in Brno, the provincial capital of south Moravia and the second largest city in today's Czech Republic, on April Fools' Day in 1929. "That has its metaphysical significance,"[3] he remarked about the peculiar date years later, by which point his novelistic portrayals of irreverent jokes played by history on hapless individuals had brought him worldwide critical acclaim. His father, Ludvík Kundera, was a distinguished pianist, musicologist, and student of Leoš Janáček. Milan Kundera grew up in a home filled with classical music and books offering the very best in Western literature and humanities.

Initially aspiring to follow in his father's footsteps and become a pianist and music composer, Kundera changed his mind in his early twenties and in 1948 moved to Prague. He first enrolled to study literature and aesthetics at Charles University and then, after two semesters, switched to screenwriting at the Film Faculty of the Academy of Performing Arts. After graduation he remained at the Faculty as lecturer in world literature and simultaneously began publishing lyrical poetry, which instantly earned him national spotlight at the forefront of the new generation of Czechoslovakia's postwar writers. "From his initial entry into the world of literature ... Kundera, as no other author of [this] generation ..., became extremely popular and widely known."[4] It goes without saying that at the time such career advancement was impossible without active engagement in the KSČ and wholehearted dedication to its principles. Kundera had what it took. His early work complied with the precepts of Soviet socialist realism and celebrated important Party symbols such as the heroic martyrdom of Julius Fučík.[5] He joined the KSČ in 1948 together with many other idealistic young Czechs enchanted by its progressive agenda and unperturbed by its violent tactics and subservience to Moscow. "I too once danced in a ring," he later wrote about this time; "the Communists had taken power ..., and I took other Communist students by the hands or shoulders."[6]

In 1950, the year the KSČ unleashed terror in show trials and executions of prominent government officials such as Milada Horáková, Kundera's advancement stalled: "I said something I should not have said, was expelled from the Party, and had to leave the ring dance."[7] He spent some time working as a laborer and jazz musician, but the setback was temporary. In the thaw following Stalin's death and Khrushchev's secret speech at the Twentieth Congress of the Communist Party of the Soviet Union in Moscow in 1956, Kundera was readmitted into the KSČ and soon emerged as one of the leading reformist writers calling for freedom of artistic expression, end of censorship, and general democratization of Czechoslovak socialism.

Marxist in ideological orientation, these reformist writers "[shared] a vision of a reconstituted socialist order based on humanist and pluralist principles."[8] They coalesced especially around *Literární noviny*, the official weekly of the Writers' Union, whose thematic scope extended far beyond literary criticism to problems of national history, official ideology, and economic planning, and whose circulation—one hundred and thirty thousand in the mid-1960s—gave it tremendous public influence. Kundera contributed to *Literární noviny* and other similar periodicals frequently and by now exclusively in prose as opposed to lyrical poetry, which was inextricably bound up with his erstwhile revolutionary zeal and which he therefore abandoned as unsuitable for his mature, more pragmatic worldview. By the late 1960s, he had established himself as one of the country's most influential oppositional public intellectuals and shapers of political consciousness—rightly feared by Novotný and other Stalinists in the KSČ.

Heralding Czechoslovakia's cultural renaissance during the Prague Spring, the publication of Kundera's first novel, *The Joke* (1967), turned him into a household name.

> *The Joke* belongs to the golden classics of Czech prose. Those who did not live through the era ... will never understand how much of a popular hero an author of such a book could be in the Czechoslovak Socialist Republic at the time.[9]

Kundera completed the manuscript in 1965, but it was held up by censors and released only once the reformist wing in the KSČ had started to gain some traction. Magnifying his status as a leading intellectual critic of the regime was his opening address to the Fourth Congress of the Writers' Union on June 27, 1967, where he surprised everyone by declining to read a preapproved statement pledging the writers' ongoing commitment to the Party's cultural policy and instead delivered his own speech urging major changes, above all open dialogue. "Any intrusion into the freedom of thought and words ... is a scandal in the twentieth century," he told the delegates; "the words 'socialist literature' will not have a positive meaning until they involve ... an emancipatory overcoming [of heretofore existing boundaries]."[10]

Unfortunately, instead of such changes history had other plans. In August 1968, it subjected Kundera precisely to the sort of prank whose essence, a sudden reversal at the hands of forces entirely beyond one's control, he would go on rendering in endless variations throughout all his subsequent work: following the Soviet invasion he was expelled from the KSČ again, had to resign from the Film Academy, and became persona non grata in Czechoslovakia. He remained highly active on the intellectual scene, including as the main adversary of fellow dissident Václav Havel in a pitched polemic about the significance of the Prague Spring in the months after its defeat.[11] But in 1970 the Party banned him from publishing, proscribed his work, and left him with only two options: to leave or go underground. From his second novel, *Laughable Loves* (1970), up to and including his latest one, *The Festival of Insignificance* (2015), all Kundera's books thus first came out abroad, mainly in Éditions Gallimard in France, where he has lived since 1975 and where the Socialist Party leader François Mitterand awarded him citizenship the very afternoon he became President in 1981.

In emigration, the magnitude of Kundera's reputation quickly surpassed that of his official standing at home, except in the opposite direction. Whereas the Czechoslovak regime condemned him as a traitor and revoked his passport, French, British, and American audiences welcomed him with open arms as one of the most compelling Eastern European dissidents: a valiant Moravian knight bearing the flag of liberalism in the fight against Marxism-Leninism. It was from Kundera's 1983 essay "The Tragedy of Central Europe" that the US Department of State first learned that in invading Czechoslovakia the Soviet Union kidnapped part of the West; Secretary Shultz promptly began citing the piece in support of President Reagan's strategy to roll back the Soviet empire.[12] In the 1980s, Kundera received such prestigious distinctions as the American Common Wealth Award, Prix Europa-Littérature, Jerusalem Prize, Los Angeles Times Book Prize, Austrian State Prize for European Literature, and what at least in the United States counts as the ultimate honor: a Hollywood film adaptation of his novel *The Unbearable Lightness of Being* (1984). Due in no small part to the exposure generated in cinemas, this book became a genuine global bestseller—including on the black markets around the Soviet Bloc. "I know people," one Polish writer recalled its popularity during the Solidarity era, "who had made enough money from [its] secret photocopying ... and illegal sale to buy a few cars. Others had gone to jail.... Sometimes they were one and the same person."[13]

Amidst Kundera's skyrocketing celebrity, however, scarcely anyone had noticed his profound dismay with his Western reception. In Britain, the first English translation of *The Joke* cut out entire chapters, rearranged the rest, and mutilated the original beyond recognition. Enraged, Kundera published an angry protest letter comparing his editors to Soviet censors.[14] Initial French translations were no better. The film adaptation of *The Unbearable Lightness of Being* was an even greater disaster: "Did I like [it]? In no way was it my film," Kundera distanced himself from the movie, which had flattened his complex story into a dumb procession of erotic scenes and anti-Soviet propaganda for mass market consumption; "it was alien to me."[15] Around the same time, Milan Jungmann, Kundera's former editor-in-chief at *Literární noviny*, nonetheless asserted that commercial success was Kundera's principal motivation in writing the book, that he had prostituted his artistic talents to Western bourgeois cliches and voyeuristic obsessions, and that the novel was a cheap caricature of socialist Czechoslovakia.[16]

Not just Kundera's Western audiences, then, but also his fellow dissident writers, not to mention Communist censors throughout the Eastern Bloc, took to stereotyping him in ways that deeply distressed him. Was he truly devoted to Western liberalism and market capitalism? Did his novels pour scorn on socialism? Were they even political novels? Few cared to ask. The answers were widely assumed to be self-evident.

In response, Kundera began exercising vigorous authorial control over his message: at first through corrective public interventions, then increasingly through withdrawal and silence. His efforts to guide his readers, police editorial intrusions, and shape journalistic and critical interpretations of his books may have no parallel among contemporary novelists. In 1985, he stopped giving interviews and later announced that "except for dialogues co-edited by me, *accompanied by my copyright*, all my reported remarks since then are to be considered forgeries."[17] After the Hollywood production of *The Unbearable Lightness of Being* he prohibited all future film, television, and stage adaptations of his works. He added that his life's work does not consist of everything he has ever written, but only of what he personally deems important, and that "The only thing that matters to me ... is my novels."[18] As for the rest, whether his poetry, plays, or cultural and political essays—including his 1967 address to the Writers' Union, Prague Spring polemic with Havel, or reflection on "The Tragedy of Central Europe"—he summarily dismissed it as juvenile, incidental, or failed.[19]

Kundera's most conspicuous and sustained act of withdrawal, however, has been his reaction to the demise of Communism in Czechoslovakia in 1989. The Velvet Revolution inaugurated a decade of sweeping political and economic changes led by President Havel and Prime Minister Klaus, respectively a great admirer of Western liberalism and a disciple of the Chicago school of neoclassical economics, under whose tenures the country adopted liberal democracy and free markets and integrated itself into core Western structures including the EU and the North Atlantic Treaty Organization: just the sort of transformation Kundera should have welcomed with enthusiasm based on his stereotypical Cold War reputation. Yet he not only declined to return to his native country but has, indeed, increasingly distanced himself from it over the last quarter century—almost in proportion to its rise as one of the genuine success stories of Westernization in the former Eastern Bloc. In *Immortality* (1990) he dropped the specific Czech context common to all his preceding novels. Soon thereafter he started writing in French and forbade anyone from translating his subsequent books into his native tongue, reserving the right for himself—mainly, it seems, to keep his Czech audiences waiting indefinitely. Today he visits the Czech Republic only rarely and always incognito, having sworn his circle of local friends to secrecy. When a major international conference honoring his achievement took place in his hometown of Brno in 2009, on the occasion of his eightieth birthday, Kundera turned down the organizers' invitation and let them know that he considers himself a French author whose work should be classified as French literature.

Why has Kundera responded to his native country's celebrated attainment of the liberal-capitalist end of history only with absence and growing disdain? Bitter memories of persecution, gratitude to the French for taking him in, deep love of their culture, new friendships and loyalties forged in Paris, even the grumpiness of old age all probably have to be factored in, as do the veneration and mistreatment Kundera continues to receive in, respectively, his adopted and original homeland. Whereas in France his oeuvre recently came out in the exclusive *Bibliothèque de la Pléiade*, a moment of canonization placing Kundera next to Cervantes, Balzac, and Rabelais in the pantheon of French and world literature, in the Czech Republic researchers from the state-funded Institute for the Study of Totalitarian Regimes (ÚSTR) made global headlines with an article accusing him of denouncing a Western agent to the Communist secret police in 1950, a model example of character assassination on the shabbiest of evidence.[20]

But Kundera's failure to return home may very well stem from something else, an additional set of reasons ignored by most of his interpreters up to now: namely that his affection for Western liberal-capitalist society has been vastly overdrawn, that he did not perceive its victory in Czechoslovakia as a triumph, and that he found the euphoria of the Havel and Klaus years misguided. After all, Kundera's old argument with Havel about the meaning of the Prague Spring pivoted precisely on this issue: whether or not Dubček's democratic socialist experiment, regardless of its premature death, briefly placed Czechoslovakia at the center of world history by revealing a pathway to full human self-realization. Unlike Havel, Kundera firmly believed that it did, and his novelistic career was born in the context of this belief. Lest it be forgotten, *The Joke* was written by a card-carrying KSČ reformist, and the Party's progressive faction authorized it for publication because it embodied "the official policy of the day, which was ... the *exposure of past errors.*"[21] If Kundera's novelistic debut had any political agenda at all, it was not to condemn Czechoslovak socialism, as is commonly assumed, but to facilitate its renovation by pointing out the absurdities of its Stalinist perversion.[22]

Could it be, then, that the Velvet Revolution as a particular phase of liberal-capitalist globalization left Kundera largely unimpressed? Ordinary Czechs and Slovaks would spend a decade drifting on top of its white cloud, almost touching heaven the way Adam's finger does God's in Michelangelo's famous fresco, before falling back to earth and discovering that political reality was as ugly and dark as ever. By the mid-2000s the massive theft—dubbed "tunneling"—of national industrial assets by a few crafty entrepreneurs during Klaus's economic privatization had surfaced, and Havel was busy making a fool of himself begging the United States to invade Iraq even before President George W. Bush decided to do so under false pretexts. *Laissez-faire* and the pursuit of liberty, American-style, had revealed themselves in their full glory, dumbfounding the masses in the former

Czechoslovakia to the raucous laughter of history. Did Kundera hear a faint echo of this laughter already in November 1989, in the memorable rattling of keys with which tens of thousands of demonstrators in Prague's public squares issued a symbolic death knell to their Communism leaders?

"Spare me your Stalinism!" or the Knight Sheds His Armor

That Kundera's novels, especially the ones written before 1989, detail life in Communist Czechoslovakia is indisputable, of course. *The Joke* relates the humorlessness of the regime at the peak of its revolutionary zeal in the early 1950s, depicting KSČ members as agelasts unable to laugh at an innocuous jest. Ludvík Jahn pays the price. A witty and popular university student, he experiences a dramatic downfall when Markéta, a beautiful fellow Communist, keeps responding to his romantic advances only with priggish letters blindly reciting Party slogans, finally exasperating him to the point that he sends her a postcard with a playful note: "Optimism is the opium of the people! A healthy atmosphere stinks of stupidity! Long live Trotsky!" Ludvík ends up dismissed from the university by a student tribunal, expelled from the Party, and conscripted into a penal battalion in the coal mines.

Often, Kundera's material comes straight from the historical record, which endows his fiction with a journalistic dimension. *The Book of Laughter and Forgetting*, for instance, opens with a well-documented, extensively photographed moment from the Party's seizure of power in Czechoslovakia in February 1948: the appearance of Klement Gottwald, leader of the KSČ, and his closest comrades including Vladimír Clementis on the balcony of a Baroque palace in Prague's Old Town Square to address masses of supporters below.

> It was snowing and cold, and Gottwald was bareheaded. Bursting with solicitude, Clementis took off his fur hat and set in on Gottwald's head. ... Four years later, Clementis was charged with treason and hanged. The propaganda section immediately made him vanish from history and, of course, from all photographs. Ever since, Gottwald has been alone on the balcony. Where Clementis stood, there is only the bare palace wall. Nothing remains of Clementis but the fur hat on Gottwald's head.[23]

In this journalistic role, as eyewitness portraits of Czechoslovakia's Stalinist system, Kundera's novels often equal and even surpass history books. Ludvík Vaculík, fellow dissident novelist and author of the "Two Thousand Words" manifesto, somehow did not get around to reading *The Joke* until well after the Velvet Revolution, but when he finally picked it up the authenticity of the world inside its covers sent chills down his spine: "The description of the atmosphere of the fifties, the monstrosity of the Party spirit, will seem untrue to today's reader," Vaculík noted in his diary, but "I felt in it the horror of that time. ... [Nobody since] has written as precise and apposite a work about that regime."[24] KSČ officials no doubt felt the same after reading *The Book of Laughter and Forgetting*, which is why they stripped Kundera of citizenship right upon the novel's publication in 1979. His report of Clementis's disappearance caused outrage by exposing the Orwellian politics of memory in Stalinist Czechoslovakia, not to mention the purges during which the country's Communist Revolution devoured many of its children.

Given such historical settings and official responses, it is not surprising that from the outset Western audiences have thought of Kundera as a dissident writing politically engaged novels deriding the Communist system. "Since his books refer to the injustices and bad faith of the Communist regime in Czechoslovakia, must this not be what his fiction is *about*? That is precisely how *The Joke* has been received in the West."[25] Subsequent works such as *The Book of Laughter and Forgetting* reinforced this perception. After the fall of Communism in Europe in 1989, the stereotype yielded a predictable consequence: growing concerns about Kundera's ongoing relevance. Noting that "Czech Communism collapsed twenty-five years ago," a recent review of Kundera's work asked pointedly "what happens to his fiction once the backdrop of Soviet oppression no longer throws his dark jokes ... into bright relief."[26] The worry was no less clear for being left discreetly unstated: if the defining feature of Kundera's novels has been their anti-Stalinism, the only place appropriate for him today is in the museum, next to the Stalinist system itself.

However, all such intimations of Kundera's obsolescence are misplaced, as is their underlying source: the traditional perception of his fiction as political art ridiculing Stalinism. This widespread perception fails to note several key points. Aside from Kundera's own problematic Communist past, the most obvious one is the marked shift in the setting of his novels since the end of the Cold War. Whether *Immortality* (1990), *Slowness* (1995), *Identity* (1998), or *The Festival of Insignificance* (2015), all unfold almost exclusively in France: at a chateau in the eighteenth century, at a hotel on the coast of Normandy, in the Luxembourg Gardens in present-day Paris. Insofar as Stalinist Czechoslovakia crops up in *Ignorance* (2000), it does so only in the memory of one of the characters, an émigré named Irena returning home after the Velvet Revolution. In other words, if Kundera used to populate his novels with KSČ members and tell their stories in order to lob literary hand-grenades at Stalinism, he stopped right when Communism fell and has been busy doing other things since then.

What is much more significant, however, is that even during the Cold War, at the peak of KSČ's normalization efforts, Kundera never considered himself a political novelist to begin with, notwithstanding the Communist milieu permeating his fiction from that period. The red star above the head of the white lion in the Czech coat of arms was shining bright and clear, tens of thousands of Soviet soldiers were drinking vodka and dancing *kazachok* in barracks around the country, and Kundera was busy writing tales about Prague doctors and artists doomed by the August 1968 invasion, to use the

example of *The Unbearable Lightness of Being*, but he nonetheless repeatedly and vehemently denounced any and all readings reducing his books
to anti-Stalinist tracts. "'Spare me your Stalinism, please. *The Joke* is a
love story!'" he angrily interjected during a 1980 television discussion when
one of the panelists referred to his first novel as "'a major indictment of
Stalinism.'"[27] Insofar as Kundera was concerned, his fiction was not political so much as politicized, and his message to those in the West interpreting
him through the anti-Stalinist prism was clear:

> If you cannot view the art that comes ... from Prague, Budapest or
> Warsaw in any other way than by means of this wretched political code,
> you murder it.... And you are quite unable to hear its true voice. The
> importance of this art does not lie in the fact that it pillories this or that
> political regime, but that, on the strength of social and human experi-
> ence of a kind people here in the West cannot even imagine, it offers new
> testimony about mankind.[28]

This testimony pertains to issues much more fundamental than any particular ideology or sociohistorical order, which are relevant only to the extent that they embody them and allow them to emerge. "I had been repeating
ad nauseam," Kundera recalled his efforts to educate his French readers and
critics about what really drives his fiction, that "the historical situation is not
the novel's proper subject matter; its value ... lies in shedding new, exceptionally sharp light on the existential themes that fascinate me...."[29] Comprehending Kundera's novels as no more than images of Stalinism amounts
to losing sight of these essential themes: letting them become occluded and
drowned out by their incidental historical instantiations.

> Certainly, politics and history are present, but only as a cache of con-
> crete situations (situational traps) revealing the only thing a novelist can
> possibly care about: the inexhaustible complexity of existence. (...) To
> read Kundera's novels as socio-political documents ... means to muti-
> late them and defile their values.[30]

For Kundera, the reduction of a work of art to its currently opportune political dimension, habitual in the reception of his novels on both sides of the
Iron Curtain, constitutes just about the greatest crime against it. "Nothing
worse could be happening to Central European art. Nothing worse can be
happening to the novel."[31]

Kundera's fiction thus can be interpreted as a scathing analysis of
Stalinism only insofar as the Stalinist order encapsulated certain basic
problems of existence inherent to all Western modernity and present in its
other historical and political manifestations as well, not least, as will be
seen, in the hegemony of liberal democracy, market capitalism, and mass
media culture after the end of the Cold War. His inquiry into these problems

makes Kundera's oeuvre, including its pre-1989 portion, as relevant as ever. Indeed, attempts to cast him as an anti-Communist writer whose novels are now passé need to be read in the context of the current hegemonic order: as attempts to marginalize one of its most perceptive and inconvenient critics. For the implications of Kundera's fiction for Western liberalism today are just as subversive as they were for Communism thirty or forty years ago: both narratives surface as epic jokes in which modern Europeans heroically proclaiming their emancipation from all self-imposed constraints in the context of a perfectly rational order descend, to the wild amusement of history, into ever greater alienation, irrationality, and oppression.

The Joke of Modern Rationality: Forging Happy Tomorrows—in a Gulag

Where does the critique of contemporary Western society emerge in Kundera's work? What are the existential themes propelling his fiction? It does not take a detective to discover them. He lists them in his extranovelistic notes: "revenge, forgetting, seriousness and unseriousness, the relation of history and the human being, the estrangement of one's action, the ambivalence of sex and love, and so on."[32] To these several others may be added, such as memory, identity, knowledge and ignorance, art and kitsch, the meaning or meaninglessness of temporal existence, and the yearning for justice and redemption. Many are immediately apparent from Kundera's titles: *Immortality, Ignorance, Identity, The Book of Laughter and Forgetting, The Festival of Insignificance.*

For the purpose of fleshing out Kundera's critique of Western liberal-capitalist society as the self-proclaimed end of humankind's intellectual evolution, his thoughts on knowledge and history offer the best point of departure. In Kundera's perspective, human reason is fundamentally limited, but it is just as intrinsic to modern Westerners intoxicated by the achievements of the scientific and industrial revolution not to be aware of the limits. The result is intractable conflict: history as a cruel jest foiling all human designs. Certain of their omniscience, modern doctrines of progress yield their opposites, in which the horrors of total control, irrational terror, and mass exclusion unfold under the banner of reason, peace, freedom, and happiness. "In the course of the Modern Era, Cartesian rationality has corroded ... all the values inherited from the Middle Ages. But just when reason wins a total victory, pure irrationality (force willing only its will) seizes the world stage...."[33] Kundera communicates this view not only through the doomed fates of his protagonists, whose actions spawn consequences exactly contrary to their original intentions, but especially through his writing style, which blends polyphony, irony, and metafictional philosophical interludes with actual historical events. His novels thereby foster multiperspectivism, rebel against homogenizing certitudes, and reveal their status as flawed human fabrications.

The notion of history as a ruthless force grinding all to dust lies at the very heart of *The Joke*, with which Kundera began his novelistic career and introduced its guiding formal and thematic characteristics. In and through the story of Ludvík's downfall, Kundera portrays a much larger collapse:

> the *debacle of modern rationality* face to face with the ruse of history, which transforms the noblest human intentions into their most brutal opposites. ... Ludvík ... belongs to the postwar generation which wanted to extend the rule of reason over human history. The deep irony of the 'dialectic of the Enlightenment' ... consists in the fact that the vision of rational control and planning of history lead to the irrationality of the gulag. ... The characters of *The Joke* have no luck saddling the logic of history; it throws them out of the saddle and crushes them with its hoofs. (...) The semantic gesture of *The Joke* fans out into a requiem for modern utopias, which ... sought total control of human society.[34]

Ludvík's demise serves as a miniature illustrating the fiasco of modern historical teleologies: like thousands of victims of Czechoslovak Communism in the 1950s and 1960s, including its most loyal servants such as Clementis or, for that matter, Kundera, he looks on powerlessly as the ideal society he himself helped to create morphs into its antithesis and mercilessly spits him out.

The root cause of this dialectic, Kundera hints, is precisely the modern presumption that history is a meaningful process amenable to rational analysis and mastery. Only when Ludvík begins to doubt this presumption and awaken to the inadequacy of the human mind does he commence to achieve some reconciliation with his grim ordeal. After realizing near the end of the novel that "the *entire* story of my life was conceived in error, through the bad joke of the postcard, that accident, that nonsense," it dawns on him that errors of this sort

> were so common and universal that they didn't represent exceptions or faults in the order of things; on the contrary, they constituted that order. What was it, then, that was mistaken? History itself? History the divine, the rational? But why call them history's *errors*? They seem so to my human reason, but if history really has its own reason, why should that reason care about human understanding, and why should it be as serious as a schoolmarm? What if history plays jokes?[35]

History is rationally inexplicable and uncontrollable for Kundera: light in the sense of devoid of any deeper meaning. But because modern Westerners, heirs to the Christian myth of God as the hidden Lord of all temporal affairs, find this lightness unbearable and insist on the presence of underlying purpose, the historical process persistently frustrates their plans and expectations, including the common belief in progress toward justice righting all wrongs. This belief, Ludvík surmises, is a delusion. "In reality the opposite is true: everything will be forgotten and nothing will be redressed. The task of obtaining redress ... will be taken over by forgetting."[36]

It is not only through Ludvík's conclusions, however, that Kundera conveys the message about human finitude and history as a jester that keeps on confounding, surprising, and laughing. He does it above all through the overall structure of *The Joke*: not a continuous first-person narrative, but a polyphony of monologues by four different characters, whose voices alternate according to the schema A-B-A-C-A-D-(A-B-C). Reflecting Kundera's conviction that the spirit of modern prose fiction "is the spirit of complexity" that says to readers, "'Things are not as simple as you think,'"[37] this polyphonic structure reveals the irreducible plurality and relativity of truth in the consciousness of his protagonists. Each of them embodies and operates within a specific linguistic-existential code shaping his or her conceptions of self, others, and the world at large. The idiosyncrasy and limits of each individual code emerge only in relation to the rest. *The Joke* is nothing if not a constellation of mirrors arranged to illuminate each other according to a delicate mathematical pattern.[38]

The polyphonic composition is inseparable from Kundera's use of irony—in the classical Greek sense of *eironeiá* as the blocking of one viewpoint opening up another—in portraying his characters.[39] Ludvík's postcard turns from an act of lighthearted play into an act of treason precisely by migrating into the radically different linguistic-existential code represented by Markéta and the Party. Ludvík ends up mocked by history because of his human inability to foresee, let alone control, this migration: the ease with which an idea, once released into the world and left to float in its river of randomly shifting contexts, acquires thoroughly new and unanticipated meanings. Insofar as the conflict triggering his demise is a conflict of interpretations of a simple text across incommensurable speech situations, polyphony and irony stem directly from the limits of language: *The Joke* tethers human ignorance and its consequences to the irreparable flaws in the instrument of human (mis)communication.[40] For Ludvík as for Kundera's other protagonists, both in *The Joke* and beyond, "loss of certainty about the content and meaning of words ... is ... a distinctive attribute of [their] alienation [from history and society]."[41]

The existential themes and formal elements first unveiled in *The Joke* recur throughout all Kundera's fiction. Stylistically, "Usually an author writing his first novel is not guided by a carefully thought-out personal aesthetic," Kundera remarked nineteen years after completing the book, but "When I look back at *The Joke* ... I find in it at the core everything I would strive for in my later novels."[42] This includes irony and polyphony, the fount of *eironeiá* in his writings. Over the course of his career, their reach and intensity have increased to such proportions as to spill out of his stories and engulf them from the outside, turning Kundera into a scandal bound to impress every novelist worth the name: the scandal of a writer reflexively interrogating, undermining, and escaping all traditional literary genres. "His endlessly cunning irony" renders "his art ... a thorough transgression" and "a project of exceptionally audacious emancipation."[43] From *The Joke* onward, Kundera's novels display "ever more pronounced abandonment of traditional ... plot, whereby [their] unity is no longer constituted by fabula, suzet, story, or action but by variations on a few main themes connected in a labyrinthically complex polyphonic composition...."[44] This composition is inspired by Kundera's musical background, specifically his passion for Janáček, and represents his greatest aesthetic transgression: "one of Kundera's most important contributions to the modern novel is precisely the extent to which he has musicalized its art."[45] Particularly in *The Book of Laughter and Forgetting* and *Immortality*, it erupts into sprawling, richly orchestrated metafictional sonatas in which movements performed by voices imagined and real, past and present—including Milan Kundera entering the story as one of the characters—harmoniously come together in periodic evocations of the same handful of basic motifs.[46]

Thematically, the insistence with which Kundera repeatedly probes the question of history suggests a lifelong obsession. Indeed, it is not Ludvík in *The Joke*, Tamina in *The Book of Laughter and Forgetting*, Tomáš and Tereza in *The Unbearable Lightness of Being*, or Agnes in *Immortality* who represent Kundera's principal characters, but history itself. Its enigma spans his entire oeuvre, whose individual books and protagonists merely mark its eternal return in subtle variations. If in *The Joke*, his opus no. 1, Kundera introduces history largely in the peripheral role of a sparse stage set against whose background Ludvík focalizes the main theme of man's estrangement from his deeds, in *The Book of Laughter and Forgetting*, opus no. 5, the stage set becomes the main theme.

> The Prague Spring ... is ... described ... as a fundamental existential situation: man (a generation of men) acts (makes a revolution), but his action slips out of control, ceases to obey him (the revolution rages, kills, destroys); he thereupon does his utmost to recapture and subdue the disobedient act (a new generation starts an opposition, reformist movement), but in vain. The act, once out of our hands, can never be recaptured.[47]

The dialectic of history turning on its masters emerges directly from the course of Czechoslovak and international politics, as does the deep source of this dialectic: modernity's boundless pride of knowledge, the mistaken assumption that instrumental reason can explain human nature and history, liberate human beings from all constraints, reconcile all their divisions, and achieve a perfectly harmonious order. The February 1948 coup setting up the monstrous joke of Czechoslovak Communism, Kundera stresses in this vein, came not from the unenlightened and backward segment of the nation but from the more sophisticated, progressive, and *modern* half:

the more dynamic, the more intelligent, the better. Yes, say what you will, the Communists were more intelligent. They had an imposing program. A plan for an entirely new world where everyone would find a place. (...) And then those young, intelligent, and radical people suddenly had the strange feeling of having sent out into the world an act that had begun to lead a life of its own, had ceased to resemble the idea it was based on, and did not care about those who had created it.[48]

In combination with his polyphonic compositional style, Kundera's fascination with the nature of man's historical existence endows his art with the distinctive qualities of historiographic metafiction. As the meditation on history that is the Kunderian novel unleashes polyphony to ironize not just its protagonists but itself, whether via essayistic digressions relativizing its own truth or by drawing its author into the circle of its characters, it reveals historical reality in all its plasticity and contingency: as a symbolic-linguistic artifact. This is, after all, the real subject of the passage about Clementis in *The Book of Laughter and Forgetting*: not the past, but its representation as a process of narrative construction commonly associated with fiction writing. No doubt Kundera would endorse the dictum that history is "a species of the genus Story."[49] His highly self-conscious approach to novelistic composition follows in the footsteps of Hermann Broch, Franz Kafka, Robert Musil, Jaroslav Hašek, and Witold Gombrowicz; particularly the "polyhistoric" method of Broch's trilogy *The Sleepwalkers*, which blends narrative, verse, aphorism, essay, and reportage, has been repeatedly acknowledged by Kundera as a major source of influence.[50] In Kundera's native land, metafiction has been in short supply: "the character of Czech prose inclines rather toward unreflected, spontaneous story-telling,"[51] which hides the principles and wellsprings of literary art. In stark contrast, Kundera's work serves a constant reminder that "the modern novel is not only a narrative of a story, but also a story of narrative itself."[52]

This reminder culminates in *The Curtain*: "a novel about the novel" or "a novel squared," in which "Kundera definitively transcend[s] the formal and aesthetic divide between fiction ... and reflection."[53] Subtitled *An Essay in Seven Parts* and marketed as literary criticism, it is nonetheless indistinguishable from Kundera's novels, only the heroes are great European writers and the action is the development of modern Western prose fiction. Without specific *a priori* expectations about what kind of truths *The Curtain* is supposed to purvey, expectations shaped by its dust jacket, library cataloguing, bookstore shelf placement, and magazine reviews, one would be unable to tell its genre: a history or a novel? It is both. Kundera thereby perfectly illustrates one of the main tenets of Whitean narrative theory: "History is no less a form of fiction than the novel is a form of historical representation."[54] That he includes *The Curtain* in his authorized oeuvre, which is restricted only to those of his works he deems artistically relevant, primarily his novels, further underscores his keen awareness of the aesthetic dimension of historical writing.

Kundera's fiction and essays have had profound influence on postmodern political philosophy. His reflections on the art of the novel constitute the epigraph to Richard Rorty's *Contingency, Irony, and Solidarity* and directly inform Rorty's anti-foundationalist vision of liberal democracy as a polis which derives its moral authority from novelists rather than philosophers and for which the novel is the genre "most closely associated with the struggle for freedom and equality."[55] This influence is not surprising given the deep fount of all Kundera's writings: his conviction that after the Death of God, in a world deprived of metaphysical warrants, "nobody owns the truth and everybody has the right to be understood."[56] For Kundera novelistic space is a realm of relativity, uncertainty, ambiguity, and tolerance where multiple perspectives exist side by side, each equally valid within its own frame of reference. It is devoid of absolute claims and final conclusions. A novel written in order to illustrate some thesis is a contradiction in terms. "Nothing is more foreign to me," Kundera stated in this regard, for "A novel does not assert anything; a novel searches and poses questions."[57] Its wisdom lies not in affirming the world but in subverting it: revealing, through imagined characters and situations, that it can be other than it is.

This, then, is the defining mission of modern prose fiction according to Kundera, its sole morality: to defamiliarize the familiar and problematize the unproblematic. "Like Penelope, it undoes each night the tapestry that theologians, philosophers, and learned men have woven the day before."[58] What emerges when the novelist tears through the "curtain of pre-interpretation" and shatters "the nonthought of received ideas" is reality "in all the comical nakedness of its prose": reality demystified, a human text.[59]

The Novel as a Negation of Idyllic Consciousness

That this conception of the novelistic art cannot be anything other than a sworn enemy of Stalinism goes without saying and is abundantly clear from Kundera's scathing treatment of Czechoslovakia's Communist regime in his pre-1989 works. "[G]rounded in the relativity and ambiguity of things human, the novel is incompatible with the totalitarian universe."[60] What his Anglophone readers have understood less well, or not at all, is that for Kundera "this incompatibility is ... not only political or moral but *ontological*"[61] and that, *as an ontological formation*, the totalitarian universe extends far beyond Stalinism. It encompasses any "world built on sacrosanct certainties,"[62] including the one erected on the certainties of liberal democracy and market capitalism and proclaiming the unification and conclusion of humankind's history on their basis: the Western world after the Cold War.

This project has its own totalizing dynamic. It "has been accompanied by a process of dizzying reduction" channeled and amplified by the mass media, which "distribute throughout the world the same simplifications and stereotypes easily acceptable by the greatest number, by everyone, by all mankind"[63]—the nonthought of empty news images, political slogans, and advertising and entertainment campaigns. Today even more so than thirty years ago, when Kundera first spotted it, this homogenizing "common spirit of the mass media, camouflaged by political diversity, is the spirit of our time," and it runs "contrary to the spirit of the novel."[64] It should come as no surprise, then, that Kundera's prose fiction carries subversive implications for present-day Western society and its global ambitions.

These implications are most visible in his post-Cold War works, but they inhere in all his novels, including his earliest ones. The reason is that contemporary Western liberalism espouses the same lofty assumptions about knowledge, history, and the scope of human possibility as used to underlie Soviet Communism, in whose guise they have represented one of Kundera's core existential themes since *The Joke*: that history is progress, that its *logos* and *telos* are rationally ascertainable, and that sufficiently enlightened social engineers can hasten the advent of universal perfection through more or less radical policies formulated on their basis. In other words, much like Communism, liberalism, too, is a specimen of idyllic consciousness, which Kundera considers the backbone of modern historical imagination, keeps mocking in his novelistic inquiries, and defines by its yearning for "the condition of the world before the first conflict; or beyond conflicts; or with conflicts that are only misunderstandings, thus false conflicts."[65]

Kundera remembers this yearning well from his own past as a lyrical poet in Czechoslovakia after World War II, when he joined hands with other students, artists, and intellectuals to build the idyll of the KSČ:

> that garden where nightingales sing, ... that realm of harmony where the world does not rise up as a stranger against man and man against other men, but rather where the world and all men are shaped from one and the same matter.[66]

Just as intimately familiar to him is the eventual result of those efforts: a society of lonely, isolated individuals—"captive minds," as Czesław Miłosz famously described them—paralyzed by paranoia and terror where everybody spied on everybody else and nobody believed a word of the official slogans about fraternal unity and happy tomorrows. It was the shocking rise of this society in Czechoslovakia in the early 1950s that led Kundera to renounce Soviet Communism, disown his lyrical past, turn to prose fiction, and eventually find his permanent artistic home in the novel as an eminently anti-idyllic literary form characterized by relativism, polyphony, and ironic laughter. In the Prague purges, during which Czechoslovakia's Communist Revolution got away from its hapless makers and began executing them at random, Kundera glimpsed the deep joke of history for the first time: the way idyllic visions of "an entirely new world where everyone would find a place"[67] engender, by virtue of the necessarily limited perspective of their human progenitors, the gulag and the gallows for those who do not fit in. In Czechoslovakia after February 1948, some "people … immediately understood that they did not have the right temperament for the idyll and tried to go abroad. But since the idyll is in essence a world for all, … instead of going abroad they went behind bars."[68]

Idyllic consciousness is not specific to Communism, however, and in interrogating it Kundera grapples with much more than just his and his native country's dark past: he addresses a set of ideas whose roots lie deep within Europe's cultural heritage and feed into all Western modernity, not only *The Communist Manifesto*.[69] The archetype of idyllic discourse is biblical eschatology: the Judeo-Christian myth of history as the story of salvation. During secularization at the dawn of the modern era this archetypal narrative was stripped of its religious content, but its eschatological form remained intact and became reoccupied with new categories appropriate to the Enlightenment.[70] Faith was replaced with reason, divine providence with human progress, and the transcendent Kingdom of God prophesied to redeem mankind at the end of time with immanent perfect society to be actualized through science and technology. If modern idyllic consciousness means "a systematic interpretation of universal history in accordance with a principle by which historical events and successions are unified and directed toward an ultimate meaning," then its "very existence … emerged from the faith in an ultimate purpose."[71] None illustrates this better than Hegel, who defined world history as the progress of rational Spirit, Spirit as the Divine Idea, and his philosophy as "the true *Theodicæa*, the justification of God in history."[72] His conception of history profoundly influenced the intellectual climate in nineteenth-century Europe in all its ideological diversity. When Reinhold Niebuhr reflected on the nature of modern historical consciousness a hundred years later, by which point the titanic clash of Western idylls—the Thousand-Year Reich, the New Soviet Man, the New World from across the Atlantic—was well underway and laying waste to Europe, he instantly noticed the remarkable "unity which transcends warring social philosophies. (…) Modern men of all shades of opinion agree in the belief that [history] is a redemptive process."[73]

In 1989, only a few months before the fall of the Berlin Wall, the long list of these men grew longer with the addition of a new name: Francis Fukuyama. Right from the opening paragraphs of his famous analysis of the final decade of the Cold War, he asserts that world history is neither random chaos, nor a congeries of local microhistories, nor again merely a sum of its parts, but a manifestation of a single "larger process at work, a process that gives coherence and order to the daily headlines."[74] This deep process is not cyclical and self-defeating, as in the Platonic conception of time as the moving image of unmoving eternity in endless revolution, but linear and progressive, unfolding toward an absolute end: "an unabashed victory of economic and political liberalism" as "the triumph of the West, of the Western *idea*."[75] Historians unaware of this *telos* have no way of "distinguishing between what is essential and what is contingent in world history"[76] and are doomed to superficial interpretations, ones missing the true import of the changes in international relations during the 1980s. Fukuyama, however, has no difficulty grasping their buried meaning:

> What we may be witnessing is not just the end of the Cold War, or the passing of a particular period of postwar history, but the end of history as such: that is, the end point of mankind's ideological evolution and the universalization of Western liberal democracy as the final form of human government.[77]

That this universalization is as yet incomplete, with most of the world outside Europe and North America—the "most advanced outposts ... at the vanguard of civilization"[78]—still clinging to different forms of political and economic organization, is inconsequential; it has no bearing on the underlying logic of history, which will continue propelling the world toward eventual convergence with iron necessity. Just as in biblical eschatology, in Fukuyama's instance, too, the belief that temporal affairs express a hidden purpose results in the ability not only to explicate the past but, first and foremost, prophesy the future: Western liberalism "is the ideal that will govern the material world in the long run."[79]

This future is idyllic exactly in the sense in which Kundera defines the term: as the condition of the world before the first conflict, beyond conflicts, or with conflicts that are only misunderstandings. According to Fukuyama, "human history and the conflict that characterized it is based on the existence of 'contradictions,'"[80] such as in the relationship between masters and slaves, humans and nature, and bourgeoisie and proletariat. But in "the state that emerges at the end of history," which is "liberal insofar as it recognizes and protects through a system of law man's universal right to freedom, and democratic insofar as it exists with the consent of the governed," none of these divisions remains: "all prior contradictions are resolved and all human needs are satisfied."[81] Progress toward liberalism is thus progress out of and beyond strife—or, alternatively, a gradual *return* to and *recovery* of a primordial harmony lost at the beginning of history thanks to human ignorance and obscured for millennia by irrational political and economic systems. The fall of Soviet Communism as the last one of these misguided systems "does not ... imply the end of international conflict *per se*," Fukuyama qualifies his prediction; Western liberalism has yet to spread globally, until which point "Conflict between states still in history, and between those states and those at the end of history, [remains] possible."[82] But the tendency and its ultimate result are nonetheless clear: "the diminution of the likelihood of large-scale conflict between states" and "the growing 'Common

Marketization' of international relations."[83] When the entire world, following the light of reason and civilization shining forth from the capitals of Western Europe and North America, finally stumbles out of the darkness of history and arrives at its end, war will disappear. It "will be replaced by economic calculation, the endless solving of technical problems, environmental concerns, and the satisfaction of sophisticated consumer demands."[84]

The Hegelian origins of this narrative lie in plain sight: Fukuyama openly celebrates the German philosopher and his teleological conception of history. Since this conception also informs Marxism, the ideological archnemesis of Western liberalism during the Cold War, part of Fukuyama's argument involves divorcing Hegel from Marx:

> It is Hegel's misfortune to be known primarily as Marx's precursor, and it is our misfortune that few of us are familiar with Hegel's work from direct study, but only as it has been filtered through the distorting lens of Marxism.[85]

Luckily, Fukuyama discovers a ready-made solution to this problem in French philosophy, specifically in the lectures by Alexandre Kojève, which "save Hegel from his Marxist interpreters and resurrect him as the philosopher who most correctly speaks to our time."[86] Crucially, the Marxist distortion alleged by Fukuyama pertains only to the substance of the end of history, *not* to the notion that history has a redeeming end in the first place: a presupposition both he and Kojève share with Marx, all three adopt from Hegel, and Hegel inherits from generations of European philosophers and theologians going back to the Old Testament. Fukuyama's liberal narrative thus retains precisely the element that constitutes the deep target of Kundera's ironic treatments of Communism: idyllic consciousness as a general feature of Western modernity.

Fukuyama is hardly the only Western liberal in the grip of this consciousness. The most powerful outburst of idyllic imagination in Anglophone thinking about international politics occurred not at the end of the twentieth century but at the beginning: in Woodrow Wilson's quest to rid the world of war by remaking sovereign states and the international system as a whole in the image of American democracy. This project did not derive from the biblical archetype; it *was* the archetype. Wilson interpreted all political reality and his role in it directly through the prism of Protestant eschatology:

> he regarded universal history as a progressively unfolding struggle between Christ and Satan; the United States as God's designated vanguard in this struggle; World War I as the apocalyptic climax of the struggle; and his statecraft as the divinely ordained pathway to the Millennium of freedom, peace, justice, and material plenty. ... [C]ollective security and the League of Nations ... signified the fulfillment of the biblically prophesied Kingdom of God on earth, *in hoc sæculo*.[87]

Although his efforts failed, his vision became "the bedrock of American foreign-policy thinking," the origin of the "Wilsonian Century," and the cornerstone of America's "Wilsonian" diplomatic culture.[88]

Fukuyama simply extended it into the post-Cold War era, where the idea of history as American-guided liberal progress to global harmony and prosperity has continued to thrive as a common denominator uniting all Republican and Democratic presidents.[89] None of them has had to explain it to the electorate, raised for centuries on patriotic Puritan myths of America's universal mission, special election, and manifest destiny. The only thing left for pundits to do was to see who could make these old beliefs even more instinctively digestible. Thomas Friedman handily won the contest when, in his "Golden Arches Theory of Conflict Prevention" arguing that "No two countries that both have a McDonald's have ever fought a war against each other,"[90] he de facto gave the liberal idyll the shape of a cheeseburger. Leading the Western world in constitutional freedoms as much as obesity rates, Americans happily discovered that achieving global peace was quite simple after all: merely a matter of converting humanity to their greasy fast food.

Kundera's literary critique of idyllic consciousness militates against the liberal teleology of history in all the above varieties, whether those speaking the sophisticated language of biblical exegesis or Hegelian philosophy, as in the cases of Wilson and Fukuyama, or those requiring no brain but only a stomach, as in the case of Friedman. The warning that human-made heavens on earth always end up building little hells on the side for all the inevitable misfits, which Kundera issues through his portrayals of Communism, enables one to resist the liberal-capitalist paradise, seemingly as inclusive as people's democracies once purported to be also, with a question its prophets pretend does not exist: who will be in *its* gulag?

The answer is easy enough to glean from Kojève's identification of the eventual "universal homogeneous state" with the "American way of life," elaborated by Fukuyama as "liberal democracy in the political sphere combined with easy access to VCRs and stereos in the economic."[91] The end of history is consecrated to markets, profits, and consumption. To survive its arrival and gain entry into the post-historical future, one must be ready to adopt private self-interest as the highest virtue, define it in material terms, and comprehend all dimensions of life—whether politics, education, health, art, or anything else—transactionally, through the prism of commercial exchange. Above all, as Friedman's and Fukuyama's references to corporate logos and audiovisual technology hint, one must embrace the virtual world of the postmodern media culture and pledge unquestioning obedience to its arbiters: powerful business elites dictating mass consciousness through the manipulation of news, advertising, and entertainment images.

These arbiters or "imagologues," as Kundera refers to them, "influence our behavior ... just as in the past we have been ruled by the systems of ideologues."[92] In his post-Cold War fiction, Kundera culminates his critique of the West by turning from Communist ideology to liberal-capitalist "imagology" as the main source of oppression and the explicit target of his irony.

Against the Tyranny of Liberal Capitalist Imagology

"Imagology! Who first thought up this remarkable neologism?"[93] It does not really matter, Kundera answers, for the word

> finally lets us put under one roof something that goes by so many names: advertising agencies; political campaign managers; designers who devise the shape of everything from cars to gym equipment; fashion stylists; barbers; show-business stars dictating the norms of physical beauty....[94]

The term aptly summarizes the diffuse culture industry governing every aspect of life in the West today: from "our political opinions and aesthetic tastes ... [to] the color of carpets and the selection of books."[95]

Kundera does not resort to the neologism only because of its descriptive power. He adopts it above all for its near-homonymy with "ideology" and in order to communicate the key point of his critical analysis of contemporary Western society: imagology captures the survival and evolution of ideology beyond the end of history and into the ostensibly post-historical and post-ideological era of liberal-capitalist globalization. On the surface, ideology and imagology may appear separated by the same chasm as lies between the historical past and the post-historical future in Fukuyama's thesis: whereas "ideology belonged to history, ... the reign of imagology begins where history ends."[96] Under the surface, however, they are connected: for Kundera imagology represents not only a secret mutation of ideology but its perfect and absolute form. "[He] emphasizes the insidious way in which imagology claims to transcend ideology rather than partake of it by exploring the imagological claim to eliminate ideology in the name of a universal value system," and in the course of this exploration he reveals that "the elevation of imagology to the level of a transparently obvious portrayal of how the world works is not an escape from the clutches of ideology but the most sublime and effective manifestation of it."[97] This finding directly negates the self-understanding of the West after 1989, which casts its guiding principles in post-ideological terms: as plain truths, what remains after all ideological distortions have been stripped away, releasing humanity from its long history of alienation and uniting it in a harmonious cosmopolis of peace, commerce, and authentic freedom.

"Imagologues," Kundera notes, "existed long before they created the powerful institutions we know today."[98] The origins of the phenomenon reside in early twentieth-century Europe, at the peak of the ideological age, and are associated particularly with Nazi propagandists and their spectacular, carefully staged mass rallies. "Hitler had his personal imagologue, who used to stand in front of him and patiently demonstrate the gestures to be made during speeches so as to fascinate the crowds."[99] The subsequent rise and evolution of imagology may be traced using the example of Soviet Marxism:

> Some one hundred years ago in Russia, persecuted Marxists began to gather secretly in small circles in order to study Marx's manifesto; they simplified the contents of this simple ideology in order to disseminate it to other circles, whose members, simplifying further this simplification of the simple, kept passing it on and on, so that when Marxism became known and powerful on the whole planet, all that was left of it was a collection of seven slogans so poorly linked that it can hardly be called an ideology. And precisely because the remnants of Marx no longer form any *logical* system of *ideas*, but only a series of suggestive images and slogans, ... we can rightfully talk of a gradual, general, planetary transformation of ideology into imagology.[100]

Born out of ideology, imagology slowly displaces and replaces it by hollowing it out until all substance of rational thought has vanished and only a shell of empty, mindless, perfectly modular signs remains. The process is driven by the same impulse as motivates marketing campaigns: the desire to appeal to the greatest number of people and achieve global monopoly. To raise the "objecti[on] that advertising and propaganda cannot be compared, because the one serves commerce and the other ideology," is to "understand nothing."[101]

As the process unfolds, Kundera stresses that the relationship between reality and sign, politician and imagologue undergoes a crucial metamorphosis: an inversion. In the past, reality determined images and slogans, which had to abide by it, were measured against it, and could be discarded as illusions. "Reality was stronger than ideology."[102] The politician controlled the imagologue. "If [Hitler's] imagologue, in an interview with the press, had amused the Germans by describing Hitler as incapable of moving his hands, he would not have survived his indiscretion by more than a few hours."[103] Today, however, images and slogans—Kundera singles out the pervasive talk of human rights and the stereotype of a laughing and waving statesman surrounded with children—determine political reality, which must comply with them regardless of their status as pure illusions devoid of any concrete content.[104] It is in this sense that imagology has surpassed ideology: "imagology is stronger than reality."[105] The human "I" itself has been divested of its foundational status and redefined into a function of its image. As Kundera points out in an aside even more pertinent now, in the age of Facebook, than when he wrote it, it is no longer tenable

> to believe that our image is only an illusion that conceals our selves, as the one true essence independent of the eyes of the world. The imagologues have revealed with cynical radicalism that the reverse is true: our

self is a mere illusion, ... while the only reality ... is our image in the eyes of others. (...) A person is nothing but his image.[106]

Politics and life in general have become entirely a matter of striking correct poses and uttering correct phrases.

The decisive shift inaugurating the reign of imagology took place when Bob Woodward and Carl Bernstein exposed the Watergate scandal. Their investigative reports leading to President Nixon's impeachment proceedings and resignation strike Kundera as "a great historic transition, a milestone, an unforgettable moment, a changing of the guard," in which "a new power had appeared, the only one capable of toppling the former professional power brokers, until then the politicians."[107] Ever since then the polis has been ruled by imagologues and the media rather than by politicians. "The politician is dependent on the journalist," journalists "are ... dependent ... on those who pay them," and "those who pay them are the advertising agencies that buy space from newspapers and time from radio and TV stations."[108]

The ideological implication of imagology is decidedly conservative. In sharp contrast to doctrines articulated in the nineteenth century and enacted a century later, yielding what Eric Hobsbawm called the "Age of Extremes" full of violence and conflict, imagology is a system of peaceful stasis. Unlike traditional liberalism or Marxism, it makes no attempt to transcend the status quo but instead works to preserve it and freeze existing injustices and inequalities indefinitely. Whereas "ideology was like a set of enormous wheels at the back of the stage, turning and setting in motion wars, revolutions, reforms, ... the wheels of imagology turn without having any effect upon history,"[109] which has been officially declared over: terminating in global political and economic liberalism.

Insofar as change still occurs in the world, it takes place only in the sense of cyclical succession of artificial systems of ideals and anti-ideals organized by imagology in order to distract attention away from the persistence of suffering and oppression. Put differently,

> The word "change" ... has been given a new meaning: it no longer means *a new stage of coherent development* (as it was understood by Vico, Hegel, or Marx), but *a shift from one side to another*, from front to back, from the back to the left, from the left to the front (as understood by designers dreaming up the fashion for the next season).[110]

As the frequency of these shifts increases and the wheels of imagology accelerate to dizzying speeds, rendering anything new—products, headlines, political platforms—instantly obsolete, distraction becomes permanent. Any remaining potential for real change evaporates.

What makes the stasis especially difficult to disrupt is imagology's uncanny and unprecedented ability to affirm itself through the democratic process:

Public opinion polls are the critical instrument of imagology's power, because they enable imagology to live in absolute harmony with the people. ... [They] are a parliament in permanent session, whose function is to create truth, the most democratic truth that has ever existed.[111]

With masses withdrawn from unmediated reality and trapped in the virtual world of empty representations, poll results never negate or undermine imagology's rule; assent is the only possible outcome. Emancipatory critique becomes foreclosed, stasis terminal. "Because it will never be at variance with the parliament of truth, the power of imagologues will always live in truth," to the point that even Kundera, despite "know[ing] that everything human is mortal," confesses, "I cannot imagine anything that could break this power."[112] At best, resistance and subversion earn one the label of a retrograde ideologue: a dangerous enemy of freedom and democracy. At worst, they end up commodified into best-selling products, such as t-shirts imprinted with the face of Che Guevara, illustrating imagology's boundless capacity to absorb even the most violent forms of protest and make them serve its purposes.[113]

The reign of imagology is therefore total, and not merely thanks to its unmatched skill in neutralizing dissent. It is total also in the sense of leaving no islands of refuge. The photographic lens is to the contemporary West what God was to medieval Europe: omnipresent and omnipotent, the ultimate source of political authority and personal identity alike. "God's eye has been replaced by a camera. The eye of one has been replaced by the eyes of all. Life has changed into one vast orgy in which everyone takes part," and this "universal orgy ... has nothing to do with delight but merely serves solemn notice to all that they have nowhere to hide and that everyone is at the mercy of everyone else."[114] In its post-historical liberal-capitalist apotheosis saturated with mass media technology, the Enlightenment project of rational emancipation thus yields a global prison: Bentham's Panopticon perfected into a carceral society of planetary proportions, in which "all of us live under the gaze of cameras" and even "when we want to protest against anything, we can't make ourselves heard without [them]."[115] This is the ultimate joke told by Kundera, attuned to the whimsies of history like only a real April Fool can be: liberal-capitalist freedom from oppression results in the oppression of liberal-capitalist freedom. In the Panopticon, disciplining power becomes its own end: blind, irrational force automated to function independently of who exercises it, regardless of their purpose, and so efficiently that its actual performance ceases to be necessary.[116]

Since the 1980s, Kundera has been repeating this joke through ever more explicit analogies of liberal-capitalist imagology to Communist ideology.

What makes reading Kundera's novels written in France ... most interesting is that we find here *exactly the same dispositions*, the same subjective and collective attitudes, repeating themselves in his eyes in the West, where ideology has been superseded by the rule of the Spectacle ... and where the place of imposed dogma has been taken up by the tyranny of (ostensibly "democratic") opinion.[117]

The celebrated revolutions of 1989 were largely apparent: yet another myth propagated by Western imagology. They put an end to Communism but not to coercion and domination. Kundera asserts their illusory nature especially pointedly in *Ignorance*, whose expatriate protagonists Irena and Josef experience profound disappointment when they arrive in Prague after the fall of the Iron Curtain. Irena realizes that Franz Kafka has been packaged into a tacky tourist attraction, which silences the revolutionary art and radical political implications of his novelistic explorations of man's enslavement in modern bureaucratized society every bit as effectively as the ban previously imposed on him by the KSČ. Josef is even more direct in his appraisal of the new "freedoms" brought to Central Europe by political and economic liberalism:

> The Soviet empire collapsed because it could no longer hold down the nations that wanted their independence. But those nations—they're less independent than ever now. They can't choose their own economy or their own foreign policy or even their own advertising slogans.[118]

Genuine freedom and autonomy, scarce under Communism, have become scarcer still with the region's incorporation into Western trade and political structures.[119] No wonder Kundera did not bother returning to the land of his birth.

Recovering the Forgotten Democratic Socialist Legacy of the Prague Spring

Kundera's thoughts on imagology bear a clear stamp of the intellectual climate in which he formulated them: French post-structuralism in the 1980s. They echo not only Foucaldian ideas about regimes of truth, surveillance, and carceral society, but especially Baudrillard's argument about the precession of simulacra in the postmodern age. Just like Kundera, Baudrillard asserted that in Western society artificial imitations of reality, particularly visual representations, have proliferated to the point of "substituting the sign of the real for the real,"[120] wiping out all empirical bases for emancipatory critique.

This context is now three decades old, but Kundera's musings about imagology, politics, and oppression have hardly gone out of date. On the contrary, like the vintages of Chenin Blanc deposited into cellars around Savennières when he first arrived in France and landed at the nearby University of Rennes, they have become more valuable with the passage of time. The march of capitalism from Western Europe to the former Eastern

Bloc and beyond—Fukuyama's "common marketization" of international relations—has conquered and homogenized societies far more swiftly and successfully than totalitarian dictators of yesteryear. Amidst endless liberal proclamations about the need to protect and foster diversity, expressions of difference have been on retreat. As Kundera stated in 2007,

> In a period when the Russian world tried to reshape my small country in its image, I worked out my ideal thus: *maximum diversity in minimum space*. The Russians no longer rule my native land, but that ideal is even more imperiled now.[121]

Since the collapse of the Soviet empire, it has lost even more ground to its opposite: the ideal of minimum diversity in maximum space, which informs the liberal-capitalist fantasy of global convergence to the American way of life as much as it once did the Marxist-Leninist dream of a universal brotherhood of New Soviet Men.

Nowhere is the annihilation of politics by imagology illustrated and the shape of liberal-capitalist cosmopolis foreshadowed more vividly than in the contemporary United States. Global leader in finance, entertainment, and information technology alike, the country evinces staggering economic inequality where the richest one percent own more wealth than the bottom ninety percent and have captured the political system to serve their narrow interests.[122] Advertising itself at home and abroad as a liberal democracy "of the people, by the people, for the people," America is in fact a corporate plutocracy "of the 1%, by the 1%, for the 1%," as Joseph Stiglitz recently put it in a provocative counter to Abraham Lincoln's famous words from the Gettysburg Address.[123] Imagology has played an essential role in sustaining the former appearance over the latter reality. In the recent ascent of billionaire entrepreneur and television personality Donald Trump to the White House it has scored its most magnificent victory yet. After entertaining the masses with a campaign practically indistinguishable from his reality TV series *The Apprentice*, Trump, one of America's largest commercial brand names, purchased the Presidency of the United States, added it to his corporate portfolio, and did it all through the established channels of democratic electoral process. To reject the result, therefore, would paradoxically mean rejecting the procedures and institutions of representative government.

Kundera demystifies the contemporary liberal-capitalist order and cuts through its purportedly post-ideological veil of images as deftly as Adorno, Foucault, Baudrillard, and other leading critical theorists of late Western modernity. Indeed, he does it even more effectively: using the language of the novel, much more accessible to the general public than their complicated analyses. As a repository of emancipatory resistance, this makes Kundera twice as dangerous. Unfortunately, he is by no means exempt from the workings of imagology, which surrounds him and appropriates him for its purposes as inevitably as it does all other dissident novelists, such as Don

DeLillo. For Kundera is not just a storyteller, of course, but above all a story: a prominent public myth forged by the West for the West in the 1960s and 1970s. This myth, to return to Kundera's standard reception discussed at the outset of this chapter, casts him as a heroic artist dreaming of life, liberty, and happiness in the depths of an evil socialist empire, taking a courageous stand against its tyrannical rulers, managing to flee their armies, and eventually fulfilling his dream in exile. It is a small but important part of a larger symbolic narrative propounded by the West in a self-serving effort to justify its global predominance: the narrative of the Cold War, and of history in general, as universal progress to political and economic liberalism as the sole viable foundation for society in the long run.

Problematizing this hegemonic representation of Kundera is deeply inconvenient, and not just because the valiant knight of liberal capitalism is rather too prone to removing his shiny armor, stripping down to his underwear, and exposing himself as his own hilarious negation in a metamorphosis worthy of his most beloved character: Don Quixote de la Mancha. It is uncomfortable especially because in the liberal eschatology of the Cold War Kundera is tightly interwoven with many other myths, which cannot survive the collapse of his orthodox reputation intact; they are bound to be compromised also. Indeed, the scandal of Kundera as a critic rather than advocate of Western liberalism is liable to spread rather quickly all the way to the Prague Spring itself, one of the most treasured symbols in the entire Western imagology of the Cold War era.[124]

This is because Kundera indicates unmistakably that rather than a movement to replace the Soviet utopia of collective existence with the Western utopia of individual freedom and *laissez-faire*, as the event is ordinarily portrayed, the Prague Spring embodied an alternative to both systems: democratic socialism as a pragmatic, critically minded third way "inspired by the postrevolutionary skepticism of adults" tired of living "smothered beneath ideological idiocy."[125] Reminiscing on this alternative decades later, Kundera related its spontaneous appearance in Czechoslovakia in the early months of 1968 as follows:

> The Prague Spring began: gleeful, the country rejected the lifestyle imposed by Russia; the State borders opened up, and all the social organizations (the syndicates, unions, associations), initially meant to transmit to the people the Party's will, went independent and turned themselves into unexpected instruments of an unexpected democracy. A system was born (with no advance planning, almost by chance) that was truly unprecedented: the economy 100 percent nationalized, agriculture in the hands of cooperatives, nobody too rich, nobody too poor, schools and medicine for free, but also: the end of the secret police's power, the end of political persecutions, the freedom to write without censorship, and consequently the blooming of literature, art, thought, journals.[126]

Whether this model would have sustained itself had Moscow not sent any tanks to kill it, nobody can be sure, not even Kundera as one of its intellectual leaders: "I cannot tell what the prospects might have been for [its] future...; in the geopolitical situation of the time, certainly not great; but in a different geopolitical situation?"[127] But two things are beyond any doubt: that for Kundera "the second the system existed ... was magnificent"[128] and that American liberalism today bears as little resemblance to this remarkable system as Soviet Communism did half a century ago.

Notes

1 Ludvík Vaculík, "Dva tisíce slov," *Literární listy* 17, no. 18 (27 June 1968): 1–3. Within weeks the manifesto garnered signatures of over one hundred thousand Czechoslovak citizens.

2 Antonín Novotný quoted in Ladislav Verecký, "Milan Kundera: Spisovatel, který se skrývá," *Lidové noviny*, 29 November 2001, 12.

3 Kundera quoted in Marie Němcová Banerjee, *Terminal Paradox: The Novels of Milan Kundera* (New York: Grove Weidenfeld, 1990), 3.

4 Milan Jungmann, "Kunderovské paradoxy," in Michal Přibáň, ed., *Z dějin českého myšlení o literatuře 1970–1989*, vol. 4 of *Antologie k Dějinám české literatury 1945–1990* (Prague: Ústav pro českou literaturu AV ČR, 2005), 322.

5 Milan Kundera, *Poslední máj* (Prague: Československý spisovatel, 1955). See also idem, *Člověk zahrada širá* (Prague: Československý spisovatel, 1953).

6 Milan Kundera, *The Book of Laughter and Forgetting*, trans. Aaron Asher (New York: Harper, 1996), 91.

7 Ibid., 92.

8 Jan Mervart, "Fenomén Literárních novin," in Jan Mervart, Petr Dvorský, and Martin Kučera, eds., *Inspirace Pražské jaro 1968* (Hradec Králové: Sumbalon, 2014), 169.

9 Verecký, "Kundera," 12.

10 Milan Kundera, "Nesamozřejmost národa," *Literární noviny* 16, no. 38 (22 September 1967): 3.

11 For Kundera's exchange with Havel, see Kundera, "Český úděl," *Listy* 1, nos. 7/8 (1968): 1, 5; Havel, "Český úděl?" *Tvář* 4, no. 2 (1969): 30–33; and Kundera, "Radikalismus a exhibicionismus," *Host do domu* 15, no. 15 (1969): 24–29.

12 Cf. Květoslav Chvatík, "Mé setkání s Milanem Kunderou," in Aleš Haman and Vladimír Novotný, eds., *Hommage à Milan Kundera: Pocta Milanu Kunderovi: Sborník k 80. spisovatelovým narozeninám* (Prague: Artes Liberales, 2009), 26. For Reagan's strategy, see John Lewis Gaddis, *Strategies of Containment: A Critical Appraisal of American National Security Policy during the Cold War*, revised ed. (New York: Oxford University Press, 2005), 342–378. Kundera's essay was widely reprinted. In the United States, it appeared in *The New York Review of Books* 31, no. 7 (26 April 1984): 33–38.

13 Marek Bieńczyk, "Číst Kunderu v době Solidarity," in Bohumil Fořt, Jiří Kudrnáč, and Petr Kyloušek, eds., *Milan Kundera aneb Co zmůže literatura? Soubor statí o díle Milana Kundery* (Brno: Host, 2012), 204.

14 See Milan Kundera, author's note to *Žert* (Brno: Atlantis, 1996 [1967]): 324–326.

15 Milan Kundera, "Můj přítel Jireš," *Iluminace* 8, no. 1 (1996): 6.

16 Jungmann, "Kunderovské paradoxy." See also Peter Steiner, "Spory o symbolický kapitál," in Fořt et al., eds., *Kundera aneb Co zmůže literatura?* 217, 221–222. As Verecký ("Kundera," 12) notes, Jungmann was under the spell of socialist

realism and failed to grasp that Kundera did not strive to mirror Czechoslovak reality. Jungmann eventually recognized this and, not long before his death, retracted his criticism. See Jungmann, "Můj vztah k dílu Milana Kundery," in Fořt et al., eds., *Kundera aneb Co zmůže literatura?* 234–236.

17 Milan Kundera, *The Art of the Novel*, trans. Linda Asher (New York: Harper, 2000 [1986]), 133. [Emphasis original.]

18 Kundera, author's note to *Žert*, 321. See also Jan Němec, "Milan Kundera jako spisovatel," *Host* 26, no. 9 (2010): 73–74.

19 Kundera, author's note to *Žert*, 319–321.

20 Adam Hradilek and Petr Třešňák, "Udání Milana Kundery," *Respekt* 19, no. 42 (13 October 2008): 38–46.

21 Alfred French, *Czech Writers and Politics 1945–1969* (Boulder, CO: Eastern European Monographs, 1982), 239. [Emphasis original.]

22 Cf. Lucio Lombardo Radice, *Gli accusati: Franz Kafka, Michail Bulgakov, Aleksandr Solzenitsyn, Milan Kundera* (Bari: De Donato, 1972), 348.

23 Kundera, *Book of Laughter and Forgetting*, 3–4.

24 Ludvík Vaculík, *Hodiny klavíru: komponovaný deník 2004–2005* (Brno: Atlantis, 2007), 102–103, 119.

25 David Lodge, "Milan Kundera, and the Idea of the Author in Modern Criticism," *Critical Quarterly* 26, nos. 1/2 (1984): 110. [Emphasis original.]

26 Jonathan Rosen, "Does Milan Kundera Still Matter?" *The Atlantic* 316, no. 1 (July/August 2015): 40.

27 Milan Kundera, author's preface to *The Joke*, trans. Michael Henry Heim (London: Faber and Faber, 1982), vii.

28 Milan Kundera, "Comedy Is Everywhere," *Index on Censorship* 6, no. 6 (1977): 6.

29 Kundera, author's note to *Žert*, 325.

30 François Ricard, "Metafyzika románu," interview by Maxime Rovère, *Host* 27, no. 8 (2011): 71.

31 Kundera, author's note to *Žert*, 326.

32 Ibid., 325.

33 Kundera, *Art of the Novel*, 10–11.

34 Květoslav Chvatík, *Svět románů Milana Kundery*, 2nd ed. (Brno: Atlantis, 2008), 50–51, 64. [Emphasis original.]

35 Milan Kundera, *The Joke*, trans. Aaron Asher (New York: Harper, 1992), 288. [Emphasis original.]

36 Ibid., 294. [Emphasis original.]

37 Kundera, *Art of the Novel*, 18.

38 For a detailed discussion of the novel's "geometry," see Kundera, *Art of the Novel*, 86–87. See also Chvatík, *Svět románů*, 16, 51–56, and Lubomír Doležel, "'Narrative Symposium' in Milan Kundera's *The Joke*," in *Narrative Modes in Czech Literature* (Toronto: University of Toronto Press, 1973), 112–125.

39 Ondřej Sládek, "O fikci a skutečnosti: Několik poznámek ke Kunderovu umění románu," in Fořt et al., eds., *Kundera aneb Co zmůže literatura?*, 156.

40 Květoslav Chvatík, "Milan Kundera and the Crisis of Language," *Review of Contemporary Fiction* 9, no. 2 (1989): 28–29.

41 Tomáš Kubíček, *Středoevropan Milan Kundera* (Olomouc: Periplum, 2013), 29.

42 Milan Kundera, "Chopins Klavier," *Neue Zürcher Zeitung*, 16 November 1984, 35.

43 Adam Thirlwell, "Skandální lehkost tohoto bytí," *Host* 27, no. 8 (2011): 76.

44 Helena Kosková, "Francouzské romány Milana Kundery," in Haman and Novotný, eds., *Hommage à Kundera*, 29.

45 Guy Scarpetta, *L'âge d'or du roman* (Paris: Grasset, 1996), 31. For Janáček's influence, see Milan Kundera, *Můj Janáček* (Brno: Atlantis, 2004).

46 The striking shift in Kundera's style beginning with *Slowness* does nothing to the polyphonic structure. It merely announces a transition from the sonata

to the fugue: a shorter form of polyphony characterized by monothematism and contrapunt of two or more voices. See Massimo Rizzante, "Umění fugy," *Host* 27, no. 8 (2011): 81–82.

47 Kundera, *Art of the Novel*, 39.
48 Kundera, *Book of Laughter and Forgetting*, 10–12.
49 W. B. Gallie, *Philosophy and the Historical Understanding* (New York: Schocken, 1964), 66.
50 See especially Kundera, *Art of the Novel*, 47–67.
51 Miroslav Balaštík, "Otázka románu," *Host* 23, no. 8 (2007): 3.
52 Ibid.
53 Sylvie Richterová, "Opona: Kunderův román o románu," *Host* 21, no. 9 (2005): 10. See Milan Kundera, *The Curtain: An Essay in Seven Parts*, trans. Linda Asher (New York: Harper, 2007).
54 Hayden White, *Tropics of Discourse: Essays in Cultural Criticism* (Baltimore, MD, and London: Johns Hopkins University Press, 1978), 122.
55 Richard Rorty, "Heidegger, Kundera, and Dickens," in *Essays on Heidegger and Others* (Cambridge: Cambridge University Press, 1991), 68; idem, *Contingency, Irony, and Solidarity* (Cambridge: Cambridge University Press, 1991).
56 Kundera, *Art of the Novel*, 164.
57 Milan Kundera, "The Most Original Book of the Season," interview by Philip Roth, *New York Times Book Review*, 30 November 1980, 78, 80.
58 Kundera, *Art of the Novel*, 160.
59 Ibid., 164; Kundera, *Curtain*, 92. In the words of Jiří Trávníček, "'Nic není více skryto lidskému zraku než životní próza,'" *Host* 20, no. 10 (2004): 40–42, Kundera's novels in this sense "transcribe *the essential* … (permanently affixed characteristics) into *the social* (characteristics born through actions and behaviors of figures, through their mutual interconnections)." [Emphasis original.]
60 Kundera, *Art of the Novel*, 14.
61 Ibid. [Emphasis original.]
62 Kundera, "Most Original Book," 80.
63 Kundera, *Art of the Novel*, 17–18.
64 Ibid., 18.
65 Ibid., 131. See also Milan Kundera, *Slova, pojmy, situace* (Brno: Atlantis, 2014), 13.
66 Kundera, *Book of Laughter and Forgetting*, 11.
67 Ibid.
68 Ibid.
69 Cf. Eugene Narrett, "Surviving History: Milan Kundera's Quarrel with Modernism," *Modern Language Studies* 22, no. 4 (1992): 10.
70 For a detailed analysis of this process, see Milan Babík, "From Providence to Progress: Secularization Theory," in *Statecraft and Salvation: Wilsonian Liberal Internationalism as Secularized Eschatology* (Waco, TX: Baylor University Press, 2013).
71 Karl Löwith, *Meaning in History: The Theological Implications of the Philosophy of History* (Chicago: University of Chicago Press, 1949), 1, 5.
72 Georg W. F. Hegel, *The Philosophy of World History*, trans. John Sibree (Armonk, NY: Prometheus Books, 1991 [1900]), 457.
73 Reinhold Niebuhr, *Faith and History: A Comparison of Christian and Modern Views of History* (London: Nisbet, 1949), 1–2, 4.
74 Francis Fukuyama, "The End of History?" *National Interest* 16 (1989): 3.
75 Ibid. [Emphasis original.]
76 Ibid.
77 Ibid., 4.
78 Ibid., 5.
79 Ibid., 4.

80 Ibid., 5.
81 Ibid.
82 Ibid., 18.
83 Ibid.
84 Ibid.
85 Ibid., 4.
86 Ibid. Fukuyama refers to Alexandre Kojève, *Introduction to the Reading of Hegel: Lectures on the "Phenomenology of Spirit,"* ed. Allan Bloom, trans. James H. Nichols (New York: Basic Books, 1969).
87 Babík, *Statecraft and Salvation*, 16.
88 These three appraisals come, respectively, from Henry Kissinger, *Diplomacy* (New York: Simon and Schuster, 1994), 52; Frank Ninkovich, *The Wilsonian Century: U.S. Foreign Policy since 1900* (Chicago: University of Chicago Press, 1999), 5–6; and Lloyd E. Ambrosius, *Wilsonianism: Woodrow Wilson and His Legacy in American Foreign Relations* (New York: Palgrave Macmillan, 2002), 7.
89 Cf. John G. Ruggie, *Winning the Peace: America and World Order in the New Era* (New York: Columbia University Press, 1995), 2, noting that "the first two post-Cold War presidents, George Bush and Bill Clinton, articulated visions of the new era that may be characterized as broadly Wilsonian in rhetoric and aspiration." For the Wilsonian foundations of George W. Bush's foreign policy, see Tony Smith, "Wilsonianism after Iraq: The End of Liberal Internationalism?" in G. John Ikenberry et al., *The Crisis of American Foreign Policy: Wilsonianism in the Twenty-First Century* (Princeton and Oxford: Princeton University Press, 2009).
90 Thomas L. Friedman, "Foreign Affairs Big Mac I," *New York Times*, 8 December 1996, n.p.
91 Ibid., 5 no. 3, 8.
92 Milan Kundera, *Immortality*, trans. Peter Kussi (New York: Grove Weidenfeld, 1991), 116.
93 Ibid., 114.
94 Ibid.
95 Ibid., 116.
96 Ibid.
97 Stephen Ross, "The Abdication of Culture: The Ideology of Imagology in Milan Kundera's *Immortality*," *Modern Fiction Studies* 46, no. 2 (2000): 337, 339.
98 Kundera, *Immortality*, 114.
99 Ibid.
100 Ibid., 113–114. [Emphasis original.]
101 Ibid., 113.
102 Ibid., 114.
103 Ibid.
104 "The fight for human rights," as Kundera puts it, "[has become] a kind of universal stance of everyone toward everything, a kind of energy that turns all human desires into rights." (Ibid., 322.)
105 Ibid., 114.
106 Ibid., 127.
107 Ibid., 111.
108 Ibid., 113.
109 Ibid., 115.
110 Ibid., 116. [Emphasis original.]
111 Ibid., 115.
112 Ibid.
113 Cf. Adorno's notions of "tolerated negativity" and "negatively useful" in his analysis of capital's ability to mobilize even apparently contradictory cultural elements in its service. See Theodor W. Adorno, "Culture and Administration," *Telos*, no. 37 (1978): 93–111.

114 Kundera, *Immortality*, 31.
115 Milan Kundera, *Slowness*, trans. Linda Asher (London: Faber and Faber, 1996), 72.
116 Michel Foucault, *Discipline and Punish: The Birth of the Prison*, trans. Alan Sheridan (New York: Vintage, 1977), 201–202.
117 Guy Scarpetta, "Politický Kundera," in Fořt et al., eds., *Kundera aneb Co zmůže literatura?* 165. [Emphasis original.]
118 Milan Kundera, *Ignorance*, trans. Linda Asher (London: Faber and Faber, 2002), 155.
119 Ross, "Ideology of Imagology," 352, indeed concludes that Kundera regards imagology as "a system of totalitarian domination ... [even] more effective than anything a purely political system like those characterized by Communist eastern Europe could ever manage."
120 Jean Baudrillard, *Simulacra and Simulation*, trans. Sheila Faria Glaser (Ann Arbor: University of Michigan Press, 1994), 2, originally published as *Simulacres et simulation* (Paris: Éditions Galilée, 1981).
121 Kundera, *Curtain*, 31. [Emphasis original.]
122 The statistic comes from Nicholas Kristoff, "An Idiot's Guide to Inequality," *New York Times*, 24 July 2014, A27.
123 Joseph E. Stiglitz, "Of the 1%, by the 1%, for the 1%," *Vanity Fair*, no. 609 (2011): 126–129.
124 According to Natasa Kovacevic, "History on Speed: Media and the Politics of Forgetting in Milan Kundera's *Slowness*," *Modern Fiction Studies* 52, no. 3 (2006): 634–655, one of Kundera's central concerns in his post-1989 fiction is precisely to recover subaltern histories of Eastern European Communism from underneath the hegemonic narrative of the Cold War propagated by the Western culture industry. "Recognizing ways in which [Western] media have helped reduce the communist histories to images of torture, labor camps, dictatorships, and, worst of all, lack of consumer goods, Kundera highlights their consequent erasure within the teleology of globalization and capitalist development" and, without seeking to restore the past, attempts to stimulate "a revival and a rethinking of the communist legacy (and its 'crushed potentials')." (Ibid., 635, 649.)
125 Milan Kundera, *Encounter*, trans. Linda Asher (New York: Harper, 2010), 117.
126 Ibid., 120.
127 Ibid.
128 Ibid. Cf. Scarpetta, "Politický Kundera," 169.

Conclusion

Fiction as a Path to Factual Reality

When one day in the spring of 2014 Salman Rushdie visited Colby College, stepped up to the lectern in Lorimer Chapter, and began talking about the role of literature in contemporary global society, it was a memorable moment for many. The assembled students experienced a rare encounter with a living legend: a novelist whose *Midnight's Children* (1981) received the Best of the Booker as the finest winner in the award's forty-year history. The deans congratulated themselves on successfully luring the legend to campus, thereby settling Colby's prestige wars against Bowdoin once and for all time—until rumors started circulating a week later that Bowdoin was going to host Kim Kardashian. Even Rushdie himself found the occasion unforgettable, albeit for more somber reasons. It was on that day, April 17, that Gabriel García Márquez passed away in Mexico City. Rushdie never met Gabo, as he affectionately referred to him during the lecture while reminiscing on his life and work, except once, sort of, at a party hosted by Carlos Fuentes, who—finding it unacceptable that their paths should never cross—dialed Gabo's number, handed the phone to Rushdie, and ushered him into an empty bathroom. There the British Indian literary lion finally got to converse with his Colombian counterpart while sitting on the edge of a toilet seat.

For Colby's resident international relations faculty members in the audience, the lecture was memorable for an additional reason: the audacity with which Rushdie trespassed on their professional turf. Although invited to speak about censorship and persecution, Rushdie quickly steered his lecture toward a different theme: the irreplaceability of fiction for the purposes of understanding world affairs. "If you want to know what actually happened in Iraq, what it was really like to be there fighting that war," he referred to the military campaign initiated by the United States in 2003, the place to go to was not the State Department, newspaper archives, history books, or any other kind of scholarship, but Phil Klay's *Redeployment* (2014), a collection of short stories which "tell you more in the course of less than two hundred pages than you ever learned from the news."[1] The same held for any other international dispute, whether in Gaza, Afghanistan, Kashmir, or elsewhere around the globe; Rushdie rattled off an entire list of conflict zones and novelists, many of them local to the areas in question and untranslated into English, before repeating his main advice: "Read outside your own world. Use reading as a way of learning the world."[2] The point was clear: the chief repository of real expertise about international affairs was prose fiction. Colby's international relations experts, at any rate the traditionalists among them, the ones with course syllabi and reading lists composed entirely out of factual literature, probably felt a little upset, irritated, dismissive, or all at once.

If this was indeed their internal response to Rushdie's claims, it stems from a fundamental misunderstanding of the relationship between fact and fiction in narrative representations of world affairs: a set of ill-conceived and largely unarticulated assumptions whose excavation, analysis, manifestations, and debunking have guided this book. According to these assumptions, which pervade the mainstream—American, social-scientific—approach to the study of international relations, factual and fictional accounts of world politics constitute separate domains, and the discipline lies squarely within the former. However, this book has revealed that international relations scholars have more in common with novelists than they realize. Whether they write about the shape of the international arena or the history of their discipline, as the chapters on anarchy and E. H. Carr have demonstrated, their compositions feature copious amounts of open invention: an entire treasure trove of content over and above empirical data. This "content of the form," as Hayden White and other narrative theorists discussed at the outset of this study call it, is purely aesthetic in that it does not refer to anything other than or outside itself. It is a product of human *poiēsis*, which makes reality intelligible by configuring singular existential statements into meaningful wholes, and it inheres in narratives regardless of the truth value of these statements, strictly on account of the narrative form, whether one has filled it with verifiable facts, as academics do, or with invented persons and occurrences, as novelists might.

The presupposed dichotomy between factual and fictional narrative representations of international politics breaks down further upon noticing that novelists frequently do not invent facts but draw them from the actual historical record. If international relations academics routinely employ the formal artistry of narrativization, figuration, and emplotment proper to fiction, in other words, fiction writers often craft their stories out of the documentary material proper to social-scientific inquiry into world affairs. This is true not only about novelists working in the realist-naturalist mode emphasizing observation and eyewitness testimony, such as Henri Barbusse in *Le Feu* (1915), but also about novelists problematizing this mode of literary and historical representation: Don DeLillo and Milan Kundera, for example, whose historiographic metafiction dealing with key international political events and processes such as 9/11, the Prague Spring, or capitalist globalization was discussed in the latter half of this book. Their works make it evident that even patently and flagrantly anti-realistic prose fiction marked by radical formal invention is no flight from political reality, but just the opposite: an intense beam of light projecting further into its depths in search of its as yet unsuspected possibilities. After all, many novelists, including the greatest ones, have journalistic backgrounds. Gabo started out as a newspaper reporter, understood reportage as a literary genre, and never tired of repeating that he saw his turn to fiction writing as an extension of his journalistic career, not a break from it.

In light of these considerations, the assumption that narratives about international affairs can be neatly divided into two mutually exclusive categories, factual and fictional, emerges as a myth. All narratives are fictions. This is not to say that they are identical and cannot be differentiated. Recall White's tropology of narrative discourse, which splits the process of poetic composition into three layers, identifies four principal strategies within each, and uses the resulting matrix of combinations to classify texts according to a multitude of narrative styles. But none of these styles is any more factual than the rest. If narratives utilizing a particular blend of poetic moves claim special authority or even monopoly over accurate representations of the world, it is all the more important to subject such narratives to critical tropological analysis, map their nonempirical dimension, and expose them as rhetorical acts.

Academic International Relations as a Rhetorical Performance of Western Hegemony

Between novelists and social scientists writing about international relations, only the latter habitually refer to themselves as experts or specialists, invoke privileged access to the reality of world affairs, and allege to be producing unique knowledge uncontaminated by any kind of nonfactual agenda— knowledge superior even to the insights of statesmen, diplomats, and other actual practitioners, who are said to have skin in the game and therefore cannot be trusted. The academic discipline of international relations is nothing if not a closed cult seeking to dominate and arbitrate serious thinking and writing about world affairs. Its exclusiveness is attested by the height of the walls one must scale in order to gain admission: a decade's worth of undergraduate and graduate coursework, examinations, and tuition leading to the terminal degree, plus written blessings from the cult's ruling priests that the candidate has been vetted and approved to join the professoriate. Fiction writing knows no such walls, or at any rate none so high. Anyone is free to compose a novel. Prerequisites are minimal, consisting of little more than writing proficiency and some *Sitzfleisch*. They certainly do not involve any lengthy academic training or ornate diplomas.

Tropologically, the cult of mainstream academic international relations displays considerable uniformity. Although not entirely devoid of variations, its narrative style comprises a distinctive blend of Mechanistic, Tragic, and Conservative inclinations. Chapters 2 and 3 demonstrated these signature elements in the ways the discipline's leading neorealist and neoliberal scholars figure forth the space of international relations and the history of their field, both of which are empirically unavailable and ontologically stable only to the extent that they are sustained through repeated rhetorical performances.

The Mechanistic mode of formal argument is not specific to academic international relations, of course. It animates all Western scientific imagination, which pictures the world as a complex clock driven by immutable laws and seeks to explicate them in an effort to gain control over nature and society. For Kenneth Waltz, John Mearsheimer, Robert Keohane, and other eminent representatives of the American science of international relations, the essential law propelling the clockwork of world politics is the principle of sovereign states pursuing power in an arena without any overarching authority. Scholars and practitioners forging ahead without heeding this essential law are deemed not only useless, but positively dangerous: as dangerous as engineers forging ahead without heeding Newton's laws of gravity. International agreements, institutions, and other edifices erected on their false ideas are ticking bombs bound sooner or later to collapse and result in disaster, much like the latter's bridges.

Disciplinary history is written accordingly: to suit and support the present. Past thinkers such as E. H. Carr are celebrated and included in the field's genealogy insofar as they have contributed to the mapping of the international mechanism and the forces that make it tick, whether by noticing the primacy of sovereign states, the anarchical nature of the international arena, or the crucial role of power. That they often made other profound intellectual discoveries, including ones flatly rejecting Mechanism in favor of more Contextualist or Organicist modes of inquiry, is brushed aside as irrelevant—in keeping with the Mechanistic attitude that, in international relations as in writings of dead scholars, it is imperative to identify central trends and patterns and disregard everything else.

The Tragic and Conservative dispositions of mainstream scholarship are intertwined with its Mechanistic conceptualization of the international stage in terms of anarchy, whose structure is seen as an insurmountable obstacle to any lasting progress and cooperation in world affairs. Anarchy forces all states to practice power politics based on narrow self-interest and national security considerations and discourages them from pursuing any kind of foreign policy—variously referred to by standard literature as utopian, idealist, or universalist—seeking to transcend the established order. The twentieth century was replete with such efforts; it witnessed numerous bids to transform the world, whether they bore the flag of American liberal internationalism, Soviet Communism, or German Nazism. The result is well known: an age of total war taking the human race to the brink of nuclear omnicide. Formulated during this age, in the dark shadows of the

Great War, World War II, and the Cold War, contemporary mainstream international relations theory is a discourse of frightened survivors urging the audience to learn from the catastrophe of the years 1914–1991, abandon any eschatological dreams, accept the divided state of the world, and focus on managing rather than ending conflict, lest catastrophe returns to destroy even the survivors.

In the context of recent Western history, few would deny the wisdom of this Tragic and Conservative conception of politics among nations. Its soberness and skepticism signal remarkable progress of European consciousness from the exalted Romantic narratives of salvation that in the first half of the twentieth century justified acts of unspeakable barbarism as perfectly civilized—even noble—stepping stones to heavens on earth. But one must remember that the proper context in which to appraise the tropological style of mainstream international relations literature is much broader than the West; it is the world at large. After all, its name and intellectual aspirations to general laws give unmistakable evidence that the discipline does not restrict itself to any particular region but presents itself as a fount of authoritative expertise about the entire globe. In the global context, the Tragic and Conservative wisdom of majority international relations literature serves to freeze the deeply stratified international political economy, protect the elite at the top, keep the billions at the bottom in their lot, and prevent emancipatory change.

With this finding, this book has run its full course and returns to its beginning, where it first announced its metatheoretical project to examine academic international relations not just as a body of literature about political power, but as a form and practice of political power in its own right. Analyzed through the lens of Whitean tropology of factual representation, this literature emerges as an expression of Western hegemony. The type of power it encapsulates is linguistic-discursive power: the power to utter words, weave them into stories, and thereby constitute the very fabric and parameters of international political reality.

This sort of power is much more diffuse, ambiguous, and harder to track than country GDPs, population sizes, armed forces personnel, fighter jet squadrons, nuclear stockpiles, and other measures of the two prevalent conceptions of power with which most international relations scholars have been mesmerized: economic and military power of sovereign states. But it is also far more elemental, immediate, and ubiquitous than either of these. Its origins coincide with the birth of the human species; not for nothing does the Bible open with, "In the beginning there was the Word." And storytelling, along with the building of memorials for the dead, is one of the few genuinely universal practices shared by people across all time and place.

> [N]arrative is present in every age, in every place, in every society; it begins with the very history of mankind and there nowhere is nor has been a people without narrative. ... [N]arrative is international, transhistorical, transcultural: it is simply there, like life itself.[3]

Given how obsessed contemporary international relations scholars have been with immutable patterns and regularities in world politics, and given that among these regularities none strikes them as more essential than the pursuit of power, one would expect the most permanent and fundamental dimension of power—the power to speak the political world into existence—to represent the chief focus of their inquiries. That precisely the opposite has been the case is ironic.

Toward a New Fiction of International Relations

Luckily, there is always going to be Alonso Quijano with a shaving basin on his head to remind us that the right story can turn even a lowly village fool into a noble knight. The difference between them is a matter of poetic imagination, whose capacity to see reality otherwise is infinite, recognizes no constraints of either nature or tradition, and transforms sinks into helmets, windmills into fighting giants, and madness into chivalry with hilarious ease—to the horror of every worldly authority. Since the early seventeenth century, when Don Quixote first departed on his journey of adventure, the stream of writing fed by this imagination has swelled into a large, fast river: the river of the art of the novel. Its currents cut into all foundations of knowledge, submerge them in alternative perspectives, and dissolve them in the bottomless depths of human possibility.

Not that all prose fiction writers have always approached their task in this manner, with the intention to undermine certainty and common sense. Examples of affirmative literature and thesis novels abound. Indeed, every modern state has a flock of poets singing its praise. Particularly in totalitarian and authoritarian orders such flocks are easy to spot, not least thanks to the plumage of state prizes adorning their chests, and official literature—much like locomotives, cement, or baby formula—is produced according to five-year plans. In Communist Czechoslovakia, Marie Pujmanová became a darling of the Stalinist regime thanks to her socialist realist prose fiction, not to mention her vocal calls for maximum punishments during the Prague show trials in the 1950s. In contemporary liberal societies, the flocks are recognizable by mass market success and sales figures. Instead of catering to the ruling political party, they are subservient to the dominant trends of late capitalist culture, whose narcissistic forms and obsessions they adopt to the point of becoming indistinct from them. Witness the *Fifty Shades of Gray* trilogy: e-mail sex correspondence parading as literature.

Such prose fiction, however, does not belong to the art of the novel as understood by this book and many contemporary novelists, whether Márquez, Rushdie, Franzen, DeLillo, or Kundera. Particularly the latter has made it explicit that novels are what they are by virtue of unsettling received truths, raising doubt, and inviting questions, not providing answers, and that what propels the literary tradition inaugurated by Cervantes is precisely the negation of tradition. The history of the novel is the history of protest—and of freedom, imagination, and courage necessary to mount it. In its most recent expressions, this protest turns against narrative itself and surfaces in historiographic metafiction such as DeLillo's *Falling Man* and Kundera's *Curtain*. It is in these works that the poetic constitution of political reality—world as story—becomes most visible.

For this reason, the art of the novel, particularly historiographic metafiction, is of inestimable value to critical international relations theorists. Their efforts to denaturalize the world order and expose it as a product of dynamic social forces coincide with the art's defining mission to problematize reality and lay bare its rhetorical plasticity. To this extent, critical international theory should stop confining itself to factual scholarly literature, recognize that it has a major ally in the novel, and engage with it. Including historiographic metafiction on course syllabi and enlisting it in support of critical analyses of international relations would be a good start, but the engagement need not end there. It ought to proceed much further, to the point where critical theorists not only read fiction but also begin writing it in the sense of producing scholarship utilizing *novel*—unorthodox, experimental, rebellious—forms subverting standard tropological protocols of academic international relations discourse. If critical theory aims to counter hegemony, and if one of the sites of hegemonic power is the nonempirical content of the form of mainstream narrative representations of international political reality, it would seem that their project requires no less.

Notes

1 Salman Rushdie, unpublished address in Lorimer Chapel at Colby College (Waterville, ME), 17 April 2014, author's notes.
2 Ibid.
3 Roland Barthes, *Image, Music, Text*, trans. Stephen Heath (New York: Hill and Wang, 1977), 79.

Bibliography

Aaron, Daniel. "How to Read Don DeLillo." In Frank Lentricchia, ed., *Introducing Don DeLillo*. Durham, NC: Duke University Press, 1991.

Abel, Marco. "Don DeLillo's 'In the Ruins of the Future': Literature, Images, and the Rhetoric of Seeing 9/11." *PMLA* 118, no. 5 (2003): 1236–1250.

Acton, Lord. "Letter to Woodrow Wilson, May 10, 1899." In Arthur S. Link et al., eds., *The Papers of Woodrow Wilson*, vol. 11. Princeton, NJ: Princeton University Press, 1971.

Adorno, Theodor W. "Culture and Administration." *Telos* 1978, no. 37 (1978): 93–111.

Ambrosius, Lloyd E. *Wilsonianism: Woodrow Wilson and His Legacy in American Foreign Relations*. New York: Palgrave Macmillan, 2002.

Amis, Martin. *The Second Plane: September 11: Terror and Boredom*. New York and Toronto, ON: Knopf, 2008.

Anatol, Giselle Liza, ed. *Reading Harry Potter: Critical Essays*. Westport, CT: Praeger, 2003.

———, ed. *Reading Harry Potter Again: New Critical Essays*. Westport, CT: Praeger, 2009.

Ankersmit, Frank R. *Historical Representation*. Stanford, CA: Stanford University Press, 2001.

———. "Historiography and Postmodernism." *History and Theory* 28, no. 2 (1989): 137–153.

———. *Narrative Logic: A Semantic Analysis of the Historian's Language*. The Hague: Nijhoff, 1983.

———. "Reply to Professor Zagorin." *History and Theory* 29, no. 3 (1990): 275–296.

Ankersmit, Frank, Ewa Domańska, and Hans Kellner, eds. *Re-figuring Hayden White*. Stanford, CA: Stanford University Press, 2009.

Antonio, Robert J. "The Origins, Development, and Contemporary Status of Critical Theory." *The Sociological Quarterly* 24, no. 3 (1983): 325–351.

Aristotle. *Poetics*. Translated by George Whalley. Edited by John Baxter and Patrick Atherton. Montreal, QC, and Kingston, ON: McGill-Queen's University Press, 1997.

Art, Robert J., and Robert Jervis. *International Politics*. 2nd ed. Boston, MA: Little, Brown, 1986.

Ashley, Richard K. "Political Realism and Human Interests." *International Studies Quarterly* 25, no. 2 (1981): 204–236.

———. "The Poverty of Neorealism." In Robert O. Keohane, ed., *Neorealism and Its Critics.* New York: Columbia University Press, 1986. First published in *International Organization* 38, no. 2 (1984): 225–261.

———. "Untying the Sovereign State: A Double Reading of the Anarchy Problematique." *Millennium: Journal of International Studies* 17, no. 2 (1988): 227–262.

Aust, Stefan. *Baader-Meinhof: The Inside Story of the R.A.F.* Translated by Anthea Bell. Oxford and New York: Oxford University Press, 2009.

Axelrod, Robert. *The Evolution of Cooperation.* New York: Basic Books, 1984.

Axelrod, Robert, and Robert O. Keohane. "Achieving Cooperation under Anarchy: Strategies and Institutions." In David A. Baldwin, ed., *Neorealism and Neoliberalism: The Contemporary Debate.* New York: Columbia University Press, 1993.

Babík, Milan. "George D. Herron and the Eschatological Foundations of Woodrow Wilson's Foreign Policy, 1917–1919." *Diplomatic History* 35, no. 5 (2011): 837–857.

———. *Statecraft and Salvation: Wilsonian Liberal Internationalism as Secularized Eschatology.* Waco, TX: Baylor University Press, 2013.

———. "'X' Ten Years On: The Fictions of George F. Kennan's Recent Factual Representations." *Review of International Studies* 42, no. 1 (2016): 74–94.

Baelo-Allué, Sonia. "9/11 and the Psychic Trauma Novel: Don DeLillo's *Falling Man.*" *Atlantis: Journal of the Spanish Association of Anglo-American Studies* 34, no. 1 (2012): 63–79.

Bain, William. "Deconfusing Morgenthau: Moral Inquiry and Classical Realism Reconsidered." *Review of International Studies* 26, no. 3 (2000): 445–464.

Balaštík, Miroslav. "Otázka románu." *Host* 23, no. 8 (2007): 3.

Baldwin, David A., ed. *Neorealism and Neoliberalism: The Contemporary Debate.* New York: Columbia University Press, 1993.

Barthes, Roland. *Image, Music, Text.* Translated by Stephen Heath. New York: Hill and Wang, 1977.

Baudrillard, Jean. *Simulacra and Simulation.* Translated by Sheila Faria Glaser. Ann Arbor, MI: University of Michigan Press, 1994. Originally published as *Simulacres et simulation.* Paris: Éditions Galilée, 1981.

Begley, Adam. "The Art of Fiction CXXXV: Don DeLillo." In Thomas DePietro, ed., *Conversations with Don DeLillo.* Jackson: University Press of Mississippi, 2005.

Benjamin, Walter. "The Work of Art in the Age of Mechanical Reproduction." In Hannah Arendt, ed., *Illuminations,* Translated by Harry Zohn. New York: Schocken, 1969.

Bernstein, Richard J. *The Restructuring of Social and Political Theory.* New York: Harcourt Brace Jovanovich, 1976.

Bieńczyk, Marek. "Číst Kunderu v době Solidarity." In Bohumil Fořt, Jiří Kudrnáč, and Petr Kyloušek, eds., *Milan Kundera aneb Co zmůže literatura? Soubor statí o díle Milana Kundery.* Brno: Host, 2012.

Bleiker, Roland. *Aesthetics and World Politics.* London: Palgrave Macmillan, 2009.

———. "The Aesthetic Turn in International Political Theory." *Millennium: Journal of International Studies* 30, no. 3 (2001): 509–533.

Booth, Ken. "Security in Anarchy: Utopian Realism in Theory and Practice." *International Affairs* 67, no. 3 (1991): 527–545.

Boxall, Peter. *Don DeLillo: The Possibility of Fiction.* New York: Routledge, 2006.

Boxer, Sarah. "One Camera, Then Thousands, Indelibly Etching a Day of Loss." *New York Times,* 11 September 2002, n.p.

Brockes, Emma. "View from the Bridge." *Guardian*, 23 May 2003, sec. Features & Reviews, p. 20.

Brown, Chris. *Understanding International Relations*. 2nd ed. Basingstoke: Palgrave, 2001.

Bueno de Mesquita, Bruce. *The War Trap*. New Haven, CT: Yale University Press, 1981.

Bull, Hedley. *The Anarchical Society: A Study of Order in World Politics*. 2nd ed. Basingstoke: Macmillan, 1995.

———. "*The Twenty Years' Crisis* Thirty Years On." *International Journal* 24, no. 4 (1969): 625–638.

Burchill, Scott, et al. *Theories of International Relations*. 2nd ed. Basingstoke: Palgrave, 2001.

Burchill, Scott, and Andrew Linklater, eds. *Theories of International Relations*. 5th ed. Basingstoke: Palgrave Macmillan, 2013.

Bush, George W. *Public Papers of the Presidents of the United States: George W. Bush, 2001*, vol. 2. Washington, DC: GPO, 2003.

Buzan, Barry. "From International System to International Society: Structural Realism and Regime Theory Meet the English School." *International Organization* 47, no. 3 (1993): 327–352.

Buzan, Barry, and Richard Little. "Why International Relations Has Failed as an Intellectual Project and What to Do about It." *Millennium: Journal of International Studies* 30, no. 1 (2001): 19–39.

The Cambridge Modern History. Vol. 7. New York: Macmillan, 1902.

Campbell, David. *National Deconstruction: Violence, Identity and Justice in Bosnia*. Minneapolis: University of Minnesota Press, 1998.

———. *Writing Security: United States Foreign Policy and the Politics of Identity*. Minneapolis: University of Minnesota Press, 1992.

Caporaso, James A. "Across the Great Divide: Integrating Comparative and International Politics." *International Studies Quarterly* 41, no. 4 (1997): 563–591.

Carr, David. "Narrative and the Real World: An Argument for Continuity." *History and Theory* 25, no. 2 (1986): 117–131.

Carr, Edward Hallett. "An Autobiography." In Michael Cox, ed., *E. H. Carr: A Critical Appraisal*. New York: Palgrave, 2000.

———. *Conditions of Peace*. London: Macmillan, 1942.

———. *Dostoevsky, 1821–1881: A New Biography*. London: Allen & Unwin, 1931.

———. *The Future of Nations: Independence or Interdependence?* London: Kegan Paul, 1941.

———. *A History of Soviet Russia*. 14 vols. London: Macmillan, 1950–1978.

———. "Karl Mannheim." In *From Napoleon to Stalin, and Other Essays*. Basingstoke: Macmillan, 1980.

———. *Karl Marx: A Study in Fanaticism*. London: Dent, 1934.

———. Letter to R. W. Davies, 9 December 1959. Quoted in R. W. Davies, "Edward Hallett Carr, 1892–1982," *Proceedings of the British Academy* 69 (1983): 504.

———. Letter to Stanley Hoffmann, 30 September 1977. Quoted in R. W. Davies, "Edward Hallett Carr, 1892–1982," *Proceedings of the British Academy* 69 (1983): 487.

———. *Michael Bakunin*. London: Macmillan, 1937.

———. *Nationalism and After*. London: Macmillan, 1945.

———. *The New Society*. London: Macmillan, 1951.

————. *The Romantic Exiles: A Nineteenth-Century Portrait Gallery.* London: Victor Gollancz, 1933.

————. *The Twenty Years' Crisis, 1919–1939: An Introduction to the Study of International Relations.* London: Macmillan, 1939.

————. *The Twenty Years' Crisis, 1919–1939: An Introduction to the Study of International Relations.* 2nd ed. New York: Harper & Row, 1946.

————. *What Is History?* New York: Vintage, 1961.

Chartier, Roger. "Quatre questions à Hayden White." *Storia della Storiografia* no. 24 (1993): 133–142.

Chvatík, Květoslav. "Mé setkání s Milanem Kunderou." In Aleš Haman and Vladimír Novotný, eds., *Hommage à Milan Kundera: Pocta Milanu Kunderovi: Sborník k 80. spisovatelovým narozeninám.* Prague: Artes Liberales, 2009.

————. "Milan Kundera and the Crisis of Language." *Review of Contemporary Fiction* 9, no. 2 (1989): 27–36.

————. *Svět románů Milana Kundery.* 2nd ed. Brno: Atlantis, 2008.

Clark, Ian. *Globalization and International Relations Theory.* Oxford and New York: Oxford University Press, 1999.

Claude, Inis L. *Swords into Plowshares: The Problems and Progress of International Institutions.* 4th ed. New York: Random House, 1971.

Coker, Christopher. *Men at War: What Fiction Tells Us About Conflict, from The Illiad to Catch-22.* New York: Oxford University Press, 2014.

Conte, Joseph M. "Don DeLillo's *Falling Man* and the Age of Terror." *Modern Fiction Studies* 57, no. 3 (2011): 557–583.

Cox, Michael, ed. *E. H. Carr: A Critical Appraisal.* New York: Palgrave, 2000.

Cox, Robert W. "Gramsci, Hegemony and International Relations: An Essay in Method." *Millennium: Journal of International Studies* 12, no. 2 (1983): 162–175.

————. "Social Forces, States and World Orders: Beyond International Relations Theory." In Robert O. Keohane, ed., *Neorealism and Its Critics.* New York: Columbia University Press, 1986. First published in *Millennium: Journal of International Studies* 10, no. 2 (1981): 126–155.

Cowart, David. "DeLillo and the Power of Language." In John N. Duvall, ed., *The Cambridge Companion to Don DeLillo.* Cambridge: Cambridge University Press, 2008.

Cozette, Murielle. "Reclaiming the Critical Dimension of Realism: Hans J. Morgenthau on the Ethics of Scholarship." *Review of International Studies* 34, no. 1 (2008): 5–27.

Cvek, Sven. *Towering Figures: Reading the 9/11 Archive.* Amsterdam and London: Rodopi, 2011.

Danchev, Alex. *On Art and War and Terror.* Edinburgh: Edinburgh University Press, 2009.

Danto, Arthur C. *Narration and Knowledge.* New York: Columbia University Press, 1985.

Davies, R. W. "Edward Hallett Carr, 1892–1982." *Proceedings of the British Academy* 69 (1983): 473–511.

DeCurtis, Anthony. "Matters of Fact and Fiction." *Rolling Stone*, 17 November 1988, 113–121, 164.

Deets, Stephen. "Wizarding in the Classroom: Teaching Harry Potter and Politics." *PS: Political Science and Politics* 42, no. 4 (2009): 741–744.

DeLillo, Don. *Americana.* Boston, MA: Houghton Mifflin, 1971.

———. "The Artist Naked in a Cage." *New Yorker*, 26 May 1997, 7.

———. "'An Outsider in This Society': An Interview with Don DeLillo." By Anthony DeCurtis. *South Atlantic Quarterly* 89, no. 2 (1990): 281–304.

———. *Falling Man: A Novel*. New York: Scribner, 2007.

———. *Great Jones Street*. Boston, MA: Houghton Mifflin, 1973.

———. "'Ich kenne Amerika nicht mehr.'" Interview by Christoph Amend. *ZEIT-Magazin Leben*, no. 42, 10 October 2007.

———. "In the Ruins of the Future: Reflections on Terror and Loss in the Shadow of September." *Harper's*, December 2001, 33–40.

———. "An Interview with Don DeLillo." By Kevin Connolly. In Thomas DePietro, ed., *Conversations with Don DeLillo*. Jackson: University Press of Mississippi, 2005.

———. "An Interview with Don DeLillo." By Maria Nadotti. Translated by Peggy Boyers. Edited by Don DeLillo. *Salmagundi* no. 100 (Fall 1993): 86–97.

———. "An Interview with Don DeLillo." By Thomas LeClair. *Contemporary Literature* 23, no. 1 (1982): 19–31.

———. *Mao II*. New York: Vintage, 1991.

———. "Der Narr in seinem Zimmer." *Die Zeit*, no. 14, 29 March 2001, n.p.

———. "Seven Seconds." Interview by Ann Arensberg. *Vogue*, August 1988, 337–339, 390.

———. *Underworld*. New York: Scribner, 1997.

———. *White Noise*. New York: Viking, 1985.

———. "'Writing as a Deeper Form of Concentration': An Interview with Don DeLillo." By Maria Moss. In Thomas DePietro, ed., *Conversations with Don DeLillo*. Jackson, MS: University Press of Mississippi, 2005.

Der Derian, James. *Virtuous War: Mapping the Military-Industrial Media-Entertainment Network*. 2nd ed. New York and Abingdon: Routledge, 2009.

Devetak, Richard. "After the Event: Don DeLillo's *White Noise* and September 11 Narratives." *Review of International Studies* 35, no. 4 (2009): 795–815.

Dickinson, G. Lowes. *The European Anarchy*. New York: Macmillan, 1916.

Doležel, Lubomír. "'Narrative Symposium' in Milan Kundera's *The Joke*." In *Narrative Modes in Czech Literature*. Toronto, ON: University of Toronto Press, 1973.

Domańska, Ewa. *Encounters: Philosophy of History after Postmodernism*. Charlottesville, VA and London: University Press of Virginia, 1998.

———. "Hayden White: Beyond Irony." *History and Theory* 37, no. 2 (1998): 173–181.

Donnelly, Jack. "Realism." In Scott Burchill and Andrew Linklater, eds., *Theories of International Relations*, 5th ed. Basingstoke: Palgrave Macmillan, 2013.

Doran, Robert. "Humanism, Formalism, and the Discourse of History." In Robert Doran, ed., Introduction to Hayden White, *The Fiction of Narrative: Essays on History, Literature, and Theory, 1957–2007*. Baltimore: Johns Hopkins University Press, 2010.

———. "The Work of Hayden White I: Mimesis, Figuration and the Writing of History." In Nancy Partner and Sarah Foot, eds., *The SAGE Handbook of Historical Theory*. London: SAGE, 2013.

Dray, William H. "On the Nature and Role of Narrativity in Historiography." *History and Theory* 10, no. 2 (1971): 153–171.

———. Review of *The Content of the Form*, by Hayden White. *History and Theory* 27, no. 3 (1988): 282–287.

Dunn, Frederick S. "The Scope of International Relations." *World Politics* 1, no. 1 (1948): 142–146.

Dunne, Tim. "Theories as Weapons: E. H. Carr and International Relations." In Michael Cox, ed., *E. H. Carr: A Critical Appraisal*. New York: Palgrave, 2000.

Duvall, John N. "The Power of History and the Persistence of Mystery." Introduction to John N. Duvall, ed., *The Cambridge Companion to Don DeLillo*. Cambridge: Cambridge University Press, 2008.

———. "Introduction: From Valparaiso to Jerusalem: Don DeLillo and the Moment of Canonization." *Modern Fiction Studies* 45, no. 3 (1999): 559–568.

Duvall, John N., and Robert P. Marzec. "Narrating 9/11." *Modern Fiction Studies* 57, no. 3 (2011): 381–400.

Edmundson, Mark. "Not Flat, Not Round, Not There: Don DeLillo's Novel Characters." *Yale Review* 83, no. 2 (1995): 107–124.

Eliade, Mircea. *The Myth of the Eternal Return, Or, Cosmos and History*. Translated by Willard R. Trask. Princeton, NJ: Princeton University Press, 1991 (1954).

Else, Gerald F. *Aristotle's Poetics: The Argument*. Cambridge, MA: Harvard University Press, 1963.

———. *Plato and Aristotle on Poetry*. Chapel Hill: University of North Carolina Press, 1986.

Elton, Geoffrey. *The Practice of History*. London: Methuen, 1967.

Esslin, Martin. *The Theatre of the Absurd*. Garden City, NJ: Doubleday, 1961.

Evans, Richard. "Truth Lost in Vain Views." *Times Higher Education Supplement*, no. 1297, 12 September 1997.

Falk, Richard. "The Critical Realist Tradition and the Demystification of Interstate Power: E. H. Carr, Hedley Bull and Robert W. Cox." In Stephen Gill and James H. Mittelman, eds., *Innovation and Transformation in International Studies*. Cambridge: Cambridge University Press, 1997.

Finney, Patrick. "Hayden White, International History and Questions Too Seldom Posed." *Rethinking History* 12, no. 1 (2008): 103–123.

Fořt, Bohumil, Jiří Kudrnáč, and Petr Kyloušek, eds. *Milan Kundera aneb Co zmůže literatura? Soubor statí o díle Milana Kundery*. Brno: Host, 2012.

Foucault, Michel. *Discipline and Punish: The Birth of the Prison*. Translated by Alan Sheridan. New York: Vintage, 1977.

Fox, William T. R. "The Uses of International Relations Theory." In William T. R. Fox, ed., *Theoretical Aspects of International Relations*. Notre Dame, IN: University of Notre Dame Press, 1959.

Franzen, Jonathan. "Perchance to Dream: In the Age of Images, a Reason to Write Novels." *Harper's*, 1 April 1996, 35–54.

Frei, Christoph. *Hans J. Morgenthau: An Intellectual Biography*. Baton Rouge: Louisiana State University Press, 2001.

French, Alfred. *Czech Writers and Politics 1945–69*. Boulder, CO: Eastern European Monographs, 1982.

Friedman, Thomas L. "Foreign Affairs Big Mac I." *New York Times*, 8 December 1996, n.p.

Frye, Northrop. *Anatomy of Criticism: Four Essays*. Princeton, NJ: Princeton University Press, 1957.

Fukuyama, Francis. "The End of History?" *National Interest* 16 (1989): 3–18.

Gaddis, John Lewis. *George F. Kennan: An American Life*. New York: Penguin, 2011.

———. *Strategies of Containment: A Critical Appraisal of American National Security Policy during the Cold War*. Revised ed. Oxford and New York: Oxford University Press, 2005.

Gallie, W. B. *Philosophy and the Historical Understanding.* New York: Schocken, 1964.

George, Jim. *Discourses of Global Politics: A Critical (Re)Introduction to International Relations.* Boulder, CO: Lynne Rienner, 1994.

Germain, Randall. "E. H. Carr and the Historical Mode of Thought." In Michael Cox, ed., *E. H. Carr: A Critical Appraisal.* New York: Palgrave, 2000.

Gilpin, Robert. "The Richness of the Tradition of Political Realism." In Robert O. Keohane, ed., *Neorealism and Its Critics.* New York: Columbia University Press, 1986.

———. *War and Change in World Politics.* Cambridge and New York: Cambridge University Press, 1981.

Ginzburg, Carlo. "Just One Witness." In Saul Friedländer, ed., *Probing the Limits of Representation: Nazism and the "Final Solution."* Cambridge, MA: Harvard University Press, 1992.

Goodman, Ellen. "Our Charmed Life Has Gone Forever." *Guardian Weekly,* 20 September 2001, 31.

———. "Our Reality Show: We No Longer Have the Luxury of Feeling Safe." *Pittsburgh Post-Gazette,* 14 September 2001, A15.

———. "Shattering the Luxury of Our Charmed Life." *Seattle Times,* 14 September 2001, n.p.

Gossman, Lionel. *Between History and Literature.* Cambridge, MA: Harvard University Press, 1990.

Gramsci, Antonio. *Selections from the Prison Notebooks.* Edited and translated by Quinton Hoare and Geoffrey Nowell Smith. New York: International Publishers, 1971.

Gray, Richard. *After the Fall: American Literature Since 9/11.* Chichester: Wiley-Blackwell, 2011.

———. "Open Doors, Closed Minds: American Prose Writing at a Time of Crisis." *American Literary History* 21, no. 1 (2009): 128–151.

Guzzini, Stefano. *Realism in International Relations and International Political Economy: The Continuing Story of a Death Foretold.* London: Routledge, 1998.

Hallett, John [E. H. Carr]. "Karl Marx: Fifty Years Later." *Fortnightly Review,* no. 319, March 1933, 625–638.

Happe, François. *Don DeLillo: La fiction contre les systèmes.* Paris: Belin, 2000.

Harris, Robert R. "A Talk with Don DeLillo." *New York Times Book Review,* 10 October 1982, BR26.

Haslam, Jonathan. "E. H. Carr's Search for Meaning, 1892–1982." In Michael Cox, ed., *E. H. Carr: A Critical Appraisal.* New York: Palgrave, 2000.

———. *The Vices of Integrity: E. H. Carr, 1892–1982.* London and New York: Verso, 1999.

Havel, Václav. "Český úděl?" *Tvář* 4, no. 2 (1969): 30–33.

Hegel, Georg W. F. *The Philosophy of World History.* Translated by J. Sibree. Armonk, NY: Prometheus Books, 1991 [1900].

Herz, John H. "Idealist Internationalism and the Security Dilemma." *World Politics* 2, no. 2 (1950): 157–180.

Himmelfarb, Gertrude. "Telling It as You Like It: Post-modernist History and the Flight from Fact." *Times Literary Supplement,* 16 October 1992.

Hobbes, Thomas. *Leviathan.* Edited by Edwin Curley. Indianapolis, IN, and Cambridge: Hackett, 1994.

Hoffman, Mark. "Conversations on Critical International Relations Theory." *Millennium: Journal of International Studies* 17, no. 1 (1988): 91–95.

―――. "Critical Theory and the Inter-Paradigm Debate." *Millennium: Journal of International Studies* 16, no. 2 (1987): 231–250.

Hoffmann, Stanley. "An American Social Science: International Relations." *Dædalus* 106, no. 3 (1977): 41–60.

Hollis, Martin, and Steve Smith. *Explaining and Understanding International Relations.* Oxford: Clarendon Press, 1990.

Horkheimer, Max. *Critical Theory.* Translated by Matthew J. O'Connell et al. New York: Herder & Herder, 1972.

Horkheimer, Max, and Theodor W. Adorno. *Dialectic of Enlightenment.* Translated by John Cumming. New York: Herder and Herder, 1972.

Howard, Gerald. "The American Strangeness: An Interview with Don DeLillo." In Thomas DePietro, ed., *Conversations with Don DeLillo.* Jackson: University Press of Mississippi, 2005.

Howe, Paul. "The Utopian Realism of E. H. Carr." *Review of International Studies* 20, no. 3 (1994): 277–297.

Hradilek, Adam, and Petr Třešňák. "Udání Milana Kundery." *Respekt* 19, no. 42 (13 October 2008): 38–46.

Hurd, Elizabeth Shakman. *The Politics of Secularism in International Relations.* Princeton, NJ: Princeton University Press, 2008.

Hutcheon, Linda. *Narcissistic Narrative: The Metafictional Paradox.* London and New York: Routledge, 1984 [1980].

―――. *A Poetics of Postmodernism: History, Theory, Fiction.* New York and London: Routledge, 1988.

―――. *The Politics of Postmodernism.* 2nd ed. London and New York: Routledge, 2002.

Huxley, Aldous. *Brave New World.* Scranton, PA: Harper Perennial, 1989 [1946].

Iggers, Georg. "Historiography between Scholarship and Poetry: Reflections on Hayden White's Approach to Historiography." *Rethinking History* 4, no. 3 (2000): 373–390.

Isaacson, Walter. *Kissinger: A Biography.* New York: Simon & Schuster, 1992.

Jackson, Richard. *Writing the War on Terror: Language, Politics and Counter-Terrorism.* Manchester: Manchester University Press, 2005.

Jahn, Beate. *The Cultural Construction of International Relations: The Invention of the State of Nature.* London: Palgrave, 2000.

Jameson, Fredric. *Postmodernism, or, The Cultural Logic of Late Capitalism.* Durham, NC: Duke University Press, 1991.

Jeffery, Renee. "Beyond Banality? Ethical Responses to Evil in Post-September 11 International Relations." *International Affairs* 81, no. 4 (2005): 175–186.

Jenkins, Keith. "A Conversation with Hayden White." *Literature and History* 7, no. 1 (1998): 68–82.

―――. "An English Myth? Rethinking the Contemporary Value of E. H. Carr's *What Is History?*" In Michael Cox, ed., *E. H. Carr: A Critical Appraisal.* New York: Palgrave, 2000.

―――. "'Nobody Does It Better': Radical History and Hayden White." *Rethinking History* 12, no. 1 (2008): 59–74.

―――. "On Hayden White." In *Why History? Ethics and Postmodernity.* London: Routledge, 1999.

————. On "What Is History?": From Carr and Elton to Rorty and White. London: Routledge, 1995.

Jervis, Robert. "Cooperation under the Security Dilemma." *World Politics* 30, no. 2 (1978): 167–214.

"Jerusalem Prize for Don DeLillo." *Publishers Weekly*, 3 May 1999, 245, no. 18, 17.

Jingsheng, Wei. *The Outrage to Stand Alone: Letters from Prison and Other Writings.* Edited and translated by Kristina M. Torgeson. New York: Viking Penguin, 1997.

Jones, Charles. "E. H. Carr: Ambivalent Realist." In Francis A. Beer and Robert Hariman, eds., *Post-Realism: The Rhetorical Turn in International Relations.* East Lansing: Michigan State University, 1997.

————. E. H. Carr and International Relations: A Duty to Lie. Cambridge and New York: Cambridge University Press, 1998.

Jungmann, Milan. "Kunderovské paradoxy." In Michal Přibáň, ed., *Z dějin českého myšlení o literatuře 1970–1989*, vol. 4 of *Antologie k Dějinám české literatury 1945–1990.* Prague: Ústav pro českou literaturu AV ČR, 2005. First published in *Svědectví* 20, no. 77 (1986/87): 135–162.

————. "Můj vztah k dílu Milana Kundery." In Bohumil Fořt, Jiří Kudrnáč, and Petr Kyloušek, eds., *Milan Kundera aneb Co zmůže literatura? Soubor statí o díle Milana Kundery.* Brno: Host, 2012.

Junod, Tom. "The Falling Man." *Esquire*, September 2003, 177–181, 198–199.

Kakutani, Michiko. "A Man, a Woman and a Day of Terror." *New York Times*, 9 May 2007, n.p.

Kansteiner, Wulf. "Hayden White's Critique of the Writing of History." *History and Theory* 32, no. 3 (1993): 273–295.

Kauffman, Linda S. "The Wake of Terror: Don DeLillo's 'In the Ruins of the Future,' 'Baader-Meinhof,' and *Falling Man*." *Modern Fiction Studies* 54, no. 2 (2008): 353–377.

Kellner, Hans. "A Bedrock of Order: Hayden White's Linguistic Humanism." *History and Theory* 19, no. 4 (1980): 1–29.

————. "Hayden White and the Kantian Discourse: Tropology, Narrative, and Freedom." In Chip Sills and George H. Jensen, eds., *The Philosophy of Discourse: The Rhetorical Turn in Twentieth-Century Thought*, vol. 1. Portsmouth, NH: Boynton/Cook Publishers, 1992.

Kennan, George F. *Around the Cragged Hill: A Statement of Personal and Political Philosophy.* New York: Norton, 1993.

————. The Kennan Diaries. Edited by Frank Costigliola. New York and London: Norton, 2014.

————. Papers. Seeley Mudd Manuscript Library, Princeton University.

————. ["X," pseud.]. "The Sources of Soviet Conduct." *Foreign Affairs* 25, no. 4 (1947): 566–582.

Keohane, Robert O. *After Hegemony: Cooperation and Discord in the World Political Economy.* Princeton, NJ: Princeton University Press, 1984.

————, ed. Neorealism and Its Critics. New York: Columbia University Press, 1986.

Keohane, Robert O., and Joseph S. Nye, Jr. *Power and Interdependence: World Politics in Transition.* Boston, MA: Little, Brown, 1977.

————, eds. Transnational Relations and World Politics. Cambridge, MA: Harvard University Press, 1972.

King, Gary, Robert O. Keohane, and Sidney Verba. *Designing Social Inquiry: Scientific Inference in Qualitative Research.* Princeton, NJ: Princeton University Press, 1994.

Kissinger, Henry. *Diplomacy.* New York: Simon and Schuster, 1994.

Kojève, Alexandre. *Introduction to the Reading of Hegel: Lectures on the "Phenomenology of Spirit."* Edited by Allan Bloom. Translated by James H. Nichols. New York: Basic Books, 1969.

Konstant, David. "The Function of Narrative in Hayden White's *Metahistory.*" *Clio* 11, no. 1 (1981): 65–78.

Kosková, Helena. "Francouzské romány Milana Kundery." In Aleš Haman and Vladimír Novotný, eds., *Hommage à Milan Kundera: Pocta Milanu Kunderovi: Sborník k 80. spisovatelovým narozeninám.* Prague: Artes Liberales, 2009.

Kovacevic, Natasa. "History on Speed: Media and the Politics of Forgetting in Milan Kundera's *Slowness.*" *Modern Fiction Studies* 52, no. 3 (2006): 634–655.

Krasner, Stephen D. "Compromising Westphalia." *International Security* 20, no. 3 (1995/96): 115–151.

Krebs, Ronald, and Jennifer Lobasz. "Fixing the Meaning of 9/11: Hegemony, Coercion, and the Road to War in Iraq." *Security Studies* 16, no. 3 (2007): 409–451.

Kristoff, Nicholas. "An Idiot's Guide to Inequality." *New York Times,* 24 July 2014, A27.

Kubíček, Tomáš. *Středoevropan Milan Kundera.* Olomouc: Periplum, 2013.

Kuhn, Thomas S. *The Structure of Scientific Revolutions.* 2nd ed. Chicago, IL: University of Chicago Press, 1970.

Kundera, Milan. *The Art of the Novel.* Translated by Linda Asher. New York: Harper, 2000 [1986].

———. *The Book of Laughter and Forgetting.* Translated by Aaron Asher. New York: Harper, 1996.

———. "Český úděl." *Listy* 1, nos. 7/8 (1968): 1, 5.

———. "Chopins Klavier." *Neue Zürcher Zeitung,* 16 November 1984, 35.

———. *Člověk zahrada širá.* Prague: Československý spisovatel, 1953.

———. "Comedy Is Everywhere." *Index on Censorship* 6, no. 6 (1977): 3–7.

———. *The Curtain: An Essay in Seven Parts.* Translated by Linda Asher. New York: Harper, 2007.

———. *Encounter.* Translated by Linda Asher. New York: Harper, 2010.

———. *Ignorance.* Translated by Linda Asher. London: Faber and Faber, 2002.

———. *Immortality.* Translated by Peter Kussi. New York: Grove Weidenfeld, 1991.

———. *The Joke.* Translated by Aaron Asher. New York: Harper, 1992.

———. *The Joke.* Translated by Michael Henry Heim. London: Faber and Faber, 1982.

———. "The Most Original Book of the Season." Interview by Philip Roth. *New York Times Book Review,* 30 November 1980, 7, 78, 80.

———. *Můj Janáček.* Brno: Atlantis, 2004.

———. "Můj přítel Jireš." *Iluminace* 8, no. 1 (1996): 6–7.

———. "Nesamozřejmost národa." *Literární noviny* 16, no. 38 (22 September 1967): 3.

———. *Poslední máj.* Prague: Československý spisovatel, 1955.

———. "Radikalismus a exhibicionismus." *Host do domu* 15, no. 15 (1969): 24–29.

———. *Slova, pojmy, situace.* Brno: Atlantis, 2014.

———. *Slowness.* Translated by Linda Asher. London: Faber and Faber, 1996.

———. "The Tragedy of Central Europe." *New York Review of Books,* 26 April 1984, 31, no. 7, 33–38.

———. *Žert.* Brno: Atlantis, 1996 [1967].

Lacassagne, Aurélie. "War and Peace in the *Harry Potter* series." *European Journal of Cultural Studies* 19, no. 4 (2016): 318–334.

Lebow, Richard Ned. *A Cultural Theory of International Relations*. Cambridge: Cambridge University Press, 2008.

Lentricchia, Frank. "The American Writer as Bad Citizen." In Frank Lentricchia, ed., *Introducing Don DeLillo*. Durham, NC: Duke University Press, 1991.

Levine, Daniel J. "Why Hans Morgenthau Was Not a Critical Theorist (and Why Contemporary IR Realists Should Care)." *International Relations* 27, no. 1 (2012): 95–118.

Link, Arthur S., et al., eds. *The Papers of Woodrow Wilson*. 69 vols. Princeton, NJ: Princeton University Press, 1966–1994.

Linklater, Andrew. "The Transformation of Political Community: E. H. Carr, Critical Theory and International Relations." *Review of International Studies* 23, no. 3 (1997): 321–338.

Lipson, Charles. "International Cooperation in Economic and Security Affairs." *World Politics* 37, no. 1 (1984): 1–27.

Lodge, David. "Milan Kundera, and the Idea of the Author in Modern Criticism." *Critical Quarterly* 26, nos. 1/2 (1984): 105–121.

Lombardo Radice, Lucio. *Gli accusati: Franz Kafka, Michail Bulgakov, Aleksandr Solzenitsyn, Milan Kundera*. Bari: De Donato, 1972.

Lorenz, Chris. "Historical Knowledge and Historical Reality: A Plea for 'Internal Realism.'" *History and Theory* 33, no. 3 (1994): 297–327.

Löwith, Karl. "Hegel and the Christian Religion." In Arnold Levison, ed., *Nature, History, and Existentialism, and Other Essays in the Philosophy of History*. Evanston, IL: Northwestern University Press, 1966.

———. *Meaning in History: The Theological Implications of the Philosophy of History*. Chicago, IL: University of Chicago Press, 1949.

Lyotard, Jean-François. *The Postmodern Condition: A Report on Knowledge*. Translated by Geoff Bennington and Brian Massumi. Minneapolis, MN: University of Minnesota Press, 1984.

Mannheim, Karl. *Ideologie und Utopie*. Bonn: F. Cohen, 1929.

———. *Ideology and Utopia*. London: Routledge & Kegan Paul, 1936.

Marcuse, Herbert. "The Affirmative Character of Culture." In *Negations: Essays in Critical Theory*, Translated by Jeremy J. Shapiro. Boston, MA: Beacon Press, 1968.

Martín Salván, Paula. "'The Writer at the Far Margin': The Rhetoric of Artistic Ethics in Don DeLillo's Novels." *European Journal of American Studies* 1 (2007): 1–12.

Marwick, Arthur. "Age-Old Problems: The Empiricist." *Times Higher Education Supplement*, 25 November, 1994, no. 1151.

———. "History's Men at War." *Times Higher Education Supplement*, 23 May 1997, no. 1281.

———. "Two Approaches to Historical Study: The Metaphysical (Including 'Postmodernism') and the Historical." *Journal of Contemporary History* 30, no. 1 (1995): 5–35.

Mauro, Aaron. "The Languishing of the Falling Man: Don DeLillo and Jonathan Safran Foer's Photographic History of 9/11." *Modern Fiction Studies* 57, no. 3 (2011): 584–606.

Max, D. T. "Final Destination." *New Yorker*, 11 and 18 June 2007, 54–71.

―――. *Every Love Story Is a Ghost Story: A Life of David Foster Wallace*. New York: Viking, 2012.

Mearsheimer, John J. "Back to the Future: Instability in Europe after the Cold War." *International Security* 15, no. 1 (1990): 5–56.

―――. "Conversations in International Relations: Interview with John Mearsheimer (Part I)." By Ken Booth et al. *International Relations* 20, no. 1 (2006): 105–123.

―――. "Conversations in International Relations: Interview with John J. Mearsheimer (Part II)." By Ken Booth et al. *International Relations* 20, no. 2 (2006): 231–243.

―――. "E. H. Carr vs. Idealism: The Battle Rages On." *International Relations* 19, no. 2 (2005): 139–152.

―――. "The False Promise of International Institutions." *International Security* 19, no. 3 (1994/95): 5–49.

―――. *The Tragedy of Great Power Politics*. New York and London: Norton, 2001.

Mervart, Jan. "Fenomén Literárních novin." In Jan Mervart, Petr Dvorský, and Martin Kučera, eds., *Inspirace Pražské jaro 1968*. Hradec Králové: Sumbalon, 2014.

Milner, Helen. "The Assumption of Anarchy in International Relations: A Critique." *Review of International Studies* 17, no. 1 (1991): 67–85.

Mink, Louis O. *Historical Understanding*. Edited by Brian Fay, Eugene O. Golob, and Richard T. Vann. Ithaca, NY: Cornell University Press, 1987.

―――. "Narrative as a Cognitive Instrument." Paper presented at the Midwest MLA meeting, Chicago, 1974. Quoted in idem, *Historical Understanding*, Brian Fay, Eugene O. Golob, and Richard T. Vann, eds. Ithaca, NY: Cornell University Press, 1987, 20 n. 17.

―――. "Narrative Form as a Cognitive Instrument." In Robert H. Canary and Henry Kozicki, eds., *The Writing of History: Literary Form and Historical Understanding*. Madison: University of Wisconsin Press, 1978.

Minzesheimer, Bob. "Novels About 9/11 Can't Stack up to Non-fiction." *USA Today*, 11 September 2011, D1.

Mishra, Pankaj. "The End of Innocence." *Guardian*, 19 May 2007, n.p.

Molloy, Seán. "Dialectics and Transformation: Exploring the International Theory of E. H. Carr." *International Journal of Politics, Culture, and Society* 17, no. 2 (2003): 279–306.

―――. *The Hidden History of Realism: A Genealogy of Power Politics*. New York: Palgrave Macmillan, 2006.

―――. "Truth, Power, Theory: Hans Morgenthau's Formulation of Realism." *Diplomacy and Statecraft* 15, no. 1 (2004): 1–34.

Momigliano, Arnaldo. "The Rhetoric of History and the History of Rhetoric: On Hayden White's Tropes." *Comparative Criticism* 3 (1981): 259–268.

Moore, Lorrie. "Look for a Writer and Find a Terrorist." *New York Times*, 9 June 1991, n.p.

Morgenthau, Hans J. "The Political Science of E. H. Carr." *World Politics* 1, no. 1 (1948): 127–134.

―――. *Politics among Nations: The Struggle for Power and Peace*. 5th ed. New York: Knopf, 1973 [1948].

―――. "The Surrender to the Immanence of Power: E. H. Carr." In Hans J. Morgenthau, ed., *Dilemmas of Politics*. Chicago, IL: University of Chicago Press, 1962.

"Mr. E. H. Carr: Eminent Historian of Soviet Russia." *The Times*, 5 November 1982.

Narrett, Eugene. "Surviving History: Milan Kundera's Quarrel with Modernism." *Modern Language Studies* 22, no. 4 (1992): 4–24.

Nel, Philip. *The Avant-Garde and American Postmodernity: Small Incisive Shocks.* Jackson: University Press of Mississippi, 2002.

———. "DeLillo and Modernism." In John N. Duvall, ed., *The Cambridge Companion to Don DeLillo.* Cambridge: Cambridge University Press, 2008.

———. "'A Small Incisive Shock': Modern Forms, Postmodern Politics, and the Role of the Avant-Garde in *Underworld*." *Modern Fiction Studies* 45, no. 3 (1999): 724–752.

Němec, Jan. "Milan Kundera jako spisovatel." *Host* 26, no. 9 (2010): 73–74.

Němcová Banerjee, Marie. *Terminal Paradox: The Novels of Milan Kundera.* New York: Grove Weidenfeld, 1990.

Neumann, Iver B., and Daniel H. Nexon. "Harry Potter and the Study of World Politics." In Neumann and Nexon, eds., *Harry Potter and International Relations.* Lanham, MD: Rowman & Littlefield, 2006.

Niebuhr, Reinhold. "Augustine's Political Realism." In Robert McAfee Brown, ed., *The Essential Reinhold Niebuhr: Selected Essays and Addresses.* New Haven, CT and London: Yale University Press, 1986.

———. *Faith and History: A Comparison of Christian and Modern Views of History.* London: Nisbet, 1949.

———. *The Nature and Destiny of Man: A Christian Interpretation.* 2 vols. New York: Scribner's Sons, 1941, 1943.

———. "Two Forms of Utopianism." *Christianity and Society* 12, no. 4 (1947): 6–7.

Ninkovich, Frank. *The Wilsonian Century: U.S. Foreign Policy since 1900.* Chicago, IL: University of Chicago Press, 1999.

Nishimura, Kuniyuki. "E. H. Carr, Dostoevsky, and the Problem of Irrationality in Modern Europe." *International Relations* 25, no. 1 (2011): 45–64.

Norman, Emma O. "International Boggarts: Carl Schmitt, *Harry Potter*, and the Transfiguration of Identity and Violence." *Politics & Policy* 40, no. 3 (2012): 403–423.

Novick, Peter. *That Noble Dream: The "Objectivity Question" and the American Historical Profession.* Cambridge: Cambridge University Press, 1988.

Nye, Joseph S. *The Future of Power.* New York: Public Affairs, 2011.

———. *Soft Power: The Means to Success in World Politics.* New York: Public Affairs, 2004.

Osteen, Mark. *American Magic and Dread: Don DeLillo's Dialogue with Culture.* Philadelphia, PA: University of Pennsylvania Press, 2000.

———. "Becoming Incorporated: Spectacular Authorship and DeLillo's *Mao II*." *Modern Fiction Studies* 45, no. 3 (1999): 643–674.

———. "DeLillo's Dedalian Artists." In John N. Duvall, ed., *The Cambridge Companion to Don DeLillo.* Cambridge: Cambridge University Press, 2008.

Oye, Kenneth A. "Explaining Cooperation under Anarchy: Hypotheses and Strategies." *World Politics* 38, no. 1 (1985): 1–24.

———, ed. *Cooperation under Anarchy.* Princeton, NJ: Princeton University Press, 1986.

Partner, Nancy. "The Fundamental Things Apply: Aristotle's Narrative Theory and the Classical Origins of Postmodern History." In Nancy Partner and Sarah Foot, eds., *The SAGE Handbook of Historical Theory.* London: SAGE, 2013.

Passaro, Vince. "Dangerous Don DeLillo." In Thomas DePietro, ed., *Conversations with Don DeLillo*. Jackson: University Press of Mississippi, 2005.

Paul, Herman. *Hayden White*. London: Polity, 2011.

Petersen, Ulrik Enemark. "Breathing Nietzsche's Air: New Reflections on Morgenthau's Concepts of Power and Human Nature." *Alternatives* 24, no. 1 (1999): 83–118.

Piccone, Paul. "The Future of Critical Theory." In Scott G. McNall and Gary N. Howe, eds., *Current Perspectives in Social Theory*, vol. 1. Greenwich, CT: Jai Press, 1980.

Ranke, Leopold. *History of Latin and Teutonic Nations, 1494–1514*. London: George Bell and Sons, 1887. Originally published as *Geschichten der romanischen und germanischen Völker von 1494 bis 1514*, vol. 1. Leipzig and Berlin: Reimer, 1824.

Remnick, David. "Exile on Main Street: Don DeLillo's Undisclosed Underworld." *New Yorker*, 15 September 1997, 42–48.

Reus-Smit, Christian, and Duncan Snidal, eds. *The Oxford Handbook of International Relations*. Oxford and New York: Oxford University Press, 2008.

Ricard, François. "Metafyzika románu." Interview by Maxime Rovère. *Host* 27, no. 8 (2011): 71.

Rice, Daniel F. *Reinhold Niebuhr and His Circle of Influence*. New York: Cambridge University Press, 2012.

Rich, Frank. "The Clear Blue Sky." *New York Times Sunday Book Review*, 27 May 2007, n.p.

Richterová, Sylvie. "Opona: Kunderův román o románu." *Host* 21, no. 9 (2005): 10–12.

Ricoeur, Paul. *Time and Narrative*, vol. 1. Translated by Kathleen McLaughlin and David Pellauer. Chicago, IL and London: University of Chicago Press, 1984.

Rizzante, Massimo. "Umění fugy." *Host* 27, no. 8 (2011): 81–82.

Rorty, Richard. *Contingency, Irony, and Solidarity*. Cambridge: Cambridge University Press, 1991.

———. "Heidegger, Kundera, and Dickens." In *Essays on Heidegger and Others*. Cambridge: Cambridge University Press, 1991.

Rosen, Jonathan. "Does Milan Kundera Still Matter?" *The Atlantic* 316, no. 1 (July/August 2015): 40–42.

Ross, Stephen. "The Abdication of Culture: The Ideology of Imagology in Milan Kundera's *Immortality*." *Modern Fiction Studies* 46, no. 2 (2000): 331–354.

Rothberg, Michael. "A Failure of the Imagination: Diagnosing the Post-9/11 Novel: A Response to Richard Gray." *American Literary History* 21, no. 1 (2009): 152–158.

Rowe, John Carlos. "*Mao II* and the War on Terrorism." *South Atlantic Quarterly* 103, no. 1 (2004): 21–43.

Ruggie, John Gerard. "Continuity and Transformation in the World Polity: Toward a Neorealist Synthesis." Review of *Theory of International Politics*, by Kenneth N. Waltz. *World Politics* 35, no. 2 (1983): 261–285.

Said, Edward W. *Orientalism*. New York: Vintage, 1979 [1978].

Sampson, Aaron Beers. "Tropical Anarchy: Waltz, Wendt, and the Way We Imagine International Politics." *Alternatives* 27, no. 4 (2002): 429–457.

Scarpetta, Guy. *L'âge d'or du roman*. Paris: Grasset, 1996.

———. "Politický Kundera." In Bohumil Fořt, Jiří Kudrnáč, and Petr Kyloušek, eds., *Milan Kundera aneb Co zmůže literatura? Soubor statí o díle Milana Kundery*. Brno: Host, 2012.

Schelling, Thomas C. *Strategy of Conflict.* Cambridge, MA: Harvard University Press, 1960.

Scheuerman, William E. "Realism and the Left: The Case of Hans J. Morgenthau." *Review of International Studies* 34, no. 1 (2008): 29–51.

———. "A Theoretical Missed Opportunity? Hans J. Morgenthau as Critical Realist." In Duncan Bell, ed., *Political Thought and International Relations.* Oxford: Oxford University Press, 2009.

———. "Was Morgenthau a Realist? Revisiting *Scientific Man vs. Power Politics.*" *Constellations* 14, no. 4 (2007): 506–530.

Schmidt, Brian C. *The Political Discourse of Anarchy: A Disciplinary History of International Relations.* Albany: State University of New York Press, 1998.

Scott, A. O. "In Search of the Best." *New York Times Book Review,* 21 May 2006, 16–19.

Shakespeare, William. *Hamlet, Prince of Denmark.* Edited by Philip Edwards. Cambridge and New York: Cambridge University Press, 2003.

Singer, Peter. *The President of Good and Evil: The Ethics of George W. Bush.* Melbourne, VIC: Text Publishing, 2004.

Sládek, Ondřej. "O fikci a skutečnosti: Několik poznámek ke Kunderovu umění románu." In Bohumil Fořt, Jiří Kudrnáč, and Petr Kyloušek, eds., *Milan Kundera aneb Co zmůže literatura? Soubor statí o díle Milana Kundery.* Brno: Host, 2012.

Smith, Michael Joseph. "The Prophetic Realism of Reinhold Niebuhr." In *Realist Thought from Weber to Kissinger.* Baton Rouge and London: Louisiana State University Press, 1986.

Smith, Steve, Ken Booth, and Marysia Zalewski, eds. *International Theory: Positivism and Beyond.* Cambridge and New York: Cambridge University Press, 1996.

Smith, Tony. "Wilsonianism after Iraq: The End of Liberal Internationalism?" In G. John Ikenberry et al., *The Crisis of American Foreign Policy: Wilsonianism in the Twenty-First Century.* Princeton, NJ and Oxford: Princeton University Press, 2009.

Snidal, Duncan. "The Game Theory of International Politics." *World Politics* 38, no. 1 (1985): 25–57.

Sontag, Susan. *On Photography.* New York: Farrar, Straus and Giroux, 1977.

Steiner, Peter. "Spory o symbolický kapitál." In Bohumil Fořt, Jiří Kudrnáč, and Petr Kyloušek, eds., *Milan Kundera aneb Co zmůže literatura? Soubor statí o díle Milana Kundery.* Brno: Host, 2012.

Stephanson, Anders. "The Lessons of *What Is History?*" In Michael Cox, ed., *E. H. Carr: A Critical Appraisal.* New York: Palgrave, 2000.

Stiglitz, Joseph E. "Of the 1%, by the 1%, for the 1%." *Vanity Fair* no. 609 (2011): 126–129.

Stone, Dan. "Paul Ricoeur, Hayden White, and Holocaust Historiography." In Jörn Stückrath and Jürg Zbinden, eds., *Metageschichte: Hayden White und Paul Ricoeur: Dargestellte Wirklichkeit in der europäischen Kultur im Kontext von Husserl, Weber, Auerbach und Gombrich.* Baden-Baden: Nomos, 1997.

Streitfeld, David. "Don DeLillo's Gloomy Muse." *Washington Post,* 14 May 1992, C1.

Šuch, Juraj. "Niekoľko poznámok k dielu Haydena Whita." *Filozofia* 55, no. 10 (2000): 809–819.

Suganami, Hidemi. *On the Causes of War.* Oxford: Oxford University Press, 1996.

Sylvester, Christine. *Feminist Theory and International Relations in a Postmodern Era.* Cambridge: Cambridge University Press, 1994.

Tabbi, Joseph. *Postmodern Sublime: Technology and American Writing from Mailer to Cyberpunk*. Ithaca, NY: Cornell University Press, 1995.

Thirlwell, Adam. "Skandální lehkost tohoto bytí." *Host* 27, no. 8 (2011): 76.

Thucydides. *History of the Peloponnesian War*. Translated by Benjamin Jowett. Amherst, NY: Prometheus Books, 1998 [1881].

Thurschwell, Adam. "Writing and Terror: Don DeLillo on the Task of Literature after 9/11." *Law and Literature* 19, no. 2 (2007): 277–302.

Tickner, J. Ann. "Hans Morgenthau's Principles of Political Realism: A Feminist Reformulation." *Millennium: Journal of International Studies* 17, no. 3 (1988): 429–440.

Tjalve, Vibeke Schou, and Michael C. Williams. "Reviving the Rhetoric of Realism: Politics and Responsibility in Grand Strategy." *Security Studies* 24, no. 1 (2015): 37–60

Topolski, Jerzy. "Historical Narrative: Towards a Coherent Structure." *History and Theory* 26, no. 4 (1987): 75–86.

Toulmin, Stephen. *Cosmopolis: The Hidden Agenda of Modernity*. New York: Free Press, 1990.

U Department of Homeland Security. Citizenship and Immigration Services. *Learn About the United States: Quick Civics Lessons for the Naturalization Test*. Washington, DC: GPO, 2013.

Trávníček, Jiří. "'Nic není více skryto lidskému zraku než životní próza.'" *Host* 20, no. 10 (2004): 40–42.

Vaculík, Ludvík. "Dva tisíce slov." *Literární listy* 17, no. 18 (27 June 1968): 1–3.

———. *Hodiny klavíru: komponovaný deník 2004–2005*. Brno: Atlantis, 2007.

Varon, Jeremy. *Bringing the War Home: The Weather Underground, the Red Army Faction, and Revolutionary Violence in the Sixties and Seventies*. Berkeley, CA: University of California Press, 2004.

Verecký, Ladislav. "Milan Kundera: Spisovatel, který se skrývá." *Lidové noviny*, 29 November 2001, 12.

Wæver, Ole. "The Rise and Fall of the Inter-Paradigm Debate." In Steve Smith, Ken Booth, and Marysia Zalewski, eds., *International Theory: Positivism and Beyond*. Cambridge and New York: Cambridge University Press, 1996.

Walker, R. B. J. *Inside/Outside: International Relations as Political Theory*. Cambridge and New York: Cambridge University Press, 1993.

Wallerstein, Immanuel. *The Modern World-System*. 3 vols. New York: Academic Press, 1974–1989.

Walsh, William H. "Colligatory Concepts in History." In W. H. Burston and D. Thompson, eds., *Studies in the Nature and Teaching of History*. New York: Humanities Press, 1967.

Walton, Gary. "The Triune Trope of the 'Falling Man' in Don DeLillo's *Falling Man*: The Commodification of 9/11 Trauma." *Kentucky Philological Review* 24 (2009): 42–48.

Waltz, Kenneth N. *Man, the State and War: A Theoretical Analysis*. New York: Columbia University Press, 1959.

———. "Structural Realism after the Cold War." *International Security* 25, no. 1 (2000): 5–41.

———. *Theory of International Politics*. Reading, MA: Addison-Wesley, 1979.

Weber, Cynthia. *Simulating Sovereignty: Intervention, the State, and Symbolic Exchange*. Cambridge: Cambridge University Press, 1995.

Weldes, Jutta. "Going Cultural: *Star Trek*, State Action, and Popular Culture." *Millennium: Journal of International Studies* 38, no. 1 (1999): 117–134.

———, ed. *To Seek Out New Worlds: Science Fiction and World Politics.* New York: Palgrave Macmillan, 2003.

Wells, H. G. "The Country of the Blind." *The Strand Magazine* 27, no. 160 (April 1904): 401–415.

Wendt, Alexander. "The Agent-Structure Problem in International Relations Theory." *International Organization* 41, no. 3 (1987): 335–370.

———. "Anarchy Is What States Make of It: The Social Construction of Power Politics." *International Organization* 46, no. 2 (1992): 391–425.

———. *Social Theory of International Politics.* Cambridge: Cambridge University Press, 1999.

Whalley, George. "On Translating Aristotle's *Poetics.*" In Aristotle, *Poetics*, trans. George Whalley, ed. John Baxter and Patrick Atherton. Montreal and Kingston, ON: McGill-Queen's University Press, 1997.

White, Hayden. "Age-Old Problems: The Theorist." *Times Higher Education Supplement*, 25 November 1994, no. 1151.

———. "The Aim of Interpretation Is to Create Perplexity in the Face of the Real: Hayden White in Conversation with Erlend Rogne." Interview by Erlend Rogne. *History and Theory* 48, no. 1 (2009): 63–75.

———. *The Content of the Form: Narrative Discourse and Historical Representation.* Baltimore, MD, and London: Johns Hopkins University Press, 1987.

———. "A Conversation with Hayden White." Interview by Ewa Domańska. *Rethinking History* 12, no. 1 (2008): 3–21.

———. *The Fiction of Narrative: Essays on History, Literature, and Theory, 1957–2007.* Edited by Robert Doran. Baltimore, MD: Johns Hopkins University Press, 2010.

———. *Figural Realism: Studies in the Mimesis Effect.* Baltimore, MD, and London: Johns Hopkins University Press, 1999.

———. "Figuring the Nature of the Times Deceased: Literary Theory and Historical Writing." In Ralph Cohen, ed., *The Future of Literary Theory.* London: Routledge, 1989.

———. "Hayden White on 'Facts, Fictions and Metahistory': II. A Discussion with Hayden White." Interview by Richard J. Murphy. *Sources: Revue d'études anglophones* 2 (Spring 1997): 3–30.

———. "Historical Fiction, Fictional History, and Historical Reality." *Rethinking History* 9, nos. 2/3 (2005): 147–157.

———. "Human Face of Scientific Mind: An Interview with Hayden White." By Ewa Domańska. *Storia della Storiografia* no. 24 (1993): 5–21.

———. "Interview: The Image of Self-Presentation." By Hans Kellner and Ewa Domańska. *Diacritics* 24, no. 1 (1994): 91–100.

———. *Metahistory: The Historical Imagination in Nineteenth-Century Europe.* Baltimore, MD, and London: Johns Hopkins University Press, 1973.

———. "An Old Question Raised Again: Is Historiography Art or Science?" *Rethinking History* 4, no. 3 (2000): 391–406.

———. "The Politics of Contemporary Philosophy of History." *Clio* 3, no. 1 (1973): 35–54.

———. "Response to Arthur Marwick." *Journal of Contemporary History* 30, no. 2 (1995): 233–246.

———. "A Response to Professor Chartier's Four Questions." *Storia della Storiografia* no. 27 (1995): 63–70.

———. *Tropics of Discourse: Essays in Cultural Criticism.* Baltimore, MD, and London: Johns Hopkins University Press, 1978.

Whitworth, Sandra. "Gender in the Inter-Paradigm Debate." *Millennium: Journal of International Studies* 18, no. 2 (1989): 265–272.

Wight, Martin. *Power Politics.* Edited by Hedley Bull and Carsten Holbraad. Leicester: Leicester University Press, 1978.

———. "Why Is There No International Theory?" *International Relations* 2, no. 1 (1960): 35–48, 62.

Wight, Martin, and Herbert Butterfield, eds. *Diplomatic Investigations: Essays in the Theory of International Politics.* Cambridge, MA: Harvard University Press, 1966.

Will, George F. "Shallow Look at the Mind of an Assassin." *Washington Post,* 22 September 1988, A25.

Williams, Michael C. *The Realist Tradition and the Limits of International Relations.* Cambridge: Cambridge University Press, 2005.

Wilson, Peter. "E. H. Carr's *The Twenty Years' Crisis*: Appearance and Reality in World Politics." *Politik: Danish Journal of Political Science* 12, no. 4 (2009): 21–25.

———. "Radicalism for a Conservative Purpose: The Peculiar Realism of E. H. Carr." *Millennium: Journal of International Studies* 30, no. 1 (2001): 123–136.

Index

Made in United States
North Haven, CT
03 February 2022

15593470R00135